Drawn *by the* Current

Books by Jocelyn Green

THE WINDY CITY SAGA

Veiled in Smoke
Shadows of the White City
Drawn by the Current

The Mark of the King
A Refuge Assured
Between Two Shores

Drawn by the Current

JOCELYN GREEN

BETHANYHOUSE

a division of Baker Publishing Group
Minneapolis, Minnesota

Published by Bethany House Publishers
11400 Hampshire Avenue South
Minneapolis, Minnesota 55438
www.bethanyhouse.com

Bethany House Publishers is a division of
Baker Publishing Group, Grand Rapids, Michigan

Printed in the United States of America

Library of Congress Cataloging-in-Publication Data
Names: Green, Jocelyn, author.
Title: Drawn by the current / Jocelyn Green.
Description: Minneapolis, Minnesota : Bethany House Publishers, a division of
    Baker Publishing Group, [2022] | Series: Windy city saga ; 3
Identifiers: LCCN 2021040498 | ISBN 9780764233326 (trade paperback) | ISBN
    9780764239809 (casebound) | ISBN 9781493435982 (ebook)
Subjects: LCGFT: Christian fiction. | Novels.
Classification: LCC PS3607.R4329255 D73 2022 | DDC 813/.6—dc23
LC record available at https://lccn.loc.gov/2021040498

Scripture quotations are from the King James Version of the Bible.

The epigraph Scripture quotation marked NIV is from THE HOLY BIBLE, NEW INTERNATIONAL VERSION®, NIV® Copyright © 1973, 1978, 1984, 2011 by Biblica, Inc.® Used by permission. All rights reserved worldwide.

This is a work of historical reconstruction; the appearances of certain historical figures are therefore inevitable. All other characters, however, are products of the author's imagination, and any resemblance to actual persons, living or dead, is coincidental.

Cover design by Dan Thornberg, Design Source Creative Services

Author is represented by Credo Communications, LLC.

Baker Publishing Group publications use paper produced from sustainable forestry practices and post-consumer waste whenever possible.

22 23 24 25 26 27 28   7 6 5 4 3 2 1

Captivating! *Drawn by the Current* explores the human depths of tragedy, loss, and what it means to survive. How the appearance of calm waters in those we love often masks hidden sorrows churning beneath. Beautifully written and rippling with secrets, Jocelyn Green's latest novel in her WINDY CITY SAGA triumphs!

Kate Breslin, best-selling author of *As Dawn Breaks*

Once again, Jocelyn Green takes us on a historical adventure worth neglecting dinner and sleep for. Readers will sink into this story and drown in the pages of Jocelyn Green's epic story-telling talent! A+++ and throw in another + for good measure!

Jaime Jo Wright, multiple award-winning author of *The House on Foster Hill* and *On the Cliffs of Foxglove Manor*

Drawn by the Current leads readers on an engaging journey of intrigue and romance, perfectly blended with a splash of Chicago history from the early 1900s. Jocelyn's fictional work successfully crosses over to be equally enjoyable—and consequential—to readers of the several non-fiction narratives previously published about the *Eastland* Disaster.

Ted Wachholz, Executive Director and Chief Historian, Eastland Disaster Historical Society

An incredible story of sacrifice, protection, and redemption, *Drawn by the Current* is another breathtaking, page-turning winner by one of my all-time favorite authors, Jocelyn Green. Olive's tale is at the top of my list of best reads this year!

Kimberley Woodhouse, bestselling and award-winning author of *A Deep Divide* and *Forever Hidden*

Praise for the WINDY CITY SAGA

"Historical romance fans will devour this newest novel from beloved author Jocelyn Green. An evocative tale about surrendered dreams and life's unexpected bends in the road, *Shadows of the White City* satisfies in every way!"

—Tamera Alexander, *USA Today* bestselling author of
Colors of Truth and *A Lasting Impression*

"History breathes new life in Jocelyn Green's latest—a masterwork of immersive storytelling set against the backdrop of the 1893 Chicago World's Fair. *Shadows of the White City* is a dazzling spectacle—worthy of the grand exhibition itself!"

—Kristy Cambron, bestselling author of *The Paris
Dressmaker* and *The Butterfly and the Violin*

"A powerful and compelling novel about one family's dramatic resurrection after the devastation of the Chicago fire."

—Elizabeth Camden, author, *Carved in Stone*

"With her trademark insight and skill, Green weaves an enthralling story with characters who beautifully combine the best of intentions with their own faults and flaws in a perfect echo of life. *Shadows of the White City* is a symphony of second chances sure to touch your heart and soul."

—Roseanna M. White, bestselling historical romance author

"In *Veiled in Smoke*, Green frames a story of loss and redemption with sensory details, a nuanced historical backdrop, and an intelligent eye for flawed and utterly engaging characters. A thoroughly enriching and thoughtful reading experience by an absolute master of inspirational fiction."

—Rachel McMillan, author, *The Mozart Code*

"Venture into all the magic, intrigue, romance, and even danger of the Chicago World's Fair. *Shadows of the White City* is a delightful—though at times heartrending—read written by one of my favorite authors, the talented Jocelyn Green."

—Michelle Griep, Christy Award-winning author
of *Once Upon a Dickens Christmas*

In memory of those who lost
their lives on the SS *Eastland*.

And to their loved ones who survived,
and the generations that followed.

Kindred spirits alone do not change with changing years.

—L. M. Montgomery,
Anne of the Island

My help comes from the LORD,
the Maker of heaven and earth.

—Psalm 121:2 NIV

CHAPTER ONE

CHICAGO
FRIDAY, JUNE 11, 1915

Olive Pierce chided herself for the tingle of nerves in her fingertips. She was twenty-nine years old and had been working for MetLife's main Chicago office for the last seven. She had no cause to feel anything less than confident.

Wind nipped her ankles and tugged at her hat as though nudging her to get moving. Putting the courthouse behind her, she crossed Washington Street to the twenty-one-story Conway Building where she worked. The white granite gleamed in the morning sun. Unseen from the street, an inner courtyard brought light to every interior office as well. The Conway had opened earlier this year, shrinking the commute from her apartment to just over a block. All the tenants renting office space were enjoying a major upgrade from wherever they'd been last.

It was a sign, Olive told herself. The time was right for her career to get an upgrade, too.

Bolstered, she breezed through the doors and into a space awash with sun pouring through skylights. Her heels clicked over Tennessee marble as she crossed the two-story rotunda surrounded

11

by shops and cafés and caught an elevator that carried her to the fifteenth floor.

She could do this, she reminded herself, and closed the few remaining yards to the MetLife office.

Greeting the two secretaries already at work, Olive passed between their desks and dropped her things off in her own office. After smoothing her hair, she wove back through reception and hesitated at the door to the corner office.

"Olive?" Gwendolyn Walsh slapped the return on her typewriter carriage and continued hammering the keys, a honey-blond curl bouncing beside her cheek. "Mr. Roth is expecting you. Go right on in, sweetie."

Olive had long ago given up trying to correct the young secretary, who had been calling her *sweetie* ever since she was hired fresh out of college three years ago. Still, Olive hoped her boss hadn't overheard. She was a professional life insurance agent, after all, and if she was going to be promoted, it wouldn't be for being sweet.

A throat clearing behind her turned her attention to the other secretary, Blanche Holden. At fifty-five years old, her hair was as white as her name, but her brown eyes snapped with the spirit of a woman half her age. "Go get it, Olive."

That was more like it.

"Thanks, ladies." With a deep breath, Olive entered her boss's office.

"Well, good morning, Miss Pierce," Edgar Roth said. "You're looking rather fetching today."

Olive's smile froze. *Fetching* was not the look she'd been going for when she'd dressed in the white shirtwaist, green jacket, and matching skirt. Capable. Ready for action. *That* was what she meant to project.

"You chose your ensemble to match your eyes, I expect? Smart. Not every girl can pull off your coloring, my dear, but I daresay you almost make a man forget about your hair."

12

It wasn't even red, for pity's sake. It was auburn. A deep auburn that Anne Shirley would have been more than happy with.

"If you please, Mr. Roth, I have far more to offer than my eyes and hair." Instantly, her cheeks burned. "I'd like to discuss my career at MetLife."

"Absolutely." He smiled, creasing a face lined and tanned from hours at the Chicago Golf Club. "But before we get started, I need my first cup of coffee." Dark eyebrows lifted toward a slightly receding hairline. When she didn't respond, he glanced pointedly toward the door. "I believe it's just through there."

If her cheeks weren't already scarlet, she was sure they would be by now. "I don't—I'm not—" Olive sputtered. "I don't make the coffee here." This man had been her boss for six months. He ought to know that.

"Is that any reason not to pour me a cup?" His injured expression triggered her temper.

"As a matter of fact—"

"Pardon me, Mr. Roth." Gwendolyn appeared in the doorway, cup in hand. Bless her. After placing it on his desk, she sashayed away.

Olive sat opposite him and collected herself while he sipped. "Mr. Roth," she tried again, "I want to be very clear about what I do here. You are aware that I am not a secretary. I'm an insurance agent. I help clients choose the best plan to fit their needs and budgets. I survey their medical histories to make sure we're giving them the best rates possible."

Mr. Roth watched her as if half amused.

Simmering, she plunged ahead. "When a MetLife client dies, I activate the process of verification and the prompt payment of death benefits for the bereaved. And I do it with all the tact and compassion the situation requires."

"Of course you do. You're a nurturer. It's what you women are good at. I hear Blanche sends our clients birthday and Christmas cards."

"She also subscribes to every church newsletter in the city. If any clients are sick, she's the first to find out and send a card."

Mr. Roth nodded. "That's the sort of thing that makes you women suited for the work you're doing. Nurturing."

"If you'll pardon my bluntness, sir, that's not all I'm good at. I've been doing this for seven years. I can do more. I want to do more."

"Seven years! You don't look old enough to have been working that long. What's the matter, you don't want to get married and have a family?"

The question stung, not just for the implication that something was wrong with her, but because she could not imagine he would ever ask her colleague Howard Penrose, who was two years older than she was, why he wasn't married. She exhaled. "Seven years *is* a long time. My point exactly."

"Oh. You're not quitting on me, are you? Some fellow proposed finally?"

"Not a bit." Olive's smile came easily. "I have a proposal of my own. You're aware that Howard is the only insurance investigator in our office. You may not be aware that he was promoted after only a year on the job, and yet—" She spread her hands, allowing her own tenure to speak for her. "Train me to be an investigator, too."

She'd be good at it. Really good. She was her father's daughter, after all. As a reporter and editor for the *Chicago Tribune*, Nate Pierce had always been asking questions, searching out all angles. Growing up in and out of her aunt's bookstore might have fueled Olive's imagination, but it was her father's blood in her veins that instilled a hunger for truth.

"I'll be able to fill either role," she went on. "Selling policies when that's needed, investigating when Howard has too much to handle on his own." She tried not to hold her breath. "I'm not just a nurturer. I'm a creative thinker and a problem solver."

Mr. Roth's eyebrows drew together. Pushing away his mug, he

dropped his elbows to the desk and tented his fingers in front of his blue serge suit. "I appreciate your loyalty to the company. I do. But your caring spirit, which is a strength in certain capacities, would be a weakness in the field. I need investigators who think with their brains, not with their hearts."

Balderdash. "You don't believe women use their minds?"

He patted the air to calm her, further agitating her instead. "What you've proposed is too unconventional for my taste."

She swallowed. "If putting a woman in the role is an acquired taste, there's only one way to acquire it." Another smile. This time, not as easy. "Look, Mr. Roth. The Chicago Police Department hired ten women two years ago. Alice Clement serves as a bona fide detective. If the police trust a woman detective, surely MetLife can trust me to be an insurance investigator."

The wariness playing across his face threatened to melt the metal from her spine. "The police can do whatever the blue blazes they want. This is my office. I don't see the need for it."

"It's a new era, Mr. Roth. Women may not have won the vote nationally yet, but we can vote for president in the state of Illinois as of two years ago. Why not embrace the change?"

"Embrace the change?" He chuckled and stood. "The only change I'd like to embrace is for my employees to do as I ask without a fuss."

He thrust his empty mug into her hand.

<hr>

If Blanche hadn't pried Mr. Roth's mug from Olive's grip so quickly, Olive might have been tempted to spit in it.

"Well, based on those flaring nostrils of yours, I don't need to ask how it went." The secretary cocked her head toward the coffee counter in the back of the reception space.

Olive followed her past the doorways to Howard's office, her own, and the records room, then crossed her arms, a huff of frustration escaping her.

15

"I'm sorry, Olive. You deserve every chance that Howard had to prove yourself an investigator. If there were anything I could say to secure that for you, believe me, I would. But you will *not* serve that man coffee. At least not as long as I'm here."

A stab of guilt pricked Olive. "It's not that I think I'm too good to do it," she said. "It's just that if he doesn't recognize the work I do as it is, this will only . . ." Unwilling to insult either Blanche or Gwendolyn, she looked for a safe place to land her next words and found none.

"Confuse him further?" A smile warmed Blanche's faintly lined face. Her wedding ring glinted as she poured the steaming brew into Mr. Roth's cup. "I completely understand. This isn't in your job description, but it is in mine. It's best to stick to our roles, or he'll never learn to keep us straight."

"Exactly." Olive exhaled, thanked Blanche, and returned to her office, leaving the paneled door partway open to the reception area. She still felt defeated—and she was—but at least she also felt a little more understood.

The rest of the morning passed without appointment or incident. Olive tried not to glare at the ivory wall separating her office from Howard's. He wasn't here. Was he in the Union Stock Yards, investigating a death that had only been made to look like an accident? Or at the railroad tracks, looking into a suspected suicide on the rails? Maybe he was at the morgue, conferring with a medical examiner over a cold metal table. Was it natural causes, or was the dead man murdered by the new spouse who stood to gain a fortune from his death?

She glanced at the clock. She, too, had somewhere to be today, even if it was just lunching with her friend. After jabbing a pearl-headed pin through her hat, she scooped up her handbag.

"I'm taking lunch," she told Blanche on her way out. "See you in an hour."

"Oh, wait!" Blanche called after her. "I'm so sorry I forgot to tell you, but your friend Claire called while you were with Roth.

She said she's very sorry, but she's ill and won't be able to meet for lunch."

Olive formed a new plan. She could wash out her Thermos, fill it with chicken noodle soup at a café downstairs, and take the train out to Claire's house. "I may be back a little later than usual from my lunch break, then. But I've no appointments until two, and I'll work later this evening to make up for any time over an hour."

"Bringing lunch to her, are you? Take your time. In fact, she and her husband are your clients, correct? This calls for a get-well card." With a flourish, Blanche withdrew one from a drawer, added her own warm wishes inside, then handed the pen to Olive. "Pay your MetLife customer a house call."

Olive laughed. "You really are the best. If Mr. Roth should ask where I am, tell him I'm out nurturing."

CHAPTER TWO

Claire didn't answer the door right away. Perhaps she was resting, hoping the knocking would cease and the caller would leave her alone. Maybe she needed sleep more than soup.

Still, Olive waited. Wind swept through the covered front porch, whispering through the folds of silk net that banded her hat and swaying the ferns hanging from the ceiling. A white picket fence surrounded the yard, which was as green and well-kept as the park across the street. In the garden in front of the cedar-shingled bungalow, peonies drooped on their stems.

She supposed she could leave the Thermos and card, but selfishly, she wanted to see her best friend. When Claire married five years ago, she quit working for Olive's aunt, Sylvie, and moved into Warren's new house in the West Division, just over a mile from the Sears, Roebuck and Company complex in North Lawndale. She went from selling books to selling clothing and housewares by writing advertising copy for the catalogs, and Warren packaged orders. Since then, her visits with Olive had dwindled to once-a-month lunches.

Lately, Claire had been canceling more often for various reasons. Olive missed her.

She knocked again on the cherry-red door, this time hard enough to make the preserved boxwood wreath shiver. Because maybe Claire wasn't in bed but sprawled on the floor somewhere. Maybe she needed help, and she was all alone.

"Claire?" she called. "It's Olive. I've brought you some soup. May I come in?" She jiggled the knob, ready to enter without an invitation if the door was unlocked.

Movement slurred from somewhere inside. Curtains parted at the front window and then fell back into place.

With a click, the door opened several inches, revealing half of Claire. A velvet headband crowned carefully pinned dark curls and matched the pink embroidery on her high-waisted linen dress. A little too perfect for someone staying home sick from work. But then, that was Claire. Some women relaxed their personal grooming habits after getting married. Claire's only seemed to improve.

"Olive. You didn't need to come all this way."

"Nonsense. We do have a lunch date, after all, and I don't mind the change in venue one bit. Blanche said you're sick, so I picked up some chicken noodle soup." She held up the Thermos. "Still hot."

Claire's forehead puckered as she hesitated. "Lucky for you, I'm not contagious." With a subtle sigh, she stepped back, opening the door wide.

Olive gasped. Claire's arm was in a cast and sling, and one side of her face was purpled and swollen.

"I guess soup won't do you much good after all!" Olive stepped over the threshold and handed Claire the card from Blanche.

The living room smelled of lemon dusting polish. Hazelnut-brown accent pillows, perfectly placed on the pistachio uphol-stered sofa, matched the two imitation leather craftsman arm-chairs facing the upright piano against one wall. Across from the sofa and flanking the fireplace, bookcases held the volumes Claire had sold to Warren when she'd worked at Corner Books & More.

Olive could still remember the day Warren Sterling came to the shop and asked twenty-four-year-old Claire what she would expect to find in the bookcase of a well-read, intelligent man. *What would impress you?"* he'd asked. She'd drawn up a list, and he'd purchased ten volumes that day. He kept returning to the store, buying her recommendations. By the time he'd acquired them all, they were both smitten. They married eight months later, just before Claire's father died of cancer. It had been a miracle that Mr. Monroe was able to walk Claire down the aisle.

Catching her own reflection in the glass doors enclosing the books, Olive turned back to Claire. "Tell me everything."

"It looks worse than it is." Her friend's smile didn't chase the shadows from her indigo eyes as she led Olive through the living and dining rooms and into the sunny kitchen. Small jars of basil, oregano, and mint flourished on the windowsill. "I am hungry, though. Want to share?"

"You bet I do. Sit." Olive removed her gloves and hat and set about arranging lunch for them both. "Now spill it, sister."

Olive *had* a sister, and a brother, too, but both Hazel and Walter were more than a decade older, so she'd grown up more like an only child. Ever since primary school, she'd been closer to Claire than she had been to either sibling, and since Claire's mother died giving birth to her, Claire had no sisters or brothers, either.

"It's almost embarrassing." Claire hooked a finger into the wedding ring she wore on a chain around her neck since she'd lost too much weight for it to stay on her finger. "I was carrying a basket of laundry down the stairs, missed a step, and went tumbling. Just imagine it. Dirty clothes flying through the air, me shrieking like a tomcat and catching myself wrong on my arm—and face."

"Dangerous business, laundry. Was Warren home, at least?"

Claire tucked the ring inside her bodice and leaned over her bowl for her first taste of soup. "Yes, thank goodness. It happened yesterday after work. He insisted I stay home today. By Monday, the swelling will have gone down enough that my clumsiness won't be a livid advertisement to anyone who walks by." Gingerly, she touched a fingertip to the puffy bruise. "You can agree I'm not fit to be seen in public today."

Olive could see why Claire thought so, at least. Claire was

stunningly beautiful and always had been, with a creamy complexion, glossy black hair, and a Sears model's lithe silhouette. In fact, the catalog illustrators often used her for inspiration. It was probably hard for Claire to go out looking less polished than a fashion-plate, even if those fashions were the frugal styles of her department store employer.

Olive, on the other hand, was the chummy sidekick with her mother's curvy build. She was named for a small, round garnish, for goodness' sake.

Peering at the uncarpeted stairs, Olive frowned. "Were you dizzy? Is that why you fell?"

Claire dipped her spoon into the soup and fished up a thick egg noodle. "Maybe a little. I don't know, it happened quickly."

Olive considered this. There were all kinds of reasons for dizzy spells. Pregnancy was one of them.

As if reading her mind, Claire met Olive's gaze. "It isn't—there's no baby, if that's what you're thinking. Not anymore."

"Do you mean—" Olive's heart sank to her stomach. "After Christmas? There was another?" Claire had miscarried in December. There had been two miscarriages before that one, too.

A hand drifting to her middle, Claire watched a finch at the feeder outside the window. "Almost three months along this time. I'm starting to think I'm never going to carry to term. Warren never even knew about the pregnancy this spring. I couldn't bear having to tell him we'd lost another one." She blinked back tears.

Her own eyes hot and sticky, Olive reached across the table and held her friend's hand. "You mean you've been all alone in your grief?"

"Not anymore." Sniffing, Claire squeezed Olive's fingers and tried on a bright but ill-fitting smile.

"I wish I'd known sooner," Olive murmured.

"It wouldn't have made a difference."

"Not for the baby, but for you. I could have been there for you. When I ask how you are, I want the truth. Unvarnished."

"I'm sorry. You do realize that I make a living making things sound good, don't you?" Claire smirked and tapped the Sears catalog on the table.

"Point taken. But *you* realize that you aren't selling me anything, right? If friends can't be honest with each other, that friendship isn't worth much."

A stricken expression stole over Claire. "Oh, Liv. Your friendship is worth more to me than you could possibly under—"

The front door burst open. "Claire?" Warren's deep voice ricocheted off the walls. "The door was unlocked. Is someone else here?"

By the time he finished his question, however, his long strides had brought him to the kitchen to see the answer himself. His grey eyes softened, but if there was any warmth in his greeting, his neatly trimmed mustache concealed it.

Olive smiled up at him. "Hello, Warren, nice to see you." It would have been nicer if he'd waited a little longer before interrupting them. If Claire hadn't confided in him about her most recent miscarriage, then it was obvious she needed Olive's companionship.

"Olive." He straightened the necktie cinching his celluloid collar. "I wasn't expecting you."

"Neither was I, dear." Claire was on her feet, taking his homburg from him. "She popped over with soup and surprised me. Is there any soup left, Olive? Warren, would you like some?"

He ran a pocket comb over his hair, not that any strands were out of place. It was cropped as short as his mustache and was the sandy brown of a Boy Scout uniform. "No, no thanks. I told you I'd have a toasted ham and cheese sandwich instead. Did you forget I said I'd be home at 12:30 to check on you?"

More like he was home at 12:30 for her to feed him, broken arm or not.

Disapproval flickered over his face. "You're not wearing your grandmother's watch. That heirloom isn't just jewelry, darling. It's meant to help you keep track of time."

Claire hurried away, returning with the gold timepiece.

Warren pinned it to the broad lapel of her dress. "She told you about the accident?" he asked Olive.

Nodding, Olive cleared the table, then packed up the Thermos she'd brought. "That was quite a tumble she took. If you need anything, Claire, while you're recovering, please call me. I can bring meals if cooking is too much or help with any housework that seems beyond you."

Warren responded for her. "That's generous of you, but she has me. I'll see to all her needs. She'll be back to her old self in no time."

Claire's smile wobbled. "That's right. And I'll be sure to be more careful, too."

SATURDAY, JUNE 12, 1915

The aromas of onions and garlic permeated Olive's third-floor apartment on the corner of Clark and Randolph. The smell of homemade lasagna was the smell of Saturday night, comfort, and family. With the weather being unusually cool and wet this summer, the hot food didn't feel out of place.

Dinner was over, and Olive poured coffee for her uncle Kristof— this being completely different from serving Mr. Roth—and sent him to the living room with the newspaper while she and Sylvie tackled the dirty dishes together. He hummed as he went, probably some piece he'd conducted as the maestro of the Chicago Symphony Orchestra last season. Or perhaps a line he'd been drilling with the master classes he was teaching this summer.

"Be honest, now." Sylvie smiled, lines fanning from her deep brown eyes as she snapped open a dish towel. Light glinted on the beautiful silver hair bound at the nape of her neck. "How do you like having the place to yourself, with your mother splitting her summer vacation between Walter's family and Hazel's?"

Olive had adjusted to the situation much quicker than she ought to admit. "I just hope she's having a good time and that everyone's taking care of her." She plunged her hands into the sudsy water.

"She's not an invalid, Olive." Sylvie chuckled, her humor still intact at age sixty-five. "I'm quite certain they aren't tasking her with hard labor and that when she needs help with buttons or laces, her grandchildren are only too eager to assist. Just as you always were."

Olive smiled. She was still willing to assist her mother, whose burns of long ago had left her hands scarred. Walter and Hazel had both moved out of state with their families, Walter to a small town in Indiana, where he was a professor at Taylor University, and Hazel to New York City, where her husband was a clothing buyer for major department stores across the country. Hazel had invited Meg to move in with her right after Nate died, but she was so much better off here with Olive, Sylvie, and Kristof in the city she grew up in and the same building that housed the family bookstore, Corner Books & More.

Diagonally across the street were the colonnaded City Hall and County Courthouse, both standing twelve stories high. Three stories taller than that was the Beaux-arts style Sherman House Hotel right next to Olive's apartment. Though dwarfed by its towering neighbors, the bookstore's building was still home.

Sylvie stacked another clean, dry plate in the cupboard. "It seems to me this summer would be an excellent time to have some fun yourself. Here we are, taking up your Saturday nights when you ought to be out with—someone else."

"You didn't marry until you were in your forties, and it was worth the wait, too." Still scrubbing at baked-on tomato sauce, Olive sent her aunt a wary look.

"But I always had Meg and Beth. You should be with friends, too, at least some of the time."

"I'm right where I want to be, I promise," Olive assured her. "Besides, I saw Claire yesterday."

"Oh, good. How is our own Diana Barry doing these days?"

Meg had painted the double portrait hanging above Olive's fireplace mantel and called it *Anne and Diana* after the bosom friends in L. M. Montgomery's bestselling books. The beaming faces with impish grins, however, were clearly auburn-haired Olive and raven-haired Claire when they were girls. Bosom friends, then and always.

"We didn't get to chat nearly as much as I would have liked," Olive admitted and told her about Claire's broken arm. "Warren came home for his lunch while I was there."

Sylvie rinsed the lasagna pan, then bunched the towel into its corners. "It may not seem like it sometimes, but Claire needs your friendship. That hasn't changed just because she's married."

"I know you're right." The elevated train, the El, roared by a block away. Living inside the Loop the El made around Chicago's business district, Olive had grown used to the sound. "I still wish we had more time together. Even on the telephone, she doesn't seem to speak freely."

"That doesn't sound like her. Why, do you remember how good she was with the customers in the bookstore?"

Olive remembered. She also recalled that after Nate had succumbed to a long bout of pneumonia in late 1912, it was Claire who had come every day for two weeks, making sure both Olive and Meg were eating, and banishing dust from the entire house. Having grieved her own father, and her grandmother nine years before that, she seemed to know what to do.

During the month that followed Olive's and Meg's move into Sylvie's apartment building, Claire came every weekend. She tethered Olive, allowing her to mourn her father but keeping her from sinking too deeply. If Olive drowned in grief, who would help her mother? It was only because Claire had been the life raft for Olive that Olive could be the same for Meg.

Now Claire was the one grieving again. She shouldn't have to bear the loss of her babies alone.

"All the more reason to keep reaching out to her." Sylvie's words drew Olive back into the conversation. Before she could voice her agreement, however, Kristof called over his newspaper that Rozalia had come by that day.

"I'm sorry I missed her!" Sylvie hung the dish towel to dry and left the kitchen, Olive following. Her footsteps imprinted the oriental rug as she crossed the living room and eased into one of the buttoned leather club chairs that had belonged to Nate.

Sylvie sat with Kristof on the sofa, its upholstery a near match to the butter-yellow curtains behind it. Striped paper in dove and pearl grey made the walls a suitable backdrop for a few of Meg's paintings. "What did she have to say?"

Lowering rays of sun winked on Kristof's silver hair as he searched his pocket. "She brought us these. Two tickets to the annual employee picnic for Western Electric's Hawthorne Works facility." Rozalia, whom Sylvie had raised since she was four years old, now worked at Hawthorne in Cicero, a suburb west of Chicago.

"I've heard about this from some of my clients who work there," Olive said. "It's a huge event. Five steamships have been chartered to carry the group across the southern tip of Lake Michigan to Michigan City, Indiana. They're expecting more than seven thousand people to go. Employees and their families, neighbors, and friends."

"Seven thousand!" Sylvie exclaimed. "It's hard to believe so many people work for the same company."

Olive could believe it. She'd been to Cicero to visit Rose. The main building at Hawthorne Works looked like a medieval fortress, but there were dozens of separate buildings spread over a campus of more than two hundred acres, like a town within a town. Hawthorne even had its own police and water supply. Rose's husband, Tobias, worked as a manager for one of the train stations in Cicero, but Rose and their daughter Izabelle worked as telegraph operators at Hawthorne. Rose also taught night classes for immigrant employees who wanted to improve their English.

"From what I understand," Olive said, "it's much more than a picnic. There are games, dancing, amusement park rides, and a parade."

A day with Rose sounded lovely, to say nothing of the festivities. Her favorite childhood memories were of sharing rides with Rose on a camel and on the Ferris wheel at the World's Fair when she was seven years old and Rose seventeen. But the bond with her cousin had loosened over time and distance as Rose started her own family.

"July 24," Kristof read from the ticket. "Far enough away that we can make arrangements. It sounds like a date to me." His smile to his wife was warm with affection. "Soon after that, Rose and her family will head to California for the Exposition, and then on to Poland to visit her husband's family. This will be our last chance to see them until summer's end."

"If Nadine can't mind the store while you're gone, I'll fill in for her," Olive offered. The young woman Sylvie employed only worked one or two weekends a month.

"Oh, she'll be working, all right," Sylvie confirmed. "That's her last day. She's going to have a baby, and her husband doesn't want her working anymore, which means I'll need to hire and train someone new."

"But not on the day Rose invited us to spend with her family," Kristof said.

"You should all go," Olive agreed. She would just stay home.

CHAPTER THREE

WEDNESDAY, JULY 21, 1915

"No one wants to think about the eventuality of death," Olive told her two newest MetLife clients, "but you're doing the right thing by preparing for it." Rising, she shook both of their hands and then walked the young husband and wife out of her office, through reception, and to the corridor, where she bid them a warm good-bye.

A low whistle greeted her as she headed back toward her office. "What is that, the third sale this week?" Howard Penrose leaned against the mahogany doorframe to his own office. Suit jacket unbuttoned to reveal a striped vest, he hooked a thumb into his trouser pocket. Hazel eyes flashed beneath a thatch of brown hair that could do with a little trimming. "You were made for this."

She straightened her jacket and lifted her chin. Nearing him, she cast a pointed glance to the mess on his desk, a mess she could be helping him with. "I was made for more than this, Howard. Just wait and see."

"I'm not holding my breath."

His response trailed her to her own desk, but she paid it no mind. It had been almost six weeks since Roth had denied her a promotion. In that time, she'd resolved to do her job the best she knew how, which was simply business as usual.

Blanche was in a meeting with Mr. Roth, and there was no tell-ing how long that would last, especially if he sent her out for coffee refills. Olive may not do coffee, but she honestly didn't mind filing when Blanche was busy. So rather than dropping manila folders of closed cases on Blanche's desk, Olive scooped them up, carried them to the records room, and filed them alphabetically. When she inserted the last one from her stack, she drew a quick intake of breath at the sight of another.

Murphy, Ernest. She hadn't known the elderly gentleman had passed. His kind, vein-mapped face burst upon her vision. Before he'd gotten sick, he'd made a habit of visiting the office every Christmas, dressed in the same tweed suit and paisley bow tie. He brought the staff bottles of his homemade Christmas punch and soaked up as much companionship as he could in return. Olive whispered a prayer for those who had known and loved him. She'd have gone to his funeral if she had known.

Howard must have processed this case. Curious, she scanned the file to see when he passed—in May—and who his beneficiary was. *Raymond Murphy.* This name had been added after the policy was originally purchased, according to the amendment. Perhaps a son or a brother. The amount paid to him was little more than a thousand dollars.

Hadn't she come across a Raymond Murphy in another closed case? It had caught her attention because the last names hadn't matched between insured and beneficiary. That wasn't unusual, with married names changing with each generation, but still. She'd seen Raymond Murphy before.

She riffled through the folders. *Samson . . . Sartori . . .*

There it was. *Schmidt, Mathilda.* If Olive recalled correctly, Mathilda had been a widow for some time before she died last Oc-tober. She opened the file and flipped to the listed beneficiary. Her husband, the primary, was marked as deceased. The secondary, who received nearly two thousand dollars, was Raymond Murphy via another amendment.

Neither of these two policies had paid out all that much upon the insureds' deaths. Mathilda and Ernest were both in their seventies when they passed, and no one depended on them for income, so that wasn't surprising.

Still, something about it was odd.

Was the game afoot, as Sherlock Holmes would say?

Olive studied both files. The initials in the bottom corner of the last page of both amendments belonged to Gwendolyn, indicating she was the one to type them up. After closing the filing cabinet drawer, Olive turned off the light and left the room.

"Gwendolyn." Olive paused at the secretary's desk and waited for her to stop typing. Gracious, but the clatter from that Underwood No. 5 was the worst she'd ever heard. It ought to be replaced, like Blanche's had been.

As if reading her mind, Gwendolyn smiled and said over her clicking keys, "That's the sound of productivity, sweetie!"

"Well, stop being so productive for just a moment, if you please."

Gwendolyn laughed, but after she *zing*ed the return carriage, she obliged. "How can I help?"

Spreading the files on the desk, Olive showed her what she'd noticed. "I see you typed these amendments. Do you remember amending Ernest's policy in 1913 to name Raymond Murphy as a secondary beneficiary?"

Lips buttoning to one side, Gwendolyn inspected her initials in the corner, then reviewed the paperwork. "I don't remember anything special about either of these. It looks like the policy was sold to Ernest by an agent named Miles Knapp twenty-five years ago."

"He's the same agent who sold Mathilda's to her, as well, in 1895," Olive said. "Mr. Knapp passed on before you were hired. But Mathilda's policy was amended in 1914."

Gwendolyn dipped into a bowl of peppermint candies she kept on the corner of her desk. She placed one in Olive's palm before unwrapping another and tucking it into her cheek. "You know, sometimes the elderly outlive all the family members who might have been beneficiaries. Maybe this Raymond, Ernest's relative, happened to be kind to Mathilda. He could have been a maintenance man in her building who stopped to talk with her when she was lonely, or even a waiter she enjoyed chatting with at her favorite diner. It's not unheard of."

The theory made sense. Older people were lonely and grateful for any human contact they could get. Olive hadn't known Mathilda, but if she was anything like Ernest, she was probably the type to leave a surprise blessing for someone in her life, relative or not.

That was probably it.

Maybe.

Blanche emerged from Mr. Roth's office as Olive thanked Gwendolyn for her time. On the way to return the files to the records room, Olive paused behind Blanche's desk and opened the folders once more. Something was off. She just didn't know what.

She spun her bracelet watch on her wrist to check the time. *Blast!* Her next appointment was due to arrive. Hurrying back to her desk, she chewed the last of the melting peppermint, slipped the files in her top desk drawer, and locked it as her next clients came through the door. The mystery of Raymond Murphy would have to wait.

Chapter Four

Thursday, July 22, 1915

There was only one reason Claire would call Olive the day before they were scheduled to meet in person. And it wasn't to say she was excited.

"Change of plans?" she asked and deflated when Claire confirmed it. "Please don't do this, Claire. Not on your birthday." She kicked off the pumps she'd worn to the office and tucked her stockinged feet beneath her on the club chair in her living room. Stray bits of ribbon she'd used to trim Claire's gift just minutes ago tumbled from her skirt.

"You know I'd come if I could." Claire spoke so quietly that Olive strained to hear her above the traffic outside. A train rumbled past the courthouse across the street. "I'm not feeling well. Not well enough to have fun, at any rate. We'll celebrate another time, I promise. Soon."

Olive doubted it. She'd tried to arrange another lunch date twice since she visited Claire at her home last month, but each time Claire had a different excuse. Finally, on the last Saturday in June, when Warren was at the auto race at Speedway Park, Olive had whisked Claire to the shore for a dip in the lake.

At first, Olive couldn't understand Claire's reluctance to leave her house without her husband's permission, especially since he was out having a lark himself. The closer they got to the beach, however, the more Claire had seemed like her old self again. By the time they had changed into their bathing costumes and stood with their toes wiggling in the sand, the water lapping at their ankles, Claire was laughing from deep in her belly, heedless for once about her hair whipping freely in the wind. Her arm was still in its cast and sling, so real swimming was out of the question, but even so, their cares sailed away.

All had been right again.

Until Olive saw the bruises ringing her friend's upper arms, barely peeking from beneath short sleeves. Around the back of Claire's neck was a horizontal cut as thin as the chain she wore her wedding ring on. And in the blink of an eye, Olive could see it. She saw Warren yanking the necklace, grabbing Claire by the arms and squeezing until he crushed the blood vessels in her skin. She saw the arm in the sling and purpled face and knew it had been no accident.

Joy curled inward, dried up, and blew away. Holding her own locks out of her eyes, Olive stared, mouth dry as sand, at her battered, too-thin friend. "Claire," she had rasped. "Why didn't you tell me?"

Claire licked her lips and swallowed. "Tell you what?" But it was no question. Her hands had already flown to cover her arms. "Would it have made any difference?" She'd glanced at Olive, then fixed her gaze on the horizon, that line where endless lake met endless sky.

Before Olive could summon a reply, someone had called out to Claire, a coworker from Sears.

Terror had sprawled across Claire's face. "Oh no. Don't turn around, I can't be seen here. She'll tell Warren she saw me at the beach—dressed like this! He'll be furious. Come on, we have to go."

Too stunned to argue, Olive complied.

Shoulders rounding, Claire hid behind her hair as they kicked sand up their calves in their hurried departure. "Don't look back," she said, even as she'd done so like someone hunted.

A chill swept Olive as she remembered it. She shifted the earpiece to the other ear. "Are you all right?"

Silence crackled.

"Because you don't sound sick. Maybe a little weak, is all." Olive winced at how that sounded. "I didn't mean *weak*," she clarified. "I meant to say tired."

A chuckle tripped over the line. "You meant what you said the first time." There was an edge to Claire's tone, hinting that she realized she'd changed. No longer did her eyes sparkle or her cheeks bloom bright with life and vigor. No longer did she stand tall, shoulders squared. It hadn't happened overnight. But gradually, Olive realized now, Claire had grown into a woman who flinched. A woman who looked over her shoulder.

With reason.

A sense of helplessness reared up within Olive. She swung her feet to the floor and stood, angling toward the fireplace mantel, which had become a gallery of other people's happiness, or so it had always seemed. Wedding photographs of her parents, her aunt and uncle, Rozalia and Tobias. Even her siblings and their spouses were there. She considered the framed image of Claire and Warren. It looked fairy-tale perfect, a prelude to happily ever after.

"He hit you again? Left a mark where clothes won't cover it? Is that why you don't want to meet me at the Tea Room tomorrow?"

Claire sighed. "That's not it."

"Tell me the truth."

"I am telling the truth," Claire insisted. "He didn't leave a mark—at least not one you'd notice. He just doesn't want me to come, that's all."

"It's your thirtieth birthday! I'm your oldest friend. We always get together on your birthday!"

"Maybe if he wasn't still upset about my going to the lake—" A huff sounded over the phone. "My thirtieth is no more important than yours. Let's just plan to celebrate yours together, all right?"

Olive stifled a groan. "That's two months away, and who's to say he won't squash those plans, too?" She paused, then dared to ask, "What would happen if you said no to him and yes to what *you* want to do?"

"What would happen?" Claire's voice hardened. "I'll tell you what would happen. I'd suddenly become very clumsy and have an accident."

Dismay rolled through Olive. She was selfish to ask Claire to put herself in danger. She hated that going to lunch meant such a risk.

"It's not that I don't stand up to him," Claire whispered. "It's just that when I do, I get knocked down. On occasion, I have the sense not to get up. At least for a while. Apparently, there is only room in this marriage for one strong person, and it's Warren."

Urgency billowed hot inside Olive. She had to do something for Claire, help her somehow. If only she could reach through the wire and pull her right out of that house. "Come stay with me. You'll be safe here, especially with my family living in the same building. You could room with me, or if you'd rather have your own space, stay in Gregor's apartment on the fourth floor." Kristof's brother was traveling with a music festival this summer, and his wife had gone with him.

"Livvie." Emotion thickened Claire's tone. "You're not just my oldest friend, you're my *only* friend. Your building is the first place he'd look. If I run, he'll find me, and then things will be even worse. For me, but for you, too."

"The police, then!"

"Who do you think they'd believe, him or me? I don't know what to— He's coming."

The line clicked and went dead in Olive's hand.

A knock on the door preceded Sylvie popping her head into the apartment, her nose red and eyes watery. At the sight of Olive's expression, she stepped inside, shutting the door behind her. "Well! I came to say I'm bowing out of our game of checkers tonight. This cold is sending me to bed soon, and there's simply no arguing with it. But I see there are more important things afoot anyway. Need to talk?"

Olive did. Hanging up the telephone, she beckoned her aunt to a chair. On her way to fix another cup of tea, she set aside the wrapped present she'd been planning to give Claire tomorrow. It was a copy of *Anne of the Island,* which had just been released, to match her copies of *Anne of Green Gables* and *Anne of Avonlea.*

"It's Claire," she said on a sigh. "She doesn't need another book for her birthday. She needs a miracle."

FRIDAY, JULY 23, 1915

Olive was practically out of breath by the time she'd navigated the maze of the Sears, Roebuck and Company office complex and found Claire.

"Olive!" Claire looked past her, then all around, probably gauging how much attention the visit had earned. Every hair was in place, her timepiece pinned to her jacket, and her wedding ring sparkled where it lay against her bodice. She looked all right.

But Olive knew better.

"Happy birthday." Olive had taken a late lunch break to be here, knowing Warren would have already taken his by now. She handed Claire the package and watched as she unwrapped it.

Claire smiled. "It's beautiful, Olive, and perfect. Thank you." A wistful note of nostalgia touched her words. "But you really didn't need to come all this way today. I could have waited to get it from you later."

Olive bit her lip to keep from smiling too broadly. "The book might have waited. But this won't." Snapping open the clasp of her bag, she withdrew the ticket and pressed it into Claire's hand.

"Western Electric's annual picnic?" A laugh escaped Claire. "This is tomorrow. I don't understand."

Olive described the entire event, from the luxurious cruise to the bands and dancing and ice cream waiting on the other side of the lake. Last night, as soon as Olive had shared Claire's story, Sylvie had insisted she take the two tickets meant for her and Kristof. *"I've already decided not to go with this cold of mine,"* she'd explained, *"and Kristof is coming down with it, too. Take our tickets and get some use out of them."* Olive hadn't needed to be told twice.

"The best part is that we'll have time," Olive continued. "Time together to really talk without interruption. Time to rest."

Claire's heartbeat pulsed in the hollow of her throat. "Warren wouldn't like it."

Olive wasn't surprised. "I don't want this trip to cause even more trouble with him. So, as much as I want to spend tomorrow with you, I won't push you to do something that will only bring you more pain."

Lashes lowered, Claire's knuckles whitened as she gripped the novel. "Getting on board wouldn't be a problem, since he has an early game of golf tomorrow. But we wouldn't get back to Chicago before he's done with his game. Unless he stays out well past evening, he'd come home to an empty house." She shook her head and repeated, "He wouldn't like that. He was livid enough about me going to the beach with you."

"Was that because wearing a bathing costume exposed your bruises?" Olive asked carefully. "I don't want to persuade you to go against your better judgment. But let's say we keep all our clothes on this time. Prim and proper. And this would be an early thirtieth birthday present for me. Do you suppose he would still object then?"

Claire's finger found its way into the tiny gold circle hanging on the chain around her neck. "I've given up predicting what he will object to. But maybe that would be all right. The man I married would have said absolutely, I should go. He would have wanted me to be happy." The small fan on her desk hummed as it stirred an atmosphere grown heavy with hope and dread.

"I want you to come," Olive whispered. "But more than that, I want you to be safe. The first ship leaves the dock near the Clark Street Bridge around seven thirty. If you come, meet me at my apartment by six forty-five, and we'll walk over together."

A sigh brushed past Claire's lips as she caressed the ticket. She said nothing.

But at least she didn't say no.

CHAPTER FIVE

SATURDAY, JULY 24, 1915

"Apples, straight from Wisconsin, nineteen cents a peck! Bing cherries, one pint for one thin dime, but only for today!"

Olive walked through the shade of multiple awnings stretching from produce stands lining the riverfront. Sellers called above traffic that smelled of both fuel and horseflesh.

Claire hadn't come to the apartment this morning. That she had decided not to come was only one possible explanation. Perhaps she was running late and decided to head straight to the docks, or she'd misunderstood Olive's instruction and thought she was to meet her on the wharf at 6:45.

"Florida lemons, today! Peanuts from Mississippi, Michigan blueberries! Get 'em while they're fresh!"

Even with all the produce, the predominant smell was the river, made noxious with waste and chemicals from local factories. Once they were out on Lake Michigan, however, the air would be perfectly sweet.

Nose wrinkling, Olive held her broad-brimmed white straw hat to her head and checked her watch.

Blast! It was ten after seven. The Clark Street Bridge was only two and a half blocks from home, but she hadn't allowed for the fact that her usual brisk pace would be slowed to a throng-choked shuffle.

All around her, Western Electric employees and their guests were dressed to the nines, the men in suits and homburgs or straw hats, the ladies in layers of white and pastel finery and high-button boots. They toted picnic baskets and small children wearing smiles as wide as their sailor collars. Riding a man's shoulders, a little boy in brown knee breeches and matching cap clutched a toy boat, weaving it through the air as though it sailed the seas. Scandinavian, Czech, and Polish accents peppered the din of conversation, all of it enthusiastic. The drizzle blowing in did nothing to dampen their spirits. It was impossible not to smile along with them.

Now, if she could only find Claire. If, in fact, her friend had even come.

"Look, Papa!" The little boy pointed with his boat. "There it is!"

The SS *Eastland* towered just ahead. Four decks rose above the water, and enormous twin chimney stacks chugged black clouds into an already pewter-grey sky. The white vessel was almost the entire length of the block from LaSalle Street to Clark. Already, the top two open decks—the promenade and the hurricane—were full of people, some waving to those on the wharf below. A steam calliope played "In the Good Old Summer Time."

"One, two, three, four . . ." Still pointing, the little boy began counting the lifeboats hanging from stanchions outside the hurricane deck. There were plenty for everyone, Olive knew even without counting them herself. After the *Titanic* had sunk three years ago, maritime law made sure of that.

At last, Olive reached the steps that took her down to the wharf. The lines tying the ship to the dock creaked as they grew taut and then slack again. Engines gurgled, and the river slapped at pilings. At four and a half stories tall, the *Eastland* dwarfed the weathered brick buildings belonging to the Chicago-South Haven steamship company below. At the bottom of the *Eastland*'s gangplank, she handed her ticket to one man in a suit and derby while another clicked his hand-counter. She gripped the rope on either side of her as she climbed the slick plank to the ship's main deck.

The soft yaw of the ship loosening her knees, she searched for Claire. The air inside was thick with laughter, cologne, machine oil, cigar smoke, and a trace of mildew.

"Taffy, nineteen cents for a pound! All sorts of fruit and spice flavors! Milk chocolates, peanut butter crisps!" a mustached man called. Wearing a tray of candy attached to his suspenders and belt, he staggered among children eager for his wares.

"Claire?" As Olive approached a woman, the ship tilted again, and she bumped into her from behind. "Sorry!" She righted herself as the woman turned around. She had Claire's thick raven hair and willowy build, but it wasn't Claire.

"It's all right." The woman laughed, then pointed at the ceiling. "They seem to think it's a game, no?"

A collective "*Wheeeeee!*" sounded from above. "*All together now!*"

Olive smiled, recognizing the woman. "Mrs. Petroski? It's so good to see you again. Olive Pierce with MetLife." She had sold life insurance policies to the Petroskis a few years ago.

"Ah yes! But please call me Stella. Jakob is over there, holding our daughter, Addie. I believe last time we met, she had yet to make her first appearance." Eyes dancing, Stella rounded her hands as if holding an invisible pregnant belly. "Our boy Michael is the one sneaking a sugar wafer from the basket he's holding. He's seven now, and Addie's two and a half. Are you here as someone's guest?"

Olive explained her connection to Rose. "I haven't seen her yet today, though." Rose had called last night to explain that Izabelle and Tobias were staying home sick. Hopefully the illness hadn't spread to Rose, as well.

"I know Rozalia. Jakob and I were both her students for a while, improving our English when we first started working here.

I haven't seen her this morning either, but she may be on one of the other four ships. You might also check the parlors on this deck. You should see them regardless. They're beautiful."

"Hello, Miss Pierce!" Jakob joined them, the golden-haired toddler in his arms gripping the brim of his homburg. His walnut-brown hair shone with Brilliantine. "Here to drum up business from the timid sailors among us?" he jested.

"Oh, heavens no!" Laughing with him, Olive greeted Stella's family.

Addie poked a curl of Olive's hair. "Red!" she declared. "*Czerwony*!"

Well, so much for auburn. "Smart girl." Olive chuckled. "Raising her bilingual?"

Jakob smiled. "We speak English at home, but she picks up Polish from Stella's parents, who live with us."

"*Matka*!" Addie reached for her mother, and Jakob handed her over.

Michael tugged on Jakob's sleeve and whispered into his bent ear. His dark hair and fair complexion were a match for his mother's. After receiving a nod from his father, the little boy fished a sugar wafer from the picnic basket and held it out to Olive.

"Papa says it's okay. You can have one."

Olive took a knee and accepted the gift. "This is my favorite flavor," she told him. "Thank you."

With a small, pleased smile, the boy tipped his newsboy cap to her, and Olive took her leave.

She headed for the burnished mahogany staircase, ten feet wide at its base, situated near the cash bar selling beer and Coca-Cola out of a giant refrigerator. If Claire were already here, she'd likely be above, watching for Olive to board.

The ship leaned the other way, and Olive steadied herself on the banister until it righted. Up on the cabin deck, she swept between hundreds of passengers, pausing at the starboard wall to let a large family pass by. Other than the portholes, this deck resembled a grand hotel with its balustrades, dozens of cabins in the center, and a saloon at one end.

"I don't like the feel of it," a woman beside her murmured, clutching a young girl's hand. Her Norwegian-accented voice was almost swallowed up in the commotion of crying babies and folks vying for chairs.

"What, Mama?" Another girl, this one not more than thirteen, looked over her shoulder at the elegantly dressed lady who'd just spoken.

"I said I don't like the feel of this boat. There are too many people on this boat!"

Olive was inclined to agree. "Claire!" she shouted into the crowd as she made her way through it toward another ornately carved staircase. Gripping the banister, she climbed to the promenade deck.

Rain blew in sideways, spotting her hat and skirt as she turned about, inhaling the smell of cigars and pipe tobacco. The center of the deck was filled with deluxe staterooms, but an eight-foot-wide walkway ran the length of the vessel. At one end was a smoking room, and at the other, a five-member orchestra played mandolins and violins. Chairs had been pushed out of the way, and scores of couples were already box-stepping to the tune.

"Olive!" Claire's voice turned Olive's head.

"You came! It's a birthday miracle!"

A picnic basket slid out from beneath someone's chair, and Claire bent to retrieve it, handing it back to its owner. "I was running late, so I decided to come straight here. I was beginning to think I'd never find you. The man who took my ticket said he was allowing twenty-five hundred people on board this morning."

"We must be nearing that now," Olive said. "I can't imagine any more people squeezing on." But when she looked below, she saw a steady stream still coming up the gangplank.

"Can we go below? I'd like to dry out, if I can. Maybe the

sun will come out by the time we get to Michigan City." Her hat drooped and dripped rain onto her thin shoulders. But her eyes snapped with that old sparkle Olive loved.

"Yes, of course, you should go on down. You haven't seen Rose, by any chance?"

Claire hadn't.

"All right. How about I meet you in one of the parlors on the main deck in a few minutes? I'd like to look for Rose before I come join you. If I don't see her soon, I'll plan to find her later. You are my main priority today anyway, sister."

Claire agreed to the plan. "And, Livvie? Thanks for inviting me. Even if it rains all day, it will be perfect." Her smile flickered as she glanced down at the wharf. She stepped back from the railing. "What I mean is, I'm glad to be getting away from here. For the day. Just one glorious day."

"I had my doubts that you'd actually come," Olive confessed.

"I wasn't planning to. Let's just say I had a change of heart." She lifted the brim of her hat, revealing a gash near her hairline, the surrounding skin a royal shade of purple. It looked fresh.

The queasiness in Olive's stomach had nothing to do with the rocking ship. "What happened?"

Claire settled the hat back in place, masking the evidence with a jaunty angle of the bow-trimmed brim. "Warren hit me for no reason. At least not a real one. I realized he's just as likely to hurt me whether I come today or not. If pain is inevitable tomorrow anyway, I might as well enjoy myself today."

Claire disappeared down the stairs, and Olive turned back to the rail to watch for Rose, more uneasy than ever over her friend's circumstances. But the ship rolled toward the river, tossing her backward. Landing on her rump, she slid until she collided with a mandolin player. From the deck below, the clanking of falling bottles pinched her ears. Stunned, she stayed pressed against this strange man, neither of them speaking nor smiling nor even apologizing, until the ship corrected its roll.

Only then did the musician help her up.

"That wasn't normal," she said.

"For the *Eastland*, it is. I've played on these decks before. She's a little wobbly, but as soon as the engineers even out the ballast tanks, we'll have smooth sailing. It shouldn't be long now. They've taken in the gangplank." He tipped his cap to her, then set to playing his instrument once more.

Somewhat reassured, Olive brushed off the seat of her dove-grey skirt. When she heard her name, she turned toward the stern and saw a woman waving to her from the *Petoskey*, docked west of the *Eastland*.

It was Rose, a gauzy floral scarf tying a hat in place over her blond hair, a gloved hand at her throat. "Are you all right?" she called. The deck behind her was beginning to fill with passengers.

"Fine," Olive called back. "See you on the other side."

But as she made her way down through the cabin deck toward the main, all she could think was an echo of what she'd heard that other passenger say. *I don't like the feel of this ship.*

No sooner did her feet hit the main deck than the refrigerator tipped and crashed onto its side. The engines stopped. So did the music upstairs.

Olive crossed the slanted floor toward the forward part of the ship, where the parlors were. A man stepped into her path, his clothing oily and smudged with what she could only guess was smoke from the engine room.

"Ladies and gents!" He held up his hands. "If you would please move to the starboard side of the boat!"

Starboard side. That was the side closest to the dock. Olive attempted to comply. Through the open doors of the parlor, she spied a glass pitcher on a table, a few inches of water still inside. Judging by the slant of the water compared to the tabletop, the ship leaned more than twenty degrees. It made no sense. When

45

she'd left the promenade deck, most of the people were still on the starboard rail, waving to friends below. Why was the ship tipping toward the river, then?

"Claire?" she called out.

The cry of a little girl cut through the chatter. "Water is coming in!" The river seeped in through the open gangways, and then suddenly, the lean reversed its course.

The crowd was silent, waiting to see if the balance would hold. Olive's pulse rushed in her ears. Surely this was dreadfully wrong.

As soon as she dared, she pardoned her way through the crush of passengers and into the parlors, still calling for Claire.

"Here!" Waving, Claire stood up from a circular velvet bench in the center of the ornate room.

Olive joined her. "Come on. It's too crowded down here." There must be a thousand people on this deck alone.

"I don't mind it." Handbag looped over her wrist, Claire tightened the belt at her waist. "It's better than getting wet."

With a raised eyebrow, Olive gestured toward the dozens of picnic-goers with soaked shoes and stockings. Those who hadn't reacted as quickly bore waterlines above the hems of taffeta skirts and woolen trousers.

"Good point," Claire conceded.

"Let's at least head up to the cabin deck. We'll still be sheltered from the rain—and from the very small chance that Warren might be looking for you from the wharf."

Claire's smile suggested Olive had hit on the real issue. She checked her watch. "It's seven twenty-six. Pretty soon we'll put Chicago behind us, and I'll breathe easier."

Back through the crowds they went. At the stairs at last, they began their ascent, ragtime music sounding again from above. The fickle ship began rocking again.

"Steady, miss!" A Bohemian gentleman caught Olive as she tripped up one of the stairs. "It's like riding a bicycle, this steamship, yes? A little unbalanced standing still, but once we get on our way . . ." He made a straight motion with his free hand. "She'll right herself with a little speed. Wait and see." He released her with a smile warm and reassuring, then clasped the hand of a little boy waiting on the step below him.

"I'm sure you're right," Claire offered from Olive's other side.

The ticking of Olive's heart calmed by a fraction. "I hope so. Thank you." She had no experience with steamships, had no idea what to expect or what was reason for alarm.

"Be brave like me and Papa." The child thumped his chest, bumping his bow tie askew.

When Olive and Claire gained the cabin deck, the ship was still listing, and a collective groan filled the space. Women clutched babies tighter, digging their high heels into the floors.

The lean increased to twenty degrees again, just as it had when everyone was told to move to the starboard side of the ship. Still clutching the top of the banister, Olive closed her eyes and waited for this obstinate hunk of steel to make up its mind to sail straight. Claire's arm slipped through hers.

The sound of rushing water popped her eyes open again. The leaning had never stopped. Peering down the stairs to the main deck, she could hear what she couldn't see. Water roared through the open gangways. A few people squealed and cried for umbrellas or baskets that slid into the filthy river.

The tipping continued. It must be thirty degrees now.

"Folks! Please move to the starboard wall! Move to the starboard rail!" The disembodied instructions from above and below held notes of panic this time.

Olive locked her gaze with Claire's before they tried, along with everyone else, to climb the slippery floor to the starboard side.

It was impossible.

Olive held her breath, as did every other wide-eyed passenger in view. From outside, she could hear a man yelling frantically in an Italian accent, most likely from the wharf only twenty feet away.

"What's he saying?" she called out, still holding Claire's arm. "Can anyone make out what he's yelling?"

A teenaged girl in a frothy white dress clutched a sconce between two portholes on the starboard side. She turned a ghostly pale face to Olive. "He says, 'Get off,'" she reported. "He says, 'The boat's turning over.'"

"It wouldn't," Claire whispered.

The ship leaned farther.

CHAPTER SIX

The tipping stopped.

Claire exhaled.

Muscles taut in her bent legs, Olive waited for the floor to level. "This is no wobbly bicycle." She cut her voice low, wary of inspiring panic in a ship packed with twenty-five hundred people, most of them women and children. "It's leaning too far. When it comes back the other way, let's get out of here and get on the *Theodore Roosevelt* instead." Even with the gangplanks drawn in, she'd find a way off.

But in the split second it took for Claire to agree, it was too late. The ship rolled toward the river again.

When the slant reached what Olive guessed was forty-five degrees, she gave up calculating geometry and estimated time instead. How much did they have to get out?

Claire slid down the floorboards toward the staircase. Olive caught her, her rubber-soled pumps keeping her in place a moment longer. But rubber soles would not save her, nor anyone.

Shock swelled into a thrumming dread. "I'm sorry," Olive gasped. Claire wouldn't be here if it weren't for her.

On the promenade deck above, a piano smashed into the rail. A giant crash on the main deck—dishes falling off shelves all at once—stunned the ship into dumb silence, except for stewards and porters dashing madly for escape.

The ship kept rolling. Time and space slowly rearranged.

In one second, Olive saw her own terror reflected in Claire's dark eyes, and in the next, her friend was torn away from her, and they were both falling as stairs back down to the main deck dropped out from under them. Olive caught herself more than halfway down, gripping a newel post, feeling the risers riding against her ribs.

"Claire?"

"Right below you!"

Dangling from the rail, Olive peeked down to see her friend hanging on to posts that were now horizontal by Olive's knees.

Wood creaked. Water rushed. A baby slipped from his mother's arms and slid toward the open gangway. Then the screaming began.

Horror paralyzed Olive for only a moment. "Climb!" she yelled, bunching her skirt in a fist and using the railing posts as a ladder. A tap on her heel told her Claire was right behind her as they pulled themselves up and away from the mad rush of a thousand people lunging all at once for the stairs.

Olive scrambled to stay ahead of them. Chairs and baskets flipped end over end, one of them slamming into the side of her head as it fell. She barely registered the pain. People dropped past her, heels flying, hands clawing for purchase, and slammed into the bottleneck of passengers below.

Blood ran hot and sticky from Olive's temple. Escaping the stairs from the main deck to cabin deck, she turned to help Claire up the last few feet.

"This way." Arms linked, they stumbled toward the forward stairs that led toward the promenade deck. Scores of others had the same idea. Many had already been injured by anything not bolted down. Gashes stained arrow collars and lace chokers.

Cries and shouts buffeted her ears. They were scuttling over the bulkhead, as well as they could in the press of people, tripping over portholes that had become windows to the black river beneath. The ship groaned.

Claire held tighter to Olive's arm with bleeding hands. "I think we're about to get wet."

The lights went out.

Water exploded into the cabin deck from below, slicing past Olive, then covering her completely, filling her nose and mouth with its rancid, toxic brew.

She thrashed to the surface. As soon as she could spew out the river, someone climbed over her, pushing her down again. Flailing boots connected with her ribs, her head, reawakening the pain already there.

Olive's lungs burned with chemicals and not enough air. Blindly, she kicked as hard as she could, fighting her slim skirt. Screams and crying filtered through the water, along with pounding from those trapped in the main deck.

Breaking through a gap between chairs and people, she emerged again. She spit out the nasty water and pushed the hair away from her nose and mouth. "Claire!" she screamed, adding one more name to all the others bouncing between water and steel.

Bessie!	*Henry!*	*Mama!*
Leif!	*Stella!*	*Papa!*
Alice!	*Carl!*	*My baby!*

Olive heaved a waterlogged breath, ready to call again, only to have another passenger tackle her. Fingernails sliced through her blouse and down her back, leaving stripes of burning pain.

"Stop!" she cried. But the word only gurgled, swallowed up by the river again. Her arms were kicked so hard, she retracted them reflexively. A hand pulled her ankle down, down. Her chest screwed so tight it might burst.

An arm encircled her waist and hauled her up. "Stay with me," a man said, then barked at someone else to keep away. "You'll drown her in your own panic!" There was splashing behind her, but she couldn't see what was going on. All she knew was that this strange man had somehow seen what was happening and put a stop to it.

"Hang on to this." He slid a plank under her arms to buoy her.

Lungs still soggy, she gripped it, coughing, and called weakly again for Claire.

"Claire?" he said. Starboard portholes twenty feet above them offered scant grey light by which to see the kind man's square-jawed face. "My name is Olaf. Keep your head above water. Help is on the way, Claire, I'm sure of it."

"No." She coughed again. "Claire is my friend. I don't know where she is."

"Olive, is that you?" Claire's battered hand stretched toward her, her hair pooling about her shoulders. "You have got to stop disappearing on me!"

Heart slamming against her corset, Olive wrapped Claire's cold fingers around the edge of the plank. "All right." She blinked water from her stinging eyes and turned her head to cough again. "No more wandering off, I promise."

"Hang on, the both of you." Olaf splashed away to help someone else.

"Help will come soon," Olive said. "Thousands of people on the riverfront just watched a steamship tip over. Help is on the way even now."

"Yes," Claire said. "It must be."

Their skirts ballooned and rose to their waists as they kicked to tread water. Those who weren't pinned beneath furniture did the same, hanging on to wooden chairs and wreckage, so that the churning river resembled a cauldron of boiling water, splashing Olive's chin and cheeks. Cigarettes and hats floated by, trailed by Uneeda biscuits and Anola sugar wafers. A toy boat sailed after, bobbing in the swells. Olive whipped around, searching for the boat's owner, the little boy in a brand-new brown suit. She didn't see him, nor his papa whose broad shoulders had borne him aloft not an hour ago.

Panic surged, but Olive shoved it down and trapped the sob in her throat. She needed her wits, needed to think. She needed to silence the fear inside her. The fear outside her was loud enough. Crying all around them sounded like the sawing of violins, some muffled, and some doubling with their own echoes.

"*Matka!*" A single plaintive voice rose above the rest.

Olive whirled toward the sound of a little girl crying for her mother in Polish.

"*Matka! Matka!* Mama!"

"Addie?" Olive called. She and Claire held tight to their plank of wood as they swam until they found her. Stella Petroski's two-year-old daughter bobbed inside an upturned wooden crate, torn dress exposing scraped knees, her stockings sliding off her feet as they dangled in the water.

"You know this child?" Claire asked.

Olive explained how she did. "Remember me, Addie?" She picked up a hank of her own wet hair, though in such dim light and soaking wet, she didn't know if Addie would recognize her. "Red. *Czerwony.* I know your mama and papa."

The child sniffed, paying attention now.

"Don't worry," she told the girl. "We'll stay with you until your parents find you." Surely at least one of them would come soon.

"Of course we will," Claire added, nudging Addie's wooden crate so it floated between her and Olive.

Olive caught her eye and nodded grimly. All it would take was one swipe from a desperate passenger, and the slats would break apart beneath the child, doing little good to anyone.

"Please, Father," Olive prayed aloud, "keep this child and her family safe. Send help."

The water level rose as the ship sank to rest in the mud on the river's bottom.

The sound of Olive's breathing was loud in her ears. So was Claire's. Addie's, however, seemed too soft, too low, her cries faded to occasional whimpers.

Olive was chilled to the bone, and her muscles ached. Soon after finding Addie, she and Claire had given up the plank of wood they'd shared to some young ladies in sodden skirts who'd never learned to swim. They'd never had reason to, they said.

Olive and Claire had been treading water ever since, in a depth of at least twenty-two feet, taking turns hanging on to Addie's crate for respite. That was more than an hour ago, Olive guessed, maybe even two, but she had no way to be sure. Claire's timepiece had stopped working almost as soon as it got wet, and Olive's bracelet watch had slipped from her wrist when the cabin deck filled with water. They had no proof that time still moved forward at all. It seemed to slow, to twist and bend and turn back on itself, like this very river that engineers had reversed so its flow wouldn't contaminate the lake. Time could no longer be trusted.

"It's so quiet now," Claire whispered through clicking teeth. Her hands were no longer bleeding, but judging by the burning in her own wounds on her head and back, Olive had no doubt Claire's injuries stung. Still, they'd been lucky.

Though grateful for the reprieve from terrified screams and crying, Olive was just as horrified that many of those voices were silent now because they had slipped beneath the water, bubbles on the surface the only thing that signaled they had been here. And then those, too, were gone.

Children. Babies. Mothers. And she had been helpless to do anything about it, save guard this one lonesome child. The magnitude of loss choked her.

Other sounds drifted through her consciousness. Rain and footsteps drumming the starboard hull of the ship, which now faced the sky. Men shouting orders. But if they were coming to get her, they weren't coming fast enough.

Olive marshaled her wits. For how tired she was, it seemed a miracle her legs hadn't cramped up yet, but they couldn't keep going indefinitely. The longer they waited, the closer they were not to rescue but to their own demise.

"It's time to leave."

Claire turned dull eyes on Olive, her complexion waxen. "What?"

Olive kept her arms and legs moving underwater, her clothing slimy against her skin. "We don't know if Addie's family will find us here. We've waited long enough. I prayed for God to send her help, but what if we are the help He sent?" When Claire's brow pinched, Olive rushed on, her sentences growing short between panting breaths. "We can't wait any longer to be rescued. Do you hear me? It's time to rescue ourselves. You can swim. We both can. We'll take Addie with us."

Reaching the stairs to the promenade deck wouldn't be easy. A double row of cabins divided the deck lengthwise. Since they couldn't scale the cabin walls to reach the starboard side of them, they'd need to swim beneath the cabins in order to reach the stairwell.

Olive turned to the child. "Can you hold your breath, Addie? Show me."

The little girl's cheeks puffed out and held, but not for very long. Still, they were left with little choice.

"Look," Olive whispered to Claire, "if she gets water in her while we swim, it will only be for a little bit. The dock is only twenty feet away. Help is waiting there to set her to rights."

The wreckage shifted again, sinking. Timbers cracked, which meant they were splitting. Metal groaned and screeched. The water was cold and toxic, the air laden with ammonia. Every minute they stayed here was another minute closer to contracting pneumonia or typhoid fever, and Olive said so.

"I don't know." Claire licked the water from her lips, then spit out whatever she'd tasted.

"Well, I do," Olive insisted. "We were on our way toward the stairs that would take us to the promenade deck. We've been washed backward quite a bit, but we can still swim there. It's maybe half a block from here."

Half a block underwater, swimming blind when already exhausted, through picnic baskets and broken glass and the remains of people already drowned. And all of that with a toddler in tow.

Olive stifled a shudder and pressed on. "We follow the stairs to the promenade deck, then swim up toward the light. We should see it between the promenade and hurricane decks."

"Go, then," Claire said. "You and Addie can make it, but hurry."

A mason jar full of iced tea bobbed between them. Olive pushed it away. "We go together. Remember? No more disappearing, no more wandering off alone."

Claire rolled her lips between her teeth. "I release you."

A jolt shot through Olive. "What?" The sounds of other passengers faded as she strained to hear what her friend was saying, along with what she wasn't.

"I've been thinking. Maybe it's better this way. To stay. Not you, just me. You don't know what life is like with Warren. Although, the fact that I can't decide which is the better fate should give you a hint."

Olive shook her head, as if that could clear her mind and make sense of what was coming out of her friend's mouth. "I don't understand. You want to stay here while we escape? You want me to send help back to you?"

Claire's fingers tightened on the slats of Addie's crate, her knuckles white. "I think—I think this is how we *both* escape. You and Addie to your lives, and me from mine."

"Don't talk like that! I'm not leaving without you—"

"Oh yes, you are. Listen to me," Claire hissed. Red lines spidered the whites of her eyes. "Let this be my choice. Let me choose this ending and meet it with dignity. My parents are gone, I have no siblings, I have no children waiting for me at home. Only a man who makes my life a terror. This is the only way I can leave him. But you—you will *live*. You'll make it out of here, save Addie's life, tell Warren I'm gone, and I'll finally rest in peace."

Horror surged through Olive. "I'm not leaving you here to die!"

Addie shifted her weight in the crate. Water splashed her and set her to crying again.

"You are. You will. You have *family*," Claire said, "not to mention this little girl who needs you to get her to safety. Do you think your mother would survive losing you? How do you think your aunt would like knowing that when she gave you her tickets, she sent you to your death? What about Stella and Jakob? Is your stubbornness worth their baby's life? Because Addie doesn't stand a chance if you don't take her away yourself, and she has her entire life ahead of her."

If Olive could have paused treading water long enough to grasp Claire's shoulders without sinking, she would have. Instead, all she could do was keep moving, keep stirring the dirty water with her legs and arms. Only her words would reach Claire now.

"If I leave you here, knowing you plan to die, it would be like killing you myself. Will you hang this on me for the rest of my life?" It sounded selfish and petty, but it was also gut-level honest. "Will you so easily take from me my only friend and make me the accomplice to the crime?" Tears mingled with the water on her cheeks.

Claire's face knotted. "This wasn't a crime. It was an accide—" Her justification cut short at the sound of crying coming closer.

"Help!" It was a child's wail, at a time when most children, by now, had been silenced.

Olive spun around. Half a wooden crate bobbed in the water. With a splash and cry, the crate broke apart into useless sticks. Lunging toward the frothing water, Olive fished a boy back up to the surface. He churned his little legs, kicking Olive.

She drew him toward Addie's crate and brought his hand to find purchase there.

"Addie!" the boy cried, wet hair spiking down his forehead. His jacket gone, little Michael Petroski shivered in his wet shirtsleeves and suspenders.

Squealing with recognition, Addie patted her brother's head.

Olive's heart buckled. "Michael," she said. "My name is Olive, and this is my friend Claire. I met you earlier today. You gave me a sugar wafer. Do you remember?"

Michael nodded, his bottom lip fluted out. "Papa put Addie in the basket and told me to take her somewhere safe. But I wanted to stay behind and help him look for Mama. He finally found a crate for me to use, but it broke. I don't know where Mama or Papa are. Papa said he was going to get her."

"Papa!" Addie wailed.

Timbers creaked, and the *Eastland* groaned again.

"Will you help us?" His voice faltered on the plea. "I'm really strong, but—Papa said to get out, to take Addie and get out. And I don't know the way."

Olive looked at Claire, more determined than ever to leave. "I can get them to safety," she said, "but I can't take them both by myself."

CHAPTER SEVEN

The river burned Olive's eyes as she navigated between murky shapes. One arm holding Addie in a vise-like grip, Olive kicked and pulled her way through noxious water, aiming for the stairs and hoping she wasn't veering off course. Claire and Michael behind her, she fought the instinct to fill her lungs and tried to suffocate her imagination. The things she bumped into underwater were not arms and legs. The rods that had caught in her hair, not fingers. That was a silk scarf, not hair, that brushed her skin.

She had one chance and one job to do right now. Growing paralyzed by despair was not an option.

Addie writhed against the restraint. Olive felt her scream underwater, which could only be followed by dragging the river back into her lungs. Olive's own cinched as she realized Addie's were already filling. She couldn't think of anything else but getting the girl to air.

Had they missed the staircase? Olive shoved a shoe and a handbag out of the way. If she'd gone past it, it would be nearly another half block to the dining room with its bolted-down tables, which would tell her to turn around again.

How long until Addie lost consciousness?

How long until Olive did the same?

Was she wrong to attempt this gamble?

She sent up a desperate prayer. The moans of a shifting, sinking ship were louder beneath the water. On the other side of the floor, trapped in the main deck, people banged and shouted for help. But those weren't the only voices she heard.

They were too indistinct for her to make out the words, but they were coming from above.

Then, light. Dim but growing brighter, signaling they were nearing the end of the cabin rooms. Buoyed by the promise it held, she swam to reach it, clamping down on Addie hard enough to bruise her ribs. Small price, compared to losing her.

Arm outstretched, Olive jammed her fingers against wood, then gripped its edge, feeling the corner of it rise in a straight line. The stairs. She'd found them at last. They were a few feet away from air.

She whirled around to be sure Claire and Michael were still at her heels.

She saw only one body. Michael's.

Olive waved to him and pointed at the stairs, then up, praying he would remember that they'd rehearsed how this would go. But the boy was small and tired. He was never meant to swim without Claire there to help him along.

Her head throbbed with pent-up pressure, and her lungs felt ready to explode. She had no choice but to keep going. With a final burst of strength, she swam up and across the stairwell until she broke through the surface on the promenade deck.

"Help!" she called, sputtering and gasping. Water hit her face, but this time it was fresh, clean rain.

On the sideways deck, benches bolted to the floor jutted out, seemingly suspended in the air and floating on their backs. She lunged up and grabbed the slat of one of them. Try as she might, she could not muster the strength to hoist Addie onto the back of the bench.

"I have a child! Help! There's another below!"

The next moments were a blur of splashes and strong arms and rope being tied around Addie.

"There's a little boy coming, too." Olive's teeth chattered as she spoke to the rescuers. "I'm going to get him. And a woman my age close at hand."

But no sooner had she slipped back under the water than a wiry arm caught her and brought her back up. "I'll get him. I'll get them both." The young man could not have been more than eighteen years old. He handed her to another set of hands, which tied rope like a cradle for her to sit in.

Before she knew what was happening, the young man dove into the river, and she was rising toward the sky.

"Easy does it. We've got you, miss." A broad hand took hers and guided her to stand on the hull. The river streamed from her body, hair, and clothes, rolling back into the ship below. It was as much like being resurrected from a grave as she would ever know. Her senses had been so attuned to the muffled darkness that every detail now struck with painful clarity.

The stench of coal smoke and rotting fish. Groaning bridges, protesting beneath the weight of thousands of horrified onlookers. Police whistles. Fire gongs. Shouting and crying.

Splashing.

Grocers from the market stalls along the riverfront threw chicken coops and produce crates in the water to support survivors. Ropes, ladders, loose shelves, and chairs were being tossed in from nearby tugboats and the *Theodore Roosevelt*. Anything that would float could save a life.

Olive rubbed the heels of her hands against her burning eyes. A blanket draped her shoulders as she turned to look for Addie, ignoring the sting from where another passenger had tried climbing up her back. Hundreds, perhaps a thousand people stood on the hull. Firemen in uniform worked alongside men in suits and hats, extending ropes below. Passengers already rescued stood dazed or filed off onto a tugboat connected to the wharf. Policemen came with stretchers, leaving prints in the ashes spread on the hull, likely to offer traction, but the rain made of it a wet grey mess.

At a break in the crowd, she saw Addie on a blanket, still and slightly blue. Olive sank beside her as a doctor checked the toddler's pulse and turned her onto her side. A woman gently urged Olive away. The words *Western Electric* were embroidered on her white uniform.

"My name is Helen, and I'm a nurse. Where does it hurt?" She checked Olive's pulse, lifted her hair to inspect the cut on her temple, and then dabbed some kind of ointment there. When Olive lowered the blanket to reveal the scratches that came to the top of her corset, Helen quickly slathered those through the torn blouse, then replaced the blanket over her shoulders. "You'll heal without stitching. Can you give me your full name, please, along with the girl's?"

But coughing racked Olive. Every stifled impulse to panic now raged to the surface. Frantic for all three people she'd led through the ship, her nerves felt frayed to shreds.

"Do you see them?" Olive called to the men kneeling on boards placed atop the promenade deck railing, looking down into the water below. "A boy and a woman with black hair were right behind me! That young man went to get them."

One man gave her a thumbs up. "Reggie's got 'em!"

Addie gurgled and coughed.

"Thank God," the doctor heaved. "Thank God. Nurse, take this child and woman away."

Olive reached Addie first, gathering her into her arms and rocking her on her knees.

"Red," the girl said in recognition, peering up through tear-spiked lashes.

"Olive." She smiled and pointed to herself, correcting the name to its proper color, but honestly, Addie could call her Carrots at this point, and she wouldn't mind. "You're safe," she said. "You're going to be all right. Your brother's coming, too."

"Another live one!" The masculine shout turned Olive's attention in time to see Michael being lifted out. He retched as soon as he touched steel. But he was alive and conscious, too.

Stumbling over to Olive and Addie, he fell into their arms with silent sobs.

Rain beaded the hull and slid into the river in jagged silver streams. Men wearing grease-streaked work clothes clomped past, hoses looped over their shoulders, dragging gas tanks and carrying torches. Kneeling, they snapped on masks and began cutting into the hull. Sparks flew, and the smell of burning metal added one more fume to the air.

Olive turned back to the place from which she and the children had emerged and absently answered the nurse's questions. "The woman," she called to the men a few yards away. "Claire Sterling. Where is she?"

Helen stepped over to see. "They're bringing up a woman now," she replied over her shoulder. "Please stay back, give the doctor some room."

Olive huddled with the children, vaguely aware that someone had tucked blankets around them, too. She watched as a woman was laid out on a stretcher. Unmoving. On the other side of her, a fireman braced a priest who was leaning into an opening that had been cut into the hull. Whispered last confessions rose up from the darkness.

Beyond him, stretchers of victims were being carried off. Two priests stood on either side of the procession, dabbing foreheads with holy water as they passed and offering all they could:

Jesus, Mary, Joseph, I give you my heart and soul.

Jesus, Mary, Joseph, assist me in my last agony.

Jesus, Mary, Joseph, may I breathe forth my soul in peace with you.

From a sudden and unprepared death, deliver us, O Lo—

"Lung motor!" The doctor drowned out the ancient prayer, and a large metal apparatus with long tubes was wheeled to him. It resembled a giant bicycle pump.

Olive's own lungs stalled as she caught glimpses of a mask being placed on Claire, tubes running back into the motor. The machine hissed and wheezed with every pump.

The silence that followed was pierced with one word: "Gone."

No. Olive felt air leave her body. *Not Claire.* Rising on unsteady legs, she kept the children's hands firmly in her own and pushed through to see for herself.

They were already lifting the stretcher and carrying her away.

Olive followed it, stunned by what she saw.

"That's not Claire." Pivoting, she shouted again. "That wasn't Claire! You have to find her!"

Chapter Eight

Too much time had passed since Olive had broken free of the ship and Claire had not. She bent to speak to Michael through a burning throat. "Do you remember when Claire left you? Did she get stuck somewhere? Or did you slip away from her because you were faster?"

"I remember." His freckles stood out starkly. "She left me right after you found the stairs. She pointed at you, then at me, and back at you again. Like she wanted me to follow you up. And then she blew me a kiss—I remember that because of the bubbles—and she waved good-bye."

The bottom dropped out of Olive's stomach, and she felt herself grow wooden. This had been Claire's plan all along, then, to stay with the wreckage and become part of it. To shun rescue for a final, permanent escape.

"Miss Pierce." Helen joined them, picked up the blanket that had fallen from Olive's shoulders, and lifted it to cover her head, too. "If you please, we need you to go and take the children with you. Get out of the rain."

Were it not for the children, Olive would have stayed. She would have sat in the ashes and let the rain and wind lash her skin.

But she did have the children, and right now, they had no one else but her. Scooping up Addie with trembling, exhausted arms, she led Michael off the hull and onto the tugboat *Kenosha*, until someone helped them, at last, onto the wharf.

Thousands paced it, looking out toward wreck and river. Camera bulbs flashed. A man stood behind a motion picture camera and turned a crank. With a twinge of indignation, Olive used the blanket she wore like wings to shield Michael and Addie from view.

Nearby merchants had thrown open their doors to shelter survivors and their families. All of them now offered free coffee, sandwiches, blankets, and cots. Steadying hands and broad shoulders.

"Papa," Addie whimpered, and Olive stroked her back. She should say something to the girl but could think of nothing. "Papa, Papa!"

"Addie? Michael!"

Olive rounded toward the sound.

Head bandaged, a shoeless, soaking-wet Jakob Petroski ran toward her and gathered his children into his arms, covering their faces with kisses. He couldn't stop touching their heads, hands, feet, as if to assure himself they were really here and perfectly intact, even if their clothes were rags. Though he exclaimed over them in a mix of English and Polish, Olive needed no translation to understand the urgency and tenderness in his voice.

At last, he embraced Olive as well. "Thank you," he told her gruffly. "For my children." He looked around. "Stella?"

Olive swallowed a sharp wedge. "I—I haven't seen her." Her arms and hands suddenly empty, she pulled the blanket tighter about herself, the cuts on her back burning.

Addie took her father's face between her cold, dimpled hands. "Where's Mama?"

"I don't know. But that doesn't mean . . ." Cradling Addie, his tone was that of one fighting to keep the agony from it.

"See, Papa?" Michael spoke up. "There are so many people here. We will find her if we keep looking, yes?"

Jakob's hand almost completely covered his son's wet head.

"True. We will not give up. And speaking of finding each other—" He looked at Olive. "I know someone who will rejoice to see you again." He pointed up toward South Water Street and waved one arm wide. "Rozalia!" he called, then bowed to Olive and excused himself, ushering Michael and Addie away.

Olive looked up the stairs to the street, heart lurching when she saw Rose flying down them, scarf streaming behind her.

"Olive, thank God!" Her shoulders shook as she captured Olive to her. "I thought we lost you! We watched the whole thing, saw the ship turn right over. We thought—" She broke off, holding Olive out at arm's length. "Claire?"

Numbness began to shear away, leaving a grief that felt like fear and something like anger. "I lost her. Or maybe she's still out there, waiting for help." Rational or not, an urge to run back to the ship made her spin that direction.

Rose held her shoulders, concern pleating her brow. "Olive, you can do nothing for her right now. You will go home and rest, get out of these soaked clothes, and let your aunt and uncle see you. News of the disaster is everywhere. You can bet they're worried sick and might even be on their way to look for you themselves. I'll see you home, and then I need to get back to Hawthorne and work the switchboard. All those families, desperate for word . . ."

After helping her up the stairs to South Water Street, Rose hailed the closest vehicle. It was a customer delivery service car from Marshall Field's department store, on loan expressly for the use of *Eastland* survivors. Between the horse-drawn ambulances and thousands of pedestrians, the pace was sluggishly slow. Slow enough for Olive to turn and stare at the disaster once more. It was too overwhelming to consider the entirety of souls lost. Her thoughts cradled Claire and Stella, refusing to give them up.

"I daresay you'll have more work to do than you ever imagined," Rose murmured. Outside the window, a man wore a sandwich board advertising views from the top of a nearby building for a dime.

"What?" Olive's mind was hazing again, her body chilled and shaking.

"Life insurance, darling. Those poor families are going to need whatever benefits you helped them sign up for. And they're going to need them right away."

The words cut through Olive's mental fog. Rose was right. In all her years of considering the end of life and its implications, she'd never imagined it could come like this. Oh, she knew ships could sink from icebergs and torpedoes. She'd read all the news about the *Titanic* and the *Lusitania*. But death wasn't supposed to come all at once for good people on a ship still tied to the dock in the Chicago River on a summer's day.

Olive wasn't supposed to process the death claim for her best friend the day after Claire's thirtieth birthday.

Claire wasn't even supposed to be on that ship.

Steam rose from the claw-foot tub, smelling of the lavender oil Olive had added to it. She peeled away her layers and stepped into the bath, easing herself down and sliding low so she was submerged up to her neck beneath a thick layer of bubbles. The claw marks on her back stung. She tried not to wonder about the fate of whoever had put them there and willed herself to be numb to thoughts of Stella and Claire.

That was harder.

For a fraction of a second, her heart rate lurched at the sensation of water lapping at her chin, even though she knew it posed no threat. From the other side of the bathroom door, she could hear the teakettle whistle and then cease as Sylvie lifted it from the heat. More water, destined for tea, which in minutes would be inside her. Her stomach, not her lungs.

How could Olive be here, with her aunt fussing over her, making sure she was clean, warm, fed, and properly hydrated, while Claire, Stella, and hundreds of others were either still in the river a few blocks away or stretched out stiff with numbers tied to their toes?

Tears slipping down her cheeks, Olive took the soap and a scrub brush and set about scouring her skin to rid herself of the stench she'd brought home with her. The memories, however, she would have to learn to live with.

"This is how we both escape. You and Addie to your lives, and me from mine."

Olive scrubbed harder, until her skin turned red and raw.

"Tell Warren I'm gone, and I'll finally rest in peace."

Throwing the brush into the water, Olive wrapped her arms around her knees and held her breath, as if this could hold together all the broken pieces of her heart. If Claire's life had been so miserable that drowning was her best alternative, Olive had failed her as a friend long before today. She released a pent-up sob.

"Sweetheart?" Hinges squeaked as the door opened. Her aunt spoke her name gently, but Olive couldn't hear it and not hear Claire, too.

But you—you will live.

Olive cried harder.

Sylvie didn't ask what was wrong, nor did she ask if Olive was all right. Instead, she did what she always did when words were not enough. She set to work, gently shampooing Olive's hair.

"I invited her," Olive whispered. She had told her harrowing tale as soon as she'd arrived home. While Rose rushed back to Cicero, Kristof wrapped Olive in a fresh, dry blanket, and Sylvie staggered to the sofa, growing pale at Olive's recounting.

"It was my idea," Sylvie said now.

"Yes, but I pressed the ticket into her hand and all but begged her to come." Olive swiped a finger beneath her nose.

Sylvie was quiet for a few minutes. Then, "Is there any way she could have found another way out? You haven't seen her body. Is there reason to hope she still lives?"

Olive knew what Sylvie was thinking. She could almost hear

her quoting Emily Dickinson's line about hope being the thing with feathers that perches in the soul, singing. But if hope was a bird, it was also flighty and had all but taken wing from Olive.

The best she could do was restate the facts. "She might have found a different way out, but why do that, when she was so close to one? As for her body . . ." She swallowed. "Divers and Coast Guardsmen are recovering those, but it will take time to account for all of them. I'll go to the morgue tonight and look."

Sylvie's hands stilled on Olive's scalp.

"I have to go," Olive told herself as much as she told her aunt. "If they find her body, it must be identified and laid to rest with dignity."

"Of course," Sylvie agreed quietly. "I'll go with you."

Surely a woman of Sylvie's age should not subject herself to what awaited. "You won't like it there."

Sylvie worked her fingers through Olive's sudsy hair. "We aren't supposed to like it. But I'm going with you, and that's that. Now, rinse. There's fresh clothes on the chair." She pressed a kiss to Olive's brow, then scooped up the filthy rags from the floor and closed the door as she left.

Olive slid under the water once more.

By the time Olive had dried off and fastened the belt on her dress, she had steeled herself for the errand ahead. She would look for Claire and Stella and any other clients she could find, God rest them. Her stomach cramped. Looking for clients in narrow, black-and-white obituary columns was so much different than searching rows of expired flesh and blood.

Pinning her wet hair into a quick chignon, she reached the kitchen as a knock sounded.

Drawing himself tall, Kristof answered the door with the commanding posture befitting the maestro he was. "May I help you?"

"Who are you?" A man's voice.

Warren's.

Knees turning soft, Olive leaned on the edge of a kitchen chair before lowering herself into it. "It's okay. Let him in."

Warren pushed past Kristof and planted himself before Olive, hat in hand and every line on his brow carved deep.

"Sit down, Warren," she urged, for she could not stand to face him.

He didn't budge. A paper crumpled in his fist. "I had this feeling while out at the golf club that something wasn't right. That instinct, along with the weather, told me to go home. See to my wife. Imagine my surprise to find she wasn't there. Claire was with you this morning."

"Yes."

"You were taking her to some picnic for Western Electric workers?"

"Yes." She would accept responsibility for that. But it was he who had bruised and beaten her, driving her away from him, if only for a day. No one knew this morning that one day would turn into forever.

"I gave her the tickets, to celebrate both girls' birthdays." Sylvie's nose was cherry red, either from blowing it or from crying.

"So this disaster that everyone's talking about," Warren went on, "the one that has made the streets a snarl for miles around, you were there when that happened. Were you on the *Eastland*? Or were you on one of the other ships before they all were evacuated?"

"The *Eastland*," Olive whispered.

"So where is she?" His entire body rigid, he looked from person to person. "Is she in the bathroom? I've come to take her home. She needs to rest."

"Warren." Olive bit her trembling lip. "The last time I saw her, she was still in the ship. Underwater. I don't think she made it out."

He stepped back as though struck. "You're not telling me my wife is dead. You can't be saying my wife is dead because a steamship tipped over in twenty feet of water. I know that's not what I'm hearing."

It was excruciating, hearing him talk this way. "Warren," Olive tried again, "that is the most likely scenario."

"What is?"

"That she's gone."

He wagged his head with an incredulity that Olive understood. The entire situation was almost beyond belief.

She pressed on. "I'll go with you myself and help you look for her."

"No." He tapped his straw boater against his leg, crushing the brim in his fist. "I've been there myself. There's an information bureau set up at 214 North Clark Street with posters on the windows, listing the names of people already accounted for. I saw yours, Olive, but not hers. So I looked in the morgues, both the floating one on a barge on the north side of the river and the one in the basement of the Reid Murdoch Building. She wasn't there. I would have recognized her. Don't you think I would know my own wife?"

Suddenly disoriented, Olive's own grief stalled and stuttered. Could he be right? Was she wrong to give up on Claire's life so easily?

"You won't object if I look for her here," Warren stated.

Olive bristled. "You think I'm lying to you? About this?"

He rubbed the back of his neck. "I'm saying I need to see for myself that she isn't resting in her best friend's apartment. That's all."

Put that way, Olive understood. "All right, Warren. Go ahead and look."

He headed down the hall, ducking in and out of rooms, searching for a wife who wasn't there.

"Poor man," Kristof said. "I wouldn't give up hope yet if I were him, either." The way he looked at Sylvie, it was obvious he was thinking that but for the grace of God and the cold that kept her home, it could have been him searching for his wife.

Warren did not look hopeful when he emerged. "The whole

building," he said. "I need to look in every apartment here and the bookstore, too."

It was a bold admission of distrust, as well as an invasion of the entire family's privacy. On the other hand, he was desperate to find his wife, clinging to even the slimmest possibility.

"Of course you do," Olive said at last, and her aunt concurred.

Kristof agreed to escort Warren. At the door, Warren turned back to point a finger at Olive. "If I find that you're keeping her from me—"

Kristof clapped his shoulder. "No one is keeping your wife from you."

Warren sagged but remained riveted on Olive. "If any harm has come to her, make no mistake, I blame you. You're the reason she left the house at all today. Last night, we agreed she would stay home."

A chill poured down Olive's spine. He had no idea—or would not admit—that his abuse of Claire was the real reason she'd fled and the reason she'd decided to stay gone forever. She bit her tongue before she could say so.

"No matter where Claire is, I don't want her to see you ever again," he added. "I don't want to see you, either. We're done."

Kristof turned him around, and they left.

Olive never wanted to see Warren again, either. Folding her arms, she curled in on herself.

Sylvie joined her at the kitchen table, looking older than her sixty-five years.

"It's not your fault," Olive reminded her. It was so much easier to absolve her aunt of guilt than it was to absolve herself.

"If it isn't mine, it certainly isn't yours."

Olive tried to absorb this and waited for some kind of release from the tightness within. It didn't come. Fire bells still gonged outside. Windows muffled the thousands still gathered two blocks away but didn't silence them.

Losing Claire wreaked havoc in Olive's soul. She was numb one moment and boiling with emotion the next. Memories bobbed like flotsam, and she could not decide which pain to choose: to gather and embrace them or to let them drift away.

Sylvie balled her handkerchief in her fist and leaned back in her chair, her expression twisted in grief. "I wish I knew what to say," she choked out. "Shall I cover the painting? Take it down?"

Olive regarded the portrait of Anne and Diana above the living room mantel. "Thank you, but no. I want her there with me. I want her here."

The door opened, and Kristof poked his head inside. "I'm heading out to wire your family in Indiana and New York to let them know we're all safe, since the phone lines are jammed. I'm sure their newspapers will carry the story, and I'd rather not have them wondering if any of us were involved, since they know Rose works for Western Electric. Warren has finished searching and is headed home."

"How is he?" Sylvie asked.

"Hard to say. I can't imagine he really expected to find Claire hiding anywhere in the building, but confirming it must have been sobering for him. He hopes to find her at home by the time he gets there, and if not, he'll check the morgues again come morning. I told him we'd do anything we could to help him during this time of sorrow. Not that I can think of a single thing that might be of use to him, aside from prayer. That, he'll need in spades."

To this, Olive could agree.

Sylvie coughed into her handkerchief, rattling her frame. A sigh caught in her throat, and she cleared it. "Do you want me to stay here with you, dear? Or would you like to come back to our apartment?"

Kristof's expression suggested that wasn't wise. "I've got a sore throat myself. For your own sake, Olive, we should delay our hospitality."

A sore throat, a cough. That was how it had begun with her father. "Please go rest," Olive told them. As much as she dreaded

74

being alone with her thoughts, neither could she allow her aunt and uncle to risk their health.

After they left, she could not get warm. Shivering, she pulled on a sweater and went to the couch to curl up under a crocheted blanket. Aside from the aching in her head and back, she felt weak and cold, but that, too, was no surprise. She'd felt this way after her father died, too. She had learned then that grief was physical.

If she thought she could be of some help at the wharf, she would go. But men with megaphones had made it clear that extra people would only choke the efforts of emergency services and the Red Cross. The best thing to do, they'd said, was stay out of the way.

A rapid-fire knock assaulted the door.

Had Warren come back, now that she was alone? Pulse spiking, she pushed herself off the couch, blanket falling to the floor. She went to the telephone, ready to call for help if it became necessary, then remembered the lines were jammed.

The knocking came again, more urgent than before. The doorknob rattled, and sweat pricked over Olive's skin. "Warren?" If he was agitated enough to try entering on his own, there was no way she was letting him in.

But the voice that replied was not his. "Livvie! Hurry!"

Stunned, Olive threw open the door.

A ghost entered and closed the door behind her, locking it again with pale, bruised hands, the stench of the river in her hair.

CHAPTER NINE

"Claire!" Olive pulled her friend into her arms, reassuring herself she was real, not some figment of hope her mind had supplied. A clammy chill pressed into her body from Claire's, lighting every nerve afire.

In an instant, Olive took the wet blanket from Claire's shoulders and wrapped her in the one she'd just discarded.

"Michael and Addie," Claire said, sinking into the sofa. "Are they safe?"

Olive sat beside her and took her friend's hands to warm them in her own. "Yes, they're with their father now. But, Claire—I thought—I thought you were dead, that you wanted to die!"

"I know," she whispered. "I'm so sorry, Olive. I needed you to think that. And now I need you again, or I won't stay alive for long."

Olive scrambled to make sense of what Claire was telling her. "Warren's been here. He searched the entire building for you. He isn't persuaded you're dead."

"The curtains, please." Claire looked worriedly at every window, and Olive hurried to close the drapes before returning to the sofa. "I know that, too," Claire continued. "I've been watching for him to come, as I knew he would. I waited until he left so I knew it was finally safe to come to you." Her wide eyes were shot through with red. "He can never know I've been here today. If he asks again, you can't tell him."

"I doubt he'll come back." If he did, Olive wasn't sure how she'd deceive him. She wasn't in the habit of lying, and as a general rule despised dishonesty. But this—surely this was different.

"You're chilled to the bone and halfway to pneumonia," Olive said and announced she would draw a bath.

After turning on the water in the bathroom, Olive prepared a mug of tea and pressed it into Claire's hands.

"Tell me everything," she prompted. "Convince me this is real, or I'm bound to think I'm dreaming. Were you lying to me when you said you wanted to stay and die?" A twinge of anger injected her tone, despite her profound relief. "Was my grief part of this elaborate scheme?"

"No, Livvie." Claire sipped from the mug. "Before we found Michael, that really was my plan. But I needed to see him to safety—or within reach of it, at least—and I was bracing myself for the coming confrontation with Warren. The closer we got to the light, though, I realized there was a third option. I didn't have to die. And I didn't have to go back to my husband."

"You'll let him think you're dead." He might not want to believe it, but he'd have to accept it eventually. Some of the bodies might never be recovered. The *Lusitania* had sunk two months ago, and many people still hadn't been found.

Claire nodded. "Louisa May Alcott once wrote that she'd rather be a free spinster and paddle her own canoe. That's what I want. To be free, even if it means I live alone. At least I'll be steering my own course." She inhaled. "My life was spared today when I could have been one of those poor souls lined up on the warehouse floor. As God is my witness, I vow not to waste it. Claire Sterling is dead. I can be someone new. I'll start over somewhere else. I can live again." She paused and took a shuddering breath. "All I have to do is leave. But I can't do it without you, Liv. I can't go back to my house."

Running water sounded faintly from the bathroom. Olive had thought she'd lost Claire once today. Now she would lose her again, but this time so that she could truly live.

"Of course I'll help you. But you're in no condition to leave until you've rested and recovered."

Claire's mouth set in a grim line. "One night," she said. "That's all I can bear, and then I'm gone."

The bath would be ready soon. "I'll get you some clothes to change into." Olive rose and for the first time noticed that Claire was barefoot.

"We'll talk more when I'm clean and dry." Claire padded to the bathroom doorway and waited until Olive handed her a stack of clothing. "You can't tell your family I'm alive, you know," she added. "You can't tell anyone."

The burden of this secret grew heavier. "Are you sure? Warren would never come back and has no reason to interact with my family here, nor with Rozalia's family in Cicero. They're about to travel to San Francisco, and my mother is visiting Walter's family right now. The news of your life being spared would be such a comfort to them all, especially since you wouldn't have been on the *Eastland* without the ticket from Rose and the gift of using it from my aunt and uncle."

"No, you can't. It's too risky. I'm sorry to do this to you and to them, but you absolutely cannot breathe a word of this to anyone. Your secrecy means my freedom. I'll be in your debt forever." The smile she dredged up was shaky, and she slipped into the steaming bathroom.

Olive had kept secrets before. Birthday and Christmas gifts, for example. Girlhood confidences that had felt sacred at the time. The financial circumstances of each one of her MetLife clients. Her own longings for a family of her own when she felt born to take care of her mother. None of those secrets had been lies of omission. This one was.

Her thoughts zigzagged with questions and possibilities, taking sharp turns at every obstacle. How could she keep this from her family? Where would Claire go? How would she live alone on such short notice?

How long would they have to hold their breath this time until Warren would assume his wife was dead?

After the river-soaked clothes had been washed, wrung, and hung to dry, after a meal had been eaten, Olive and Claire shared a blanket on the couch.

"He's going back to the morgue in the morning," Olive whispered.

"Good. Perfect. Then that's when you'll go to my house and bring back the money I've stashed away. There's a spare key under the geranium pot at the back door. Go early enough that you can watch from the park across the street for when he leaves. Then let yourself in and try not to let our neighbor Mrs. Feinstein see you. It will take you one minute to find the money and get out again. He'll never know you were there."

Olive's gaze drifted to the cut and bruise near Claire's hairline, then back to her glinting blue eyes. "All right. Where do you keep it?"

Her mouth quirked to one side. "Inside *Anne of Green Gables*, the hardcover. It's in a basket with the rest of my books, which I keep under the bed. Warren didn't think my novels were impressive enough to display in the living room. He never read a single one of those books, by the way. Never intended to. From the start, they were only for show. When Warren admires something, he wants to own it for how it makes him look. That's not the same as love. I learned that the hard way."

Olive set her teeth, trapping a cry on her friend's behalf. But the time for mere words was long past. If Claire was ready to act, so was she. "All right, so I look for *Anne of Green Gables* under your bed."

"Exactly. Flip to chapter two, and you'll see a hole I cut out of the rest of the pages. The money is nested inside. I knew he'd never look there."

A dark chuckle escaped Olive's lips. "No, I don't suppose he would. How long have you been saving for this?"

Claire retied the ribbon at the end of her braid. "I wasn't. I didn't know what I was saving for. I just knew, as soon as Warren tightened his control on our money, that someday I'd want something and I wouldn't want to ask him for permission to buy it."

That made it sound like she'd been saving for a pair of shoes or a fur coat too extravagant to be sold by Sears. It did not sound adequate for starting a new life. "Is it enough?"

"It will have to be, at least for now. Don't worry, Liv, this is it. I'm going, and I'm not looking back."

As much as Olive longed for Claire's success, she wondered if she fully appreciated the magnitude of her quest. She'd need lodging, food, money for utilities. A job, and fast. Money for transportation to that job.

"Just don't take any clothes from my closet while you're there, or anything else you think I might like to have with me. He'll suspect if he notices things missing. It has to be a clean break, with nothing but that money and the clothes on my back." A wrinkle formed between her eyebrows. "Well, if you don't mind. They're yours, after all."

"Keep them," Olive said. "I'll send more outfits with you when you go tomorrow, and I won't take no for an answer. Consider it a loan until you can buy your own, if that makes you feel better."

Claire's smile faltered. "I'll feel better once I put Chicago behind me. Aside from you, there's nothing here for me."

The twisting Olive felt was merely a physical reaction to the idea that being her best friend for two decades was not enough reason for Claire to stay. But logic ruled. Claire had been trapped in an abusive marriage, and this was her best chance out of it. Olive would be a fool not to recognize that.

Still, she had to ask. "I suppose you've considered divorce?"

Claire spread the blanket higher over her lap. "Warren would sooner kill me than sign papers dissolving the marriage. He told me so. He said the only way for me to leave him would be in a hearse."

"Claire!" Olive gasped.

"God's truth. His very words." Claire took the fringe of the crocheted blanket and began braiding the strands together. Unraveling them. Twisting them into fuzzy cords.

"He's insane to talk like that."

"Maybe he is, but no one else sees it. He's calculating, shrewd, and manipulative. He built his entire life as if it were a Sears kit, with every piece in its place. If he's not in control, he's not happy and won't let anyone else be, either. I thought a baby would please him, especially a son, to carry on his name. But I know now that wouldn't have changed who he is. It would only have given him another target." Her fingers stilled and clasped. "I could never be glad I lost my babies. But I am relieved they never had a chance to suffer at their father's own hand."

Olive grasped her shoulder. "He won't have a chance to hurt you again, either."

"That's the goal."

Night proved to be a long and broken thing. After the phone lines were restored, Sylvie called and offered to come sleep in the same apartment so Olive wouldn't be alone, but Olive refused in order to keep Claire's secret safe.

Olive rested on her stomach so as not to disturb the ointment Claire had applied to the scratches on her back. Then she realized that Sylvie had known something Olive was just learning. That the dark and the quiet were powerful magnifiers of grief and trauma, and that dreams would not be kind. She and Claire, who chose the floor in Olive's room rather than the bed in Meg's, took turns waking each other from nightmares.

SUNDAY, JULY 25, 1915

Only the slightest tremor betrayed Olive's nervous energy as she handed the money to Claire. Weak sunshine struggled through the curtains, casting a pale ribbon on the living room rug.

Thanking her, Claire counted it, then added some to a handbag and folded the rest, which she tucked inside her shoe. Church bells pealed for an eleven o'clock mass a few blocks away. "Any trouble?"

Aside from the overall deception in which she was actively participating? "None. Everything happened just as you said it would, and I was careful to place the key precisely where it had been after locking up behind me." She glanced toward the street, checking again for Warren without fully opening the drapes.

Outside, police were stationed in a two-block perimeter around the *Eastland*, which meant Olive could see some of the officers from her apartment. Aside from their whistles and the newsies, Chicago seemed eerily quiet. The White Sox and the Whales had both canceled their doubleheader baseball games. River traffic had almost completely stopped.

"Good." Claire stood back from the window. "I'm sorry I had to ask you to do this for me, but I couldn't do it without you."

A lump formed in Olive's throat. She was sorry for many things, but not for helping Claire. "I'll miss you."

A packed bag at the door contained Claire's clothes from yesterday, washed and dried, and as much of Olive's as she could spare. Beside it, a small wicker basket held food.

Hornets swarmed in Olive's belly. In moments, Claire would leave from the rear entrance of the building and step into the cab Olive had called to meet them in the alley.

"Will you at least call me once you've landed wherever it is you're going?" Olive asked.

"Probably not, Liv. Any place I can afford isn't likely to come with its own telephone, and I don't want to risk going to an exchange and talking where I could be overheard."

There was nothing left to do but walk her downstairs.

The taxi was already there by the time they reached the back door. Olive wrapped her friend in a fierce embrace. "Don't let this be forever." She stood back, searching Claire's face.

"No, of course not."

"Promise you'll find a way to let me know once you've settled in your new place. You don't have to tell me where you are, just that you're all right."

"I do. I will." A tear slipped down her wan cheek. "Don't worry, Liv."

But they both knew that she would.

Chapter Ten

Monday, July 26, 1915

Olive's fingertips were grey as she waved to Gwendolyn on her way into Mr. Roth's office. The residue on her skin came from tracing newspaper columns of disaster coverage, including lists of the deceased, the missing, and descriptions of the unidentified. The five major dailies still covered her desk, their headlines imprinted in her mind.

River Yields 810 Bodies
Engineer and Captain Tell All: Admit Boat Was Listing Long
Before Disaster
Greatest Inquiry in History of US to Find Who Is to Blame
Many Children on Eastland, Witness Tells Coroner Jury
Who Is to Blame?

The news had traveled far and wide, even eclipsing coverage of Europe's war, which had dominated the front pages for months. It seemed the whole world knew what had happened, and yet no one understood how it could have.

Today's headlines would line tomorrow's bird cages. But for the victims and their families, the *Eastland* disaster had altered life irrevocably. Olive was one of the lucky ones. This morning she'd awakened with the cries of the dying and the survivors still ringing in her ears.

The question now, at least for her, was not how or why the tragedy happened, but what next?

"Mr. Roth." Without waiting for an invitation, Olive marched to his desk. By now, everyone in the office knew she'd been on the *Eastland*, which had granted her a certain degree of respect.

Rising, Mr. Roth shook her hand. Through the window behind him, she could see laundry strung up to dry on the rooftop of City Hall. It had all been found in the river, she'd learned yesterday while getting the typhus vaccination the public health department was providing *Eastland* survivors. The city had disinfected the clothes that, once dry, would fill an office designated for lost and found.

Olive didn't want to think about how many of those dresses and trousers would never be claimed.

"How are you feeling this morning?" Roth resumed his seat.

Like a caged animal, she did not say as she sat across from him. *Like I'll come out of my skin if you don't let me help.*

Instead, she told him, "Ready to work." It was seven o'clock in the morning, well before the usual open of business, but there were mountains of caseloads to process. She pointed to the wall dividing Roth's office from Howard's. "Howard has more work investigating death claims than one person can possibly handle. Let me shoulder some of that load."

"He ought to be here by now. Gwendolyn," Roth called, jowls quivering. "Telephone Howard's place, will you? I want him here on the double. He should have known that." He rubbed his jaw, then tugged his necktie. "I need him out at Cicero right away," he muttered to Olive. "We're making house calls this time. There's no way I'm going to wait for those family members to come to the office given what they've already been through. Some of them probably don't even speak English, anyway."

"Send me," Olive said. "Not instead of Howard, but with him.

I'll accompany him at first, then split off and cover more ground on my own. I'll arrange for translators when necessary, and we'll get the claims started for these families twice as fast."

Not every *Eastland* victim had been a MetLife client, but enough of them were that it made the urgent work overwhelming, even with the other MetLife branches in Chicago working toward the same end.

"Sir," she pressed, "many of the victims were wage earners not just for their spouses and children, but for elderly parents living with them, as well. The longer the families go without their benefits, the more they'll be in danger of losing their homes, right on the heels of losing their loved ones. It is not to be borne, as long as we can help it. And I can, sir. I can help, if you'll only let me."

"Most of the cases will be clear-cut. But if the papers are to be believed, more than five hundred passengers have yet to be recovered, or at least accounted for. Confirming these as deaths rather than missing persons will be more complicated."

"I expect it will." She sat bolt upright, her spine straight. "Which is why you'll need more than Howard working on it."

"These immigrant families keep very much to themselves. They have their own newspapers in their own languages. Their own undertakers. They may resist a barrage of questions from an unknown insurance investigator."

She nodded. "That only makes sense. Who do you think will have better rapport with the grieving family members?"

"You're saying that as a woman, they'll trust you more?"

"No. I'm saying that as someone who was on the *Eastland* myself, I'll be less of an outsider to them. I was *there*." Images seared her mind. "I care, not just as a life insurance agent, but as a fellow survivor."

He paused, apparently weighing his next words. "I am so sorry for that, you know. Did you lose someone, too?"

Her tongue cleaved to the roof of her mouth. She hadn't anticipated lying to her boss today.

"You went with a friend, didn't you? I thought Gwendolyn said that. I don't mean to pry. I do hope she escaped with you."

Olive lowered her lashes, studying the midnight weave of her skirt. She'd worn black today, the same dress she'd worn to her father's funeral, out of respect for Chicago's dead hundreds. She couldn't tell him Claire lived, but neither would she say she was missing or dead. Heat crept up her neck and into her cheeks.

"I shouldn't have brought it up," Mr. Roth backpedaled. "That was wrong of me. Do let me know, though, if there's anything I can do."

Looking up, she forced memories from Saturday to recede. They'd never go away, she guessed. But she would push them into the dark corners of her mind as often as necessary. "You can let me get to work. Consider it a trial period. If you're not pleased with my work after the next several weeks, I'll remain an agent only. If you are pleased, and if I've proven my competency as an investigator . . ."

Rising, he went to the door and leaned out. "Did you reach Howard?"

"Not at home," Gwendolyn replied. "But I tried the employee gymnasium downstairs and caught him there. He said he'd be here in forty minutes. He has an appointment with the barbershop on the twelfth floor before work."

"Another forty minutes wasted." Scowling, Roth turned back to Olive. "How would you feel about learning the basics now?"

She uncapped her pen and flipped to a fresh sheet of paper in her notebook. "I'm ready."

"Just so I'm clear"—Howard tossed to the ground a cigarette that would not stay lit—"I show up early to work on a Monday morning, but not early enough by Roth's standards, and you've weaseled your way into my job. Do I have that straight?"

His ire baffled her, considering where they were.

"Look around you, Howard." She kept her voice low, though the umbrella they shared offered a modicum of privacy. Rain blotted the sidewalk, and wind billowed her skirt out before her. "There's enough work for both of us."

In the neighborhoods radiating out from Hawthorne Works, rowhouses and bungalows thrown into mourning were marked by sprays of flowers and black ribbon crepes on their paneled front doors. In the last block they'd canvassed, nineteen residents had been claimed by the *Eastland*. In this one, one out of every three or four homes bore crepes on front doors that remained wide open for visitors to come inside and pay their respects.

Every family that had received a coffin—or more than one— from their undertaker kept it in the center of their parlors until the funeral. Most of the families being Catholic, every corner of the parlor seemed stuffed with votive candles at which loved ones and visitors knelt and prayed for the souls of the dead. It made it far easier for Olive and Howard to identify which homes already had bodies and death certificates to go with them, which launched the process that would send the beneficiaries their checks. Olive entered every candlelit parlor with the deepest reverence and still felt she was intruding on an intensely personal time. Still, the clients so far had been grateful for her heartfelt condolences and the help MetLife could set in motion.

"I'm ready to split up," Olive told Howard, nodding a greeting to a passing policeman, whose slicker was beaded with rain. The open doors of the bereaved made it a snap for thieves to quietly enter and slip out again with valuables, which was why an extra force of Cicero police officers patrolled the neighborhoods. "You take one side of the street, I'll take the other?"

"Apparently I don't have a say in the matter. So, by all means, jump on in. Just be a doll and don't make messes I'll have to clean up later." Howard stomped off like an insecure, overgrown child.

Refusing to be rattled by him, Olive consulted the chart on

her clipboard to see if the next crepe-marked house matched an address on her list of MetLife clients. Blanche had listed them by street, not alphabetically, so when Olive's gaze fell on the Petroski surname, she wasn't expecting it.

Visions of Stella as Olive had last seen her flooded her mind, quickly followed by those of Michael, Addie, and Jakob. Grief pulled at her, but she fought against it. Right now, she had a job to do.

The Petroski bungalow was seafoam green with cedar-shingled gables. Marigolds added sunshine to the dreary day from the garden edging the front of the house. Olive climbed three steps to the covered porch, closed her umbrella, and quietly stepped past the crepe of fragrant lilies.

Her stomach hollowed as she entered the sacred space. A closed coffin presided in the center, encircled by seated mourners. Ice dripped beneath the bier into pans, the rhythmic sound an insistent knocking of time. Pushed to the edges of the room, tables and benches were stippled with candles of every width and height. Their tiny flames bent with the whispered prayers of those kneeling before them.

Olive signed a guest book near the door, then sat in an open chair. The man next to her held his head in his hands, elbows supported on his knees. He sat up and turned to her, dark crescents beneath his red-rimmed eyes.

"Mr. Petroski," she whispered, masking her dismay at the change in him.

"Please. You must call me Jakob. These are Stella's parents, Mr. and Mrs. Adamski." He indicated the elderly couple seated on the other side of him, their ashen faces thatched with care.

Pressure swelled at the base of her throat as Olive leaned forward and clasped each hand. "I'm so sorry about Stella. You have my most sincere condolences." If they spoke little English, they may not understand her words, but surely they'd hear the sentiment behind them.

"Stella?" Coarse grey brows knitting, Mr. Adamski crooked a finger at the coffin. "Henryk. My son. Not Stella."

Olive looked to Jakob to confirm what he was saying.

Another pair of visitors stepped into the parlor, bearing a covered dish. Jakob rose and took it with thanks, then turned back to Olive. "Right. It's Stella's brother, Henryk."

She followed him into the kitchen, where he set the dish on a counter crowded with others.

"Henryk Adamski?" Hooking the umbrella handle over her wrist, she consulted the list on her clipboard. "Did he live here?"

Leaning against the counter, Jakob ran a hand over his jaw. "He moved in with us about a year ago. Henryk, Stella, and I pooled our wages to provide for the entire household, all seven of us."

Olive began filling in a form. "I'll get his policy claim processed right away."

"Stella's missing."

The words sank to the bottom of Olive's gut. Pen stilling, she looked up. "She hasn't been identified at the morgue?" The first temporary morgues had been moved to a central location at the Second Regiment Armory building.

"We've been there, Stella's parents and me. We've all looked. She wasn't there."

The back door opened, and in a rush of sunshine, Michael and Addie spilled in, both wearing their Sunday best but rumpled enough to suggest they'd burned off some energy outside.

"Red!" Addie cried and promptly hugged Olive's legs.

Olive gathered her close before tousling Michael's hair. She had not expected that seeing them again would bring such a bittersweet sting.

"Did you find our mama?" Michael asked.

She swallowed. "No."

Apparently hearing the commotion, Mrs. Adamski appeared in the doorway of the kitchen, scolding in Polish while brushing

Addie's blond hair out of her face. After licking her thumb and wiping a smudge of dirt from Michael's cheek, she grasped their hands and paraded them back into the parlor, where Olive had no doubt they would be tasked with sitting quietly until they reached their limit once more.

"Have you called the hospitals, Jakob?" Olive asked.

"Every one of them. There are no Stella Petroskis registered anywhere, and no unidentified patients, either."

"I'll check them again in person," Olive promised. "I can only imagine the confusion a sudden influx may have caused in record keeping."

In the pause that followed, neither acknowledged that Stella could very well be one of the hundreds of bodies the divers were still recovering.

"Do you have a photograph of her that you could part with while I search?" she asked.

Jakob produced one from the breast pocket of his faded black suit. Stella had been caught unaware, it seemed, as if someone had spoken her name and taken her picture as soon as she looked up. Beneath the brim of her hat, bending in the wind, her smile was natural.

"That was taken at last year's picnic," he said. His throat seemed to close around the words.

"It's beautiful. Could you spare it for a few days?"

"If it will help. Whatever you need to do to find her, just let me know."

It was too early to assume that her body was not still in the river. But it wasn't too early to rule out other possibilities.

"I need a list of her friends and coworkers," Olive told him. "I'll need to talk to anyone who interacted with her. I'll want to look at the guest book for Henryk's wake, too, to see if any names are there that aren't already on the list you provide me."

As sincere as he seemed about helping, just now he looked stricken and overwhelmed.

"Tomorrow," she added. "I'll come back tomorrow, and we'll go over it then."

Michael silently stole back into the kitchen, his trousers sagging at his waist. He slipped his fingers into Olive's. "Are you going to find her?"

"I am."

CHAPTER ELEVEN

TUESDAY, JULY 27, 1915

Twenty-four hours after learning Stella was missing, Olive could claim no ground gained. Only ground covered.

Traffic echoed her clanging thoughts as she hopped off the streetcar on Dearborn Street and headed toward the corner at Madison. It was already nearly five o'clock when she'd telephoned the *Chicago Tribune* office, but the secretary had said if she hurried, she might catch a photographer who was currently stuck in a meeting with the editor-in-chief.

Olive needed this to work. After a day of dead ends, she needed one single open door through which to guide her investigation.

Starting at six o'clock this morning, she'd taken Stella's photo to each area hospital and showed it to every nurse on duty. No one had seen or heard of Stella Petroski. After leaving business cards with the medical staff, she'd gone back to Cicero to find the organizers of the picnic. She wanted to see if they had taken any photographs that might be helpful, but they'd been waiting until they arrived in Michigan City to use their film.

Then she visited with Jakob and began interviewing the friends and family on his list. Preparing to meet with folks whose English might not be fluent, she had even arranged yesterday with Blanche for an interpreter to meet her. Today, however, that interpreter never showed.

Still, she'd been able to ask a handful of young women about anything out of the ordinary they'd noticed with Stella before Saturday. These questions never would have occurred to her had it not been for Claire. The most likely scenario was that Stella died in the river and her body hadn't been found. But waiting for that discovery while doing nothing felt like an unforgivable waste of time. If Olive could cross off the possibility that Stella didn't want to be found, it would be better than nothing.

And so far, *nothing* was exactly what she'd found.

A horn honked, and Olive leapt back onto the curb, waiting for a Packard to pass. She shifted her satchel to the opposite shoulder, adjusting the strap over her navy suit jacket. The papers had listed more confirmed dead today, along with a reminder that hundreds were yet unrecovered. None of the descriptions of the seven people still unidentified at the morgue matched Stella, either. Perhaps Olive's eagerness to help had made her investigation premature. But everything in her cried "Hurry!" and accused her of already being too late.

Late. Out of habit, she checked her wrist before remembering her watch had been lost in the river. Something within her, however, resisted replacing it. She wasn't ready to wear a reminder that she'd been given more time on this earth while, for hundreds of others, time had run out.

But she didn't need to see a clock to know she'd better hustle if she wanted to catch the photographer before he went home.

At the corner of Dearborn and Madison Streets, the grey stone of the seventeen-story Tribune Building beckoned to her. At a break in traffic, she darted across the road, pushed through the doors of plate glass, and stepped into the grand lobby with its soaring ceiling and double curving staircase of veined Carrara marble. Bronze relief panels at her left and right showed the evolution of the *Chicago Tribune*, and above the entrance, all the way to the ceiling, were Tiffany glass mosaics.

As soon as she inhaled, memories of her father burst upon her. Every time he'd come home from work, this was the combination he'd worn on his lapels: men's aftershave, ink from both pens and printing presses, and the air that stirred within these walls. She'd visited often then but hadn't had a reason to come here since he died. Now that she was here—using his worn leather satchel, no less—she could almost hear him giving her his classic newsy advice. *"Ask the right questions of the right people. Do not rush to unproven conclusions. Do not settle for half-truths but pursue the whole truth instead."*

That was exactly what she was here to do.

Past the business and advertising offices, she stepped onto the elevator sixty feet back from the entrance.

She was so eager that when the door opened on the third floor, she rushed headlong out of it.

"Oh!" She reeled back, but not before she'd clipped a strange man in the chest with the brim of her straw hat, which now twisted at a ridiculous angle. "I'm so sorry. I didn't see you. Which I suppose is difficult to believe, given the fact that you're—" To say *so tall* would be an understatement. He had at least nine inches on her, which put him well north of six feet.

"Standing right in front of you?" His broad hands still cupped her elbows, steadying her. He looked down at her with ice-blue eyes that could no doubt freeze water into glaciers, had he a mind to.

When she lifted her arms to adjust her hat, his hold fell away. "A Viking," she blurted.

Though disguised in a deep blue suit and striped tie, he was a square-jawed, blond-haired, stern-faced Norseman from the land of Thor, with a physique built from swinging hammers or battle-axes, or rowing dragon-headed longships, or whatever it was Vikings did.

Faint lines webbed from the corners of his eyes. "I've been called worse," he said.

"I'll just bet you have," she muttered, already wary. But that had more to do with Warren than with the man before her. Just because Warren abused Claire didn't mean every man in her age bracket was a total reprobate.

"What was that you said? I didn't quite catch it."

Blast. "Never mind."

An eyebrow lifted. "Well, then. Do you need any help finding where you're headed?"

As if she didn't know every square foot of this floor from the editors' offices to the etching room, the dark rooms, the art department, library, biographies, and the local news reporters' room down the hall, from which she could hear more than a dozen clacking typewriters even now. She'd even seen what few had: the mammoth printing presses churning twenty feet below the sidewalk.

But how would he know that? It was a perfectly legitimate question. Courteous, even.

Willing her quills to flatten, she fixed a smile in place. "I know where I'm going."

He held her in his gaze a beat too long. "I believe you do." He took a step back, presumably to let her pass. "Watch your step."

Only then did she notice the files scattered over the floor. He must have dropped them to catch her when she barreled into him.

She knelt to help gather the mess she'd made. Photographs fanned beneath her gloved fingertips, black-and-white images of the one theme that interested her right now. "You took these?" The elevator doors closed without them, and a mechanical whir signaled its empty descent.

He took a knee beside her and opened a manila file folder, placing photographs inside it. "I did."

"When I called not twenty minutes ago, I was told I might catch a photographer before you left for the day."

"You caught me? As I recall, it was the other way around."

"Regardless. Were you in a meeting with an editor just now?" She needed to be sure this was the same photographer the secretary had told her about.

He confirmed he had been.

"Perfect. And are these your photos from the *Eastland* disaster?"

"They are. This batch I took yesterday."

Olive fished in her satchel for a business card and thrust it at him. "Olive Pierce, MetLife. Do you have photographs from Saturday, showing survivors coming off the ship? I'm looking for evidence that a client of mine survived. If she's in one of your photos, the case would be closed for MetLife and opened by the police as a missing person."

He palmed her card and read it before slipping it into his vest pocket. He extended a hand, and they shook right there, both still on their knees. Folks researching in the library across the hall must have enjoyed the view from the interior windows.

"Erik Magnussen," said the Viking photographer, introducing himself. "I don't have photos from Saturday, but Jun Fujita of the *Chicago Evening Post* has a scrapbook of the hundreds he took. He happened to be there when the ship tipped. I'm happy to ring him for you if you'd like to meet."

It wasn't what she'd expected, but it was a lead, nonetheless. "Thank you, but there's no need for that. I have a directory. I'll ring him myself." With all the photos safely back in place, she stood, and he did the same. "I'll be on my way, then. I apologize for running into you like that. I have a tendency to . . . step lively."

"I'll just bet you have." He tipped his hat to her like a gentleman, but she could have sworn he winked.

Spotting Mr. Fujita was easy. As he approached Corner Books & More, Olive opened the door for him. Locking it behind them, she made sure the sign was turned so no customers thought they were still open.

"Olive Pierce. Thank you so much for coming, Mr. Fujita."

He bowed to her, then shook her proffered hand. "It was an easy walk, and the weather is fine, at last."

Only two blocks separated the bookstore and the *Chicago Evening Post* office on Washington Street, the same distance between his office and hers in the Conway Building. But as her office was closed for the evening, and his floor was being cleaned right now, they'd settled on this location.

"This is your family's store?" Mr. Fujita doffed his homburg and surveyed the space.

Olive wondered what he made of it. To her, it was as familiar as the house she'd grown up in. A Chicagoan named Frank Lloyd Wright had brought a new, simpler style in vogue, but Sylvie stood staunchly by Victorian wallpaper and velvet curtains. She had, however, updated the colors. Above wood paneling that went from floor to chair rail, the walls were now covered with a mustard-gold paper embossed in a marigold pattern, and the drapes were a soothing moss green. The copper-tiled ceiling stamped with medallions hadn't changed since the store was rebuilt after the Great Fire. Electricity lit the chandeliers as well as the table lamps placed near armchairs throughout the store.

"My grandfather founded it in the last century and passed the baton to my aunt when running it became too much for him. My mother painted all the character portraits hanging on the walls." Olive led Mr. Fujita to the bistro area, where chairs sat upended on the tables. She flipped two of them down again. "Please, have a seat."

First, he placed a bulging scrapbook on the small round table. When it was opened, it took up almost the entire circumference. He seated himself on the other side of the table and hung his homburg on the upturned leg of a nearby chair. "Take your time. You know what you're looking for more than I do."

"And you know your work better than anyone." She handed him the photo Jakob had given her. "Do you happen to recall seeing this woman in any of the images you developed?"

He took the photo from her and studied it. "I couldn't say for certain. Everything I took and processed is in this book, though." He handed Stella's likeness back to her.

She kept it on the table and turned her attention to oversized pages stiff with photos. The number of photographs he'd processed and mounted from the disaster was astounding. "Do you have a book like this for other major news events, too?"

"No." His gaze did not meet Olive's but instead roved over the images, coming to rest on one that made her breath hitch and knot. A portly fireman, perhaps in his fifties, in his undershirt and suspenders, held the limp body of a child whose head lolled back. The fireman's mouth was agape, his eyes wide with horror and disbelief. In this one expression, Mr. Fujita had captured the feeling of all who were there that day.

Her gloves still on to keep her fingerprints covered, she turned the pages and saw what he had seen. A solemn parade of survivors passing over the *Eastland*'s hull, onto the tugboat *Kenosha*, and finally onto the wharf. Welders cutting holes in the hull, and other men lifting people through them. A girl on a stretcher, hooked up to a Pulmotor. A diver inside the sunken ship. Another girl, slumped forward, her hair flipped over her head and streaming water. The caption Mr. Fujita had penned beneath it in small block letters read, *Too late.*

Eyelids burning, Olive stood and spun away from the table. It was too hot in here. She couldn't breathe. Crossing to one set of drapes, she parted them and opened the window a few inches to permit a breeze.

It wasn't enough. Desperate to feel the movement of air, she flipped a switch on the fan that stood on the broad windowsill. There she stood, gulping that stream of oxygen, dust motes and all. Adrenaline spiked through limbs that, mere days ago, had thrashed and kicked to keep her head above water.

Moments melted together as she prayed for composure and for the grace to confront in photographs what she was loath to meet in her dreams. She wasn't here to relive her own ordeal. She was here to work.

Mr. Fujita watched her as she returned to the table but made no comment.

Using the magnifying glass he offered her, Olive enlarged each face and the emotion written in their expressions. "Did you know any of the passengers?"

"I did not know any of them. But I knew all of them," he told her. "I know what it is to leave one's homeland behind in search of a better life in America. I came from Japan; they came from Poland, Bohemia, Germany, Sweden, Norway. Where we came from matters less than the dream we all shared and the hard work we're willing to put into it. What I do *not* know, Miss Pierce, is what it's like for all of that to disappear in the course of minutes. Two. Two minutes was all it took for the ship to roll onto its side. I saw it happen. It didn't even make a splash."

It seemed impossible that this steamship—four and a half stories tall, a city block long, carrying twenty-five hundred souls—had made no more than an outward ripple in the water.

"There was splashing on the inside. For a while."

Mr. Fujita squinted at her. "You were there. With children?"

"A seven-year-old boy and a two-year-old girl. I'm looking for their mother." She tapped Stella's photo again. "This is going to take me a while. Feel free to find a book to help pass the time, if you'd like."

With that slight bow of his, he pushed back his chair, smoothed the tie beneath his vest, and went browsing.

Page after page, Olive searched. Every black-and-white figure looked so much the same. Their wet hair streamed down their backs and over their shoulders, in some cases obscuring their faces.

Their features twisted into expressions of pain too private for public viewing.

Those passengers who had been on the promenade and hurricane decks when the *Eastland* tipped and had the good fortune of climbing over the rail and walking off the hull were not much easier to identify. Some still had broad-brimmed hats and umbrellas shielding them from the camera's eye. Their mouths were open with shouts or covered by their hands. Watching. Waiting. Agonizing.

Identical blankets from Marshall Field's covered survivors on the wharf. Truly, if anyone had wanted to hide in a crowd, this would have been the perfect place for it.

A few pages later, Olive halted on a clear image of a woman reaching to accept a blanket. It was Claire.

She flipped farther into the scrapbook, looking for more pictures with her friend in the frame. A few dozen images later, she was satisfied there was only the one.

If Warren ever saw this, he would know Claire hadn't died in the river.

Mr. Fujita returned. "You found her?" He eased into the chair, his thumb holding his place in a book.

"I didn't find who I was looking for. But this woman." She touched a fingertip to the image. "She's the one I was with that morning. May I purchase this picture from you, Mr. Fujita? What would you consider a fair price?"

"It is yours. It's your memory and hers, not mine." He slipped the stiff square from the corners that mounted it to the page and handed it to her.

"Thank you." Tucking it under Stella's photo on the table, she kept searching for Stella. In vain.

Later, after Mr. Fujita had left with his scrapbook and Olive had closed up the store for the night, she returned to her apartment. But she didn't feel alone, not with all of those images branded into her mind. Before tonight's meeting, she had her own experience to haunt her. Now she had hundreds more.

Her head ached with the pressure of all it held, and her chest felt bruised from her heartbeat. She'd disregarded the stinging stripes on her back all day, but when she changed out of her work clothes, dark red tracks on her chemise revealed that ignoring wounds didn't mean they were not there.

Throwing on an old shirt, she took the soiled white cambric to the bathroom and rubbed a wet bar of soap over the spots, then scrubbed the fabric together. Under a stream of cold water, the blood stains faded but didn't disappear. She scoured the fabric until her hands were chapped and she could no longer stand the feel of water on her skin. Sweating, she turned off the faucet.

Olive squeezed her eyes shut and braced her hands against the sink. She heard water dripping from the chemise onto the hexagonal-tiled floor. She heard the splashes of the drowning. She heard their screams. She heard crying, and at last realized it was her own.

CHAPTER TWELVE

THURSDAY, JULY 29, 1915

"You look like you could use this." Entering Olive's office, Blanche handed her a steaming mug of coffee.

Stifling a sigh, Olive wrapped her hands around the mug and thanked the stalwart secretary.

"You've been through so much, Olive. It hasn't even been five days since you almost—since the disaster." Blanche was making allowances. She shouldn't have to. With a bob of her chin, she added, "Today is a new day."

"With no mistakes in it yet," Olive quipped, unable to resist channeling Anne of Green Gables. The key word in that quote, however, was *yet*.

With a generous smile, Blanche returned to her desk in the reception area, and Olive returned to rehashing yesterday in her mind. The day after her meeting with Mr. Fujita had begun well enough, with a consultation with Red Cross workers. They'd sent their own people to Cicero to gather data on victims and survivors so they could cut checks. Olive cross-referenced their records with hers and learned that the bodies of five missing clients had been recovered and identified since Olive had been to Cicero on Monday.

None were Stella. It was a relief that she wasn't proven dead, but even after combing through Mr. Fujita's scrapbook Tuesday night, Olive couldn't prove she was still living, either.

Regardless, that was five closed cases, thanks to the cooperation of the Red Cross, and five death claim benefits that were now being processed.

Compelled by the news, Olive had used the MetLife car to drive out to Cicero yesterday to pay respects to those families and see if any others had been found. Only when she arrived and heard the church bells tolling did she remember that it was Black Wednesday, the day all the funerals were held. Hawthorne Works was draped with black bunting, and neighborhoods were decked in wreaths. The entire town in mourning.

She wouldn't chase after people with paperwork on such a day. Besides, all the forms she'd packed, the ones requiring beneficiary signatures, were nowhere in her satchel or the car. Abandoning that task, she had attended the mass funeral.

When she'd returned to the car, it wouldn't start. It was completely out of fuel, even though Howard had told her it still had a quarter of a tank, plenty for a twelve-mile round trip.

Olive buried her face in her mug, drinking so she wouldn't groan aloud at the memory. By the time she'd arrived back at the office yesterday, she'd missed a meeting with Roth and Howard she didn't even have on her calendar. All the forms she distinctly remembered packing were sitting in a neat pile on her desk.

This coffee could stand to be a whole lot stronger.

Resolving to leave yesterday behind her, she set the mug aside. The *Tribune* rustled as she turned the page. Today's news was crowded with relief tallies and accounts of yesterday's funerals. One photograph showed seven coffins stacked in two rows. An entire family, perished.

Olive parsed the notices and obituaries, looking for MetLife clients, whether they'd perished on the *Eastland* or elsewhere, so she could start processing the death benefits even if the bereaved had not yet contacted the office.

A single line arrested her.

"No." Her hands turned cold as blood rushed to her galloping heart. She read it again.

STERLING——Claire Elizabeth Sterling, aged 30, beloved wife of Warren Sterling, was laid to rest in Mount Hermon Cemetery, North Lawndale. Burial private.

Questions exploded in Olive's mind. She hadn't yet heard that Claire had gotten safely out of Chicago. Had an accident befallen her before or during her escape? She'd gone unchaperoned. Did she encounter some unsavory character, unprotected and alone?

Her gut told her that whatever happened to Claire had not been accidental or a random act of violence. Warren might have been watching Olive's apartment building Sunday and followed Claire to the train station. He could have killed her, just as Claire said he would if he found her. If Warren wanted it to be a matter of record that she'd died on the *Eastland*, he'd have to forge a death certificate, but that wouldn't be complicated. The county coroner had been so overwhelmed with cases, she'd learned, that on Saturday he ordered a rubber stamp to use on all the certificates, declaring the date and cause of death the same for everyone. Warren was smart enough that he could have gotten a blank death certificate, had another stamp made, and no one would be the wiser.

Pinpricks of sweat dotted her skin. He could have done it. He could have gotten away with murder.

And since Claire was insured with MetLife, he'd be paid for it, too.

With a shaking hand, she brought the phone to her ear and called the switchboard at Sears, Roebuck and Company. "Shipping department, please," she directed.

Seconds ticked past while Olive waited to be connected, giving her enough time to realize she had no idea what she'd say when

Warren answered. All she knew was that she had to see if this was some huge mistake.

"Shipping," a man answered.

"Warren Sterling, please," Olive tried.

"He's not available. May I help you with something instead?"

Olive gripped the telephone tighter. "Thank you, but I really need to speak with Warren personally. It's important."

A grunt filtered over the line. "Lady, he buried his wife yesterday. Whatever you have to say can't be more important than that. Today is his last day off before he reports back to work tomorrow. If there was a problem with your order, I'm happy to handle it for—"

"Claire Sterling? She works in advertising there at Sears. Are you certain she's the one you're talking about?"

A pause. "I'm sorry, ma'am, if you knew her. But yes, that's the Mrs. Sterling who died."

She slammed the earpiece into the fork. It wasn't true. Claire had survived, and Olive had proof of it with the photo from Mr. Fujita. If she was dead, it wasn't from drowning.

She dialed Claire's house and let it ring for what seemed like minutes. Finally, a click, then another, as the line opened and then immediately closed.

Warren was home, all right.

"I have to go."

Blanche swiveled in her chair as Olive hurried out of her office. "Will you be back in time for your meeting with Roth? He won't be happy if you miss two in a row."

Olive heard her speak but didn't register what she said. "I have to see a client."

Then she stopped herself. What was she doing? If Warren had murdered Claire and Olive went alone to his house to question him, what would stop him from killing her, too? She was rushing into a trap. Even if she left the address with Blanche, Warren could kill her and dispose of her body before Olive missed her next meeting. She had to be smarter than that.

She couldn't go alone. But she couldn't let it alone, either.

Seating her hat in place, she silently calculated the options. Kristof wasn't back to his full strength after his cold, and he was sixty-six years old besides. If there was any sort of physical struggle with Warren, her uncle could get hurt. She hoped they wouldn't come to blows at all, but she didn't know how volatile Warren might be right now.

Where was the Viking when she needed one?

Swallowing her pride, she did an about-face and marched past Blanche and Gwendolyn to Howard's office. She smoothed a fold in her accordion-pleated black skirt. "Howard. I need you to come with me to visit a client in North Lawndale. Please."

He barely looked up as he flipped through an issue of *Photoplay* with movie starlet Mary Pickford on the cover. "What, right this second? Thanks for the advance notice."

"Please. It's urgent." She approached his desk.

Howard smirked. "A matter of life and death? In this business, it usually is." When she didn't respond, he lifted the dark fringe of his lashes, assessing her. "Listen, you had a bad day yesterday. Missing our meeting with Roth, forgetting your forms . . ."

Olive held up a hand. "What did you say?"

His face darkened to a guilty shade of red.

She felt hers heat to match it. There was only one way he could know about that. "Did you take the forms from my satchel?"

"Settle down, would you?" He leaned back in his chair. "I needed some for my own cases, and Gwendolyn and Blanche were both on the phone. So I went to ask you for some, but you weren't there."

She must have been in the toilet room on the other side of the building. "You couldn't have waited for me to return?"

"How was I to know how long you'd be? Anyway, I saw them poking out of your satchel, and I grabbed them. I took them back to my office to check how many I needed. I kept about seven, and then, when I returned the rest to your desk, your satchel was gone."

Olive stared at him. "I was probably waiting for an elevator. You could have poked your head out of the office and seen me."

He offered an elaborate shrug. "You could have checked your bag one more time. Just like you should have checked the fuel gauge on the car."

Olive crossed her arms. "So it's my fault you took the forms right out of my bag?"

"It's your fault you didn't notice in time."

"You didn't also happen to reroute the interpreter yesterday for your own purposes, did you?"

His frown held genuine confusion. "No. Wow. Sounds like your day was even worse than I realized. That doesn't mean I'm going to help you with your errands now, though. I have my own work to do." He slid the magazine beneath his appointment book.

Only with a monumental effort did Olive keep her temper in check.

Unfolding her arms, she tried again. "It's Claire. My friend I took on the *Eastland* with me. She was buried yesterday." She felt her skin heat and cool and could just imagine the mottling that bloomed on her neck. "I need to go see her husband, who is also my client. But I don't think I should go alone. He blames me for what happened and said he never wants to see me again."

Howard clasped his hands behind his head. "So you need me."

"And you owe me after that stunt with the forms yesterday. Are you going to come with me or not?"

Howard knocked on Warren's front door while Olive waited beside him on the porch. Two wooden rockers creaked in the breeze.

"I still say you ought to leave this entire case to me," he muttered. "In fact, better yet, leave all of them to me. They're too emotional for you."

She peered at him from beneath the straw brim of her hat. "Why? Because I was there?"

"That too. But you know what I mean. Selling insurance policies is one thing. But investigating claims, coming face-to-face with death and grief among the survivors—that takes not just brains but a certain kind of strength."

Unbelievable. Did he not think it took strength to escape the *Eastland*, bringing a child with her? Olive's instinct told her that his remarks had less to do with her than they had to do with him. "Honestly, Howard, nothing would change for you if I get a promotion. There's work enough for two investigators."

"But not for long." He huffed a quiet laugh. "If women take men's jobs from them for less pay, what will be next? Before you know it, you'll be parading around in trousers, too. It's unnatural. It isn't the God-given order of things."

Hogwash. Before she could form a response that might reassure him about his job security, however, he took a step closer to the window and squinted to see inside. "You sure this guy is even home? Or are you wasting my time?"

"I called him from the office, and he answered," she told him.

"So he knows we're coming?"

"I didn't have a chance to tell him. Before he hung up."

Howard rolled his eyes. "Splendid." He knocked again, louder this time. "Mr. Sterling, my name is Howard Penrose. I'm here from Metropolitan Life Insurance. I'm sorry to disturb you in your time of loss." He glanced at Olive and added quietly, "If he wants his money, he'll come."

The last thing she wanted was for Warren to get paid for Claire's death. "We'll need to rule out any suspicious circumstances before closing the case."

"And by suspicious, you mean aside from a steamship tipping over, right? The entire thing smells fishy to me, if you'll pardon the pun. Did you read what the steamship company did to the *Eastland* that made it even more top-heavy?"

She had. They had covered the upper decks of rotting wood with several tons of concrete and added all those lifeboats—for all the good they did—which added at least ten more tons of weight at the very top. To make it *safer*.

Movement inside the house captured her attention. A few footsteps, and the lock clicked. The door opened.

Olive had expected to see a monster. The man leaning against the doorframe, however, was stubbled and wearing only an undershirt and a pair of pajama bottoms. A dark brown bottle dangled from his hand. Blue half-moons hung beneath his glassy eyes.

She looked away from his state of undress. This man was no threat. He was raw and exposed. A wreck.

Howard raised his hands as if to form a shield for Warren. "How about you throw on a robe, Mr. Sterling?"

Heat wrapped Olive's neck as she paced away from the door, giving them some semblance of privacy while they talked. Her fingertips rested on the porch railing while she looked absently out at the park across the street. A flake of white paint caught beneath her fingernail.

Warren returned wearing actual trousers and a rumpled shirt, the bottle no longer in sight. "Come in." He motioned to the living room, then finished buttoning his shirt as Howard and Olive stepped inside.

"Why are you here?" Warren demanded of Olive as soon as they were all seated. He took the sofa, and Olive and Howard the armchairs. "I told you not to come around. Ever."

"Mr. Sterling," Howard interjected, "Miss Pierce and I are here as agents of MetLife."

"I'm also here as a friend," Olive tried. "I was in your wedding, for goodness' sake. Claire was like a sister to me. I was so sorry to learn of her burial in the newspaper." She couldn't keep the censure from her tone.

"I don't owe you anything, Olive. No explanation, no personal visit."

Howard leaned forward. "That may be, on a personal level, but as far as life insurance goes, we do require some details. Here, you look like you could use this." He pulled a cigarette from the silver case in his pocket.

"He doesn't smoke," Olive whispered automatically. Too late, she registered the faint odor despite the breeze from the open windows.

Howard kicked an empty Lucky Strikes carton toward her. "Evidence to the contrary. Something a *real* investigator would notice."

Warren accepted the cigarette while Howard lit it. "It seemed like a good time to start."

"In any case," Howard went on, "we do need to see a copy of the death certificate."

Warren took a drag, then left them. When he returned, he handed the paper to Howard before collapsing onto the couch. Olive leaned over to inspect it. Just as she'd thought, it had been stamped with the cause and location of death.

DROWNED, JULY 24, 1915
FROM STEAMER *EASTLAND*
CHICAGO RIVER AT CLARK STREET

It wasn't true.

"I thought you couldn't find her body," Olive said.

Warren squinted at her, then rose and shut the blinds over the piano with a snap she felt in her chest. "I looked again. And again. And there she was." Smoke unfurled between his words.

"You're sure?"

He tapped ash into a tray. "You don't think I know my own wife?"

What Olive knew, but didn't say, was that it grew harder to identify bodies the longer they'd been out of the water. She had been to the morgue herself, looking for Stella or other clients. The coroner's assistant she'd spoken with confirmed her sense that the bodies looked more like each other than they looked like themselves. The skin changed color to the same green-grey. The facial features lost their distinctness. The people working at the morgue had laid nets over the bodies and sprayed insect repellent in the air as quickly as they could, but some flies had managed to get through and lay their eggs first. Those bodies . . . Olive was still trying to wipe those images from her memory.

"How did you know it was her?" Howard asked Warren.

Warren's expression twisted into something like revulsion. "She had a head injury, which is why I couldn't find her at first." He inhaled deeply on his cigarette, then blew out the smoke and coughed. "It was bad. Something fell on her. That's not how I wanted to remember her." Tears leaked down his unshaven cheeks, and he palmed them away.

If he was lying, he was a master at it.

Olive didn't know what to think. Everything about Warren, from his perfect home to his model wife, was intended to support the Sterling reputation. But what one saw was a veneer, constructed to impress. Everything about him was false.

Except, Olive conceded, the brokenness she saw in him, the kind that couldn't be faked.

"So how did you identify her?" Howard prompted.

Warren exhaled. "When I stopped looking at faces and looked for other clues, it was easy." He reached into his pocket, then set two things on the coffee table.

One was a wedding ring on a chain. The other was an heirloom timepiece.

Olive picked them up, inspecting them. The engraving inside the ring was their wedding date. The timepiece was one of a kind. The hands had stopped at 7:29.

"You recognize these, too?" Howard asked her.

She told him she did, even as she floundered to make sense of it. What had Claire been wearing when she came to Olive's apartment Saturday afternoon? A grey skirt. A once-white shirtwaist. A cardigan sweater, but no French linen jacket. At the time, Olive had assumed Claire had shed the jacket in the water to be free of its weight. But the photo from Mr. Fujita showed her still wearing it and her jewelry while accepting the blanket.

Olive's pulse thudded in her ears. "She was wearing these when you found her?"

"No. That's why it took me so long. They were having trouble with thieves coming in, pretending they were looking for loved ones and picking the valuables off them instead. So when Claire was brought in, they took off her jewelry, put it in a bag, and marked it with a number that matched the tag on her toe. When I finally found someone who would listen to me, I described these two pieces, and they found them. When they took me to where she was in the row of bodies—" His voice broke on the words, and he sought solace in the cigarette once more before putting it out. "No wonder I didn't recognize her at first. But she was wearing that French linen coat I got her for her birthday last year."

Olive's head spun. Her palms grew slick on the wooden arms of the craftsman chair.

Howard took a form from his briefcase. "We are sorry for your loss, Mr. Sterling. MetLife is committed to a timely processing of your claim."

"No." She couldn't be part of this. Standing, she cast her gaze heavenward, but it caught on the oak beams crossing the nine-foot ceiling. Like bars, she thought. Like a cage. She was trapped in deception and had no idea how to make it right without courting danger for herself or for Claire, if she were indeed still living. "This isn't right."

With a word to Warren, Howard stood and led her by the elbow until they were standing on the front porch again. "You're losing it, Pierce. I realize she was your friend, but that's no reason to forsake all semblance of professionalism. Your emotions are getting in the way. You see? You're proving my earlier point."

Olive fumed, because she knew that was exactly what this looked like. "This has nothing to do with professionalism," she began. "I have reason to believe there's something he's not telling us. I don't trust him. If you're such a superior investigator, then do your job and look into this death further before you send that man a check. Please," she added. "Please, don't take his word for it."

"Do you have any proof that what Mr. Sterling said is untrue?"

She did. But if she showed Howard the photograph, either he wouldn't believe the woman in the photo was Claire, or he would show it to Warren to explain why MetLife wasn't honoring the life insurance claim. Warren's story would fall apart. If he had murdered Claire after the photo was taken, taking the jewelry himself, Olive had no idea what he'd do to cover his tracks. If he had simply misidentified the body as Claire, the photo would prove that she was still alive, and he'd hunt her with a vengeance.

"I asked you a question," Howard pressed. "If there's something you need to tell me . . ."

Unspoken words clogged her throat. God forgive her, but she clamped her lips shut and kept them there.

CHAPTER THIRTEEN

"Aunt Sylvie?" Olive knocked on the door to her aunt's apartment.

She'd been later than usual coming home tonight, leaving work only when security asked her to. She didn't relish returning to an empty apartment, where she'd be alone with her guilt for keeping Claire's secrets and her fear of revealing them.

The door opened, and Olive held up the slip of paper she'd found beneath her apartment door. "I got your note." She tried to smile. "You wanted to see me?"

"Come in, come in!" With warm hands, Sylvie pulled Olive inside and then into an embrace so comforting, she didn't mind the brief pain it caused her back. "I read the news," Sylvie said. "About Claire. God rest her!"

Olive tried to speak, but all that came out was a broken sigh. Tears welled and spilled over.

Sylvie released her, then guided her to sit in the kitchen, which was papered in crimson-and-ivory chintz. From the parlor, the Victrola quietly played a record of violin music. "Kristof is at a rehearsal right now, so it's just you and me. And Lizzie and Jane." She gestured to the tortoiseshell cats curled up together in a wing chair by the fireplace. "Do you want to talk?"

Oh, how Olive wished she could. "I don't know what to say." Nor could she predict the consequences of confiding the truth.

Sylvie folded her arms over a bottle-green shirtwaist with broad ivory cuffs and collar. "How on earth could you go on working today after seeing news like that? When you didn't come home at your usual time, I worried."

"I'm sorry. I figured since Mom isn't home waiting for me, I might as well work late when I can. So many of the victims were MetLife clients. And so many people who never considered life insurance before are now making it a priority." Olive had sold policies to five new clients this week in between her investigations.

"I can well imagine. Is there any point in my telling you not to work too hard?"

Olive had to laugh. "In this scenario, would you be the pot or the kettle?"

The end of the table held a stack of flyers advertising a full week of special events to celebrate the upcoming sixty-fifth anniversary of Corner Books & More. Months of careful planning had gone into daily themes, such as Jungle Day, during which the store would host two local authors: Edgar Rice Burroughs, who wrote the wildly popular Tarzan stories, and Upton Sinclair, whose novel *The Jungle* was still causing a stir over Chicago's stockyards and the urban poor.

Olive folded a flyer into thirds to stuff into an envelope. Without Nadine's help, it was little wonder Sylvie brought work home with her.

"You can't deny that you, Uncle Kristof, and my own parents have all handed down a legacy of regular dedication unbound by regular business hours. I'm only following in your footsteps," she said.

"Pish!" Sylvie waved a hand but then began folding flyers, too.

In a separate stack beside the envelopes were sheets of stickers created by the Chicago Board of Trade for businesses to put on every piece of mail. Part of a new marketing campaign to bolster tourism, each sticker proclaimed *Chicago: The Summer Resort*. But the accompanying images—a steamship on one, a girl up to her neck in water in another—turned Olive cold.

"How are you set for food, dear?" Sylvie asked. "Can I feed you something?"

"Thanks, but I'm not hungry. I couldn't eat a thing today."

Sylvie folded another flyer. "I understand. And I'm sure you want nothing more than to go home and kick off your heels. Just remember to call your mother while you're at it. She telephoned the store today, asking where you've been in the evenings and why on earth you haven't called her yet." She raised an eyebrow.

Olive didn't have an excuse. At least, not one she wanted to name. She had never lied to or kept secrets from her mother before, and she didn't want to start now.

"You can talk to us, you know." Abandoning the flyers, Sylvie turned her full attention to Olive. "We do know a little something about surviving a disaster. We didn't lose a loved one to the Great Fire, by the grace of God, but we lost everything else. The aftermath was an ordeal, at least for me. Surviving wasn't as simple as it sounds. Talking helped, I found."

A deep breath filled and released Olive's chest. "I feel like I should be handling it—my memories, my experience—better than I am," she confessed. She told her aunt about her tug of war between insomnia and nightmares, the way small things shook her, and that memories had an immediacy and intensity that sometimes overwhelmed her. "This can't be normal."

Sylvie squeezed her hand. "On the contrary. Those are all normal reactions to a completely abnormal experience. Not to mention the added element of grief for Claire and all those who died so senselessly. But trust me when I say that you won't always feel the way you feel right now."

"To tell you the truth, I'm trying not to do a lot of feeling at all so I can concentrate on work. There's so much to do."

"I've noticed. And I understand the urgency of your job, and I support you. But please, whenever you want to talk or cry or be angry, I'm here for you."

Rising, Olive thanked her. She was exhausted and certain it showed.

"Well, then. This is from your mother." Sylvie stood and hugged Olive. Stepping back again, she fished something from her pocket. "I nearly forgot. A piece of your mail was delivered to the store by mistake today."

Olive accepted a business-sized envelope and examined the return address, handwritten in neat block letters.

ANNE OF GREEN GABLES FAN CLUB, ILLINOIS CHAPTER
724 WHITE WAY OF DELIGHT
LAKE OF SHINING WATERS, IL

"I knew you enjoyed the Anne books," Sylvie was saying, "but I didn't know your admiration was enough for you to join a club, especially considering how busy you are. What does this fan club do?"

Olive snapped her gaze up. "I wouldn't know. This is the first correspondence I've received from them. It's probably just an invitation to join."

"Well, if it sounds good, let me know about it, would you? It might be a wonderful thing to start a Chicago chapter and have them meet at the store. We could discount all of L. M. Montgomery's novels and short story collections and serve raspberry cordial at the meetings. We did something similar for fans of Jane Austen when you were a little girl, and it proved to be a big hit."

But Olive wasn't thinking about book clubs. She was thinking about Anne Shirley, Diana Barry, the fact that the fan club's address was entirely fictional, and the way this handwriting looked suspiciously like Claire's.

❖

Alone in her apartment, Olive locked the door and tossed her hat onto the kitchen table. Unbuckling the straps around her ankles, she stepped out of her shoes, dropped onto the sofa, and tore open the letter. It was dated Wednesday, the day Warren had laid a body in the ground.

> Dear Olive,
>   I am safe and well.

The rest of the words blurred until Olive swiped at her eyes and kept going.

> My hostess is generous, but I don't want to impose on her hospitality much longer. She has children, and I don't want to put them all in danger with my presence. (Besides that, you know how little ones talk. I can't risk that.)
>   I need more funds. There is jewelry in the chest on my vanity. I didn't have you take it when you went to fetch the cash because Warren might have become suspicious if he saw it was gone. But by now, I know he thinks I'm dead. I saw the notice in the newspaper. I can't describe what a release I felt to see in black and white that Claire Sterling is no more. She really isn't, Olive. I'm a new person with a new last name I chose for myself. Barrymore. Perfect, right?
>   I know I said I wouldn't ask anything more of you, but I underestimated how much money I'd need to start over. Forgive me, dear, but I need you to get my jewelry for me. Enter the same way you did before, when Warren is at work. You'll be fine. We both will.

What followed was a detailed list of the items Claire deemed worth the risk of taking. She then told Olive where and when to meet her inside Central Station on Michigan Avenue on Friday. Tomorrow.

> Your bosom friend,
> Claire Barrymore
>
> P.S. Burn this.

Snakes coiled in Olive's middle. After reading the letter again and memorizing the instructions, she knelt at the empty fireplace in the living room and set fire to the paper. The edges blackened and curled, and tiny flames leapt higher.

Claire knew. She knew Warren thought she was dead and seemed relieved but not surprised. She had to understand the coroner had attached her name to a body that wasn't hers.

No. Claire didn't just know these things. She'd planned them. Somehow, before coming to Olive's apartment Saturday, she'd found a body whose build was similar to her own and whose face had been rendered unrecognizable by injury, and had planted her jewelry on it. She'd even dressed the body with her jacket. It was the only way she could be sure Warren would stop looking for her.

Who, then, was buried in Claire's grave? Which family was still searching for their daughter, wife, sister, or mother? The Petroski family flared in her mind. Had Olive's search for Stella been futile because she'd already been buried as someone else?

The small fire burned itself out, leaving only ashes behind, and yet Olive still stared at it as if she might find answers there. Keeping Claire's secret wasn't supposed to hurt anyone else. But every day she kept quiet was another day an entire family was without peace, not to mention the life insurance benefits to which they were entitled.

How could Olive keep up this ruse, knowing an innocent family suffered for it? And how could she reveal the truth, knowing Warren would hunt Claire if she did?

She couldn't stay here in a trance. She had to do something with her hands to help her think.

Rising, she headed to the kitchen with a fresh wave of energy and washed her hands before turning on the oven. She still wasn't hungry, but that didn't mean that Claire wouldn't be tomorrow. Olive might not have all the answers, but at least she could bake. She pulled a bowl from the cupboard and mixed ingredients to form the dough for baking powder biscuits.

This was what she did. She helped. Since she was a child, she'd felt her life's purpose was providing whatever the people she loved needed most. This conviction had taken root early in life, as soon as she'd learned her sister Louise had died days before Olive was born. Louise had been eight years old.

"God took one daughter but gave me another," her mother had told her. *"I don't know what I would have done without you."* Olive had realized that she was there to fill in for Louise. Her job was to take care of her mother.

Over the years, her perception evolved and broadened. Her job was to take care of everyone.

Helping others made her feel good. Valuable. The fact that she didn't feel those things right now meant she wasn't succeeding. Sylvie was working longer hours than she ought to since Nadine had left, and Olive hadn't eased that burden. Meg didn't need her nimble fingers to fasten buttons or work liniment oil into her scars, since she had Walter's family—or was it Hazel's turn by now? The Petroskis needed her to find Stella, and she hadn't.

Olive dipped a biscuit cutter in flour before slamming it into the rolled-out dough and twisting to cut a circle, then repeated the process. Soon, Claire would be gone for good to some mysterious new town, where she would make new friends and a new life for herself. But first, she needed Olive one more time.

Just one more time.

Heat blasted Olive's face and neck as she opened the oven door and slid a baking sheet inside. Checking the clock, she folded her arms and leaned against the counter, forehead aching. Never had she been in a position where helping one person meant hurting another. Compassion for Claire meant injustice for the woman buried in her place.

The telephone rang, startling Olive from her thoughts. Quickly washing her hands again, she rushed to pick up the call.

"Olive, thank goodness I caught you!" Meg's voice reached through the line and touched Olive in the way only a mother could. "How are you?"

"Hi, Mom," was all Olive could say before her throat tightened. "I miss you." Until this moment, she hadn't realized how much.

"Should I come home? Say the word, darling, and I'm on the first train back to Chicago."

"No," Olive said firmly. "Hazel would never forgive me for stealing you away from her."

"Hazel understands that her little sister's best friend just died in an accident that never should have happened. Never. The news we're getting out here gets worse and worse. I keep thinking of you right in the thick of it, grieving for Claire, trying to process the claims of hundreds more. Tell me right now if I should come home. I could at least make sure you're eating."

A small smile lifted Olive's lips. "Aunt Sylvie's got you covered there. She gave me a hug from you, too. I do miss you, Mom, but I'm not at home very much right now anyway. You might as well keep your plans with Hazel's family. I'm sure they're pulling out all the stops for you in New York City. Are you there already? Or are you still in Indiana with Walter and his brood?" He and his wife Maria had four children now, the youngest just eight months old.

"The plan is for Walter to accompany me up to New York next week. But it's not too late to change those plans."

"Don't change a thing," Olive insisted.

A beat of quiet followed before Meg said, "I'm so unspeakably sorry about Claire."

A hollowness spread inside Olive as she found herself at a crossroads. She could let her mother believe Claire was dead, or she could tell her the truth. Meg was hundreds of miles away. There was no way she could let it slip to Warren. Olive couldn't imagine the solace to be had in telling the whole truth to one person, just one person, and who better than her own mother?

"I've worried over you ever since I received the telegram Saturday," Meg went on before Olive had formed a response. "You've always been my rock, Olive, the one I could rely on. I hate that I'm not there for you now, as you've been my right hand—literally—

122

since you were a wee thing in braids and pinafores. I realize you're a grown woman, but if I stay with Walter and then visit Hazel, will you truly be all right?"

Olive watched the steam curling over the oven and set her jaw. She was not about to add to her mother's worries or make her feel guilty for being away.

"I'll be fine," she replied.

The truth would have to wait.

Chapter Fourteen

Friday, July 30, 1915

It wasn't breaking and entering if she had a key. It wasn't illegal to retrieve a friend's jewelry for her if acting on that friend's instructions.

Even so, Olive felt like a thief as she let herself in through Warren's back door.

Using public transportation, she'd gotten to the park across the street early enough to watch him drive away around six o'clock this morning. Once he was gone, she had studied the neighbors' houses until she was certain no one watched from windows.

She'd slipped in unnoticed. She was safe now. She could breathe.

But when she entered the bedroom Claire had shared with Warren until six days ago, her breath stalled all over again. The bed was rumpled, and a lump on one side smelled strongly of violets. Edging closer to it, Olive peered through the shadows until she recognized what it was. Claire's pillow had been dressed with her nightgown and sprayed with her perfume. By the way it was shaped, Olive guessed Warren had held it close.

Heart thudding, she turned away from the evidence of Warren's private grief and hurried toward Claire's vanity. On the skirted stool, Olive set down the basket of food she had baked for her friend and removed the jar of blackberry jam. She opened the lid and dropped inside the jewelry identified on Claire's list. Wedding rings that had belonged to her grandparents and parents. One amethyst and diamond ring. An antique bracelet with rubies and empty prongs where other gems had been. One gold chain with an emerald pendant. Two hair combs encrusted with sapphires. Leaving the costume jewelry, Olive screwed the lid back on and rolled the jar in her hands until all the pieces sank to the bottom.

She could not have been inside the house longer than two minutes, but it still felt too long. Basket hooked over her arm, she locked the rear door again, then replaced the key in its hiding spot. Birdsong trilled in the silver maple as Olive made her way toward the front of the house. Thankfully, there was no traffic, and she didn't see or hear neighbors or even dogs. If she hurried, she could catch the 6:25 train unseen, be at work by seven, and take a longer lunch than usual to meet Claire.

As she rounded the front corner of the house, a breeze swayed the hem of her skirt, and long blades of dewy grass brushed her ankles. The fact that the lawn needed mowing as much as the gardens needed weeding was yet more proof of Warren's state of mind.

Shadows veiled the front of the bungalow. Olive slowed her gait as she passed Claire's neglected flower beds. Melancholy drifted over her as she recalled planting tulip and daffodil bulbs with Claire the very autumn the Sterlings married. She'd never seen Claire happier than she was that day, bright with hope, smudged with dirt, locks of hair twirling madly on a gust of wind.

"This is it, Liv," Claire had said then. *"This is where I'm putting down my own roots with a home of my own. A family of my own. A big one."*

Olive had laughed with her at the overwrought metaphors of nurturing and cultivation that followed. Then Claire had quoted something about magic and earth from a brand-new children's story called *The Secret Garden*, proving once again why Claire had been so wonderful at the bookstore. But trading books for Sears catalogs, she'd said, was a small price to pay for her happy ending with Warren and all the happy beginnings that would follow.

Oh, Claire.

"Yoo-hoo!"

Olive winced and slowly turned around.

"Yoo-hoo, Olive, is that you?" Mrs. Hilda Feinstein was hurrying toward her, newspaper under one arm. Beyond her, Olive could see the delivery boy pedaling his bicycle away.

Blast! Hilda was sure to tell Warren she'd seen Olive here this morning. Olive turned back to the garden. She bent, uprooted a thick-stalked weed, and tossed it on the overgrown lawn. By the time Hilda reached her, she'd ripped out four more.

"Mrs. Feinstein." Olive straightened, brushing dirt from her hands.

"Call me Hilda, dear." Dressed in a bright floral housecoat and slippers, she propped a fist on her ample hip. Silver wisps escaped the coral kerchief wrapping her head. "It's a crying shame about poor Claire, isn't it? I couldn't believe it when I read it in the paper. You never know when the good Lord will call you home, do you? Here one day, and then—wham! Gone the next! But you know all about that, don't you? Still working at MetLife? What a booming business it must be for you now, although one can't rightly say one is pleased about it. You were the only friend I saw come calling on Claire for quite some time, did you know that, dear?"

At last, she paused for breath and noticed the pile of weeds. "Oh, what a nice thing you're doing. Claire was always so particular about her garden. It's a shame to watch nature reclaim it. What a lovely way to honor your friend, dear. But you'll get filthy in no time flat, if you don't mind my saying so. You might have thought to dress for the job, it seems to me."

"I wasn't planning on weeding," Olive confessed. "But now that I'm here, I couldn't leave it without a little attention."

"Not planning to weed? Then why make the trip?" Before Olive could reply, Hilda spotted the basket bearing tins and two canning jars. "You're full of Christian charity to bring the bereaved refreshment like this. I've got a roast going today that I'll bring him later."

When she reached toward the basket, Olive stepped in front of it. All Hilda had to do was hold one jar of blackberry preserves to the light, and she might find the sparkle of gold inside.

"Would you mind very much," Olive began, "if I borrow a spade and some gardening gloves? Perhaps an apron? I'm headed straight to work after this, so I'd better not show up wearing dirt."

"Of course." Hilda beamed. "I've got just what you need. Back in a jiffy!"

As soon as she left, Olive turned her back to Hilda's house, bent to the ground again, and dug a shallow hole with her hands. She dropped the jewel-laden jar into the earth and covered it with dirt.

"You couldn't wait, could you?" Hilda clucked her tongue as she returned and extended the apron.

Olive accepted it with thanks and tied it around her waist. "I want to make the most of the little time I have before I need to catch the train to work." She pulled on the stiff gardening gloves and took the spade.

As Olive suspected she would, Hilda hefted the basket and poked through it. "I'm not criticizing you, dear, but you might have thought to bring something other than four tins of tea and coffee. Although it would be an improvement over his current drink."

Olive smiled. "There's no tea or coffee there. I just reused the tins, you see. Baking powder biscuits and cookies."

"Ah!" Hilda chuckled. "Well then, that does explain the preserves!" She lifted out the other jar, squinting at the seeds. "Raspberry. Divine. I see no card here, though. How is he to know whom to thank?"

"No thanks are expected at a time like this. I'll just empty the basket onto the front porch and trust he'll find it when he gets home." Kneeling on the long apron that covered her skirt, Olive set to work rooting out dandelions.

"Nonsense. They'll be no good after sitting in the heat all day. As I plan to deliver dinner once he's home, I'll take your contribution home with me now and add it to the roast. Together, it will make a fine meal."

Olive looked up to find that Hilda had already stacked the tins, holding the tower of baked goods steady beneath her chin. With any luck, Hilda might forget to mention Olive and take all the credit for herself.

"Thank you." Olive watched her clutch the jar of raspberry preserves. "I'll just leave these on your porch when I'm done with them, all right?"

"Absolutely, dear. What a dedicated friend you are."

Hilda had no idea.

Eyes crinkling in a parting smile, the woman shuffled away.

Olive attacked the weeds with the gusto they deserved. Shadows shortened as the sun rose higher. By the time she called the job done, the front beds were noticeably better, if not perfect. She unearthed the jar she'd buried and tucked it back into the basket. After moving the pile of weeds off the lawn, she wiped her face with a clean patch on the apron, returned Hilda's gardening tools, and tugged on her white cotton gloves before grasping the basket again.

A last glance at Claire's gardens gave her the satisfaction of seeing the results of her work. The pile of dandelions, carpetweeds, and crabgrass bore testament that she'd accomplished something. Could she say that about her efforts to find Stella Petroski?

Not yet. But soon, perhaps, she'd see that the truth about Stella was dug up, too.

◆

Olive wasn't late to work, so when Blanche met her at the doorway between the office and the marble corridor outside, she couldn't mask her surprise.

"He's been here ten minutes already," Blanche whispered, beckoning Olive a few feet farther down the hall.

"Who?" Olive shifted the basket to her other hand, glad the linen napkin covered the jar inside.

A thin white eyebrow arched. "You cannot miss him. Gwendolyn sure didn't. She served him coffee, sugar, and charm like a waitress on her bottom dollar."

Aha. Through the doorway, Olive spied a man whose long limbs were currently folded to fit the buttoned sofa in the reception area. Even with his nose stuck in a book, he was easy to recognize. "The Viking is here."

Blanche hid a smile in the tight corners of her lips. "I told him Howard could help him with whatever he needs, but he insisted on seeing you. He has your card."

"He's a photographer for the *Tribune*," Olive offered. "I met him when I was looking for photographs of the *Eastland* disaster. I best not keep him waiting."

Blanche following, Olive strode back into the reception room, removing her hat and tossing it in the basket she still carried. "Good morning. Mr. Erickson, is it?"

Closing the book, he stood, a small smile bending his lips as he looked down at her. "Magnussen. Erik Magnussen, although my shortest friends do call me Mr. Erik, so you were close."

He was close. Close enough that surely he smelled the wind and sun-warmed earth that clung to her. Smelling like an actual garden wasn't nearly as enchanting as smelling of the flowers that grew in them.

"Your shortest friends?" she queried. A strand of auburn hair dropped to her shoulder.

He plucked a piece of grass from it. As it fluttered to the floor, she brushed a few blades from her skirt, too. *Drat.*

"Boys at the Lincoln Park Boat Club. I give them lessons in rowing, and they help me clean the shells and sculls."

That explained the strain at the shoulders of his dark khaki suit.

"But I didn't come here to talk about them." He picked up a mug from the magazine-topped end table.

"Of course. Let's head on back."

Once in her own office space, Olive tucked the basket beneath her desk and removed her white gloves. Dirt lined her fingernails.

Mr. Magnussen set his half-full mug on the edge of Olive's desk, then pulled up a chair. "For a city girl, you sure do seem down-to-earth." Amusement sparked in his eyes.

She held up her hands and turned them back and forth. "Don't I just? I squeezed in a bit of gardening this morning on the way to work. I didn't intend to bring it with me."

"In that case." He tapped his cheek and discreetly pointed to hers.

So eager was she to wipe the smudge away, she practically slapped her face. "Better?"

He shook his head.

She rubbed harder.

He shifted, withdrawing a handkerchief from his jacket pocket, presumably to help her.

Olive fumbled for her own kerchief and finished the job herself. "That ought to have done it."

Mr. Magnussen cleared his throat, probably to cover a chuckle. "I'll say."

She thoroughly wiped her hands on the handkerchief before tucking it out of sight. "At least you can't say I'm afraid to get my hands dirty. Now, what can I help you with this morning? In the mood to buy a life insurance policy?"

"If I had a single soul who relied on my income, I would be."

He had to be a few years older than she was, yet he wore no wedding ring. She found it curious that he had no dependents.

"Actually, I brought something you might be interested in." He held up the book he'd been reading.

Gwendolyn appeared in the office and inserted herself at his side, honey-blond hair in perfect Marcel waves, her fair complexion flawless. Not a speck of dirt or grass anywhere on her. "*The Hound of the Baskervilles*," she read from the cover. "Sounds thrilling! Care for a warm-up?" She lifted the coffeepot.

Mr. Magnussen covered his mug with a hand. "I'm fine, thanks. But I think Miss Pierce here could use a cup."

What was that supposed to mean? Just because she'd brought the great outdoors indoors didn't mean she wasn't thinking clearly. In fact, she felt she'd been pretty sharp this morning with Hilda Feinstein. Aside from allowing herself to be seen in the first place.

She raised a brow. "If you're a fan of Sherlock Holmes, have you read the newest, *The Valley of Fear*? It arrived in bookstores this spring. It was an awfully long time to wait for a new Sherlock novel from Doyle. I've been enjoying Mary Roberts Rinehart very much in the meantime. She's grossly underrated."

"Is that so?" He laid the book on the desk , his expression an invitation to elaborate.

"Her aunt owns a bookstore," Gwendolyn interrupted. "Olive lives in an apartment above it."

"So she knows detective fiction by osmosis?" Mr. Magnussen jibed.

"I read," Olive said. "I actually read." She raised her mug toward Gwendolyn. "I think I will have some of that, if you don't mind."

"Sure thing, hon." But the smile the secretary flashed while she poured was aimed at Mr. Magnussen.

He missed it entirely, focused on Olive instead. "I brought you pictures," he said once Gwendolyn had gone, and he opened the book to reveal a small stack of photographs.

"I thought you said you didn't have any." She sipped the hot brew slowly, wrinkling her nose at the bitterness unsoftened by cream.

"None that I personally took. I was at a regatta in Peoria that day. But another photographer let me borrow these to see if they could help you. If you met with Jun Fujita, you've already seen hundreds. But you never know. You might spot something here that helps."

"By all means." Olive nudged her typewriter to one side.

He set the photographs on the desk between them. "Your card says you're an agent. Is this part of your typical duties?"

"Nothing is typical right now, Mr. Magnussen. But to answer you more directly, I'm trying to earn a promotion to investigator. I'm looking for a missing client of mine." Even though she strongly suspected Stella had been buried in Claire's place, she studied the images for any clues.

"What are you looking for, exactly?"

"My client."

"Just one person?" he prodded.

Her gaze moved from the first photo to the next. "Other clients who were missing have since been identified and located. Stella Petroski is the only case of mine that hasn't been closed yet. She left behind a husband, two children, and both parents."

He took another drink of coffee before loosening his green silk necktie with the air of a man who'd like to fling off the suit jacket, roll up his shirtsleeves, and get to work. "See anything?"

There were only a couple dozen photos here. Olive could tell fairly quickly that Stella wasn't in them.

"I don't," she admitted, "but thank you all the same for bringing these over. That was thoughtful."

"Thoughtful, but not helpful." He gathered the photos into a neat stack and slipped them between the pages of his novel. "Here's an idea. Why don't we meet for lunch today?"

She blinked at him, confused that his question sounded so much like a statement. It must be that his Viking blood made him prone to taking the reins of a situation. Still, she couldn't puzzle out why he would issue such an invitation at all.

"Lunch?"

"A working lunch," he clarified. "The sooner you find Mrs. Petroski, the better."

"And you think eating together will help her how?"

"We can go over your notes together. I can be a sounding board for your theories and help you think of new angles, new avenues of investigation you may not have tried yet."

She tilted her head, and that strand of hair she'd forgotten to repin tickled her neck again. This time, she repaired it. "You've read that many detective stories, have you? Think you can channel the great Sherlock Holmes himself?"

"On the contrary, Miss Pierce. You can be Sherlock. I'm happy to play the role of Watson. You must admit, two heads are better than one."

"I already have two heads, thank you very much." She jerked a thumb toward Howard's office. If she was to compare notes with anyone, it ought to be her MetLife colleague. Not that he took her seriously, especially after she hadn't noticed quickly enough that Warren had started smoking. "Regardless, I'd rather just use my own. Besides, I already have plans for lunch today."

Mr. Magnussen stood when she did and reseated his hat. "I'll bet you have."

Olive matched his knowing smile with her own. "But I do thank you for stopping by."

"Perhaps a rain check, then," he said. "If I can do anything to help—"

"I'm sure you're a first-rate photographer, but what I'm doing here doesn't conform to the conventions of fiction. I appreciate the offer just the same."

She wondered if he was accustomed to being turned down by a lady, for any reason, and decided it highly unlikely. Poor, beautiful Viking. It must be disorienting for him.

The telephone on Blanche's desk rang, drawing Olive's attention. The secretary answered it, then put the caller on hold before turning to Olive. "I have Mr. Jakob Petroski on the line for you."

Olive swallowed. "Send it through, please."

Mr. Magnussen shook her hand. "Until next time, then," he said, and took his leave.

Resuming her seat at her desk, Olive answered the phone. "Jakob."

A heavy sigh traveled over the wire. "It's been six days," he replied. "That's too long."

Olive agreed. It had been entirely too long. "Jakob, you won't like hearing this, but you would be wise to prepare yourself for the possibility that she's among the bodies still to be recovered from the river."

"I would feel it if her soul had left the earth," he countered. "I would know, somehow, if the woman I love had died. How to explain it? Like something inside me would come untethered. Besides, didn't you read in the paper last month about that young woman who was found after being missing for eight days? She'd had a memory lapse, they say, but she's fine now. So I won't accept that my Stella is dead unless I see the body."

There was no point in arguing with how he felt.

"Did you talk to everyone on your list?" he prompted.

"I did, and then some." She didn't need to remind him that he'd already asked her this yesterday when she'd called him with an update.

"Did you learn anything new?"

"I did, in fact. I spoke with a druggist in Cicero who told me Stella had come in asking for headache powders a few times during the last two months." Thanks to Mr. Platek's meticulous records, he was able to tell Olive the exact dates.

"Headache powders? Was she ill?"

"Mr. Platek didn't think so. She never came with a prescription and just bought the most common remedy." Olive had cross-referenced the dates of the purchases with her notes from an interview with a neighbor. If the neighbor could be believed, the days Stella bought the powders fell on weeks she had argued with Jakob at home. Olive didn't deem it necessary to tell the grieving husband this. For now, it was enough that she had written every-thing in her own notes.

"She didn't tell me she had headaches," Jakob was saying. "Why wouldn't she have told me?"

"Mr. Platek thought her ailments minor," Olive assured him. She pulled a file folder from her desk drawer and flipped through it until she found her transcribed notes from both Mr. Platek and the neighbor, Mrs. Albrecht. She laid them out side by side.

"You'll tell me if you hear anything new? Anything at all."

"Of course. I always do." She hadn't gone a day without talk-ing to him.

After hanging up the phone, she scanned her typed notes and frowned. The dates Mr. Platek had given her for the times Stella had bought the powders weren't listed, yet she was positive she'd included those. In the transcription of Mrs. Albrecht's interview, the dates of the backyard arguments were left off, too. In fact, Olive found no mention of them at all.

What in the world?

She had taken those notes herself and had carefully typed in every detail back at the office. The dates, especially, were impor-tant. The arguments could prove important, too, and now she suddenly had no record of them. Neither did she see the telephone numbers of the interview subjects or their work schedules, though she could have sworn she'd made careful note of them in the event she needed to follow up.

Going back to her file, she searched the rest of her notes, hand-written and transcribed, then moved on to other folders and did the same, just in case she'd mixed the interviews in with the wrong client's files. Then she looked through every pocket of her leather satchel.

Nothing.

In a quiet swish of linen, Blanche paused at the door to Olive's office. The secretary's arms were full of folders to be filed, and her brow was etched with concern, or at least with curiosity. "Everything all right, Olive? You look a little lost today."

No wonder. Olive had lost her notes and her confidence and felt like she was losing her wits.

"Need any help?" Blanche asked.

Must everyone insist she couldn't do this on her own? "No, thank you. I'm fine."

Even if she wasn't, she wouldn't admit that to anyone, least of all herself.

CHAPTER FIFTEEN

Beneath the soaring arched ceiling, the great lobby of the Illinois Central Station on Michigan Avenue teemed with people, but Olive recognized Claire right away. After all, the navy dress with white piping and buttons she wore had belonged to Olive until last week.

Had it really only been five days since they'd parted? Olive threaded between porters and passengers, nannies, children, maids, and matrons to reach her friend. It felt like a month had passed.

"You look well," she told Claire with a hug brief enough to be ordinary. Sunshine poured through the windows. Through the main entrance doors, a breeze carried the smell of fresh-cut grass from Grant Park just outside, far more pleasant than the inescapable fumes of locomotives. A janitor pushed a mop across the mosaic tiled floor, openly admiring Claire at the same time, while another swept discarded ticket stubs and food wrappers into a long-handled dustpan.

"Like a new woman?" Claire teased, but it was true. Her natural color had returned to lips and cheeks that had never needed rouge. She held herself straighter, taller. She didn't appear well-rested, but she had shed that hunted look.

Olive handed her the basket, now all but empty. "I thought you might like some blackberry preserves."

Claire peeled back the napkin to reveal the jar inside, then rotated it until the glint of gold shone through the glass near the bottom. "I owe you." She tucked the napkin back inside.

"We need to talk." Olive steered her toward a sandwich counter in the lobby.

Minutes later, they sat at a tiny table, Claire with a grilled cheese with tomato and bacon on sourdough, and Olive with a turkey club on rye. Other customers bustled around them, making them virtually invisible in the crowd.

The thirteen-story clock tower chimed the hour. "I have forty minutes before I need to go," Claire said. "Don't ask me where."

"I won't," Olive said. "But I will ask how your grandmother's watch and your wedding ring were found at the morgue." She relayed Warren's account of it.

Claire sipped her Coca-Cola.

"You planted the jewelry on another body?" Olive asked. "Letting people assume the worst was one thing, but . . ." She let the dismay in her voice finish the thought. Claire had taken the deception to a whole new level, entangling innocents in the web she'd spun.

"Don't scold me, Livvie," Claire whispered. "I couldn't bear that from you. You know who I'm up against. I had to make sure he stopped looking for me. And the only way to guarantee that was for him to find me. Tell me I'm wrong."

The logic wasn't. The morality of falsely marking a body, however, *that* was what had Olive's shoulders in knots.

"I want you to be safe," Olive said. She took a bite of her sandwich, not because she was hungry, but because it was what people who were having lunch did, and chewing gave her time to choose her words. "You know I do. But that woman's family deserves to know what happened to her. They deserve closure and the right to lay her to rest with her own name in her own grave."

138

Claire's expression clouded. A fly circled above her food, and she waved it away. "The papers say *Eastland* passengers are still missing. Surely the families will assume they are dead by now. It's terrible, I know. But it's not like they don't know what must have happened. They can still have memorial services for their loved ones. I realize it's not the same, but it's close. Close enough."

But it wasn't. Olive studied her friend and found guilt in the lines on her brow. Compassion for Claire kept her tone gentle as she pressed. "Families don't get paid their insurance benefits unless there is a body. Missing people are not presumed dead, legally, for years. And that doesn't even get into the emotional trauma of not knowing what happened to a loved one or her remains."

A whistle blew from within the bowels of the station, and Claire startled at the shrill sound.

"Stella Petroski is still missing," Olive said quietly. "She looked a lot like you."

A frown rippled across Claire's face. "Stella. I know that name."

"She's one of my clients. Michael and Addie were her children."

Claire's eyes misted, and the tip of her nose pinked. "Oh no." She cringed, and Olive wondered if she could see them, terrified and wet, as they had been in that dark, dead ship.

"Stella's family still doesn't know where she is. They are suspended between hope and grief."

"You think it's her," Claire choked out. "The woman buried in my place. You think it's Stella."

Olive allowed the words to hang in the air so the gravity of the situation would settle on Claire of its own accord. "I have searched the hospitals, consulted with the Red Cross, interviewed everyone who ever interacted with her or with her husband, Jakob. I've spent all week investigating, and I haven't found her. I need to find her, Claire. For Jakob, Michael, and Addie's sakes. For her parents, too. It's the right thing to do."

Claire wrapped her barely touched sandwich in the paper it came in and added it to the basket at her feet. "You're saying you want to dig her up. You won't be able to do that without permission, and what will you tell Warren to get him to agree? And then, as soon as the body is exhumed, he'll be suspicious. I chose a body whose injury made it difficult to identify anyway, and that was within twenty-four hours after she died. What do you suppose you'll find in that coffin now? You still won't know who it is, and then all you'll have accomplished is setting Warren on the prowl for me again."

Olive had considered all of this. She also knew she couldn't live with herself if she allowed the truth to remain buried. "You have a new name. You're moving to a different location that even I don't know about. What are the chances that he'll find you?"

Resting her elbow on the table, Claire bit the edge of her thumb. "Greater than zero."

"And if we don't exhume that body, the chances that her family will never know what happened to her are no less than one-hundred-percent. I'm not really asking for permission. I'm letting you know that I need to return that body to her family. It's my job." It was also her conscience. "I don't blame you for being angry or scared. I hate that this must feel like I'm betraying you."

Claire twisted awkwardly to cast about furtive glances. She pulled her gloves back on and covered the side of her face with her hand. "I'm terrified. But I don't think you're betraying me. Warren did that every time he beat me. This? This is you making a hard choice in an impossible situation. But I beg of you, Liv, give me more time."

"More time," Olive repeated, thinking of all that had already been wasted.

"For whoever is in my grave," Claire went on, "waiting a few more days won't change the outcome for her or for her family. She'll still be dead. Her family will still find out about her, with just a little more waiting. But for me? The difference of a few days will allow me to get farther away from here, find a safer place for my new life. It could mean the difference between being safe and being discovered. And make no mistake, he will kill me if he finds me now." Fear bowed her shoulders.

"I don't know if that's true," Olive protested. "You haven't seen how wrecked he is without you."

"He doesn't love me. He loves control, and I stole that from him. I humiliated him with this ruse. That's how he'll see it—that I deliberately and publicly made a fool of him. It will be in all the papers. And I'm already dead, with a death certificate and everything. Aren't I?"

Olive's mouth went dry. She couldn't deny it. If it weren't true, they wouldn't be having this conversation.

"Last I checked," Claire added, "one can't be charged with murdering a dead person."

Another train whistle split the air. Time was ticking, ticking, the minutes dropping away.

"I'll give you the weekend," Olive said at last.

"I'll take it."

Wordless moments followed, sealing the agreement. Then, somewhere in the lobby, a child let out a piercing wail, and Claire flinched at the same time Olive did.

"Are you sleeping?" Olive quietly asked.

"Are you?" But the rueful bend at the corner of Claire's mouth said they both knew the answers.

Olive finished her lemonade. "Do you still hear them? The ones who didn't get out?"

Claire exhaled. "I heard them in that child's scream. In the train whistles. Sometimes I hear them when a baby cries. I hear them, sometimes, in the silence."

"Yes," Olive said, nodding. "I know. So do I." There was a strange comfort in hearing the reflection of her own experience.

The lines in Claire's brow eased. "Good. I mean, if I'm going crazy, it's nice to know you're coming with me." She allowed herself a small laugh, and Olive joined her.

"We're not crazy," Olive added. "We're survivors."

"We escaped." Claire's expression tightened. "But I'm still trying to find safe harbor."

───◆───

MONDAY, AUGUST 2, 1915

"Olive Pierce, MetLife, for Detective Clement, please." Olive waited for the police clerk to look up from his coffee and hop to it. He didn't. "I called Friday afternoon and made an appointment to see her this morning." She tapped her toe impatiently and scanned the LaSalle Street police station.

The weekend had been one of almost unbearable anticipation building to this. How she had managed to host her regular Saturday night dinner for her family without giving away the state of her suspense had been a miracle. True, she had burned the garlic toast, but other than that, she had conquered her distraction. During the meal, Olive had asked her aunt more about her post-fire experiences, and Sylvie had carried the conversation without pressing Olive to share in equal measure. She seemed to sense that the last thing Olive wanted to do was explain herself. These days, that was getting rather complicated.

But it shouldn't be. It was simple, when one stuck to the facts, and that was exactly what she intended to do with Detective Clement.

"Pardon me," Olive said, irritated. It was early, but not pre-dawn, and the clerk had had at least one cup of coffee while she waited. "My appointment is for seven o'clock. I'd like her to know I'm here. If you can't help me with that, just point me in the right direction."

"Miss Pierce!" Like a high wind, thirty-seven-year-old Detective Alice Clement blew in from a corridor, long strands of pearls swinging with her stride. "Right on time. Come with me."

After shaking her hand, Olive followed the small force of nature, who couldn't have been taller than five foot three when not wearing heels.

Past the administrative offices, Clement turned a corner and

142

led Olive to a room full of chunky oak desks and slatted chairs. At this early hour, only two of them were filled by detectives in blue suits. On a counter beneath the windows, overturned mugs rested beside a silver coffee percolator.

Clement positioned a second chair next to her desk, which was the only surface in the room graced by a vase of pink tea roses. She sat while Olive did the same. "I understand you're working on a case. Tell me what you know." Pearl earrings softened her square jaw, and handcuffs were clipped to her belt at the hip. She was fully feminine and no less fully a detective.

Olive liked her immediately.

Clement flipped to a clean sheet of paper in her notepad and poised her pencil above it. "Fire when ready."

At last, it was time for the truth. "A woman killed in the *Eastland* disaster was misidentified and is now buried in the wrong grave. I know it takes a law enforcement officer to set in process the exhumation, and I wanted to come to you, specifically. The situation is somewhat delicate."

"Delicate in what way?" Clement asked. Sunlight glinted on her chestnut bob. She'd filed for divorce last year and was still waiting for it to be granted. If any detective could understand Claire's situation, she would.

With a deep breath, Olive told Clement what Claire had done and why.

"I was there that day," the detective admitted. "What chaos, right? What a mess. I was acting as a coroner's assistant, and I know the work was sloppy. It couldn't be helped in those conditions. There were so many dead, all at once. That coroner's stamp you mentioned—I used that myself. There were other volunteers there, too. Were we trained as coroners? Not a chance. We were just there, and we wanted to help."

She didn't mention that some passengers had been declared dead when they'd only been hypothermic, which had happened to at least two MetLife clients. Olive wouldn't bring that up, either.

"It's not hard to believe what you've told me," Clement said. "Mistakes happened without any help from an interested party. A few days ago, a girl's body was returned to the morgue because a man had taken it home, mistakenly thinking it was his daughter. He was wrong. So if Mrs. Sterling planted evidence as you say, and Mr. Sterling found it, I've no doubt the wrong body could have been buried in her stead."

"We need to return that body to the rightful family." Olive perched on the edge of her chair and kept her voice low. "But I hope we can do so without telling Warren that Claire is alive and well. He may guess it, but can we avoid telling him outright?"

The detective finished writing something, then leaned forward and clasped her pearl strands in a loose fist. "I'm sympathetic to Mrs. Sterling's situation. I am. And I'll be as discreet as possible about ordering an exhumation if it comes to that—although how discreet can bringing a coffin out of the ground ever be, right? But first, I need proof beyond your word that your friend is still alive. You understand. I need something to go on, tangible evidence before I get the ball rolling. Can you deliver?"

Olive opened her satchel and withdrew the framed photograph from her mantel of Claire and Warren on their wedding day, along with the photograph of Claire as she accepted a blanket after surviving the disaster. "That's her." She slid both images to Detective Clement, explaining the contexts. "If that doesn't give you the proof you need, take the photos to Central Station. She bought a train ticket there the day after the disaster. The ticket agent will recognize her. Janitorial staff may, too."

"I'll say." Detective Clement whistled low. "She's a looker. I'll bet the gents don't forget a dame like her. This is obviously the same woman, but how do I know this photo hasn't been altered to place her likeness in the scene with the *Eastland* in the background?"

"The newspaper photographer Jun Fujita took it for the *Evening Post*. Call him or bring it to him if you wish, and he'll confirm it."

Clement wrote a note. "All right, Pierce, I'll tell you what I'm going to do. Leave these photos with me—I'll do my due diligence and then make sure they get back to you. If everything checks out, I'll approach Mr. Sterling and tell him we have reason to believe there's been a mistake with the body."

"But you won't mention me?"

"I will not say your name," Clement said. "You have my word on that."

A sigh built where relief should have gathered. Olive didn't feel easy about any of this. Warren would remember that she'd already questioned the identification of the body. He would guess that she was the one who tipped off Clement. And he would wonder why.

"He'll be suspicious immediately," Olive said. "So he'll let you order the exhumation because he'll want answers."

"You do understand that he'll probably come to you for those? Even if I don't breathe a word about you or what you've shared with me. You were his wife's best friend. He'll expect you to know things."

He may even expect Olive to know more than she actually did. "I understand."

"Don't be alone with him, Pierce."

Olive crossed her ankles, then uncrossed them. "I don't plan to be."

"No one ever does." Detective Clement leaned back in her chair and tapped her pencil on the paper. "I'm serious about this. If what you say is true, this man is prone to violence, and the object of his frustration is no longer within reach. See that you aren't, either."

Olive was beginning to feel as though she'd painted a target on her back. "I hear you. We still need to go through with this. There's really no choice."

A lopsided smile edging her thin lips, Clement slipped Mr. Fujita's photograph of Claire into an envelope. "There's always a choice."

The smell of too-strong coffee mingled with the smoke of someone's cigarette. "What I mean is that I've made my decision," Olive clarified. "The next step is to live with it."

The detective squinted at Warren's likeness through the frame, then turned a serious gaze on Olive. "I sincerely hope you do."

❖

Now Olive was the one looking over her shoulder. Or she would be, as soon as enough time passed for Detective Clement to have approached Warren about the body.

It had been an hour since she'd left the police station. Was that long enough to check with Fujita or the train ticket agent? Was Clement on her way to the Sears complex even now?

"Olive." Mr. Roth rapped his knuckles on the doorframe to her office. "Let's chat."

Willing her complexion to remain stable, she brushed out the wrinkles from her skirt, then met him at his desk.

"Sir?"

"Sit."

She did.

Mr. Roth remained at the window facing the courthouse and City Hall. When he turned around, he wasn't smiling. "It's a new week, Olive, and I need a better one from you than the last. It may have been a mistake, allowing you to gallivant around as an investigator."

"It wasn't, sir. And I don't gallivant, as a rule."

He took his chair, then tented his fingers above the blotter covering his desk. "You've made mistakes. Missing meetings, running out of fuel, wasting precious time. Howard told me he was not impressed with your potential as an investigator, based on your visit with Mr. Sterling."

Of course he did. Frustration burned, and Olive felt its heat in her cheeks. At least Mr. Roth didn't know about the omissions she'd found in her notes last Friday. That was a mystery that still confused her, one she hadn't admitted to anyone.

"I apologize—again—for all of that. But let's not forget that I have also lightened Howard's caseload considerably. Working in tandem with the hospitals and the Red Cross, I've located and processed claims for all the clients on my list except one."

"Your reports have been uncharacteristically sloppy."

She felt the blood drain from her face. "Excuse me?"

He opened a folder. Inside was her stack of reports from last week. She'd written one at the end of each day, outlining the progress she'd made and the plan going forward. He hadn't asked for these, but she'd insisted on keeping him updated so there'd be no question of how she'd been spending resources.

"Given how adamant you are about a promotion, I thought you'd go above and beyond your usual work ethic. I expected more from you."

Bewildered and stinging with shame, she slid a report from the top of the pile. The format wasn't sloppy. The content was. Where she remembered writing specific numbers, in their place were general terms like *some*, *a few*, *several*. Instead of the full names, addresses, and phone numbers for the people she interviewed, there were only initials. In some instances, their occupations and connections to her clients were omitted altogether.

She checked the date of the report. This was the day she'd learned that a client named William Brody had been declared dead when he'd only been suffering hypothermia, and that he was alive and well. Yet there was no mention of Brody here at all.

Impossible.

On her worst day, and in her most distracted state, Olive never would have submitted a piece of shoddy work like this.

"This isn't my report." She looked through the rest and found similar unaccountable errors. Outside, streetcars clanged their bells.

Mr. Roth studied her. "Your name is on each of them. I saw you drop them off in my box last week."

"Not these," she insisted. "You said yourself you expected more from me. You should. This isn't me." She thumped two fingers on the counterfeit reports. The seven months he'd been her boss ought to be long enough for him to know that.

"Neither is missing meetings or showing up late."

It might be worse to admit to not knowing about those meetings at all. "My reports were tampered with, sir. It's the only explanation."

"That's a serious accusation. Can you prove it?"

She stared at the buff-colored wall that held Mr. Roth's framed diploma. Behind it sat Howard Penrose.

"I asked you for evidence." Mr. Roth closed the folder on the false reports. "Do you have any?"

All Olive could think of was that Howard had told her the company car had a quarter tank of fuel the day she'd driven it out to Cicero and had gotten stranded there. Had she misheard him? Possibly. Besides, she could have checked the fuel gauge herself. Then there was the matter of him taking the forms from her satchel and letting her leave without them, when he could have called her back. But he'd admitted to this. Despite his fear that his own job was at risk if she succeeded, could she prove him a saboteur?

"No," she admitted. "Not yet. But I'll redo those reports for you right away."

"I went against my better judgment, letting you partner with Howard last week and surround yourself with grieving families. You're too close to the situation, and it shows. Stick to selling and processing claims from now on. No more investigating for you. It has only caused unnecessary strain on your feminine faculties. I accept my share of blame for that."

She felt her ire rise and straightened her spine. "Pardon me, Mr. Roth. A point of clarification. I don't deny I've experienced stress on a different level than Howard, given my personal experience with the *Eastland*. I also concede that these reports are unworthy of an investigator. But feminine faculties, in general, are as capable as the male variety. If women don't do well under pressure, it might be simply because they haven't been allowed to have enough of it."

Mr. Roth leaned forward. "Take it easy at home, but when you're at work, impress me. As a sales agent. Nothing more. How's that for pressure?"

Well, she'd walked right into that one. "Will that be all, sir?" She stood, cheeks blazing. Until she had proof of sabotage, there was nothing more to say.

With a jerk of his chin, he dismissed her.

Reconstructing a week's worth of daily reports took all day and then some. A few minutes after five o'clock, Olive had called her aunt at the bookstore to let her know she'd be working into the evening but that there was no reason to worry.

That settled, she had set her nose to the grindstone once more. Whatever she handed to Mr. Roth tomorrow would be an improvement, but it wouldn't be as precise as the original reports. What on earth had happened to those? Someone had taken the reports and retyped them, replacing them before Roth noticed the switch. Would Howard stoop so low? Was it even possible for him to tamper that consistently while still keeping up with his own work? Perhaps the heavy caseload wasn't the only reason he was behind.

Rubbing at the kinks in her neck and shoulders, she indulged in an audible sigh, since she was the only one left in the office. It felt like two days had passed since she'd arrived at work this morning.

This morning. Thoughts of her meeting at the police station came rushing back. By now, Detective Clement had probably contacted Warren and requested to exhume the body. By now, Warren was probably suspicious.

Olive went to the window to peer out. Rain blurred the view. Thunder rolled, and lightning forked the sky above City Hall. A few people dashed onto trolleys while others hailed taxi cabs. Honking Tin Lizzies splashed horses and carriages as they swerved around them.

She was looking for Warren on the street. Was Warren looking for her? He wouldn't be able to see much in this storm, but he could easily spot the light. She wondered if he could identify which office belonged to MetLife.

Stepping back, she leaned against the pillar between windows and prayed Claire had found her safe place. She needed to pray for far more than that, however. Surely something was wrong with her that she had such a hard time admitting to God what He already knew. She was tangled in a web and didn't know how she'd get out. Part of her longed to beg God for help, while the other part felt she needed to navigate her own way out. If she could only think clearly and be at her absolute sharpest from here on out, she might be able to fix this.

Her lips pressed into a thin line. A headache came knocking at her skull, and she massaged her brow to chase it away. It was time to get back to work.

She returned to her desk. The sound of crashing rain surrounded her as it fell both outside the building and inside the open courtyard carved out of its center. A faint whistling, which Olive thought at first to be the wind, grew louder until the cheerful notes accompanied the janitor into the MetLife reception room.

"Hello, Harold," Olive greeted him through her open door.

"Well, hello to you too, Miss Pierce!" He rolled a large waste bin in front of him. When he bent to empty a trash can, she noticed more grey in his tightly coiled black hair than the last time she'd seen him.

"How's your back these days?" she asked, watching for signs of discomfort.

"Oh, can't complain, can't complain." But he winced a little as he said it. "I should ask how *you* been," he added with a look that said he'd already heard. She wasn't surprised. Word traveled faster among the staff in this building than it possibly could over Western Electric wires.

For a few minutes, they chatted over the thunder, each inquiring after the other's family, until Harold signaled he was ready to get back to his work. Olive wished him well and turned to her own, undisturbed by his cleaning and whistling.

When Harold paused at the door to the corridor to bid her good night, she glanced up.

"Finished? Did you get Blanche's trash, too?" She grimaced. She wasn't his boss, after all, so she had no business telling him how to do his job. "I'm sorry, Harold. If you're done, you're done. Have a good night."

"No, no, you're right, Miss Pierce. I did not empty Mrs. Holden's trash can, but only because there's nothing in it."

That couldn't be right. Olive had seen that it was almost full after lunch. "She takes out her own trash?"

"Just so."

"Did she tell you why?"

He shrugged his sloping shoulders. "Didn't tell me anything. All I know is, for the last couple weeks, whenever I check, her bin is already empty. Good night, now."

She smiled and lifted a hand, then stared at Blanche's desk. The only thing on the surface besides the blotter and typewriter was a jar of pencils and pens, the small pot of violets, and a framed photograph. Not even a paper clip was out of place. And there was her empty waste bin, gleaming in the incandescent light.

Only someone with secrets would empty her own office trash.

CHAPTER SIXTEEN

TUESDAY, AUGUST 3, 1915

The downpour finally ceased just before lunch the next day. By evening, wet streets shone gold beneath a sky the shade of a ripened peach. Streetcar and telephone lines overhead striped the streets with thin shadows.

Satchel slung across her body, Olive stood against the rounded corner of the Conway Building and peered over the newspaper she held, watching for Blanche to emerge from the bronze doors. There were far too many question marks in her life right now. Finding out what Blanche did with her trash after work would put at least one of them to rest.

Model Ts and Dodge touring cars rattled past, puffing exhaust fumes. A trolley slowed, bell ringing, beside a teeming sidewalk. Her gaze still trained on the door to the Conway, Olive guarded herself from distraction. But the city's pulse proved no match for the alarm bells in her mind.

Detective Clement had called her at work today and delivered the news she'd been expecting. Warren had agreed right away to having the body exhumed. The job was scheduled for the day after tomorrow.

Olive turned the page of the newspaper and willed her middle to calm. At least whoever was buried in Claire's place would finally be reunited with her family soon, and that was no small thing.

In the meantime, Olive had other mysteries to solve.

There she was. Her white hair mostly covered by a rolled brim hat, Blanche Holden exited the Conway Building holding a paper bag, turned east on Washington, then rounded the corner and merged with the foot traffic heading south on Clark.

Olive followed, careful to keep three or four people between herself and Blanche as they walked. Not once did the secretary turn around or slow her pace. After a few blocks, she turned east on Jackson. The El rumbled by a block south. Before reaching Dearborn, the secretary veered into a dim alley.

Pausing at the alley entrance, Olive watched Blanche toss the bag into a dumpster and continue through the narrow lane, the echo of her heels fading until she stepped into the sunshine on the opposite side.

Other than a dog digging through a pile of trash, the alley remained empty. Olive headed straight for the dumpster. According to the law, as soon as a person dropped their garbage, they abandoned it, making it no longer personal property. Olive was legally free to search it.

Now all she needed was a clothespin for her nose. The stench that had attracted the stray dog also drew a cloud of black flies. The mutt ran off, scattering rotten apple cores and tin cans full of grease.

Olive removed her white cotton gloves and tucked them, along with her folded jacket, inside her satchel. After another scan of the alley to be sure she was alone, she laid her copy of the *Tribune* on the ground, then set her father's satchel on top of it.

There was nothing for it but to begin. Olive rolled back the cuffs of her jade-green blouse, then stacked a few broken milk crates beside the dumpster. After climbing these, she stepped onto a metal ledge on the dumpster's side. Now the top edge of the receptacle was at her waist, and she could easily reach inside.

She probed for the paper bag. Slimy banana peels met her fingers, followed by orange rinds, carrot and potato peelings, coffee grounds, and something so gelatinous she blocked her imagination from guessing at it.

She leaned in farther, grasping at last the top of a paper bag, and found the bottom of it damp but not soft enough to rip apart. Triumphant, she dropped it to the ground. Before she climbed down, however, she bit her lip, thinking. She wasn't sure how often the city emptied this dumpster, but it was obvious it had been more than twenty-four hours. Unless Blanche used a different receptacle, last night's trash could be here, too.

Olive could just imagine how her next phone call with her mother would go. "Hello, Mom," she muttered to herself, "what did you and Hazel do today? A stroll in Central Park, followed by a visit to the Metropolitan Museum of Art? How lovely. Me? Oh, just digging through a dumpster, alone in a dark alley while the sun goes down on the wickedest city in America." She released a rueful chuckle.

"Well, well, well." The masculine voice sent a jolt through Olive. "You're not alone, after all, Miss Alley Cat."

Clutching the top of the dumpster, she turned to find two men in the shadows. The lapels of their suits were both emblazoned with fraternity insignias from the University of Chicago. College boys. She didn't trust them. Especially if they were trying to impress each other.

"Carry on, gentlemen," she called down to them. "Trust me, you won't want to linger here."

"How about you come with us?" The taller of the two men edged closer to her. Smooth fingers wrapped her ankle and began sliding up her silk-stockinged calf.

"Shame on you!" She kicked at him.

He dodged the blow and laughed. "We've got ourselves a wildcat here, Roy. Even better."

"Leave me alone," she tried, but her command bounced off the alley walls and landed in the gutter.

"I was thinking we could all get a drink together." The man called Roy stepped forward. "But if you'd rather stay here, nice and private-like, I suppose we can oblige."

"You would oblige me by leaving," Olive snapped. "Go on, now."

"What do you say, Jim? You ready to leave yet?" Laughing, Roy reached for her skirt. "Because, personally, I'm having a little too much fun."

Olive could change that. She hurled a fistful of rotting food at him and kicked again, this time finding her mark with the pointed toe of her high-heeled shoe.

Roy reeled back, and Jim grabbed both her ankles, yanking her off the ledge.

She crashed down onto the milk crates, smashing them to pieces. But the sensation of falling remained. Dizziness swept through her, and her balance fled in the dark. Her pulse raced and tripped and stumbled. Blood beat a tocsin in her skull. She needed to leave, to get out before the water choked her, but she'd lost her footing and could not find it again.

But she was not on the *Eastland*. She was not sideways and sinking, and so she swallowed a swelling scream.

Setting her teeth, Olive planted her hands on dry ground and pushed herself to her feet.

"That wasn't very nice." Jim closed in and flung her hat aside. He trapped her against the brick wall, scraping the scabs on her back, reopening wounds she'd been trying to ignore. It wasn't brick she felt but someone's fingernails clawing, tearing. The pain held a terror that had nothing to do with these boys. She held her breath.

Olive didn't register the thundering footsteps until they halted within yards of her.

Jim spun away from her. "Roy?"

"No. Erik. I'd say it's nice to meet you, but it isn't."

Erik Magnussen stepped in front of Olive, completely obscuring her view. Wrestling her memories into the dark closets of her mind, she swam back to the present.

"Your mothers would be ashamed of you," the towering photographer was saying, "and I can't imagine your dean would approve, either."

"What do you know about it?" Roy snarled.

Fully engaged now, Olive sidled along the wall so she could watch how this played out.

Mr. Magnussen pointed at the insignia on Roy's jacket and named the fraternity it signified. "That's only open to graduate students in sociology, in which case your dean is Dr. William Hirsch. I'd ask what you're doing here, but I already know about the department's research on the city of Chicago, and harassing women isn't within your project's scope."

Not bad. Reading detective fiction had obviously schooled him in the art of observation. At least he knew how to put it to use.

Jim threw a punch, but Mr. Magnussen caught the young man's fist in one hand and shoved him away. "Don't try that again, Jim," he said.

Jim tried it again.

This time, Mr. Magnussen didn't hold back. In one graceful move, he landed a blow to Jim's jaw that sent him staggering into Roy. "Get lost," he told them, "or I might actually hurt you." As they fled, he turned to Olive. "Are you harmed?"

She shook her head, and pins dropped from her hair onto the hat that had been trampled beyond repair. "Well, a little," she amended, adding the hat to the dumpster, "but nothing that won't heal." Her tailbone smarted from landing on the wooden crates, and she wouldn't be surprised if she found bruises later. As for the burst of panic, she could barely admit that to herself, let alone to him. "Thank you. Did you just happen to be in the neighborhood?"

"I was dropping off mail at the post office and was on my way to try to catch you at MetLife before you left for the day. I found a few more photos to show you, Sherlock." He patted a vest pocket.

156

"Then I spotted you heading this way. I tried hailing you, but you must not have heard me."

She hadn't.

He paused, hooking his thumbs in his trouser pockets. "You didn't scream even when those two rakes went from bothering you to assaulting you. You didn't call for help."

The last time Olive had needed rescuing, she had done it herself. Her chest constricted, as though she were holding her breath all over again, swimming through murky waters full of people who would never ask for help again.

"Miss Pierce? Why didn't you call out?"

She inhaled deeply, and the stench of the dumpster helped ground her. "No one would have heard me from here, given the noise from the street. I was alone, and I knew it."

"You're never as alone as you think. If you need help, there's nothing wrong in asking for it."

Olive stifled a sigh. "Duly noted."

"Have I earned the right to ask what you're doing here?"

There was no denying that he had. "I've noticed someone behaving in a way that's suspicious. More suspicious, even, than what I'm doing. This is all perfectly legal, by the way."

"I see."

She couldn't see his face the way she wanted, but she heard the smile in his voice.

"Are we finished here?" he asked, offering his arm.

"Oh no." Olive eyed the dumpster. "I've got more digging to do first. If only I hadn't smashed my makeshift steps to pieces."

Mr. Magnussen took a knee and held out a hand, even though hers was even filthier than the last time they'd met. To think she'd once been embarrassed by dirt beneath her fingernails.

"Don't be shy, Miss Pierce. You're not the only one who's not afraid to get their hands dirty."

She slipped the cleaner of her two hands inside his and took a giant step up so that she stood on his leg, careful not to put weight on her heels. "You'd better call me Olive from now on," she said, balancing on the balls of her feet.

"All part of my master plan." He gave her fingers a little squeeze.

She looked down at him, her hair tumbling over one shoulder. "I suppose I ought to call you Erik, then." Her flickering smile found an answering glimmer in his eyes.

"Or Watson. I'm here to help, if you haven't noticed. Care to tell me what all this is about?" So he was still pining after a real investigation.

"Will you send me sprawling if I say no?"

With a sly grin, he bounced his knee in answer, making her wobble, but his other hand steadied the small of her back. A flash of heat fanned through her.

"Up you go," he said, and she climbed onto the ledge where she'd perched before.

Bending over the edge, she peered inside. "It's no use," she told Erik, who was standing now, his hand still warm on her back. "What I'm searching for is buried beneath a day's worth of garbage, if it's here at all. Don't look."

"Excuse me?"

"I have to get inside, and I'd rather not have you watch the contortions required."

"Really, Olive?"

The way he said her name made it sound as though they were friends. And right now she sure could use one. "Really."

"What are you hunting for?" he asked.

She pointed to the ground near his feet. "See that paper bag? I'm looking for its twin. I'm telling you this in confidence now, Watson. I learned last night that one of our secretaries takes out her own trash every night, rather than letting our janitor do it. She's been doing this for two weeks, according to him. Which is why I followed her this evening. I found what she tossed today, but if she used this receptacle last night, too, I can find another one."

"Double the trash, double the clues."

"Exactly. So, if you please." She twirled a finger in the air, indicating that he should turn or at least look away.

Instead, both his hands came around her waist. He lifted her off her perch and set her on the ground as though she weighed no more than a sack of flour. "Hold this." Apparently recalling the state of her hands, he popped his Panama hat on her head instead. After pulling off his necktie with a swish, he stripped out of his suit jacket and draped both over her shoulders—for lack of a proper coatrack, he said—then climbed into the dumpster himself.

He could not have known that when Olive was a child, her father had done this very thing every night upon arriving home from work. She'd stood there giggling while Nate asked if anyone had seen Olive, then proceeded to transfer his hat, jacket, and satchel onto her person. With a completely straight face, he pretended not to see her while praising the fine qualities of the coatrack she was pretending to be. The mystery and magic of it was that she'd felt seen and cared for even though the joke was that she was invisible.

The same sensation took hold of her now. Only she did not feel in any way that Erik was like a father to her.

Cloaked in the warm scent of sandalwood, she gaped at him. "Why are you doing this?"

"Aside from that look on your face? Longer arms. Faster searching."

"Besides that," she said, but he ignored her, intent on the prize.

Minutes later, he had it. "Voilà. The bag is about ready to split open, but it's only paper inside, as far as I can tell. Wait a minute." He disappeared for a bit, then resurfaced. "Congratulations. It's triplets." He held a third bag aloft.

She had to stop herself from clasping her hands in delight. "I owe you one. Hand them down."

"Intriguing." He loomed over her, still cradling Blanche's trash, his white shirt looking silver in this half-light. "What do you suppose you owe me?"

"What?"

"For my rescue of this garbage. Not to mention the rescue of yourself."

He had a point. She tipped her head back to see him from under the brim of his hat. "I can't offer an even trade, given that you're probably almost never in need of rescue yourself."

His smile was easy and broad, nothing like the guarded, tight-lipped curl she'd seen him give Gwendolyn. "In that case, a cup of coffee will do."

"Down on your luck? Need a dime?" she teased.

"I want a cup of coffee with you while you're having a cup of coffee with me. At the place and time of my choosing. No more, no less. You did say you owe me."

Given the fact that cleaning his trousers and shirt—or replacing them, if they proved to be ruined—would cost far more than a cup of joe, Olive supposed it was a bargain. "Deal. Now, would you hand that evidence over, please?"

He did, then swung his long legs over the side of the dumpster and jumped to the ground. After wiping his hands on a handkerchief, he returned his hat to his head, then draped the tie around his neck and folded the jacket over his arm.

Olive retrieved her leather satchel, then carried the smelly bags of trash in her arms.

"All set?" With a comically regal air, he offered his arm once more, and she allowed him to escort her out of the alley with as much grace as if they weren't both reeking and soiled.

Horns honked, wheels crunched over litter on the road, and a merchant banged the hood of a car too close to his sidewalk market. The after-work crowd thronged the streets on their way to dinner or home.

"Before I forget." From his jacket pocket, Erik withdrew an envelope and showed her the photographs inside. "These must have been tucked into a different chapter of my book last time. See anything helpful?"

She didn't. The images showed survivors shuffling off the *Kenosha*, but none of them were Stella.

"Had to try." Sunlight touched Erik's hair with gold as he scanned the intersection. "I'm putting you in a cab from here."

"That isn't necessary," she protested. The bags weighed almost nothing, and her apartment wasn't far. "I won't be visiting any other alleys, and I'm not in that much of a hurry."

"Actually, we are. Step lively, Sherlock. We've got a date."

When she didn't respond, he turned from the street and looked at her. Taking in her raised eyebrow, his confident features shifted, which she could only hope meant he realized how demanding he sounded.

"That is," he tried again, "I really hope you don't have plans, because I have an idea that won't wait. I'd be very pleased to have that coffee with you tonight, because what I have in mind won't work at any other time."

The Viking was trying. Olive smiled.

"Are you game?" he asked.

She was.

CHAPTER SEVENTEEN

When Erik had said Olive would be picked up in a black Model T for their coffee date after she'd had time to clean up, Olive had assumed he would be the one driving it.

So much for assumptions.

The streets were full of black Tin Lizzies, but the one parked outside the bookstore had the same license plate number Erik had told her to watch for.

The man behind the wheel hopped out as soon as Olive approached. "Miss Pierce?" He straightened his bow tie and pushed a pair of spectacles up the bridge of his nose.

"I am."

"*Enchanté, mademoiselle.*" His French accent was terrible. He doffed his boater, revealing a bald crown rimmed with short dark brown hair. He bowed lavishly before reseating the hat above prominent ears. "Leopold Rousseau the First, at your service. But my friends all call me Leo. One of those friends is Erik," he confirmed. "I'm to deliver you to him posthaste."

He was barely as tall as she was, but to be fair, she was wearing pumps. The overall effect couldn't be described as handsome, but he was still appealing, in the way that the ceramic gnome in Claire's garden was appealing. One couldn't help but smile at it.

The evening was cooling quickly. She fastened the top two buttons of her cotton cardigan, the tiered skirt of her Swiss dot dress ruffling in the wind. "He couldn't come for me himself?"

The car sputtered exhaust behind him. "He's otherwise engaged right now. You'll see what I mean if we hurry. I don't blame you for being surprised, and I respect you for being suspicious. Here's a note from him."

"A note anyone could have written," she replied. "I don't have the slightest idea what his handwriting looks like."

"You're about to find out. Just read it, will you? Your chariot awaits."

Fine. She opened the note, written on *Tribune* stationery.

Dear Sherlock,

You're not being abducted. I have somewhere I need to be right now, so I sent Leo in my place to get you. You're in good hands with him, eccentric though he may be. If he's nervous, as I expect he will be around you, he's going to talk a lot. Sorry. By the time you get here, I'll be ready for that cup of coffee you promised me. I'll even let you wax poetic about Mary Roberts Rinehart.

Yours truly,
Watson

P.S. Don't be alarmed, but Leo isn't taking you to a coffee shop. Rest easy. The coffee will still be waiting.

Olive's lips quirked up. He really did enjoy mysteries. "All right, Leo." She folded the note and tucked it into her pocket. "Let's hit it."

"*Très bon.*" With a lopsided grin, Leo shut the car door once she was seated, dashed around the front of the car, and slid back in.

She waited until he'd merged with traffic before she began her interrogation. This could be fun. "How long have you known Erik?"

"Forever. He's in my earliest memories, and my memories go way back."

"Grade school?" she asked.

"Diapers." He peered at her over the rim of his glasses. "I didn't say the memories weren't blurry. I was two, he was six." He pointed to his head. "Don't let the shine fool you. I'm only twenty-nine, just prematurely balding. I hear it's a hereditary thing. Or possibly the result of trauma. Either way." He shrugged.

"Are you related somehow? Cousins?"

"Brothers."

She squinted at him, searching for a sign of jesting, but his expression remained placid. "Yet you have different last names," she pointed out, leaving the difference in physical appearance to speak for itself.

"Not by blood. We spent time in an orphanage together right here in Chicago. That's not a secret, mind you, so don't think I'm betraying his confidence. I'm no snitch."

Olive's heart sank. She couldn't imagine growing up in an institution, no matter how kind the staff or how strong the bonds between fellow orphans. "Were the two of you later adopted into the same family?"

"In a manner of speaking. Eventually." He turned a corner and accelerated. "Before that, Erik adopted me, as it were. I don't remember a time when he wasn't acting as my guardian. The first punch he ever threw? On my account." He beamed. "Someone cast my spectacles to the floor and ground the lens under his heel. You know how cruel kids can be. Erik's sense of justice being strong, he avenged me. We did strike out on our own together for a while, as newsies." He chuckled. "Such tough guys at six and ten. We thought we'd be living the dream, you know? More like a nightmare."

She wanted to know more. And judging by Erik's note and Leo's chattiness so far, she could probably draw story after story from Leo if she tried, wading into the depths of what made Erik who he was. But that would feel like cheating. She wanted to hear from Erik himself and for the revelations to be his decision. It was the difference, she supposed, between an investigation and a friendship.

Leo turned onto Michigan Avenue and crossed the bridge over the river. A mile later, they motored north on Lake Shore Drive, passing the affluent Gold Coast district where mansions lined the shore. Lake Michigan spread to the east as far as the eye could see.

The apprehension Olive had first felt about coming with Leo dissolved by the time they entered Lincoln Park. Staring at the clock at home wouldn't alleviate the agony of suspense she'd have to endure until the body in Claire's grave was exhumed the day after tomorrow. She'd gone through Blanche's trash already and found in each bag a receipt for cab fare and a receipt to a restaurant in a suburb north of the city. All three cab receipts were for the exact same amount. The totals on the restaurant receipts matched each other to the penny, as well. Olive could ask Blanche about that tomorrow at work, but for now, there was nothing else to be done.

"Our journey ends," Leo said at last, slowing the Ford to a halt in a parking area not far from the boathouse. The lowering sun burnished a long, slender body of water with Lake Shore Drive on the opposite side of it. Beyond that, the lake looked like the open sea.

Couples and families packed the park. "Is our coffee date to be a picnic?" Maybe Erik had come early to stake out a good spot.

"Of sorts." Leo opened her car door and helped her out. "Come on, we'll miss him if we don't hurry. To the lagoon!" He extended an arm like a pith-helmeted explorer of the last century.

They wedged a path through the crowd until they stood at the edge of the water.

"There he is!" Leo shouted. "You see?"

"He's in one of those skinny canoes?" Between lanes marked off with floating strings of flags, four vessels glided across the gilded water, each one rowed by two men.

"Skinny canoes!" Leo guffawed. "They're called sculls—with a *c*, not a *k*. And yes, he's there. In the second position for now, but just wait. They're saving their strength and will take over for the win. Watch."

She did. As Leo predicted, Erik's scull soon moved into the lead. When it did, a group of boys onshore went wild, jumping and whooping, shouting "Mr. Erik!" until she feared they'd go hoarse.

Erik's concentration didn't waver as he pulled the oars in and out of the water, propelling the scull backward toward the finish line.

"And that, Miss Pierce, is why he couldn't come get you himself. He'd never let down his crewmate, nor those boys who came to see him row. They seem to think he's at least half immortal."

That much she believed. "Has he no flaws, Leo?"

"Plenty," he said, then paused to cheer when Erik's scull came in first.

Olive clapped with him. She couldn't be sure, but standing this close to the finish line, she thought Erik spotted her when he scanned the crowd at the end. That smile. She wondered if it came from winning or from winning in front of her.

A quarter of an hour later, Erik emerged from the boathouse in dry clothes, much cleaner than the last set she'd seen him wearing. "You made it," he said.

"Leo made sure of that," Olive said, adding congratulations. "We could have picked a different time for the coffee date, since you're already busy tonight."

Erik lifted a Thermos. On his other hand, two mugs dangled from his thumb. "No time like the present."

"Ah." Leo bowed. "Three's a crowd. I take my leave of you. Miss Pierce, it's been a pleasure. *Au revoir.*" His impish smile brought one from Olive, as well.

"I like him," she told Erik as Leo walked away. Leaves rustled on the branches overhead, sounding like whispered secrets. The evening's last rays filtered through them, marbling the grass with gold. "His eccentricity, as you put it, carries a certain kind of charm."

"Really? He'll be insufferable once I tell him that. He likes to say he's an acquired taste."

"One which you acquired right away, from what he tells me."

The corner of his mouth hitched up. "I told you he talks a lot when he's nervous."

"But why should he have been nervous? Does driving put him ill at ease?"

Erik's blue eyes sparkled as he looked down at her. "Pretty sure it wasn't the driving. You clean up well." He looked away. "Thirsty?"

"You bet," she said, ignoring the mild-mannered compliment. "If I'd known the venue ahead of time, I'd have contributed a blanket for the cause."

"Already taken care of. This way." His elbow poked out, and she took it.

She got the feeling he enjoyed taking care of things. People, too.

He guided her down a gentle slope and onto a dock that led to the lake. On both sides of it bobbed vessels a little wider than canoes boasting cushions, pillows, garlands, and old-fashioned lanterns with candles flickering inside.

She halted. "What is this?"

"It's Venetian Night at the boat club. We might as well share that cup of coffee in a makeshift gondola out on the lake, right?"

Olive stared at the vessels bumping lightly against the dock. The sound of water sloshing against the sides brought unwelcome goose bumps. "How deep is the lake?"

"On average? Nearly two hundred eighty feet, although at her deepest it's more than nine hundred. But where we'll be, I'd say sixteen feet, twenty tops."

That wasn't as deep as the river. Then again, she was only five foot five. She could drown in half the depth that Erik had just named.

He was waiting for her response.

"The last time I was on the water, I ended up in it," she told him.

"Went for a swim, did you? I hope the water was warmer than this. With such a mild summer, it's not even sixty degrees."

"Not by choice." Her fingers and toes grew cold as she recalled her fellow passengers, happy and expectant, dressed for a summer excursion, just like the crowd swarming toward the water now.

"The *Eastland*?" Erik asked, incredulous. "You were on it when it tipped?"

She managed a nod.

"Were you on one of the upper decks?"

"Not when it rolled over."

His gaze grew so intense that she felt its burn. "Olive." Just one word, and yet it carried so much more than her name. "I can't imagine," he added at length.

"Be glad of that," she said. A passing couple shoved her toward Erik, and only then did she realize her hesitation had made them an obstacle. It was the last thing she wanted to be.

Erik reached to steady her, but his hands were still full with the Thermos and mugs. "We don't have to go on the water," he said. "It's nice in the boathouse, too. Just not my favorite place for coffee."

A laugh bubbled out of her. "Your favorite place for coffee is on the lake?"

"I didn't say it happens often."

She looked over her shoulder at the boathouse. People streamed into it, and "Maple Leaf Rag" spilled out. She doubted she'd be able to hear herself think, let alone maintain a conversation with Erik.

Olive turned back to the canoe-gondola, determined to leave the *Eastland* where it lay in the river and focus on the present instead. "Did you decorate that yourself?" A garland of colorful flags drooped and dipped into the water.

"I had help."

"From your shortest friends?"

He smiled in answer.

Olive could picture those boys pounding down the dock with armfuls of pillows. Some kind of scaffolding had been erected above the benches, draped with exotic-looking scarves. Loans from the boys' mothers, perhaps? Her guess was that even now, a lanky aspiring rower or two was watching to see how their efforts would be received.

"Work like that shouldn't go to waste," she decided. "Let's go."

"You're sure?"

"I won't let one experience hold me back from others."

Ducking beneath the makeshift canopy, Erik climbed in first and set down the Thermos and mugs. Olive tossed in one of the lines holding the canoe to the dock, then accepted his hand as she stepped into the gently rocking vessel. She sat quickly on a cushioned bench. Erik took in the other line, then sat across from her, his knees almost touching hers.

She was fine. She was dry. She was safe.

Erik rowed until they were well away from shore and from the other lantern-lit vessels. Laughter floated across the rippling water from all sides.

On the other side of Chicago, the sun was setting. Skyscrapers became silhouettes as the platinum orb dipped behind them. Bright pink striped the horizon behind downtown, and the underbellies of cumulous clouds flushed purple in a sky of deepening blue.

"I could have missed this," she mused aloud. She was glad she hadn't.

Oars stowed, Erik poured coffee into a mug and passed it to her. "What did I tell you? Best coffee spot around."

Olive agreed with him and took a sip. "Mmm. Thanks for adding cream. It's delicious." She didn't care if the caffeine would keep her up half the night. The way she'd been sleeping, it wouldn't be all that different from usual.

"I thought you might like that. I saw your reaction to the cup of straight black Gwendolyn poured."

"You don't miss much, do you?"

"Generous of you, considering I missed the fact that you're one of the *Eastland* survivors."

She waved his comment away. "It's not something I include on my business card." A breeze riffled the bright orange fringe of the scarf draping the scaffold above her.

He took a slow drink, his long fingers wrapping completely around the mug. "Serving the families of clients who lost their lives that day must be incredibly personal for you. The woman you're still looking for—Stella? Have you found her yet?"

Olive cradled the mug in her hands. The lake lapped at the sides of the vessel. "Not yet. I've got a lead, though, which I hope will close the case later this week." How clinical it all sounded. The words were absent of emotion, but she wondered if he detected the feelings pulsing beneath the surface. "Her two children—her entire family deserves to have her back. I only wish I'd found her alive."

"So you found her body. Eleven days after the disaster? How did you manage that?"

"To be honest, I haven't found her yet. But, like I said, soon that could change."

He studied her. "You found something in a photograph of the morgue, then. Or some evidence from the coroner."

"No." She drank again, grateful for the coffee. It couldn't be much warmer than sixty degrees even above the water this evening.

"Then how do you know?"

A sinking feeling pressed down on Olive at the idea of misleading him. For some reason, she found herself wanting to be honest, and for him to be honest with her.

"Chicago Police Detective Alice Clement informed me today that the grave of another woman will be exhumed on Thursday because Clement suspects a misidentification. The woman who was buried could be Stella."

It wasn't a lie. But it was half the truth, something her father would have said was equally dishonest. The canoe rocked, and she gripped the edge to steady herself.

"Was she another client of yours? The person whose identity was attached to the body in the grave? Because then you'll be trading one missing client for another."

"She was not just my client. She was my best friend." The admission slipped from her like water through a leaking boat. She was powerless to stop it. Still, she didn't regret it.

Erik's head bowed. When he looked up again, his expression was grave. "You survived, but your best friend didn't?"

Olive said nothing, choosing instead to watch the coffee slant in the mug. Wind blew harder, pressing her skirt against her shins and carrying a raft of voices from other boats. In a manner of speaking, what Erik had said was correct. Claire Sterling had boarded the *Eastland* and never disembarked. The woman who emerged, Claire Barrymore, was someone else.

But that wasn't what Erik had meant.

"I'm sorry." He covered one of her hands with his, but in the gesture she felt a small distance open between them, a gap she could bridge with the truth but didn't.

Her head swam. Had she lied to him, or hadn't she? Either way, he now believed what he needed to in order for Claire's secret to remain safe. What surprised her was how this felt like a new loss, a broken trust when it had only just begun to grow.

Stars pricked the velvet dusk. The coming night had snuffed out the sunset and muted the color in the cushions, pillows, and scarves. Lanterns in small boats across the lake shone like lonely fireflies hovering over the water.

Erik sat back. "Did you find anything helpful in the trash?"

This was territory Olive could tread with complete candor. She told him what she'd found and that while it was odd, she saw no connection to the *Eastland* cases.

"I'll ask Blanche about it tomorrow. But let's not spend all our conversation on my work, shall we? I wouldn't mind getting away from all that this evening."

"Absolutely," he said. "What's on your mind?"

"Aside from everything we just discussed?" She laughed a little, relieved to steer the conversation elsewhere. "Leo told me the two of you were newsies together at ages six and ten. How does a newsie grow up to be a photographer for the *Tribune*?"

"That's a long story."

Someone splashed and yelped, and Olive scanned the water for the source. "I like long stories." Her tone was as tight as her muscles. Willing herself to relax, she drank her coffee and shifted on the cushion to focus on the tale ahead.

She lurched sideways. Two sets of boy-sized hands gripped the side of the canoe. Heads bobbed up, gasping for air. No doubt these were the boys who'd splashed into the water from their own vessel to swim here.

"Got you, Mr. Erik!" one cried.

"Easy there, Sticks, or you'll flip us over." Erik leaned the opposite direction to compensate for their weight.

Two more boys emerged from the lake and, along with the other two, tried climbing in.

"Don't—"

But Erik's words were swallowed by the water closing over Olive's head.

Cold shocked her into stillness as she sank. Then, blindly, she thrashed in her skirts and shoes, but she couldn't gain her bearings in the pitch-black lake. Without the sun, she had no idea whether she was swimming deeper or toward the surface.

Her flailing hand connected with someone else's limb, and she recoiled, sending a stream of bubbles in a silent scream. The panic she'd managed to quell in the alley after work returned, now ten times stronger. It overpowered reason, insisting she was swimming with corpses again. That she was in danger, people were dying, and rescue remained far off.

Fingers tangled in her hair. Frantic, she swam to get free. Hands caught her arms, and she tried to beat them off, but they slid to her wrists and held them. They were calloused. They were Erik's. He guided her hands to his broad shoulders, and she wrapped her arms around his neck, hanging on to him while, with powerful strokes, he propelled them to the surface.

Water streamed away from Olive's face. Still holding tight to Erik, she coughed over his shoulder, then gulped at the air. A dark cloud sailed away like a wraith, leaving a wake of diamond studs in the sky.

"I've got you." Erik's voice was steady in her ear. "You're all right. I won't let you go."

Then the makeshift gondola was within reach. But it was not more solid than Erik, who gripped its edge with one hand while his other spanned her back. Her teeth chattered, her limbs shook.

"Olive, I'm going to help you get back in. Are you ready?"

In answer, she spun slowly around as his arm relaxed its hold. Climbing in and being pushed up by Erik would have been more awkward if they hadn't already shared their dumpster experience. As it was, she could only be grateful they managed it as quickly as they did. She scooted to the opposite side while he climbed in after her, not certain he wouldn't capsize them both all over again.

"That wasn't supposed to happen." He unfastened a shawl that had been secured to the scaffolding as a privacy screen. "Take this for now. I need to get you home."

She wrapped the shawl around her shoulders. It offered scant warmth, but at least it covered the way her wet clothing clung to her corset.

"Where are the boys?" Even her voice shook. "There were four of them, weren't there?"

"They swam away before I could catch them and make them apologize to you. Don't worry, they're fine, at least until I see them next time. I don't think they meant to dump us in the lake, but I still intend to take them to task for it."

Shame filled her. She had not been dropped from a great height into the lake, so she couldn't have been much below the surface at the start. No bulkhead had trapped her there. If there'd been any danger just now, it was less from the boys' action than from her own. She'd lost her wits and spiraled down.

"This isn't how I wanted this evening to go," Erik said again. Their lantern had been lost in the upheaval, but starlight silvered the strong lines of his face. Water dripped from his clothes and hers, puddling at their feet. "I can't begin to tell you how sorry I am."

A boom cracked the sky, and a starburst of light exploded overhead. Olive jumped. Red and orange embers trailed smoke as they fell harmlessly over the water.

"Surprise." Erik pulled on the oars, directing the vessel toward shore. "There's a fireworks show. We had the best seats for it, too, but only if we weren't both soaked and chilled."

"So this was the plan for the rest of the night?"

"Part of it. There's dancing later, too. I wouldn't have assumed you'd want to, though. I would have asked first. Honest."

She struggled to reclaim her self-possession. "And here I thought I'd only agreed to coffee."

"You did. But I figured there wouldn't be any harm in having options. The best option now, though, is getting you home."

Olive quite agreed.

◆

Later, when she was clean, dry, and warm in her bed, Olive tried to imagine the evening if it had gone according to Erik's plan. If she hadn't been dumped into the lake, and if he had asked her to dance.

But how could she, with pain that cried out to be heard? Throwing back her covers, she went to the vanity and turned on the lamp. Gathering her nightgown up to her shoulders, she angled to see her back in the tri-fold mirror.

The stripes were raw and pink where scabs had been torn away. She'd never actually looked until now, unwilling to confront the evidence left by someone who had tried to climb over her but who had failed and most likely perished. The edges puckered where they tried to close over the wounds. The scars would be deeper than skin.

When tears rolled down her cheeks and met beneath her chin, she did not wipe them away or dismiss the guilt-tinged grief behind them. She wept because these marks on her back bore witness to a truth both terrible and profound. Olive had survived, and others had not. By the grace of God, she lived. She would never understand why she had been spared when babies and children, young people, parents, and grandparents hadn't. Nor could she guess how long the disaster would haunt her, as the Great Fire had haunted her aunt.

What she knew for sure was that she would do everything she could to honor the *Eastland* victims and their families. It was the least she could do, and no less than they deserved.

CHAPTER EIGHTEEN

THURSDAY, AUGUST 5, 1915

Today was the day.

This was Olive's first thought upon waking Thursday morning, that in a matter of hours, the Petroski family would finally learn what had happened to Stella, and Warren would learn that Claire was not only alive but had deliberately deceived him into thinking she'd died on the *Eastland*.

Aside from a slice of dry toast, breakfast was out of the question.

Olive bathed and dressed, then coiled and pinned her thick hair between sips of coffee. Shadows rimmed the green eyes staring back at her from the mirror. On the phone last night, she'd told her mother she was holding up all right. If Meg had believed her, it was only because she couldn't see her.

Erik had called to check on her yesterday, too. No, she hadn't caught a cold from her plunge in the lake, she'd told him. No, she didn't need any soup to ward off any chance of a chill, just in case.

Frustration still simmered over her visceral reaction to the boyish prank. She'd known she wasn't really drowning and yet felt like she was. Talking to Sylvie about it afterward helped, but she still felt upside down and inside out. It was disorienting.

So was the fact that Erik had wanted to turn a simple coffee date into an evening that could have included dancing. It might not have meant a thing. Then again, it might have. But she'd embarrassed herself, so the point was moot.

Huffing a sigh, she unscrewed the lid of a small jar of lip rouge and dabbed some color onto her lips. Normally, she didn't use cosmetics, but she feared if she didn't today, she'd scare people with her ghastly pale complexion. Yesterday, Blanche had commented that Olive didn't look or behave as though she were well.

That had been after Olive asked if Blanche knew any good restaurants outside the city. Blanche had said no, adding that she hadn't been out of Chicago since March. Three sets of taxi and diner receipts Olive had harvested from the trash said otherwise. The secretary was definitely hiding something.

Olive was swimming in mysteries.

Her conscience pricked. She owned her share of deception, too, and hers were no little white lies about whether she frequented a greasy spoon in the suburbs. Hers were life and death.

And they'd be exposed at last, today.

***

Olive refused to be sick.

It was a courtesy that Detective Clement had called, inviting her to a meeting with the medical examiner and Cook County Coroner Peter Hoffman at the morgue. Olive would be professional. She would not be sick.

She also wouldn't eat until sometime next week.

Clamping her lips shut, she accepted the photographs of Claire that Clement returned to her and tucked them into her satchel as the little group held court over a metal table, a woman's sheet-draped body between them. Olive produced a picture of Stella Petroski.

Dr. Richards, the medical examiner, glanced at it. "These remains look nothing like any image taken in life, Miss Pierce. You recall how rushed the embalmers were on July 24 and days following. You may also recall that there was a shortage of coffins. This body was laid to rest in a pine box that was not sealed properly."

In the pause that followed, Olive's imagination leapt to fill in the blanks. Air, water, insects. All of those would have entered the makeshift coffin. "Were you able to identify who she was? Or who she wasn't? The teeth, at least, offer clues."

"You bet." Detective Clement nodded. "Claire Sterling's dentist showed us records of her having a filling in one of her molars. We didn't find any fillings here."

That much was no surprise. Breathing shallow sips of air, Olive pointed to the smiling Stella still in hand. "Mrs. Petroski has a little gap between her two front teeth. Did you see that?"

"We did not," Dr. Richards said. He folded back the sheet, and Olive steeled herself. "See for yourself."

She licked dry lips and looked, determined to narrow her focus. But even in the blurred edges of her vision, the bloating was obvious, as was the green discoloration about the wound to the woman's head. The odor was overpowering.

Muscling down a gag, she forced herself to lean in close enough to examine the mouth. The corpse's lips were peeled back, so she could plainly see that one front tooth slightly overlapped the other. This woman was not Stella.

Olive had seen enough.

"We did find another distinctive." Mr. Hoffman replaced the sheet. "Her left leg is two inches shorter than her right. It appears that she broke her femur, most likely as a child, and it didn't heal properly before she finished growing. As you can imagine, it's far easier to say who she isn't than who she is. Today we've ruled out both Claire Sterling and Stella Petroski. Do you have other missing clients?"

Olive shook her head. "Other than Mrs. Petroski, mine have been accounted for, but there are others still missing from the disaster." Employees at Western Electric had formed an information bureau and had gone through the painstaking work of creating two passenger lists. One named Western Electric employees and relatives, and the other, the rest of the passengers. The only WE employee still marked as missing was Stella Petroski. But there were four or five names still missing on the list of non-company passengers. She'd check her copy back at the office. "Does the body have any other identifying marks on it to help us?"

Dr. Richards frowned. "Any scars, birthmarks, etc., are no longer visible, if they'd ever been there to begin with. The decomposition is already too far along. The bones and teeth are really the only unchanged features."

So instead of unearthing an answer today, what they'd exhumed was another question to add to Olive's growing list. Who was this woman? Where could Stella be if not here? And what would Warren do now?

"What condition is her clothing in?" Olive asked. "May I see it, or better yet, take it with me?" Claire had swapped out some of the garments, but not all of them. There may be some small clue that could lead to a break in the case.

Detective Clement lifted her chin. "It's no good, Pierce. I already asked about that."

Olive had suspected as much. She'd write to Claire as soon as she could and see if she still had any clothing she'd taken from the body.

"I'll need a photograph of the teeth," Olive said.

"We've taken plenty of images," Mr. Hoffman told her. "I'll make sure you get a set. Unless—" He looked to Detective Clement. "Is this a police investigation now?"

"Afraid not," Clement said. "My supervisor thinks it's a lost cause and says we ought to call her Jane Doe and be done with her."

"What will happen to the body, then?" Olive asked.

Mr. Hoffman regarded her, as if measuring how much truth she could handle. "We'll keep it for a little while, but if no one claims it, it will either be buried in the potters' field, or we'll boil the flesh off and give the skeleton to the university. For science and teaching, you know. The biology department is always happy for samples."

In either case, the body would be lost forever. Her family would never learn what happened to her, never give her a proper burial or have a place to plant flowers in her memory.

"How soon do you need proof of identity before you need to dispose of the body?" Olive asked.

"You'll have to take that up with the morgue director," Mr. Hoffman replied. "But the short answer? As soon as you can."

The meeting over, the good-byes were brief and professional until Clement touched Olive's shoulder. "Mr. Sterling has already been notified," she murmured. "Watch yourself."

<hr/>

As Olive stepped inside Corner Books & More after work, her mother's character portraits stared down at her. Unnerved, she wound between display tables toward the center of the store. A shipment of new books topped the counter in organized piles, framing Sylvie in chapters and verse.

"There you are!" She slapped her pencil down on a packing list. "I was wondering if I'd get to see you tonight or if Mr. Magnussen would whisk you away for another coffee date."

"We need to talk." Olive clutched her satchel's strap where it crossed her pounding heart.

"I'd love that, dear." Sylvie stepped out from behind the counter. "Have dinner with your uncle and me this evening. It's his turn to cook, and he'll want to hear all your news as much as I do. Plus, I want to fill you in on the latest developments for the store's anniversary celebration."

Footsteps sounded from the rear of the store, and Kristof appeared. The silver tie that matched his hair added a dignified touch to the midnight-blue vest and crisply creased trousers. "Olive! Are the rumors true about a suitor?"

Sylvie thwacked him on the arm with the nearest book. "She's coming to dinner. We'll hear all she wants to share about it then. Oh! Another letter came for you today from the Anne of Green Gables Fan Club."

Olive accepted the envelope and exhaled. At least her friend had been safe when she'd posted it.

"They exhumed Claire's body today." The words burst from her. "It wasn't her. That wasn't Claire they buried."

Her aunt blanched. "What do you mean?" She leaned into the counter and gripped its edge, sending *The House of Mirth* by Edith Wharton tumbling to the rug.

Kristof bent to retrieve it, his expression drawn in somber lines. "Tell us."

Bells clanged above the front door, and Olive turned to tell the customer the shop was closed. But her mouth went dry. As discreetly as she could, she slid her mail under the book on the counter, then faced the shell of a man before her.

Warren.

His suit was wrinkled at the elbows. It was obvious he'd shaved and trimmed his mustache this morning, but the nicks on his neck testified to an unsteady hand. He either hadn't noticed or hadn't cared about the small dark brown stain spotting his collar, and neither possibility was like him.

"You knew." Warren approached Olive with two fingers outstretched, a cigarette between them.

Kristof stepped forward, shoulders squared and spine straight. "Mr. Sterling."

Warren didn't acknowledge him, even when Kristof asked him to put out his cigarette and then, receiving no response, took the Lucky Strike and snuffed it in the ashtray on the counter. His gaze was fixed on Olive alone. "You knew it wasn't her, didn't you?"

If Warren had looked poised to attack her, either verbally or physically, Olive would have taken cover behind the counter. But he didn't look strong enough to attack. He barely looked strong enough to drive himself home. In a very real way, Claire was as dead to him now as he thought she'd been then. She was gone. Perhaps worse, from his perspective, she was gone by choice.

"You stood up with us both at our wedding," Warren rasped. "Remember that day when God joined us together? You've betrayed us both by breaking us apart."

"Why would you say a thing like that?" Sylvie's question tied a knot in Olive's conscience.

As if noticing Sylvie for the first time, Warren rounded on her. "She came to visit me after the burial. She didn't believe that I'd found my wife. Now I know why."

"I asked how you could be sure it was her," Olive clarified, the knot pulling tighter, tighter. "And in light of the circumstances, my question was perfectly reasonable. There were so many dead and so much confusion afterward."

"There was nothing confusing about the jewelry that marked her as mine. Even you must admit there was no mistake about that."

Olive tried to swallow, but sharp edges hurt her throat.

"You know where she is," Warren pressed. "You're hiding her."

Kristof held out a staying hand. "Careful, young man. You're upset. I understand. But we've been through this before."

"No." Warren swiped the boater from his head and clenched the brim with both hands. "You *don't* understand. *I* don't understand how she could do this to me."

"How do you know she's still alive?" Olive asked, grasping for a way to keep him from the hunt. "As much as I would hate this fate for her, who is to say she isn't one of the missing, never to be recovered?"

"Did you plant her jewelry on that other woman's body?" Warren asked.

"No," Olive answered. "I did not."

"Then she did," Warren said. "And she could only have done that if she survived the *Eastland* disaster. I'm worried about her, Olive. She must be sick, in mind or spirit. If she didn't get the typhus vaccination after being in that river, she could be sick in body, too. Otherwise, she'd come home. She can't have enough money, wherever she is. At least tell me where to send money. A letter. Anything."

"I can't tell you what I don't know, Warren." So far, it was still true that she had no idea where Claire was. But it took every ounce of control she had not to glance at the letter that had just arrived to be sure the envelope was completely out of sight. Her palms grew warm.

A hardening flickered over Warren's features, there and then gone, before his expression drooped like melting wax. "She's my wife. My *wife*. I buried her. And now, miracle of miracles, I learn she's alive, and that she deliberately deceived me into believing otherwise." He tapped the boater against his leg with his right hand. With his left thumb, he spun his wedding band. They were nervous tics, not displays of anger or intimidation.

"Our marriage isn't perfect," he went on, "but I deserve a chance to apologize and make things right. I need to see her. If I can't persuade her to give our marriage another chance, I'll have to make my peace with that." A muscle bunched in his jaw. "But I need to talk to her, and I can't do that if you won't tell me where she is."

Olive flinched at the sudden drop in his voice, more menacing than a shout. "I told you I don't know, and that's the truth." Before she could fight the instinct, her hand flew up to cover the book that hid Claire's mail. She felt her face heat and prayed the color would not rise with it.

In one long step, Warren was there, flinging her hand away, seizing the envelope.

A plummeting dread filled Olive, but ripping it away from him would only make him more suspicious. She crossed her arms and forced her features into a neutral expression.

"Were you hiding this?" He studied the block letters.

Brow furrowing, Sylvie stepped forward. "That's bookstore

mail and none of your concern." She held out her hand. "If you please."

"It's addressed to Olive," Warren insisted.

"It is addressed to Corner Books & More, as you see." Sylvie's tone held longsuffering patience for a man clearly coming unhinged. "Olive and I are considering sponsoring a club for fans of L. M. Montgomery—the author of the *Anne of Green Gables* books," she added when the author's name brought no sign of recognition.

Olive forced herself to breathe. Did Warren recall that Claire loved those books? Did he remember that her collection was stashed beneath her bed at his request, or that Olive's family had playfully nicknamed her and Claire after the main characters? It hadn't mattered to him before. Fervently, she prayed these details would elude him now. If he ripped open the seal and read the letter . . . if Claire hadn't veiled her meaning . . .

"Mr. Sterling." Kristof took the envelope from Warren and returned it to Olive. He gestured toward the door. "The bookstore is closed."

Sylvie touched the telephone, as though ready to call the police. "Good night, Warren."

A lump shifted behind his collar. Straightening his necktie, he dipped his chin, crushed his hat to his head, and left.

Kristof locked the door and shut the drapes, cutting off the sunlight. Even at his age, he was regal in silhouette. He and Sylvie were as protective of her as they could possibly be, but if Warren ever turned vengeful, neither would be any sort of match for the younger man. Olive couldn't stomach the thought.

Willing her pulse to steady, she found her voice again. "About that talk we need to have."

Sylvie hooked an arm through hers, eyes full of wonder and just a hint of hurt. "We're listening."

Poor Kristof. While a record of Liszt's music played on the Victrola, three bowls of his Hungarian sour cherry soup sat largely untouched, the dollops of sour cream garnish spreading on the deep pink surface. Fried bread covered with cheese cooled on a platter. The meal had been no competition for what Olive brought to the table, spilling everything that had happened since the *East-land* tipped.

Finally, Olive pushed her dishes away and reread the new letter from Claire. This one was extremely brief and businesslike, offering only an updated post office box where Olive may "kindly direct any future correspondence should it become necessary." In other words, for emergencies only.

"So, this fan club has a current membership of two," Sylvie said quietly.

"I hated deceiving you," Olive choked out. "Claire begged me not to tell a soul—and I agreed, thinking it would keep you safer if you didn't have to bear this burden, too."

"All this time," Sylvie whispered. "This entire time . . . Claire's alive. Thank God." Her hands lifted before twisting together again. "But then, who is the poor soul Warren buried in her place?"

"I wish I knew." Olive folded the letter and put it back in the envelope. "I learned some identifying characteristics at the morgue today and then consulted a list of *Eastland* passengers that marks five as still missing. But two of those missing are men in their forties, and two are children under the age of ten. One was a woman named Sarah, aged twenty-seven, but she wasn't a match to Jane Doe, either."

"How do you know?"

"Jane Doe had one leg shorter than the other, likely from a childhood break that never healed properly. I talked to Sarah's mother and learned she had never broken a bone, nor suffered any abnormal growth pattern. She never even really got sick."

A somber silence descended over the table for the young woman, a picture of perfect health, gone. It was too terrible to fathom, and yet there were hundreds of other stories just as wrenching from that day.

"Well." Kristof cleared his throat. One of the cats, Lizzie, leapt onto the table, and he promptly set her back on the floor. "Claire's safe now, wherever she is, and that's something."

"Yes, for now." Olive shifted, crossing her ankles. "She may not contact me again for a long time to keep it that way. In fact, it may be best for her to make a clean break with her old life in Chicago and cut all ties."

"Including her ties with you?" The symphony playing in the parlor reached a fevered pitch, and Sylvie left the table to turn down the volume. "I find that hard to believe. I've never known two girls to be better friends than the pair of you. The bigger question in my mind is Warren. He seems repentant. And traumatized, but that's completely understandable. Is it possible they could reconcile?"

Olive chewed her bottom lip while her aunt resumed her seat, hesitant to share how awful Claire's life with Warren had become. But if she didn't give them this piece of the puzzle, they wouldn't be able to grasp the seriousness of the rift.

Olive told them.

Sylvie covered her mouth. When Lizzie jumped into her lap with an insistent purring, she let the cat stay. "If it were anyone else telling me this, I wouldn't believe it," she said. "That young man was so earnest when he came to the bookstore all those years ago, so charmingly awkward in the roundabout way he started courting Claire. I was so happy for her, for them both, especially since it was clear her father wasn't long for this world."

"Warren is not the suitor you remember. Either he's changed, or he was performing to win Claire's hand." Olive pleated her napkin into accordion folds on her lap. "Dr. Jekyll and Mr. Hyde come to mind. Obviously, Claire is determined not to reconcile with either version of her husband, since she can't have one without the other. Otherwise she wouldn't have gone to such drastic measures to be rid of him."

Kristof leaned forward. "And Warren is determined to find her. He's convinced he can do that through you, despite what you told him tonight."

"You think he'll come after Olive again?" Sylvie asked. Lizzie nested her head in Sylvie's palm, and Sylvie rubbed a thumb between the cat's ears. "She's already told him she doesn't know where Claire is."

Kristof shook his head. "He doesn't trust your word anymore, Olive. Not since you knew Claire survived the disaster and didn't tell him. I understand why you made the choices you did, but we need to be on guard. I'm not your father, and I don't pretend to be. But if he were here, he'd tell you the same thing: no more working late and walking home alone in the dark. At least not until this thing settles down."

Olive was nearly thirty years old. She did not need to hold someone's hand while she crossed the street. Then again, how could she fault her aunt and uncle for simply wanting her to be safe?

"Promise, Olive?" Sylvie pleaded. "Your mother would never forgive me if something happens to you. I'd never forgive myself."

Even if their fears for her safety were unfounded, the last thing Olive wanted was for them to worry. "I may still work late," she told them, "but I promise I won't walk home alone in the dark."

CHAPTER NINETEEN

SATURDAY, AUGUST 7, 1915

It was five in the morning when Olive jolted awake. She sat upright in bed, as if doing so could shed dreams like water from her skin. But the images were too penetrating to be wiped away so easily. Any lift that she had felt from releasing the secret about Claire to her aunt and uncle had been flattened by the dreams that weighted her slumber. In a morbid, unending parade, three women had been climbing into and out of a single coffin—Claire, Stella, and the unknown woman exhumed from Claire's grave. Each of them had reached out to Olive. In the nightmare, she'd been too far away to help any of them.

She curled on her side in that in-between space that was too early to rise and too late to expect more sleep.

Questions nudged at her, insistent. What would Warren do, now that he knew Claire was alive? Who was that woman in her grave? Once Claire received the letter Olive had sent her yesterday, would she be able to supply any of Jane Doe's clothes to help Olive in her search? Where was Stella Petroski?

The blanks that followed each query expanded into an emptiness that filled Olive. When she'd spoken to Jakob yesterday on their daily call, she'd barely been able to string two sentences together at a time. She didn't want Stella to be dead, but if they had found her body in Claire's grave, at least the family would have had closure. Now all Stella's family had were the hollows where she ought to be.

Groaning with frustration, Olive turned onto her other side. Pointless.

She flipped back the covers and rose, slipping into her robe before setting the coffee to brew.

Hungry for light, she opened the curtains to a sun already risen, then sat at the kitchen table. Still spread over the oak surface were the taxi and diner receipts from Blanche's trash. The small scraps seemed so diminished compared to the matter of missing and misidentified women, and yet they beckoned to Olive. Here was a riddle with tangible clues, one which might occupy the weekend that loomed before her. At this point, any question she could answer would be a relief to her churning mind.

She glanced at the clock and calculated. If she got started right away, she could bake shortbread cookies and a loaf of zucchini bread to take to the Petroskis before heading north to visit Flo's Kitchen, the restaurant named on Blanche's receipts. Earlier this week, she'd promised Michael and Addie she'd check on them today, and she didn't want to arrive empty-handed, even if all she could bring were baked goods. Then she could have lunch at Flo's, do a little digging there, and still be back in time to host Saturday night family dinner, as usual.

Energized now, Olive finished her morning routine, then tied an apron over a floral crepe de Chine dress cuffed at the elbows. When she found she had enough zucchini, she decided to double both recipes so she'd have enough to share with her aunt and uncle, too.

Not long after Olive placed the two loaves of bread in the oven, a heavenly smell filled her apartment.

The telephone rang in the living room. After wiping her hands on her apron, she answered it.

"Olive," Sylvie began, "I'm glad I caught you. I wasn't sure if you would be going into the office."

"Not today." Olive told her the plans she'd made.

"The diner is in Evanston? Do you know how long you'll need there? I only ask because Kristof is performing in a concert this afternoon, and I'd love to go if you wouldn't mind watching the store from three o'clock on. The Mystery Lovers Book Club is meeting then, so I don't want to close the store early. Could you squeeze that in?"

Olive told her she could.

"Good. Don't hang up yet. I have a customer here who wants to speak with you."

"What? Who?"

A shuffling sounded as the telephone changed hands.

"Olive. It's Erik Magnussen." If she wasn't mistaken, he sounded a little nervous.

Not that she blamed him, after what happened Tuesday night. He had telephoned her office again Thursday while she'd been out, but she'd been so preoccupied with the exhumation that she hadn't rung him back. "Erik. I owe you a phone call, don't I?"

"If either of us owes the other, it's the other way around. Listen, I'm here in your aunt's bookstore, picking up the latest Holmes. I still feel terrible about what happened during our coffee date. How would you feel about trying again? This time, you pick the place. And time."

Olive dabbed the end of her apron to her forehead before fanning herself. "Is this offer for coffee only?"

He chuckled. "No boat rides or fireworks this time, I promise."

Glancing at the clock again, she quickly revised her vision for how her day might go. "How do you feel about lunch?"

"In general? I'm for it."

She dropped into a club chair. "And with me, specifically, at a diner north of town while sleuthing out the evidence we uncovered in the dumpster?"

"Why, Sherlock! I thought you'd never ask."

A smile spread over her face. "Good. I'm asking. And if I may be so bold, I'll go even further. I want to drop off some cookies and bread in Cicero first. Could we include that errand along the way?" Cicero wasn't on the way to Evanston, and they both knew it. But somehow, Olive suspected Erik wouldn't mind.

"I'm at your service. Are you ready now?"

Dirty bowls and measuring cups crowded her counter and sink. Flour dusted the linoleum floor, and bits of dough were drying on the table. "Not exactly. The bread is still baking, and I need to clean the kitchen."

"I know what would make that go faster." When Olive started to protest, he interrupted her. "Don't tell me you're worried about propriety. If you trust me to drive you all over Chicago, you'll have to trust me to be on my best behavior in your apartment. Wait a minute, your aunt is waving at me."

Another pause signaled he was handing the phone back to her.

"Olive," Sylvie said, "if this nice young man wants to do the dishes, you let him. I'm hanging up now, we're tying up the telephone line."

Who was Olive to argue with her aunt?

———◆———

Olive was already flushed from the oven's heat when she opened the door to Erik, a bag stamped with *Corner Books & More* dangling from his hand. Smiling, his gaze drifted to a spot on her cheek, and she brushed away what she guessed was a streak of flour.

"Just you wait," she said. "One of these days, you'll catch a glimpse of me when I'm not smudged with flour, dirt, or garbage."

He doffed his hat as he entered and reminded her that he already had when she'd come to the Lincoln Park Boat Club.

Only to spare his feelings, she did not remind him that the shining moment of cleanliness had been rather short-lived. Cheeks blazing from the memory, she turned toward the mess in her kitchen instead. "Ready to roll up your sleeves?"

"That's why I'm here."

She tossed a dish towel his way and attacked the sink full of suds.

Flinging the towel over one shoulder, he bent over the short-bread cookies cooling on the table.

"Take one," she told him, "then get moving. We have a busy day ahead."

"You know, for a person who doesn't like asking for help, you sure make a stern taskmaster." He popped a cookie into his mouth and closed his eyes. "Oh, that's good."

Satisfaction unfurled through her. She didn't need to distribute the entire two batches of cookies. She'd let him have more once the kitchen was clean.

"I'm glad you like it," she admitted. "It took several trials and errors before we got the recipe right."

"We?" He picked a wooden spoon off the drainboard and began to dry it.

"My mother and I," she explained. "She grew up here, with a bakery down the block, so she didn't learn to bake with her own mother. But by the time I was born, my family had moved into a house north of the river. If I wanted cookies, we had to make them ourselves. She and I figured it out together."

"I gather she was the type who actually let you participate, even if it meant the process was a bit slower and not as tidy."

Olive confirmed his hunch. "She's an artist." She told him that Meg had painted the portraits in the living room, and that she lived here with Olive now that she was a widow. While he crossed the room to admire the paintings, she went on. "She doesn't mind a creative process that falls outside the lines. And I always really *wanted* to help her. Her hands were burned in the Great Fire of 1871, and the way the right hand healed, she doesn't have the use of all her fingers. So any time I could do something for her, whether it was buttoning her cuff or fixing her hair, I was glad to. I often felt in the way of my older brother and sister, and I didn't inherit

192

my mother's artistic talent. But when I was useful to her, I felt . . ." She searched for the right word. Valuable? Worthwhile? No, it was simpler than that. "I felt happy, because I had made *her* happy."

She didn't confess that when she wasn't helping someone, she often felt invisible. Overlooked. Did that make this compulsion selfish or selfless? At last, a question she didn't mind leaving unanswered.

Returning to the kitchen, Erik wiped down a space on the counter and set the dry dishes there. "The association remains."

She handed him a mixing bowl. "It does." Cracking eggs, measuring spices, and pulling sweets from the oven made her feel good, both then and now. "If we're honest with ourselves, I think we'd find that much of what we love has a lot to do with the memories we've attached to it. Would you say that's true for you and rowing?" She knew he loved it. She wanted to know why.

His expression grew thoughtful and distant. Rotating the dish towel to find a dry spot, he picked up another tin measuring cup. "Leo told you we were orphans."

"Yes." She blinked, waiting for this to relate to her question.

"I don't remember much about my parents, Soren and Inga. But my birth certificate says they were both born in Norway. My father was a sailor. He must have loved the water. So, to answer your question, I enjoy rowing for its own sake, but it's also a way to connect with my roots. So this is an association not to true memories, but to the memories I wish I had. Of family."

The quiet that followed was marked only by the gentle sloshing of water as Olive continued to scrub. "That makes sense," she said quietly. "And yet you didn't choose a maritime occupation in order to fully follow in your father's footsteps."

Erik set down the measuring cup and swiped out the bowls of a few spoons. "You noticed." A hint of a smile curved his lips. "My father's work took him far from family in a way I would never want." He stole a glance at her. "I was around twelve when I began really searching for clues about his life so I could know

193

where I came from. That's when I found an immigration document that revealed his last known occupation. I also found his death certificate. He was declared dead when I was twelve, but they never found his body. He was lost in a storm when I was five years old."

Olive's hands stilled as she tried to make sense of this.

"My parents put me in the orphanage when they were both still living," he went on. "My mother suffered from consumption—I found her death certificate, too, and then found her doctor and talked to him. She was so ill by the time I was eighteen months old that there was no way she could have cared for me. And my father took to the Great Lakes and was gone for weeks or months at a time. So technically, I was a half-orphan. For years, I still had one parent living. I just didn't know it until it was too late. I did, however, find my mother's bachelor cousin, Oscar Gunderson, when I was thirteen. He had come from Norway as a structural engineer to work on the World's Fair buildings years earlier and stayed."

"How did you find him?"

"The orphanage had my certificate of baptism. I visited the Lutheran church in Humboldt Park where I'd been baptized, checked the marriage records, and found my parents, which is how I learned my mother's maiden name. So I called every Gunderson listed in the city directory, along with every Magnussen. There are a lot of Gundersons and Magnussens in Chicago," he added with a rueful smile.

"But it's amazing that you found a relative! He took you in?"

"He did. He was well-off with the architectural firm and had a housekeeper to keep things running in his home in the Wicker Park neighborhood. Providing financially wasn't a problem, and his sense of duty was strong. Brazen thirteen-year-old that I was, I insisted he take Leo, too. To his credit, he did, and we lived together, a trio of bachelors."

"Were you happy and comfortable after that?" She resumed her scrubbing.

"An older couple in the neighborhood checked on us often while

Oscar was working or courting. Between Oscar and this couple, we learned manners, work ethic, and to trust God and people. We were an unconventional little group, but I felt like we were family nonetheless. But when I turned eighteen and Oscar married, Leo and I took our bow and left."

It wasn't a direct answer to her question, yet it was more than he could have shared, and she was grateful for that. "Did Oscar ask you to do that?" She tried to lay the question gently, aware she might be touching a tender spot. "Did his wife?"

"They didn't tell us to go, but neither did they beg us to stay. Oscar had fulfilled his obligation, and I was old enough to live on my own with Leo by then. I do keep in touch with Oscar's family, though, and see them around the holidays each year." He finished drying a bowl and set it on the counter. "I told you it was a long story. Not so much in the telling of it, I suppose, but in the living it."

Olive touched his elbow, heedless of the water dripping from her fingers, because whatever she could say would not be enough. She tried anyway. "Thank you for sharing that with me."

A muscle jerked in his cheek, and he dipped his chin. "You asked about rowing, and my answer took sail and caught the wind, didn't it? To your question: as much as I want to connect with my father's memory, I would never choose a life at sea. I would never choose the thrill and freedom of wind and waves over the chance to weigh anchor at home with a family of my own." He wiped a baking sheet dry.

A thumb pressed Olive's heart, not just for Erik, but for the riches of family with which she had been blessed, a wealth she resolved not to take for granted. She could not imagine getting to know her parents only through documents and interviews after their deaths, as Erik had done. She couldn't imagine finally finding a relative, living as a family for years, and then leaving.

No wonder he was interested in her work finding *Eastland* victims. He had more experience investigating missing persons than she did. He had known personally the pain of an absent family member and likely felt it still. Would it help him if she included him in thinking through the possible scenarios for Stella and the misidentified woman they'd unearthed?

With a grimace, she recalled the way she'd dismissed his desire to be of service as a bid to play a hero from a detective novel. He didn't seem to hold it against her, though, and for that, she was impressed.

"Leo is lucky to have you, Erik."

His smile lifted his entire countenance. "I'm lucky to have him, too. But God willing, he won't always be the only family I have."

Seconds passed in quiet as they finished their humble work. Olive found the camaraderie in their conversation and in cleaning up together so strong that it approached something like comfort.

The timer buzzed. Olive pulled the pans of zucchini bread from the oven and set them on the stovetop.

Erik stared in wonder at the golden-brown loaves as though he'd never seen fresh homemade bread, let alone tasted it.

Perhaps he hadn't. "Did Oscar's housekeeper cook or bake for you?"

"Not on your life." A laugh skipped across his words.

This was a wrong she could actually right.

After the bread had cooled a little, she cut a thick slice, slathered butter on it, and passed the plate to him. She had baked it to be shared, after all. She just hadn't known until now that she wanted to share it with him.

CHAPTER TWENTY

Perhaps it was the conversation they'd had at her kitchen sink. Perhaps it was sitting side by side in the front seat of his Tin Lizzie, like allies facing the same road together. But on the drive to Cicero, her resistance to sharing about her investigations fell by the wayside like unwanted baggage. She told him of her ongoing search for Stella and the unknown woman exhumed from Claire's grave.

"That was your lead, wasn't it?" he asked. "You mentioned it Tuesday night. I read about it in the paper yesterday. Which means your best friend Claire is missing, too." He glanced her way. "Right?"

"Yes." Clasping her gloved hands in her lap, Olive felt again that carved-out space where Claire had been in her life. "I miss her." She longed to tell him more, tell him everything.

"Are you searching for her now, too?"

"No." The answer escaped like a sigh. "That is, only in memories. I can see her here, in fact." They were crossing the Clark Street Bridge. "She used to join my family as we stood on the pedestrian part of the bridge along with hundreds of other Chicagoans, cheering the arrival of the Christmas Tree Ship. Did you ever—?"

He shook his head. "Tell me."

"It was the official start of the holiday season when, after Thanksgiving every year, a three-mast schooner full of Christmas trees freshly cut from Wisconsin arrived. The ship was decked with red bunting, and you can only imagine the smell of pine with hundreds of spruces onboard! Claire helped our family choose one and then came home with us to decorate it each year."

"Sounds like a regular Currier and Ives scene."

It did. It was a scene Olive much preferred to the view out the car's window now. The *Eastland* still lay on its side in the river. By night, it was illuminated by ten floodlights that had been affixed to the Reid Murdoch Building and by more than one hundred tungsten-nitrogen lights strung on the ship itself. By day, the vessel looked filthy and bloated. An eyesore and proof of tragedy.

"I wish they'd get that thing out of here," she muttered.

As they put the bridge behind them and headed west, images of the *Eastland* clung to Olive like barnacles. The quiet seemed appropriate after being so close to the site of so much death and suffering.

At length, Erik spoke. "If you don't want to talk about it, just say so. But why wouldn't you want to search for Claire?"

"Because Claire does not wish to be found." This was no secret any longer. "Warren—her husband—found her jewelry planted on the body that he buried. She could only have done that if she survived, and she would only have done that if she wanted people to think she was dead."

There. The truth, and almost all of it.

Erik shifted gears and slowed for a crossing horse-drawn ice wagon, then accelerated again. "But what drove her to such desperate measures? Did she give you any hints before that morning of the picnic?"

"She didn't feel safe with her husband. She bore evidence that her fear was well-founded."

Erik turned to look at her, a gathering storm in his eyes. "Tell me more."

And so she did. She explained the strange way Warren courted

Claire, how he arranged everything in his life to serve his reputation. She told Erik about Claire's broken arm, the bruises and cuts, and that when they were in danger of drowning in the *Eastland*, Claire had seen it as a way out. She shared everything she could, right up to the point when she lost sight of Claire while helping Michael and Addie to the promenade deck.

"So that's the last time you saw her," Erik said, and she didn't correct him. "You don't know where she is?"

"I do not," Olive replied. "Although I couldn't convince Warren of that when he came to the store after the exhumation." Outside the window, traffic eased as they left downtown congestion in their wake.

"Wait a minute. Was he there to shop?"

Olive laughed. "He was there for information, Watson, which he thought he could only get from me. I might feel sorry for him, but I can't get past the fact that he beat her. There is no excuse for that."

"No." Erik's tone was emphatic. "There is not."

Five miles later, they rolled into the grief-stricken Cicero neighborhood where Stella's family lived.

"That one." Olive pointed to the Petroski bungalow up ahead. "Green siding, cedar shingle gable." Weeds sprang up between the marigolds on either side of the porch.

Erik parked the car, then came around the front to let Olive out. Hinges squeaked as the screen door swung open and slammed shut again, and Michael and Addie came barreling down the stairs. They hurtled across the ragged lawn toward her.

"You came!" Michael stopped short before her, stuffing his hands into his trouser pockets while Addie wrapped her little body around Olive's leg.

"Red!" the little girl cried.

Olive knelt, kissing Addie's cheek and encircling Michael in an embrace he did not fight.

"Did you bring my mama this time?" he asked quietly, as though bracing himself for the wrong answer.

Overcome, Olive swallowed. "No," she said, "though I wish with all my heart I could say otherwise. I came because I told you I would. I wanted to see you both."

Addie buried her face in Olive's neck, pushing her off balance. With an unceremonious plop, Olive fell sideways onto her hip, and the girl climbed into her lap right there in the grass. Michael pulled away, mouth firm, a mask snapped in place over emotions he was learning to hide.

A shadow loomed as Erik approached with a tin of cookies and a loaf wrapped in paper. Before Olive could stand to make the introductions, he lowered himself from his intimidating height and sat on the warm grass beside her.

"Michael, Addie, this is Mr. Magnussen," Olive said, "my friend." It was a simple term for a simple introduction, easy for children to understand. But as soon as Olive said it, she felt it was true.

Erik's smile was gentle. "Or Mr. Erik, if that's easier. I'm very pleased to meet you both."

Michael's hand disappeared in Erik's as they shook.

Addie pressed herself more tightly against Olive, peeking at the blond giant from behind a tangle of windswept hair.

"Look, Addie," Olive whispered, "he brought cookies."

At this, the girl straightened a little, eyeing the tin in his hand.

"Are your grandparents home? Your father?" Olive asked. "We should ask first before we spoil your lunch."

Michael kicked at a fallen hickory nut, then plucked it from the grass and polished the dirt from it with the cuff of his sleeve. "We don't really eat lunch anymore. Not since Mama went away."

Olive sent Erik a worried glance. "What do you mean?"

The boy shrugged. "We eat, but we don't sit down at the table like we used to. No one will care if we eat cookies."

She looked toward the house, wondering if any of the adults inside had even noticed the children's rambunctious exit. "Still, we'd better go inside and say hello."

After handing Michael the tin to carry, Erik stood and helped Olive to her feet, still cradling the loaf of zucchini bread in his other arm. She took an extra moment to brush grass and clover from her skirt, but even if she stayed out here for an hour, she still wouldn't find the right words to bring Jakob and his in-laws.

At the porch, Erik hesitated, then handed her the bread. "I think I'll stay out here in the fresh air, if you don't mind. Say, Michael, is that a baseball I see under that rocker?"

Eyes alight, the boy scurried across the porch and under the rocker, crawling out with both baseball and glove, spider webs trailing the stitched leather. Draping his jacket over the porch railing, Erik grinned and told Olive to take her time.

Addie scooped up the cookie tin Michael had deposited on the porch and claimed Olive's free hand. "In!"

Olive opened the latch and let Addie through but remained in the doorway herself. Newspapers in English and Polish covered the couch and coffee table. "Hello? Jakob? Mr. and Mrs. Adamski?" Too late, she realized they might be resting. Grief was exhausting, after all. So was uncertainty, and this poor family had both.

It was Jakob who came to greet her, looping suspenders over his shoulders as he approached. "Miss Pierce. I forgot you said you'd come today. Please excuse . . ." He lifted a hand, indicating his own state, as well as that of the house.

"That's fine, I don't need to stay long. I came to bring you these, along with the tin Addie has." She handed over the bread. "It's zucchini. Do you like zucchini bread? I hope you do."

"How kind of you," he said. "Nothing tastes the same anymore, but this I will eat." His voice remained a low rumble, adding to her suspicion that Stella's parents were taking a nap. "Shall we visit on the porch?"

He followed her outside, barefoot. Pretending not to notice, she was quick to explain who was playing catch with his son in the front yard.

"I have not had time or the spirit for games lately." Jakob sat with the stiffness of a much older man.

"Of course not," she replied, taking the other rocker. "No one would expect that of you."

He rubbed his stubbled jaw. "Two weeks ago today."

"Yes."

"Still no body."

"No."

Leaning his head back, Jakob began pushing himself in the rocker. "I begin to wonder if this is what she wants," he whispered. "Otherwise, wouldn't we have found her by now?" He stared blankly ahead while his son caught the ball and hurled it back to Erik. "I read about that Sterling woman in the paper," he went on. "I read about what she did to make it seem like she had died. What if Stella doesn't want me to find her, either?"

"I have a hard time believing she'd willingly leave her entire family. Were you having trouble in your marriage?" Olive asked, though she'd posed the question before. "So much trouble she would abandon not just you, but her children and parents, as well?"

Jakob blinked. "I could have done better. I know I could have done better by her. Those headaches you found out about—those could have been my fault."

"Or they could have been the natural result of normal stress."

"But what if she found someone else? What if she escaped the monotony of assembling telephone parts and caring for a family intentionally?"

Before Olive could reply, Addie came out onto the porch again, shortbread crumbs between her fingers and on her cheeks. Rubbing her eyes, she climbed onto Olive's lap. In one dimpled fist, the little girl clutched a blouse that smelled faintly of perfume.

The scent seemed to trigger something in Jakob, for his expression collapsed, and he covered his face. "Oh, God," he prayed, for

Olive was certain this was not blasphemy. "God. What do I tell the children?"

Gathering Addie closer, Olive kissed the top of her head. She ached not just for the Petroski family, but for the loved ones of the unknown woman found Thursday. Wherever they were, they had to be a mirror image of Jakob's despair.

CHAPTER TWENTY-ONE

The drive from Cicero to Evanston was twenty miles, but the time passed quickly. Now that Erik had met Jakob and the children, Olive discussed the case with him in more detail than she'd ever done with Howard. As she spoke, Erik nodded, his fingers kneading the steering wheel every so often.

"Did you learn anything from Michael when you were playing catch with him?" she asked.

"What kind of sidekick would I be if I didn't?" he teased, but Olive knew that even if there had been no investigation, he still would have reached out to a boy who had lost his mother. "I learned that Stella used to play catch with him."

"Not Jakob?"

"He did, too. But it says a lot about the kind of mother she was, doesn't it? She could have delegated games of catch to Jakob, to her father, even to her brother."

"But she didn't," Olive said. "She chose to play with him when no one would have faulted her for leaving that to her male relatives."

"Michael told me she was terrible at it." Erik chuckled. "Early this summer she 'caught' his pitch with her eye. He was mortified that he'd hurt her, but she insisted it was nothing, made some crack about keeping her eye on the ball, and went right on playing

204

for another twenty minutes, even though her eye swelled up and turned purple right in front of him."

Olive blinked back the heat in her eyes. "She loved him so much," she whispered.

"Michael knew it, and I thank God for that."

Olive agreed and told him about Jakob's concern that Stella deliberately left her family. "But a woman who laughs off a black eye and keeps playing in order to make her son feel better is a mother who puts her children's interests above her own. I just can't believe Stella abandoned them. What concerns me, though, is what *they* believe."

At last, they drove through the dappled light of a maple-canopied neighborhood. Baskets of trailing pink petunias hung from lampposts. Erik rolled to a stop along the curb, and Olive peered through her window at a turreted house from the Victorian age. Only it wasn't just a house anymore. It was Flo's Kitchen, according to the painted wooden shingle squeaking on its hinges on the front lawn. A red slate roof topped clapboard siding of sunflower yellow. A wooden arbor arched in front of the entrance, its white paint disguised by vines of floppy lime-green leaves.

Erik came around to Olive's side and opened the car door. She stepped out.

"Looks cozy," she said. "Like it's still someone's home. Someone who can't wait to feed you."

Then it occurred to her that Erik may not know what that was like. He'd never come home from sledding to a mother waiting with gingersnaps and hot chocolate. He'd never been invited to an aunt's home for pot roast after church on Sunday. He'd never joined relatives for Saturday-night lasagna.

She couldn't explain why this pained her so much.

"Let's see if I can be useful here." Erik took out his camera and photographed the outside of the restaurant. "I want to get a few different angles from here, as well," he said quietly. "The street in both directions, and the buildings across the street. We may catch something in the images later that doesn't mean anything to us now."

"Good idea. But we're going to look awfully suspicious, you know."

"Not if people assume I'm taking pictures of you."

He was right. She swallowed. "So I should just—move around a bit, shall I? To stand in front of different backgrounds, but you'll be pointing the camera near me, not at me."

His lips hooked up at one corner as he brought the camera to his eye. "Don't forget to smile."

She didn't. Neither did she forget that Erik Magnussen wasn't really looking at her, so he couldn't see that her smile wasn't only for show.

She took a few steps clockwise, turning her back to the view he wanted to capture. Always facing her, he spun around her in a slow revolution. It was almost like a dance, she supposed, and thought again of the dance they might have shared but didn't.

Olive wondered if he realized that he was smiling, too.

"There," he said. "Let's see how those turn out."

"Yes, let's."

Inside, they were seated at a corner booth by a window, the bench squeaking as they each slid onto it. Erik removed his hat and set it on the bench beside him. Daisies sprouted from a milk bottle flanked by salt and pepper shakers. A crocheted valance cast pinpricks of light and shadow over the menus. One glance at the offerings proved this was far from the greasy spoon diner Olive had expected. It was good old-fashioned comfort food. No wonder Blanche enjoyed it.

A waitress came and introduced herself as Fran. Olive insisted Erik order first so she'd have extra time to decide. It didn't take long for him to land on chicken fried steak and mashed potatoes.

"Sounds good, hon." Fran scribbled it down. "You want a side with that?" Her snood barely contained wiry brown curls sparkling with strands of silver.

When Erik asked for the salad, she peered at him over the rims of her glasses. "Really? I wouldn't have guessed it. Not that you don't know your own mind, but I'd think a man of your . . . stature would want a heartier side. Something to really refuel you, you know? What is it you do, anyhow? Manual labor of some kind? Maybe you're an athlete?"

Olive sat back, enjoying this. Not only was Fran talkative, but she was also nosy. Whether this was part of the family-style atmosphere or not, it would play to Olive's advantage.

"He's a photographer," she supplied, amused at Fran's apparent confusion.

Gamely, Erik produced the camera and set it on the table.

"Always behind the camera, never in front of it," Olive said. "You'd think from the pictures he takes that I go to all these places alone."

"Well, we can't have that," Fran huffed, slipping her notebook and pencil into her apron pocket. "Can I help? Slide together, you two." She picked up the camera. "Okay?"

Erik darted a questioning look at Olive.

"Don't you want him in the picture?" Fran asked.

Olive regarded him. "I do."

That smile again. Something turned over inside her.

When he moved closer to her, the August afternoon grew warmer by ten degrees. He draped his arm across the back of the bench, his fingers brushing her shoulder. Pretending it didn't affect her, Olive kept her eyes on Fran and waited for the click.

Erik moved away then, but not so far as he'd been before. He set the camera inside his upturned hat.

"Well, if that don't beat all. A photographer." Fran scratched a spot behind her ear. "I'm usually right about folks. It's a gift. My instincts must be slipping."

"I do a fair amount of rowing, too," Erik conceded. "Your instincts are secure."

"Ha!" The laugh burst from her as she scooped out her notebook and pencil. "Now you tell me! I was wondering how pushing a pin on one of those Kodaks could possibly give your shoulders such a workout!" She looked at Olive. "Ready, sugar?"

Olive smiled. "Everything looks so good. I know Blanche Holden comes here quite a bit. I wish I knew what she orders."

"You know Blanche?" Fran beamed. "Well, how about that? One of our regulars here, and if she isn't one of the sweetest, too. Is she the one who sent you to us? Shoot." She shook her head as if this was the most generous tip she'd received all week.

"What does she like to eat?" Olive asked. It wasn't that she thought Blanche's menu choice would crack the case, but if she could just keep Fran talking, she was sure it would lead some-where. It had to. Why else would Blanche keep this hidden gem of a restaurant a secret?

"Same thing every time she comes in here, and always to go. Two breakfast specials and two coffees in Thermoses she brings herself, one with cream and sugar, one with just cream."

Olive glanced at the menu. Sure enough, breakfast was served all day. "But she doesn't eat here?"

"Used to. She used to come in every so often with Joe, God rest him."

"Joe was Blanche's first husband," Olive murmured to Erik. "She married her second husband, Darryl, less than two years ago."

"Mm-hmm." Fran fanned herself with the menu she'd taken from Erik. "Apparently, Darryl doesn't get out much. Must be why she gets the food to go, although I would like to meet him. I sure hope whatever ails him isn't serious." Her narrowed gaze strayed to the window.

Olive followed it with her own, resolving to explore the area after their meal. "Is there a hospital nearby?"

"Of sorts," Fran said. "Wouldn't it be awful for her to lose another husband so soon after the first? Shoot."

"Awful," Olive agreed. "How long has he been in treatment?"

The average person might consider the question too private to answer. Thankfully, Fran was not the average person.

"Oh, now, I may have gotten a little ahead of myself with my guesswork, but as I said, my instincts are pretty reliable. Blanche has never told me Darryl's up there." She tilted her head toward the window again. "Not in so many words. All I know is that for the last eighteen months or so, she comes here by cab, takes her orders, and walks up that hill. About an hour later, she comes back down the hill with only the Thermoses and her purse and meets a cab that arrives right about the same time she does. She must schedule the pick-up when he drops her off. Those are the facts. I'm just filling in the blanks. With my instincts." Winking, she pushed her glasses up the bridge of her nose, then jabbed her pencil at her notepad. "Know what you want yet?"

Olive ordered the breakfast special and coffee with cream, then watched Fran swish away. "It's turning out to be quite the coffee-lunch-breakfast date!"

Erik leaned in, his arm stretching across the top of the booth behind her again. She could feel the warmth radiating from him. "And what are *your* instincts telling you, Sherlock?"

"That our new and very helpful friend Fran is on to something. But not what she thinks."

"Explain."

"Darryl isn't sick," Olive said. "He comes to the office to meet Blanche for lunch once a week."

"And you're sure it's Darryl who's coming for her? I hate to sound cynical, but even if he matches the photograph I saw on her desk of the two of them together, that doesn't prove he's her husband."

She smiled in admiration. Not only had he noticed the small framed image on Blanche's desk on the single visit he'd made to her office, but he was willing to question it.

Not bad.

"In this case," Olive replied, "it's one of the very few things I am sure of. Blanche and Darryl invited MetLife staff to a modest reception after their wedding. I know Darryl. He most certainly has not been an inpatient in a facility for eighteen months, let alone one so far from where Blanche lives and works."

Erik bowed his head, lowering his voice. "And then, of course, there's the matter of the receipts you found in the trash."

"Exactly. She threw them away at work, not at home. Is that significant, or just a coincidence? Why does she take out her own trash now? Is she protecting her secrets from Darryl *and* from the janitors? How many secrets does she have?" Olive peered out the window again, toward the ivy-draped building at the top of the hill. "One of those secrets lives there."

"Nice day for a walk," Erik said.

Olive couldn't agree more.

Of all the places Olive had planned to go today, she hadn't expected to find herself at Evercrest Sanitarium. The mahogany walls inside the lobby gave her a closed-in feeling. Sunlight fractured on tree limbs and fell through mullioned windows. Framed paintings of botanicals and bodies of water hung all around the room. If the effect was supposed to be calming, it wasn't working.

Blanche loved someone here. She loved him or her so much that she went out of her way to bring this person comforting foods and coffee on a regular basis. Moreover, she felt she had to do it in secret. Why?

Misgiving threaded through Olive. Was she crossing a line to uncover what Blanche obviously wanted to keep private?

But this was what investigators did. Olive hadn't lied or done anything illegal to get this far in unraveling Blanche's riddle. And she wasn't doing this to be nosy or for a lark.

Of all the unknowns swirling in her mind, this one seemed the least important or urgent. Stella was missing. A woman's body remained unidentified. Someone was sabotaging Olive's efforts at work. And then there was Blanche, who didn't want anyone knowing what she was up to. Olive at least had to consider the possibility that some of these mysteries could be connected.

All of this ran through her mind in the time it took to reach the glass-topped front desk. Behind it, a woman in her late twenties stood and flashed a dimpled smile at Erik. The name on her badge said *Sandra*.

"Good afternoon! How may I help you?" she asked Erik, more than a trifle too eager to please. She tilted her head in that vulnerable way so many males found appealing.

Olive felt a snap of irritation. They were in a sanitarium, for pity's sake, not a church social or an ice cream parlor. No one came here to flirt.

Then she became even more irritated with herself because she realized if it had been Howard Penrose in Sandra's sights, or any man other than the one standing beside her now, feminine wiles wouldn't have bothered her.

One glance at Erik told her that he wasn't taken in by any of it.

Reassured, Olive presented her with a business card. "I'm investigating a missing persons case for MetLife Insurance. I need to see your visitor logbook."

"Our patient records are confidential," Sandra said, her dimple gone.

"I only asked to see your visitors log, which is no more than any other guest sees."

The open book was right there on the countertop, a pen lying in the gutter of its spine. Olive read the script filling the columns and rows, then began scanning the preceding pages.

There. Blanche had signed in for about an hour a few times last week. Olive consulted the receipts in her satchel. The dates matched.

Blanche hadn't used her new married name when signing in but the surname from her first marriage, Eaton. According to the log, the person she was visiting was staying in room 217. The patient's name wasn't listed.

"Tell me you have some film left," Olive murmured to Erik.

While he photographed every page where Blanche had signed her name, Olive scribbled the dates and times in her notebook, just in case anything disrupted the proper development of the images. Blanche had visited three times a week without fail all the way back to January 19, 1914. And always over the lunch hour. Also significant was the fact that no one else visited the patient in room 217. Blanche was the only person the patient ever saw from the outside world.

With a twinge in her chest, Olive flipped back several more pages and found no more entries from Blanche until January 5, 1914, when she had signed in for only thirty minutes. Olive held the page flat while Erik pushed the pin to capture it. She turned back more pages, looking through weeks, months. There was no sign of Blanche visiting before January 5.

She slid the book to the side so she could read the Guest Policy printed on a sheet of paper beneath the glass. She tapped a line of text, drawing Erik's attention to it. New patients were not allowed any visitors for their first month at Evercrest. Then they were allowed one visitor for thirty minutes only. Two weeks later, patients were allowed a one-hour visit. After that, the frequency of visits was at the discretion of the patient's doctor. The pattern matched Blanche's visits. Which meant that whoever the patient was, he or she had been admitted, most likely, on December 5, 1913.

A soft click and whir told her that Erik had taken a photo of the policy. He consulted his watch and put the camera away.

It was time to go. She had what she came for.

———◆———

Instead of dropping Olive off at the bookstore just before three o'clock, Erik announced he'd come in and check out the Mystery Lovers Book Club. Whatever qualms she felt about monopolizing his entire Saturday vanished about twenty minutes later when Warren stepped through the door.

Olive hurried to the group meeting in the back, bending to whisper in Erik's ear. "Warren's here."

At once, Erik was out of his seat, striding toward Warren with outstretched hand. Meeting him near the middle of the store, Warren clasped Erik's hand, and Erik held on as he walked Warren right back outside. Olive lost sight of them, then, and went back to helping customers. It wasn't until after the book club disbanded that Erik returned.

"He won't bother you again." He leaned a hip against the counter but kept an eye on the door.

"How can you be sure?" she asked. One couldn't control another person's actions every hour of every day, after all.

Erik took his time before replying. "Put it this way, then. That man has no business lurking around the store or around you, wherever you may be. I've made that clear to him. If you see him again when I'm not with you, call the police."

The intensity in his eyes brought her heartbeat to her throat. She couldn't guess the words those two men had exchanged, and she didn't feel the need to. She trusted Erik.

"Olive." He captured her gaze with his. "Promise you'll go to the police if necessary? I don't want him around you."

"I promise," she said. And then she invited him to join her for dinner with her aunt and uncle. "There's plenty to share." She wasn't brave enough to tell him that she longed to share it with him. That he deserved to be part of a family, and that she had a wonderful one, ready to embrace him. She didn't yet dare to suggest that she was ready to embrace him, too—as a friend, a partner. Perhaps in time, more.

"Wish I could," he said, "but I've got plans for this evening and the rest of the weekend."

"Of course," she replied, suddenly embarrassed that she'd asked for even more time than he'd already given today. "I'll see you sooner or later, then."

He tipped his hat to her. "Count on it."

CHAPTER TWENTY-TWO

MONDAY, AUGUST 9, 1915

Time was running out.

If Olive didn't learn the identity of the woman buried in Claire's place by Friday, the morgue would send the remains to be buried in an unmarked pauper's grave or donate her skeleton to science. She would be lost all over again. Her body. Her memory. All of it.

Monday was all but gone, and only Olive was still at MetLife. She'd spent hours back at Western Electric's Hawthorne Works in Cicero today, since her phone calls hadn't yielded results. Since the Western Electric information bureau had closed a week ago, Olive no longer had a central place to inquire. She'd walked for miles within the complex, asking department heads if they supervised any female employees who walked with a limp, wore a lift in one shoe, or used a cane.

They didn't. Or rather, they hadn't noticed. Most factory girls sat while working.

Olive could place a notice in the company newsletter, but that wouldn't go out again for almost a month. She asked for permission to speak to each department that employed women, since a coworker was more likely to notice a shortened leg than a supervisor. Her request was denied. The company was scrambling to keep up with demand while being short on staff and having to train new employees. They simply couldn't afford any more disruptions, especially for a ghost who was not on either of the passenger lists they'd compiled.

Jane Doe wasn't a ghost. She'd been flesh and blood, and somewhere a family was grieving her. But Olive wasn't convinced she'd been an employee. She could have been a family member, neighbor, or friend. She might not even have lived in Cicero.

Olive's feet hurt even more than her head. Since there was no one present to offend, she slipped off her heels. Hoping to clear her head, she left her office to pace the reception area, the marble floor cool against her stockinged feet.

What she really needed was coffee. At the counter in the rear corner, she flipped on a light, scooped grounds from the Folgers can, and set the percolator to brew. Inhaling the redolent aroma, she returned to her desk and picked up the reports she'd typed this afternoon. They hadn't been out of her sight since she'd written them, and still she inspected each line to see if anything was missing. She didn't know how her earlier reports had been tampered with, which accounted for her paranoia.

Nothing appeared to be missing, thank goodness.

"Nothing except for Stella and the identity of Jane Doe," she muttered to herself.

Finding a typographical error, she uncapped a pen to correct it. She'd retype it later, unwilling to let Mr. Roth see anything from her that wasn't spotless. The last thing she needed was to give her boss one more ounce of proof that her work was slipping.

The pen scratched against the paper, dry. Tossing it in the waste bin, she pulled at the drawer beneath her desktop. It didn't budge. She'd locked it a few days before the *Eastland* disaster and never had reason to open it again until now.

Bending, she withdrew from her satchel the desk key, unlocked the drawer, and remembered why she'd secured it in the first place.

Covering her extra pens and staples were the files of two separate clients whose benefits had been paid to the same person. She spread them out on her desk and looked at them again.

The percolator sputtered to a finish outside her office door. Olive went and poured herself a cup, then took her first sip while returning to her desk. She'd need all her brain cells alert for this.

"Raymond Murphy." She spoke the beneficiary's name aloud. "Who are you?"

Trading the mug for a fresh pen, she picked up Ernest Murphy's policy and studied it, paying special attention to the amendment dated November 29, 1913, naming Raymond a beneficiary. If they were related, why had Ernest waited almost twenty-three years to add him to the policy?

Olive ran her thumb over Gwendolyn's initials at the bottom of the page, signifying she'd been the one to type up the changes. She could almost hear Gwendolyn's typewriter now, clanging away with its typical force. *"My work speaks for itself,"* Gwendolyn often joked. The keys struck so hard, the letters embossed the back of every page, marking it as hers.

Except this one.

Olive grazed her fingertips over the surface and found it absolutely smooth. She inspected every page in both amendments and found the same thing.

Perhaps Gwendolyn had been exaggerating. There was one way to find out.

After another drink of coffee, Olive went to Gwendolyn's desk, turned on the lamp, and picked up the paper at the top of her outgoing stack. Sure enough, the back of the page was slightly raised by the indenting of characters from the other side. Just to be sure, Olive fed a blank sheet of paper into the Underwood No. 5 and typed a few lines before ripping it out of the machine. The result was the same. The embossing, as Gwendolyn had called it, was slight but easy to see if one was looking for it.

Gwendolyn had used this typewriter since the day she'd been hired. There was no way she had typed those amendments for Ernest and Mathilda, unless she had used someone else's machine. But that was out of the question. Staff didn't swap desks, and even if Gwendolyn had, for some reason, she would have remembered it. She would have said something when Olive asked her about these amendments weeks ago.

Whoever typed these amendments didn't want anyone to find out.

Returning to her own desk, Olive laid the amendments beside the original policies and studied them again. There was something else here, some clue she'd missed, if she could only find it. The type on the amendment was darker than on the policy, and the paper for the policy was a shade more yellow. But that was to be expected. The twenty-five-year-old policy would have faded.

There was nothing for it but to start from the top, comparing everything, beginning with the policy number.

She moved her finger over the string of digits in the original policy. 4987384. Then she did the same on the amendment. 4987384.

She focused on the three and looked at both again. They were different.

The numeral three in the Underwood No. 5 typeface had a straight line at the top, before zagging from the right end of that line down and to the left, then finishing in a backwards c. The numeral three in the amendment was more like two backwards c's stacked on top of each other.

Hurriedly, she examined the rest of the characters. The rest of the letters and numerals looked the same, but that number three—the difference was unmistakable. These amendments had not been typed on an Underwood No. 5 typewriter, the standard issue for MetLife employees.

That was, all except for one. Olive's stomach tilted. Gold lettering emblazoned the black machine on Blanche's desk: *The Oliver Typewriter Co. Chicago U.S.A.*

Three years ago, Blanche's Underwood had broken beyond repair. Their former boss decided to replace it with an Oliver typewriter to support a Chicago business and resolved to do the same whenever anyone else's machine needed replacing. So far, Blanche's was the only one that had.

Slowly, Olive made her way to Blanche's desk and inserted into the Oliver the same piece of paper she'd tested in Gwendolyn's Underwood. This time, she only typed Ernest's policy number.

And there it was. The numeral three with its perfectly rounded curves.

"Oh, Blanche," she whispered. "What have you done?"

In the silence that followed, all she heard were the faint swishes and clanks of the janitors cleaning the floor above her.

Whisking back to her office, she snatched up Mathilda Schmidt's amendment. The policy number had no threes in it, but the date of the amendment did. *January 3, 1914.* That was an Oliver three. Proof enough, in Olive's mind, that Blanche had typed these amendments and, for some unknown reason, marked them as Gwendolyn's work.

Olive let the papers flutter to the desk. Cupping her hands around her cooling mug, she leaned back in her chair. "Why?" she asked.

But there could only be one reason. Those amendments must have been fabricated in order to benefit Raymond Murphy.

Was Raymond blackmailing Blanche? Had he found out she had a loved one at Evercrest Sanitarium and demanded that she pay for his silence?

Shadows slanting across the office melted into the general darkness overtaking the space, but Olive was finally on to something. Ignoring the clock, she drained her mug and took it back to the counter to wash it. Her stomach had soured with her discoveries. She didn't want or need any more coffee.

As Olive put the mug away and cleaned out the percolator, she thought back to the day she'd found these policies and taken them to Gwendolyn. Blanche had seemed concerned that Olive had been in the records room. She'd told her not to do it again, that it wasn't her job. Olive had thought Blanche was looking out for her, but she'd been looking out for herself.

She must have wondered what Olive had seen. She must have gone back to the records room and looked for all the files she'd altered. She would have seen that two were still missing. She must have been scared.

Sweat pricked Olive's hairline as a new thought took hold. She dried her hands, hurried back to her office, and dug out those sloppy reports submitted to Roth as hers. Skimming the interview transcripts, she hunted for numbers—street addresses, dates, times—until she found the number 3 in each of them.

They were all rounded.

It was Blanche.

Stunned, Olive dropped the last report as though she'd been burned. If she had looked through Blanche's trash the first week of her investigation, would she have found her original reports?

Olive couldn't wait to tell Erik what she'd learned.

The phone rang, jarring her nerves. She answered it.

"Olive?" Sylvie's voice carried worry. "It's getting dark. You won't forget your promise not to walk home alone, will you? Take a cab. Or I can call one and have it pick you up at a certain time."

Olive cast a glance toward the window and saw only her reflection. "No, don't call a cab. I don't know how late I'll be, but I'll get a ride home, I promise."

"Are you all right?" she asked.

"I'm making progress, which is more than I've been able to say in a long while."

"But have you eaten?"

Olive assured her aunt that her stomach was well cared for, promised to stay safe, and hung up.

She wiped her palms on her skirt. She ought to go through the policies in the records room and see if more were falsified. Then again, that would take hours, and if Blanche had a hunch Olive was on to her, she might have moved them.

Outside, traffic dwindled to almost nothing as the business

block emptied for the night. A lone horn honked, but Olive barely registered it as she strode back to Blanche's desk. The drawer was locked.

Would it be trespassing to try to open it? Technically, it was MetLife property, not personal property. And Olive was investigating a MetLife case—a handful of them. Besides that, she had probable cause. She had proof of Blanche's tampering, she just didn't know why Blanche was doing it. What else was she hiding? If her secrets could, in any way, shed light on the investigations Blanche had sabotaged, Olive could waste no time in exposing them.

Kneeling on the floor, she borrowed two pins from her hair and used them to pick the lock. Inside, she found a small, framed photograph of Blanche, her first husband, Joe, and a little boy Olive knew nothing about.

Carefully, she eased into Blanche's chair and took the photograph out of the frame. On the back of the image was written, *Our son, Geoffrey, age 5. April 1898.*

Blanche had a son?

Olive flipped the photo over again. Blanche's hands were on Geoffrey's shoulders in a gesture of protection and affection that matched her smile. She would have been forty when this was taken. Which meant she'd been thirty-five when she'd given birth, unless this child had been adopted. Either way, he must have been a miracle to them. Joe's arm disappeared behind Blanche, and it was obvious that he was proud of his little family.

In the seven years Olive had worked with Blanche, she'd never once spoken her son's name.

She looked closer at the image. The little boy had wide-set eyes, ears that tipped out at the top, and a wide open, thousand-watt smile. What a charmer. He'd be twenty-two now. Olive's mind spun through possibilities. Was he still alive? Had he moved away and started his own family? Was he a prodigal son who hadn't yet reconciled with his mother?

Was he the resident in room 217 at Evercrest Sanitarium?

Olive had no way of knowing. But the fact that Blanche kept his likeness hidden did not bode well.

She reached into the desk drawer once more and pulled out a thin leather-bound notebook. Inside, three columns were marked on each page. The columns were not labeled, but the left-hand one clearly held dates. The middle column carried numbers written in dollars and cents, and the column on the far right contained what appeared to be a balance. The debt in the righthand column intermittently increased by a uniform amount and decreased by the amount in the middle column. But the payment dates were several weeks apart, sometimes months. No two entries in the middle column were the same, either.

Then pieces flew together in Olive's mind. The ledger had begun in December 1913, the same month Blanche's loved one had been admitted to Evercrest. She flipped through the pages, looking for the dates Ernest Murphy and Mathilda Schmidt had died. Three weeks after Murphy's death—time enough to process the death benefit—there was an entry. She expected it to be in the exact amount of the benefit paid to Raymond Murphy, but it was less, by $113.42. She looked for an entry two to three weeks after Mathilda Schmidt's death and found one, but the amount in the ledger was $208.59 less than the amount paid to Raymond Murphy.

That didn't mean there was zero connection.

A door slammed down the hallway from the MetLife office. Urgency rising, Olive grabbed a pen and the sheet of paper with her typing samples and copied as many ledger entries as she could, including those that followed Ernest's and Mathilda's deaths.

Her phone rang again, and she jumped. Heart thumping, she hurried back to her office. Then she paused, staring at the telephone. It wouldn't be Sylvie again. Could it be Warren? If she answered and it was him, he would know she was alone here. He wouldn't have to say a word. He could wait for her outside the building.

If she didn't answer, would he wait for her outside anyway? Or would he go to her apartment? And if he did, would Sylvie and Kristof be in danger? Chills fell like water down her spine.

Keys jangled in the lock to the door that led from MetLife's office to the corridor outside.

"Miss?" A security guard, Mr. Bennett, marched toward her, his dark skin blending in with the shadows from which he emerged. "What's going on in here? You need to get going, Miss Pierce. We're locking up for the night."

The phone kept ringing. "Would you answer that, please?" she asked him. "I don't know who it is. I don't know if I want whoever it is knowing I'm here this late at night."

With long strides, Mr. Bennett crossed through reception and entered her office, his crisp blue uniform smelling of starch. He picked up the receiver. "Conway Building, Officer Bennett speaking." His gaze fell to Olive's stockinged feet. "Who's asking?"

Olive held her breath.

"Erik Magnussen?" he repeated for her benefit. "Calling from the *Trib*?"

Relieved, Olive nodded and gestured that she'd take the call herself.

Bennett shook his head. "Miss Pierce is just leaving. We need to lock up the building." He paused, listening, and Olive slipped her heels back on and went to put Blanche's things away. She was locking the drawer when Bennett said, "Right, I'll tell her. See you soon."

"Well?" Olive returned to him and gathered all the files on her desk into one stack that she quickly shoved into her satchel.

"You know this Mr. Magnussen, I take it?"

She assured him she did.

"He's coming to pick you up, if that's all right with you. He wants to escort you home. I'll stay with you until he shows up and you confirm he's the man you're expecting."

"Good." Olive picked up her suit jacket from the back of her chair and shrugged back into it, then pinned her hat in place. Only when she turned off the desk lamp did she realize she'd left one on at Gwendolyn's desk, too.

"I got it." Officer Bennett turned it off, then gave her a wary look.

* * *

At this hour, the shops bordering the rotunda were closed and as dark as the skylights. Exiting the elevator with Officer Bennett, Olive's footsteps echoed in the cavernous space as they crossed to the bronze vestibule. Erik must have raced over from the *Tribune* building a few blocks away, because he was parking on Washington Street five seconds into the security guard's admonition not to work so late in the future. His Ford still pumping exhaust at the curb behind him, he came to the bronze and glass door.

"You feel safe with this man?" Officer Bennett asked.

"The safest," Olive said. She meant it.

With a twist of his keys in the lock, the door opened. Thanking the officer, Olive stepped into the breezy summer night.

Immediately, Erik cupped her elbow. "Are you all right? Why did you let the phone ring for so long? If I hadn't just talked to your aunt on the phone, I would have hung up much sooner. By the twentieth ring, at least." He flashed half a smile while handing her into the passenger side of the car.

Olive waited until he took his place behind the wheel to explain her rationale. "I know you said Warren wouldn't hassle me anymore, and it's not that I don't trust you. I just don't trust *him*. Honestly, I have enough to think about without spending energy being frightened of what he could do. But all alone in that office, I imagined a scenario I didn't want to invite."

Erik turned left onto Clark Street for the one-block ride home. "You did the right thing," he said. "That was smart. We need a code."

"What kind of code?" Wind brushed through the open window, carrying the smell of the nearby river.

"The kind only the two of us know about, so you don't have to answer the phone to know it's me who's calling."

"Oh! Like, one ring, then you hang up, then call with two more rings, and then call again and let it ring?"

"At which point you would pick up the earpiece so the poor man on the other end of the line doesn't imagine his own dark scenario. Agreed?" His Panama hat dropped a shadow to the bridge of his nose.

She studied his profile, measuring how serious he was. "Agreed. Were you really worried?"

The car rolled to a stop outside Corner Books & More. The glow of a streetlamp spilled over it, just barely catching the blue in his eyes. "Yes." He took her gloved hand in his. "Yes," he said again.

She pressed his fingers, at a loss for what to think, let alone say.

"Don't tell me not to," he said. "It's no use. And now, will you tell me what kept you working so late?"

At this, her voice returned. "Better yet, I'll show you." Giving his broad hand one more squeeze, she released it to retrieve the typed and handwritten notes she'd made at the office.

"The number three?" he asked. "You noticed the number three?"

"I only wish I had before. '*The detection of types is one of the most elementary branches of knowledge to the special expert in crime.*'" She wondered if he'd catch that quote from *The Hound of the Baskervilles.*

"Yes, Sherlock," he replied with a grin.

He had.

She went on to explain everything else she'd examined. "I'm trying not to jump to conclusions about Blanche's activities until I know more."

"That's wise." Erik glanced at the light in the apartment above the bookstore. "It's getting late. Your aunt will worry. But before you go, I need to ask—is there anything about Warren or about Claire you're not telling me? I get the feeling there's more to your fear than you've let on so far. I'd like to know just what kind of man we're dealing with."

Without hesitation, Olive filled in the blanks she'd preserved until now, confessing that she'd seen Claire not just once but twice since the disaster, and that in between, Claire had asked Olive to sneak some of her jewelry out of her house so she could pawn them for cash.

"Did anyone see you?" Erik asked.

She hated to tell him someone had. "This was the morning you came to my office the first time," she said. "I had dirt under my nails because Claire's neighbor came over to chat, and pulling weeds was the best excuse I could think of for being there." She went on to explain how she'd left food with Mrs. Feinstein to bring to Warren after work.

"So this Mrs. Feinstein knew you were there, and she probably told Warren, too. Did he ever mention it to you later?"

"No. It's possible Mrs. Feinstein took credit for the biscuits I made. But if he ever looked through Claire's jewelry box after that and saw that some pieces were missing . . ." Olive dragged in a breath and controlled a long exhale. "If Warren figured out that the jewelry didn't go missing until after July 24, he ought to suspect I took it. He ought to suspect I've been in contact with Claire to get it to her."

"Olive." Erik leaned back against the bench, his shoulders slanting with the gravity of what she'd just shared. "Do you know where she is?"

"I told you I don't. I never lied to you, Erik. I have no idea where she is. You have to believe me."

"I do."

CHAPTER TWENTY-THREE

TUESDAY, AUGUST 10, 1915

When Olive arrived at the bustling Conway Building the next morning, she was determined to talk to Blanche. She needed to give her coworker a chance to explain herself.

As soon as she reached the MetLife office, Blanche hurried over to greet her, silver bracelets jingling. "Roth asked to see you right away. He doesn't want you to stop at your desk. Just go directly to his office." She pressed her lips into a thin, sharp line. "For what it's worth—if anything—I'm sorry."

Olive's mouth went dry. Marching past Gwendolyn, she stiffened her spine, entered Roth's office, and closed the door behind her.

Roth smoothed his dark hair, though by the smell of it, there was enough Brilliantine holding it in place that he needn't have bothered. On his desk, the mug beside the newspaper was already empty. He exhaled. "You're dismissed, Miss Pierce."

She frowned. "I thought you wanted to speak with me."

"I am dismissing you from your position at MetLife. You're fired."

She sat in the closest chair.

"Don't make this any harder with histrionics, all right? Facts are facts. And the fact is, you knew Claire Sterling was alive, and you knew her death benefit was being processed, and you said nothing. Correct?"

She didn't deny it.

"Hiding the truth allowed a life insurance payment to be approved for Warren Sterling for his presumed-dead-but-still-living wife. Thank goodness we were able to stop the processing of the check before it was actually paid out. But you know what this is. Insurance fraud, or an attempt at it."

"That wasn't my intention—"

"Your intention is irrelevant. I'm looking at cold hard facts, Miss Pierce, and even beyond this huge infraction, in the last few weeks, you have missed meetings, botched your own investigations with sloppy reporting that had to be redone, and now I've heard from both the janitor and the security guard that you've been here late at night doing who knows what."

"I can explain."

He raised a palm to stop her. "Mr. Bennett says you were at Gwendolyn's desk and Blanche's, and that you were in your stocking feet, as if you didn't want to be heard. Now, we could sit here and argue, but whatever you say, it won't help your case. You have so successfully damaged your credibility that I won't believe you. You're terminated from your position at MetLife, effective immediately. Understood?"

She'd never be able to work at an insurance company again. Her mind whirred. "What about my open cases? Stella Petroski and the unknown woman who was buried in Mrs. Sterling's grave?"

"They go to Howard, who will close them promptly."

"But those are ongoing investigations!"

"Have you new leads? If so, I'm sure Howard will see them in your reports and follow up accordingly. But we've already wasted more than enough resources on those two. Now I'm down an agent and will have to hire another. We don't have any more time to waste on lost causes."

Defeat tightened Olive's throat. She had failed Stella and her family. She'd failed this other woman, whose battered remains had given Claire the means to escape. Neither could be properly mourned by their grieving families. Guilt lined her belly with lead.

"Miss Pierce? I asked to see inside your bag."

Heat rolled over her. She knew what he'd find. Still, she let him look.

Outside, the shoeshine boys' voices dimmed against the clamor of horses, trains, streetcars, and automobiles. The atmosphere seemed stuffed with sound, and yet this office throbbed with quiet while Roth rifled through her bag.

"Company files?" He slapped Ernest's and Mathilda's policies on his desk. "Good grief, Miss Pierce! You've been here long enough to know this is company property and not to be removed from the premises. Why did you take them home with you? To tamper with them?"

"No, no, I would never," she choked out. "These are closed cases, already processed, but let me show you what I found. These amendments both had the same—"

"I don't want to hear another word. The integrity and reputation of Metropolitan Life is on the line. If you want to avoid being taken to court, I suggest you thank your lucky stars that your only consequence is termination. It brings me no pleasure to have to do this." He flung her satchel back at her. "Leave now, before I change my mind."

———◆———

Drizzle misted Olive's face and beaded the brim of her hat. She stood on the Clark Street Bridge and watched the work crews tasked with lifting the *Eastland*, which was still resting on its side in the riverbed. Three tugboats surrounding it puffed coal-black clouds into the gunmetal sky.

The ship could not be raised. The holes in the hull hadn't been sealed up properly, so as the crew pumped water out, the river rushed right back in. The wreck could not be righted. Five hours into her unemployment, Olive felt a little something like that wreck herself. Exposed. Stagnant.

Useless.

She had failed in her duty to Stella, Jane Doe, and their families. She'd made promises she hadn't kept. She'd floundered, and now she'd fallen so completely that she'd never be able to rise up as an insurance investigator again. Like the *Eastland*, she took up space but went nowhere. She was no good to the families she'd so desperately wanted to help. What would they do now?

Drays and trucks shook the bridge as they rattled by. Nothing felt stable, not the water that flowed below or the vibrating steel beneath her feet. No longer anchored to her purpose, she felt herself drifting. Sinking.

"I almost didn't come." Howard Penrose materialized out of the mist, snapping the line of her thoughts. He shifted his umbrella to shield her, too, despite his foul mood. "To be very frank, I don't mind that you were fired, but I *do* mind that you almost dragged me down with you. I was the one who processed the claim for the Sterlings. You knew Claire was alive, and you didn't tell me. How long were you going to let that go? If we hadn't caught it and canceled it, that would have gone on my record, too. I would have looked incompetent at best and criminal at worst. Did you think of that?"

"I don't blame you for being upset," she said quietly. "Believe me, if there had been another way—"

"There was another way. You made your choice, and you had your reasons. But you didn't ask to meet with me so you could apologize. So what's this about?"

"I *do* apologize," she began. "But you're right. That's not all I wanted to say. I was on to something last night. Something big. You'll want to talk to Blanche about it yourself, but I need to tell you what I learned."

She told him everything about the policy files and Evercrest Sanitarium. "We took photographs of the visitor ledger. I can get

229

those for you soon, if you need them. But in the meantime, look at those files Roth took from my satchel this morning." She told him about the different typefaces and how she'd identified the change in the amendments and in her own reports. Under the umbrella's protection, she showed him the paper she'd typed on last night, along with her handwritten copy of some of the ledger, both of which he snapped into his briefcase.

"Will you look into it?" she pressed. "Please. I've gone as far as I can with it. An hour ago, I went to the courthouse but hit a dead end. I wanted to see the copies of Ernest Murphy's and Mathilda Schmidt's insurance policies that were filed there. Any lawful amendments ought to have been filed there, too. If I—if *you* could get a look at those policies, and if you found the amendments to pay benefits to Raymond Murphy were not on record, you would have more evidence that the policies had been falsified."

"Did you ask to see them yourself?"

"Of course," she admitted. "But since I'm no longer employed by MetLife, I wasn't allowed to. You have to look into it yourself. Find and talk to Raymond Murphy, too. His address is on file."

Howard cocked his head to one side, disdain sketched across his face. "You're in no position to tell me what I have to do. You never were, no matter how much you wanted to be."

She bit back a sharp retort that would serve no purpose. "Please. This needs your attention."

He looked down his nose at her. "I don't answer to you, Olive. I suppose next you'll tell me to keep looking for Stella Petroski, but it's over. She's gone. Her body may never be found. The best we can do is let time run its course. She'll be declared dead eventually."

"That will take years!" Pressure built, helplessness pinching her ribs with each breath. "Please, don't give up so soon. I'm sure there's something I missed, some clue in the file I overlooked that you'll catch if you only try." She gripped the railing, her gloves wet and sticking to her skin. Her incompetence clung tighter.

He shrugged, then tipped back the umbrella so he could see

the clock on the Reid Murdoch Building across the river. "I need to get back. And you need to let go." With a dip of his chin, he turned and left.

Was he right?

Rain fell harder, tapping Olive's hat and stippling the river. It drummed against the *Eastland*'s metal side. She closed her eyes, and she was right there on the hull, grasping tight to Michael and Addie. Waiting for Claire to come back. Hoping that Stella would find them.

Olive's heart rate spiked with a force that left her gasping for air all over again.

Olive had told Erik everything. But she didn't want to tell him this.

A little before five o'clock, he came to Corner Books & More and found her restocking shelves with the latest inventory shipment while Sylvie rang up purchases for the last customers of the day.

"Olive?" His approach carried a restrained urgency. "You didn't answer your phone. Tell me what's wrong."

She'd really rather not. She couldn't explain how she'd already grown to care so deeply what he thought of her. All she knew was that she couldn't abide the thought of losing his esteem, and she couldn't see her way around it.

A few lights in the store went out, and drapes snapped shut, blocking the meager sun. With a swish of her mauve gabardine skirt, Sylvie wove her way toward them. Earlier today, she'd offered Olive a job as her assistant, and Olive hadn't said no. But even now her aunt treated her gently, as though bumping into her might break her to pieces.

"I've just locked up," Sylvie said. "Take the time you need, dears. Just remember the lights when you're done, and lock up again when Erik leaves, all right?" With a warm smile, she left them alone.

Gathering her thoughts, Olive slid two copies of *Wuthering Heights* onto the shelf.

Erik took the remaining three volumes of *Jane Eyre* from her arms and placed them beside *Villette*. "It's not Warren, is it?"

She shook her head. "I was fired this morning."

His eyebrows plunged. "What?"

Tears threatened. She turned away to hide them and made her way to the closest pair of armchairs, dropping into the leather seat. On the table beside her, a lamp with a stained-glass shade scattered gold, green, and blue light in the shape of dragonfly wings.

Erik took the opposite chair, setting his briefcase on the floor. "What happened?"

Dashing the back of her hand against her cheek, she relayed every word that had passed between her and Roth and her meeting with Howard over lunch.

"I knew it might happen," she added quietly. "When I agreed to give Claire more time before requesting an exhumation. I knew I could lose my job for it and that Roth would be well within his rights to terminate me."

"But you chose to protect your friend anyway."

"I don't regret that. But now I've lost my cases." The book spines on the shelf behind him blurred. "What you must think of me. A failure."

Erik covered her hand with his. "Olive. Look at me." His voice reached out to her, lifting her chin. "I think you're loyal, brave, compassionate, whip-smart, and a fine investigator who ought to be working."

"Based on my track record?" She nearly snorted.

"Based on your methods and the way your mind works. Give yourself some credit. You've been given very little to work with in finding Stella and the identity of the woman buried in Claire's place. And the mystery surrounding Blanche? My guess is that if you'd had one more day to investigate, you would have cracked that case wide open. You were well on your way last night. All you need to do is find Raymond Murphy and his relationship to Blanche."

"Hopefully Howard will find that link."

Erik leaned back in his chair, unbuttoned his jacket, and rested his elbows on the chair arms, hands clasped. "You're not going to stop investigating just because you aren't employed by MetLife, are you?"

Olive felt a quickening inside, one that grew the longer she regarded this man who believed in the importance of her work. Who believed, it seemed, in her. "Not a chance."

"I didn't think so." His smile reflected her own. "In that case, you might be interested in seeing the photos we took on Saturday." He tapped his briefcase.

"Yes!" She sprang to her feet. "Spread them out on the checkout counter, if you don't mind," she said, already striding toward it. "That way we can get a panoramic view of the neighborhood."

Erik laid the glossy black-and-white photographs side by side, and Olive inspected them, left to right, pleased that the details had come through so clearly. There was Flo's Kitchen. Then there was the oak in the front yard, and next, the street that passed in front of it. That blur was a child pedaling by on his bicycle in front of a parked Model T.

And there was Olive at the edge of the frame, smiling as she held her hat against the wind. She hadn't thought she'd be in the picture.

The next photograph showed the adjacent view of the same neighborhood, but still with Olive on one side.

"I thought you were aiming the camera near me, not at me," she said.

"And pass up capturing that smile?"

At least he'd focused on the background, so the image of her in the foreground remained fuzzy. But the next image—

"Erik, this is a portrait!" She was centered and in sharp focus, while the trees and cars behind were not. Her eyes shone, and her expression was free of self-consciousness despite the tendrils of hair caught by the breeze. "I had no idea you were paying any attention to me."

"Then your powers of observation are slipping."

She looked up at him and found the steadiness in his gaze so serious that it belied the small smile resting on his lips.

"I like paying attention to you," he said.

Perhaps he was too near for her to think straight, because right now she could almost believe that she wasn't the only one here who could imagine a relationship that went beyond friendship. Perhaps she ought to step to the side, away from him, but then she wouldn't be able to see the rest of the photographs.

Turning back to the counter, she edged to the right to see what was next, and her pulse kicked up another notch. This was the photograph Fran had insisted on taking inside the restaurant. While Olive had been almost laughing in Fran's direction, Erik had been smiling at Olive.

"Aren't you supposed to look at the camera when someone's taking a picture of you?" she asked.

"I like looking at you." Angling to face her, he tucked an errant lock of hair behind her ear. "I like being near you. I like being *with* you."

A smile tugged up one corner of her mouth. His words were so simple, completely without guile or artifice. If he'd soliloquized with flowery praise, she wouldn't trust him farther than she could throw him. She'd wonder how long he'd practiced such a speech, and if such lines had ever worked for him with a woman before. She'd push him away, determined not to be taken in by empty romanticism.

But she didn't want to push Erik away. She wanted him in the picture with her, and in her life, even beyond these investigations that had brought them together. So when he slipped his hands around her waist, she wasn't sure if he was the one gently drawing her near, or if she had willingly closed the space between them. All she knew was that she was exactly where she wanted to be.

"I'm sorry you lost your job," he said. "But you haven't lost me."

She straightened his tie, then smoothed it down behind his vest. "So we can go on solving riddles together? I'm beginning to think you may be in this relationship just for the mysteries."

Erik's smile dispelled that notion. "I'm in it for you."

Heat washed through Olive. His gaze dropped to her lips and lingered a moment. When he bent his head, a question in his eyes, it took only a heartbeat for her to answer. There were many unknowns in her life, but Erik wasn't one of them. If she was certain of anything, it was him.

She stretched up and curved one hand around his neck, yielding to his encircling arms. His kiss, careful and soft, was no impulsive whim. Rather, it was a seal on the regard he'd been showing her almost since the moment they met.

Olive kissed him back in equal measure, fingers curling into his hair. Then she lowered her arms, tucked her head beneath his chin, and listened to the pounding in his chest.

"Maybe I should have asked you first," Erik murmured. "We can pretend it never happened if you'd rather."

"Actually, I believe I'll spend considerable time reminding myself that it did." Warmth fanned through her all over again.

Chuckling, he pressed a kiss to the top of her head. "That makes two of us."

A few moments later, something caught Olive's eye.

Pulling away from Erik, she tapped the edges of two photographs. "Did you already notice this?"

His hand settled at her waist while he looked at the images. "Tell me what you see."

"This car." She pointed to one parked on a side street. "Now look at this photo Fran took of us in the booth. Over my shoulder, you can see the front door has opened and a customer is walking in."

"The booth obscures him. All we can see is a hat."

"Yes, but look at that boater. The straw brim is bent awry." She picked up a pair of reading glasses Sylvie had on her desk and held a lens over the photograph. "See?"

"I do. What does this mean to you?"

"When Warren came to the bookstore the day of the exhumation, he was so beside himself that he crushed his boater while accusing me of conspiring against him. By the time he reseated it on his head, it didn't look much better than this."

"All right." Erik shifted, resting both palms on the counter. "But I'm sure Warren isn't the only man with a less-than-pristine boater."

"Of course. But the car." She moved the magnifier over the front bumper. "That's his license plate. That was him. Warren was following us, probably from the time we left my apartment that morning until he tried to confront me in the bookstore during the meeting. He was in the restaurant, Erik." She covered her mouth. This was so much worse than him popping over to the bookstore to spout off. "Did we talk about Claire? What did he hear?" *And what will he do next?*

Shadows darkened Erik's face. "You didn't tell me you'd been in contact with Claire until I drove you home last night. And thank goodness for that."

"Why am I not more relieved?" She rubbed the sides of her arms, suddenly cold. "You talked to him after he followed us, not before, so it's possible he's backed off since then." When he gave her a dubious look, she asked, "What exactly did you say to him, anyway?"

"You don't want to know." Erik scanned the empty bookshop. "I need to go soon for rowing practice with the boys at Lincoln Park. But before I leave, I want to check your apartment. Who's on the floor above you?"

"Kristof's brother, Gregor, and his wife live on the fourth floor, but they've been gone since early June, touring with a festival."

236

"You've got an empty apartment directly above you?" A muscle tensed in his jaw. "I'll need to check that one, too."

Borrowing the keys from Sylvie, he did, then searched Olive's home for an intruder, too. At last, he was satisfied that Warren wasn't there.

That didn't mean Warren wouldn't try later.

And it didn't mean he hadn't already been here.

The notion leapt upon Olive only after Erik had left. They'd both noticed a faint smell of smoke but had found the source by looking out the open living room window. A few men coming from the Sherman House hotel had lit up their Lucky Strikes outside Corner Books & More.

Now, Olive's confidence ebbed away. She always had with her the photo of Claire from Mr. Fujita. But she couldn't find the last letter Claire had sent to update her post office box. It was the letter Warren had spied at the bookstore the same day he learned the woman he'd buried wasn't his wife.

Where was it now? For the life of her, she could not recall if she'd burned it after reading it at her aunt and uncle's apartment. She checked the pocket of the dress she'd been wearing that day, then sifted through the mail, and found nothing. If Warren had been here in her absence and taken it, he would know at least the post office Claire used. He could find her from there.

Shaken, she rushed to the hearth and knelt, gauging the ashes still there. There were too many ashes to be from only the first letter and envelope Claire had sent. Olive must have burned the second set as well. So even if Warren had been here—and she had found no evidence at all that he had—he would have found nothing incriminating.

Nothing, that was, except for a small pile of ashes in a hearth in summer.

Dread turned sticky on her skin. Among the smooth black flakes that had once been paper was a dusting of white and grey powder. In her mind's eye, she saw Warren kneeling in this very spot, poking his finger through the charred remains of the letters, looking for clues, then sweeping it all back into a mound with his hands. She saw him tap his cigarette over the mess. She saw his smoke curling, hovering. Smelled it still.

Nonsense. The door was locked, and there had been no sign of tampering. If Warren had been careful enough not to leave a single item out of place in the apartment, surely he wouldn't be careless enough to add his own ashes to the hearth. If, in fact, those were cigarette ashes at all.

Then it occurred to her that Warren might not be the only one interested in searching Olive's apartment. If Blanche had overheard Mr. Roth say that she'd taken files home with her, wouldn't she wonder if Olive had kept other incriminating evidence? Would she go so far as to pick the lock to the apartment, just as Olive had picked the lock to Blanche's desk drawer? Olive sat on her heels, wondering. Again, she reminded herself that nothing was out of place in her apartment. And again, she saw Blanche's neat-as-a-pin desk, her empty waste bin. If anyone could search a place without detection, Olive mused, Blanche could.

More groundless imagining.

Exhaling her paranoia, Olive swept the hearth clean. These ashes weren't even worth mentioning to Erik.

With a little thrill, she touched her lips. Was he courting her now? He hadn't said so. In fact, when he bade her good night, he had only kissed her cheek and made her promise to be safe. She'd been ready to promise him more than that, and by the look in his eyes, she'd thought he had been, too. But there would be time for declarations later.

Meanwhile, she had things to do.

CHAPTER TWENTY-FOUR

WEDNESDAY, AUGUST 11, 1915

Olive had meant what she'd said yesterday. She wasn't going to quit just because she'd been fired. How was that for a bit of irony? Even more ironic was the fact that while Howard Penrose still had a job, he was refusing to do it.

At least, that was how it seemed to Olive.

"What do you mean, a dead end?" Gripping the telephone earpiece, she stood at her living room window. Beyond the courthouse, the top of the white Conway Building disappeared in fog. She imagined Howard ensconced in his office with his feet up on the desk. Convinced he ought to have found Raymond Murphy by now, she had called him this morning to end the suspense.

"Not that I answer to you," he grumbled, "but I looked up the address on file for Murphy and called the telephone number listed for that apartment building. It turns out Murphy never lived there. Furthermore, the resident who did live at that address died a few months ago. Buried with military honors, the landlord said, as a GAR veteran." The GAR was the Grand Army of the Republic, veterans who served in the Civil War.

"What was his name?"

A shuffling of papers rattled over the wire. "Fisher. Jeremiah Fisher. He wasn't a client of ours."

"Why would Murphy have used his address?" Olive began thinking aloud. "Obviously he didn't want to be found, which means he knew he was doing something wrong. Murphy must have trusted Fisher, because any insurance correspondence would have had to go through his address, including money sent after processing a death benefit. They had some kind of relationship. They must have."

Howard sighed, and in the pause that followed, Gwendolyn's typewriter clanged in the background. "It could have been a clerical error."

"I don't believe that. If that were the case, the check we sent him at that address would have been returned to us. But I'll bet it was deposited in Murphy's bank account, which you could confirm, if you haven't already. If the money reached him, it was through Jeremiah Fisher."

"Olive, the trail has gone cold. Fisher is dead. We have no idea where Murphy could be now."

"The trail is just heating up," she countered. If the telephone cord didn't tether her so, she'd be pacing her living room in her heels, unable to keep still. She'd dressed for work today, and she was ready for it. "Keep going. You can't stop now."

"Enough of this. It's over. You don't work here anymore, remember?"

"Apparently neither do you, if you're not going to pursue the connection between Murphy and Fisher!"

The words rushed out on a wave of frustration and helplessness. It was the wrong thing to say. She heard a click as Howard hung up.

Olive replaced the earpiece in the fork and crossed her arms, staring vacantly at the fog that leveled the skyline. She could have handled that better. But the nagging thought would not leave her that Howard wasn't handling it at all. He'd called it a dead end, a cold trail, when it was actually another stepping-stone to the truth.

If Howard wouldn't follow where it led, she would. After all, the next step was only a few blocks away.

The fog had lifted by the time she reached the Chicago Public Library. The Randolph Street entrance was closer, but Olive preferred to go around the five-story stone building and enter from Washington Street instead.

Inside the main lobby of white Carrara marble, she crossed over a huge seal of the city of Chicago set into the floor and climbed the grand staircase. On the second floor, three arched doorways led into the main rotunda, which was awash with light from chandeliers and the largest Tiffany dome in the world. Veined marble columns led to the dazzling mosaic ceiling, covered with flowering vines. Beneath the dome, a long mahogany counter separated the librarians from the patrons. Olive took her place in line.

A few minutes later, she requested the book containing lists of all the regiments Chicago had sent to serve the Union between 1861 and 1865. After another wait for the librarian to retrieve it from the closed stacks, Olive took the book to the Reading Room.

With its soaring floor-to-ceiling windows, this space, too, was flooded with natural light. Olive's footsteps magnified in the silent room, where the only sound was the turning of pages. She sat at a long wooden table, and her surroundings faded away as she focused on the information before her.

It didn't take long to find Jeremiah Fisher in the index. Perched on the edge of her chair, she turned to the roster of soldiers in his regiment and skimmed her gloved fingertip over the list of names, looking for Raymond Murphy. She realized there was only a small chance that their connection had been through the war. Murphy would have been too young to fight, if his birthdate in the MetLife files could be trusted. He and Fisher might have been work colleagues instead, or they might have attended the same church. Any number of possibilities sprang to mind. But this was the one most easily investigated, so it was where she would start.

"There!" Olive didn't realize she'd spoken aloud until three other readers at her table shushed her. But right there in black and white, Raymond Murphy was listed as a drummer boy in Jeremiah Fisher's regiment. He would have been fourteen at the time. It fit.

Olive sat back in her chair and let her gaze wander to the silverleaf coffered ceiling. As a GAR member, Fisher would have attended meetings here at Memorial Hall in this very building. Would Murphy have done the same?

It wouldn't be hard to find out.

Leaving the Reading Room behind her, she made her way across the library to the section dedicated to the GAR. Hoping to find a docent or officer of the veterans group, she passed through another rotunda and entered the somber GAR Memorial Hall. It was mostly empty, save for a few patrons studying displays of battle flags and other Civil War artifacts. Her grandfather's photograph was among them, along with excerpts of his memoir about being a prisoner at Andersonville. But she wasn't here to pay tribute to him today.

Still armed with the library book, she swung back into the rotunda room and crossed to the small office tucked into a corner. She couldn't see anything through the frosted-glass window, but the door was slightly ajar. She knocked on it.

"Come in."

Olive stepped inside, pleased to see Captain Jameson, a white-haired veteran she'd met during a previous visit. Smile lines creased his face when he recognized her, though it had been months since they'd last seen each other.

He stood tall in his blue wool uniform as he greeted her. "You look as though you've something on your mind. Can I help?"

"I hope so. I'm trying to track down a man listed as a beneficiary for a MetLife claim."

"That's right, you mentioned that you worked there."

"I did," Olive said but didn't add that she'd been fired. "The address on file for him is outdated. His name is Raymond Murphy, and I see he was a drummer boy in the war." She patted the book in her arms. "If he's an active member in the GAR, I assume you'd have his address. If so, would you be willing to share that with me?"

Captain Jameson ran a brown-spotted hand over his neatly trimmed beard. "Raymond Murphy? Oh yes, he's a member. Never misses a meeting."

Olive's heart skipped a beat. She'd found him. "Wonderful."

"However, the addresses we have for our members are strictly confidential. It's against policy to give out personal information. If you like, I could leave him a note that you were looking for him and ask that he update his records with MetLife. Will that do?"

It would not. If he didn't want to be found, warning him that MetLife was searching for him wouldn't go over well. Olive was searching for a suitable reply when she spotted a paper on the captain's desk. An agenda for the next meeting, to be held at ten o'clock on Monday, August 16.

The captain followed her gaze. "Oh, yes. He'll be there, if you'd like to just talk to him afterward."

"That would be perfect. You're sure he's coming?"

"He'd better. He's making a committee report." Captain Jameson smiled.

So did Olive.

Raymond Murphy would be right here five days from now. So would she.

Howard needed to be here, too, and she'd tell him as much as soon as she could call him. She was practically tying a bow on this case for him to unwrap. The least he could do was show up.

CHAPTER TWENTY-FIVE

THURSDAY, AUGUST 12, 1915

With an unladylike grunt, Olive shoved open the window in the rear of Corner Books & More and set the fan on the broad sill, then switched it on. With the mercury only at seventy-three degrees so far, the store wasn't overly warm, but she was. She welcomed the air feathering her face.

The last time she'd done this very thing had been during her meeting with Jun Fujita. So much had happened since then, yet the one thing she most wanted to change had stayed stubbornly the same.

What was finding Raymond Murphy worth when Stella remained missing?

A hand came gently to her elbow. "You look deep in thought," Sylvie said.

"Very deep," Olive admitted.

"I understand," her aunt murmured, and Olive knew she did. "How about something new to think about? That was the postman just now. This came for you." With a knowing smile, she handed Olive a package with a return address of the Anne of Green Gables Fan Club. "Off with you, now."

Olive bounded up the stairs to her apartment and opened the parcel.

A note dropped from between layers of tissue paper. Olive snatched it up and immediately realized Claire had sent this in response to her letter asking for Jane Doe's clothes.

Dear Miss Pierce,

My apologies for the delay in sending the costume pieces you requested for your next L. M. Montgomery Fan Club meeting. Your letter had gone to the wrong address and had to be forwarded. Furthermore, the enclosed clothing had been pawned (in a regrettable lapse of judgment, obviously) but I was finally able to locate and buy it back. I'm still trying to reclaim the jewelry. Again, please accept my sincerest apologies for not sending you the items sooner. I believe they'd been used to portray the scene in which Anne Shirley and her friends reenact the water voyage of the Lady of Shalott. As you recall, the canoe springs a leak and sinks. Hence the water stains.

Best wishes on all your endeavors.

> *Yours, as ever,*
> *Claire Barrymore*
> *President, Illinois Chapter,*
> *AoGG Fan Club*

A postscript identified a new post office box at which she could be reached.

Olive crossed to the living room, where light fell through the window and landed in rainbows on the rug. She ran her fingertips over a dingy white cardigan sweater. The fine crochet work held intricate floral patterns and vines cascading down the bell-shaped sleeves and dancing along the hem.

From the right pocket, Olive removed a folded square of fabric. A note pinned to it read, *This was tied around her neck.* She opened the yellow silk scarf and found the black Western Electric logo emblazoned on one corner. The company's name spanned a map of the United States, flanked by candlestick telephones and outstretched wings.

Hope flared. Now Olive knew that Jane Doe had indeed worked at Hawthorne Works and had done so for at least one year prior to July 24. During her time in Cicero, Olive had seen dozens of women with the same scarf and had learned it was the company's standard gift to ladies to mark one year of service.

Olive bowed her head over the sweater and scarf, struck with reverence for what she held and the life it represented.

"Please, God," she prayed. "I need to know who this woman is. I need your help laying her to rest. Guide my steps today. Direct my path."

She needed to manage her expectations. The last time she'd gone to Hawthorne Works, she'd been looking for a needle in a haystack. Now she knew what the needle had been wearing on July 24, but the analogy still held. It was overwhelming.

A sense of impending defeat drizzling over her, Olive leaned back against the sofa cushions and imagined how her mission would play out. As she did, her gaze traveled over the wedding photographs on the mantel. Still holding Jane Doe's sweater, Olive crossed to the fireplace and regarded the images of herself at Walter's and Hazel's ceremonies. She wore the same fixed smile, and though her siblings had been married a few years apart, the same dress in both. After all, she only had one best dress, and it still fit just fine.

She gasped. That was it!

The annual Western Electric picnic was such a grand event that employees went every year if they could. If Jane Doe had earned a scarf for one year's service by this year's picnic, that meant she'd been working at Hawthorne last summer, too. Chances were good that she'd gone to last year's picnic. This year, no one had a chance to take photographs of all the ladies in their Sunday best at their destination.

Last year, they had.

And just like Olive had worn the same dress to both her siblings' weddings, if Jane Doe had been anything like thousands of other frugal Western Electric employees, she would have worn the same finery this year that she had last year.

Olive's mind whirled. Laying the sweater back in its tissue paper nest, she burned Claire's letter, cleaned the hearth, then hurried to the satchel she'd left on a kitchen chair. She pulled out the August edition of *Western Electric News*, the monthly employee newspaper she'd picked up at Hawthorne.

She spread it over the table, though she had read every word at least three times already. It began with letters from the Western Electric Company president and the Hawthorne Works general superintendent. It carried condolences, articles, eyewitness accounts. Pages upon pages named the employees and their relatives who had died on the *Eastland*.

But the name she looked for was not among the dead. She flipped to page twenty-two, to an article titled, "What the Survivors Tell." The photograph taking up the top half of the page showed the *Eastland* docking at Michigan City for the picnic last year. According to the caption, it was taken by C. W. Robbins of the cable plant. Had he taken other photographs that day, of the ladies' beauty pageant, the potato sack races, the dance? If he hadn't, he would know who had.

Olive circled the name with her pen. For one sinking moment, she checked the columns of the dead to see if Mr. Robbins was listed. He was not. Heaven help her, she would find him by this afternoon.

◆

The end of the day, however, found her barreling back home on the streetcar without Jane Doe's identity in hand. Mr. Robbins had no leisure to show pictures to an unemployed, disgraced, former insurance agent. At least, that was what his supervisor had told her. She'd waited just outside his building section, hoping to catch Mr. Robbins alone should he leave for a break. Before she had a chance, the supervisor spied her and informed her that if she didn't leave company property at once, he'd have the Hawthorne police escort her off the premises.

Forcing back a sigh of frustration, Olive shifted on the worn leather bench as the streetcar stopped for more passengers. Commuters filled the benches and the aisle, feet planted wide while they grasped leather loops attached to the ceiling. The doors clanged shut, and cologne, perfume, and cigarette smoke thickened the air despite the open windows.

The car lurched into motion, heading east on Madison Street. When it crossed the river's south branch, smells of coal dust and chemical waste tinged the air, unlocking memories of tasting that foul water in a fight for life that Olive had won while hundreds had not. She had hoped that by now, the sensations from that day would stay buried. But smell was a powerful key. The disaster pressed in on her with an immediacy that defied all reason.

"Clark Street stop!" The conductor called out from the rear, and only then did she realize the wheels had halted. "This is Clark Street!"

Olive joined the people shuffling out of the car. Nearby, a train clattered past on the El. At the corner of Clark and Lake, she paused. This was where the thousands who had come for the picnic had gotten off too.

Pedestrians streamed around her. Memories eddied. The world might soon forget what had happened here, but Olive wouldn't. She wouldn't forget the ones who died, nor the ones still missing, nor the part she and Claire had played in that. It was the sort of regret that might be buried but would never go away.

An arm slipped around her waist and held her firm.

"Erik! I didn't see you." Yet there was no one else she'd rather encounter. She'd been so busy lately that she hadn't realized how much she missed him.

His lips edged up. "I find that difficult to believe, given that I was standing right in front of you."

She smiled at the echo of when they'd first met. His tender gaze held more than friendship, bringing a flush to her cheeks. "I'm sorry, I was distracted. What are you doing here?"

"Waiting for you. Your aunt told me where you went, and I figured you'd get off at this stop." He took her hand and pressed a kiss to it before lacing his fingers with hers. "Hungry?"

"Starved."

"Then let's grab dinner, if you have time. Lamb's Café?"

She agreed. Lamb's was in the basement of the Olympic Theater at the corner of Clark and Randolph. It was mere steps from her apartment building.

Minutes later, they were ducking under the vaudeville theatre's awning and entering the basement café. Forest-green carpet covered broad marble steps descending into the restaurant. Landscape murals made up for the lack of windows, and globe-shaped chandeliers offered their own soft light. It was the nicest place they'd been together. Olive supposed this was their first official date.

Once seated at a white linen-draped table, she updated Erik on all that had happened yesterday and today, pausing only so they could place their orders when the waiter came.

Erik remained strangely quiet as she told him of her afternoon at Hawthorne Works. "You didn't get to speak to Robbins, but would you consider your visit there a total waste?" he finally asked. On the opposite side of the café, a small jazz band began tuning their instruments.

"No." She leaned forward to be heard. "I left a business card with as many department heads as I could, scratching out the MetLife phone number and address and penning in my own. At least now they can contact me if they think of anything helpful." She doubted they would, though, especially now that they knew she no longer worked with MetLife.

He nodded. Behind him, a draft stirred the artificial greenery wrapping a supportive pillar. "Did you see Jakob?"

An ache spread from her chest as she recalled her visit to his home. "I did. He called for me at the office yesterday and learned from Blanche that I'm no longer with MetLife. Apparently she transferred him to Howard, who painted a bleak picture about the likelihood of finding Stella at this point."

A knot swelled at the base of her throat as she remembered Jakob sharing this with her on his front porch. She could still see Michael clutching his baseball, listening to everything, his little face growing dark with confusion and then darker still with understanding. Mosquito bites covered his arms and legs, and the boy scratched them harder and harder until they bled. With a harsh word, Jakob told him to stop and to see his grandmother for a lotion to make him stop itching. *"That's Mommy's job,"* the child had shouted. *"No one else can do it!"*

"What did you say to him?" Erik asked.

"I told him I wasn't ready to give up, but the way Jakob looked at me . . . he doesn't believe I'll find her, and I don't blame him."

"Well, you're closer to answers now than you've ever been. One case might be connected to the other."

"Yes, but today is Thursday," she reminded him. "At tomorrow's end, 'closer than ever' will not prevent the morgue from disposing of Jane Doe's remains."

His mouth firm in grave acknowledgment, Erik surveyed the rest of the café. Few other tables were filled. The band was only practicing, getting ready for the main event later this evening that would pack the space with diners.

Erik edged his chair closer to hers. "We need to talk about Warren. He's after you, Olive."

She licked dry lips, then sipped from her water goblet. "But you talked to him Saturday. You said he wouldn't bother me anymore."

"Yeah, well, he and I aren't seeing eye to eye."

She stared at him. In the background, the cornet blared, and the trombonist slid up and down a scale. "What does that mean? What do you mean?"

Something dark bled into the air between them. "He hired me to watch you."

She pushed a laugh past the shrinking in her middle. "What are you talking about? On Saturday? The conversation you said I didn't want to know about?"

Erik wrapped cold fingers around her clasped hands. "I'm a private detective, Olive. Warren Sterling hired me to help him find his wife, and he thought you were the only one who knew where she was."

"What?" He wasn't making sense. Or he was joking. "That's not funny. You're a photographer for the *Chicago Tribune*. I ran into you there the first day we met. There's no way you could have planned for that to happen."

"I am a freelance photographer, and that day I was trying to sell photographs of the *Eastland* wreckage to the editor. I also sell photographs to the *Daily Journal*, the *Herald*, and half a dozen other papers in the area. And I am *also* a private investigator."

"I don't understand." His words were unrelated notes, as disconnected as the band's discordant warm-up. It was noise without reason.

"Warren Sterling engaged my services after I met you that first time at the *Trib*. I had no idea it would be you he wanted me to get close to."

She yanked her hands from his and clutched the sides of her chair. The drumbeat filled the room and entered her, banging in the hollow where her heart had been. "So when you came to my office with that Sherlock Holmes novel, offering to help . . . you were already working for Warren?"

"I was."

Two syllables, barely audible. But they struck Olive with a physical force.

The buzz inside her head grew to a deafening ring that rivaled the clarinet. She wanted to leave but didn't trust her legs to carry her. She wanted to rail but could only manage a broken whisper. "How could you?"

"That's exactly what I'll try to explain, if you'll stay and hear me out. Consider how strongly you feel about helping Jakob Petroski find his wife. When Warren came to me and told me his wife was missing after the *Eastland* disaster, I felt the same way. He was desperate and broken, and he needed to know what had happened, even if the truth was hard to hear. Of course I agreed to help him. It was only after he hired me that he told me you were the one with answers and that you'd never tell him."

"So you decided to get close to me. I get it."

"No, you don't get it. That was how it started, but it didn't take long for me to realize I wanted to know you for your own sake."

"Oh, really? Was it the dirt under my fingernails or the garbage in my hair that you found so appealing?" She had never felt more mortified.

"Both. I may have approached you for Warren's sake at first, but that's not how it stayed. I care about you, Olive, more deeply than you probably want to hear right now. And I never lied to you."

"This entire thing was a lie!" She gestured back and forth in the space between them. The bond she'd thought had been there had snapped. She felt unmoored. Tossed about and seasick.

"That isn't true. Our friendship and my feelings for you are real. That was never made up. What we have together is real."

Her laughter came out choppy and a little cruel. "Whatever we had together was a mirage. What did you do, hire Leo to fill my ears with those stories?"

"Of course not. I wouldn't manipulate your feelings. I care about you far too much to toy with you."

The band was screeching now, and she felt like screeching with it. Her uncle hated this new type of music, with its improvisation and rhythms that broke all rules. It was unpredictable, he said, and that was unsettling. He was right. She hated it, too.

Rules should not be broken, in music or in relationships. And Erik had broken the most important one: honesty.

"What did you think would happen?" she asked him. "How did you think this would end?"

"The more you told me about Warren," he replied, "the more suspicious I grew of him. I dropped his case. I returned his deposit. I don't work for him anymore."

"As of when?"

"As of today. I waited as long as I dared to confront him, knowing he'd go off the rails and take matters into his own hands. That's you, by the way. He's coming for you."

She'd stopped listening after the first three words. Every nerve ending felt suddenly exposed. Heat fired her skin. "So Tuesday night, when you—when we kissed—" To think she'd gone to bed that night still thinking of how right and natural it had felt. "You were simply on the job."

Erik looked as though he'd been struck. "No, it's not like that. I shouldn't have kissed you before I told you everything, but it was real. All I could think of was how much I wanted to hold you. To show you that my feelings for you have grown too deep for words." He reached for her.

She recoiled, suddenly grateful for the cacophony that covered the tremble in her voice. "Don't you dare. Don't you dare lie to try to make me feel better so you can ease your guilty conscience. To think I actually believed you were attracted to me, too."

He caught her hands again. His fingers were so cold around hers. "I am. We can start again," he said, his eyes glittering like blue sea glass. "I'm not the only one here who's kept secrets."

"You're talking about Claire. That was different. I did it to save her life."

"Do you realize how ironic this is? Both of us did what we did because we thought we were helping Claire! We found our way to each other because of it. We'll start over, Olive. I'm sorry I hurt you. Please believe I never meant to. Please say we can begin again. If not right now, then someday."

But he had lied to her. He couldn't be trusted. "I just don't think I can."

He released her hands but didn't respond right away. "Well," he said at last. "My personal feelings are secondary to your safety. You don't have to like me, but I refuse to stand by while that man hunts you."

"What are you saying, exactly?"

"I'm saying that the only thing restraining Warren from going after you before now was the fact that I was on the case. But even that didn't deter him from following us both on Saturday. Either I wasn't getting answers fast enough for him, or he already had some idea that I cared more about your well-being—and Claire's—than about helping him exact revenge."

"That's what this is about." It was the one thing he'd said that Olive could agree with. "He doesn't want reconciliation. He wants to get even. Claire can never come back here." She'd already known it. But saying it brought a stone to her already bruised heart. She missed Claire. She missed her best friend.

"You're the closest link Warren has to her. He isn't going to leave you alone."

"What do you suggest? That I stay locked inside my apartment and work in the bookstore for the rest of my life?" Hurt hid behind her anger, sharpening her tongue. "Because I don't think you'll have time to add *bodyguard* to your list of jobs. Not that I would let you."

Olive left before the meal ever came.

CHAPTER TWENTY-SIX

When Olive left Lamb's Café, Erik had thrown money on the table and chased after her, insisting that he see her safely home. She stayed in the hall outside her apartment while he checked inside to make sure it was clear. As soon as he emerged and declared it safe, she slipped inside and locked him out.

Gritting her teeth, she set the kettle on the stove to heat, wishing that keeping her hands busy could occupy her mind and heart, as well.

No such luck.

Anger boiled, surprising her with its force. How could she be this deeply hurt by a man she'd known so briefly? She didn't understand how the loss of a man she'd kissed only once could hollow out her insides.

Fiercely, she dislodged her hairpins and massaged her scalp, trying to work out the tension stored there. The more she thought about all the little moments they'd shared—and the bigger ones, too—the more humiliated she felt for assigning meaning that wasn't there. She must have seemed like such a fool to him. She *had* been a fool.

The teakettle steamed, and she lifted it from the burner, then turned off the stove. She poured the water into a mug and watched wisps of steam rise, then dropped into a chair. Elbows on the table, she rested her head in her hands.

She was being ridiculous, she told herself. What business did she have pining for someone when she had so much work to do?

Not that he had kept her from it. Whatever his motive, he'd been a partner, willing to do whatever she needed in the investigations. Sherlock and Watson, he'd said.

"Sherlock and Watson!" Olive cried out, the irony just too much. She had belittled his offer to help her the first time he came to her office, and yet *he* was the private detective. Honestly, she had no idea how he'd kept a straight face when she'd so condescendingly pointed out that real cases weren't like the novels he read for fun. He ought to add *actor* to his résumé along with everything else.

Actor, detective, photographer-for-hire, for all your deceiving needs.

Whatever he did for his job, she'd thought of him as a friend who could be so much more.

With a gusty sigh, she sat back in her chair, stared at the door, and wondered if he would ever try knocking on it again.

Metal scraped the lock from outside.

Olive leapt up. Erik might come knocking, but he would never pick the lock.

Pulse throbbing, she looked around for a weapon. The closest thing she had was a cup of hot water and the element of surprise. She grabbed the mug, ready to scald Warren.

The handle turned. Hinges squeaked, and the door opened.

The tea sloshed as she thunked the mug back on the table. "Mom!"

Meg opened her arms, and Olive rushed into her embrace.

After gathering her composure, Olive fetched the linseed oil and sat with her mother on the couch. As she rubbed the oil into Meg's scarred hands, she asked, "When was the last time someone did this for you?"

Meg smiled, and fine lines webbed from her eyes. "I've been well taken care of, dear. I always have been. It's you I've been concerned about."

"Please tell me you didn't cut short your visit on my account."

"Not at all. We had plenty of time together in New York, and I came home exactly according to our original plan. I wouldn't miss the Corner Books & More celebration for anything."

A twinge of embarrassment tweaked Olive for not expecting her mother's return. She had completely forgotten that next week was the store's big anniversary. "I've lost track of the time," she confessed, touching her bare wrist where her bracelet watch used to be.

"You've lost far more than that."

A lump wedged in Olive's throat. "Did you talk to Aunt Sylvie?"

Meg nodded. "She and Kristof picked me up at the train station this evening."

Olive poured a little more oil into her palm and began working on Meg's other hand. "What did she tell you?"

"She told me that you and I have a lot of catching up to do."

Olive gave her an apologetic smile. "Some things are better shared in person than on the phone."

"Well, I'm here now, and I'd love nothing more than to listen. I'm all yours."

And Olive was all hers. It was like old times again, just the two of them.

She told her mother everything about Claire and Warren, her MetLife investigations, and losing her job. She even told her about Erik, since she couldn't relay the events of the past few weeks without including him and his role, too.

Meg stretched her fingers back from her palms once Olive finished massaging the oil into her skin. "Sylvie mentioned this Erik to me."

Of course she had. Her mother and aunt had made a pact long before Olive was born never to keep secrets from each other again. "What did she say?"

"She said I'd like to meet him. I do believe she's right."

This, even after Olive told her that he'd been working for Warren.

"I don't think that's likely to happen." Olive went to the kitchen to fix a cup of tea for her mother, then brought it to her in the living room and set it on the table at her side, as she had almost every night for the last few years. Later, she would help her mother with the buttons on her cuffs.

It felt good to be taking care of her mother again. It was a relief to make a difference, however small. She had tried to make a difference in bigger things, matters of life and death. She'd failed. Perhaps she had reached too high, her ambitions grander than her potential.

"Sylvie tells me you have a job at the bookstore now. If you want it." Meg turned on the lamp on the table beside her, chasing shadows to the corners of the room.

"Yes. I'm afraid I was a terrible employee yesterday, running off to chase clues."

"She understands. She and I have both solved riddles in the past. But after the dust settled, we always came back to the store our father built. When your cases are closed," Meg prodded, "will you do the same? Will you be the third generation in our family bookstore? It won't be too long before Sylvie will want to hand over the reins, especially once Kristof retires."

Olive settled deeper into the cushions, regarding her mother. She'd forgotten how diminutive Meg was. Her beauty hadn't faded as her golden hair turned silvery and her jawline softened. She had become more precious with age, or more fragile, like the porcelain teacup she cradled with both hands.

Would it be so terrible a life to be devoted to her widowed mother and aging aunt and uncle? Hazel and Walter wouldn't do it. Rozalia had her own family, as well. Olive didn't. She was in a perfect position to help her family and the store. As far as puzzles went, the pieces would fit together perfectly.

But would Olive like the picture it painted?

Would it matter if she didn't?

This was meaningful. It should be—*would* be enough. She had made a mistake when she'd allowed herself to imagine a life caring for someone other than her mother. A life that went beyond the walls of this building. Because during the last few weeks, her world had expanded beyond those boundaries, and she didn't know how to fit back inside them again.

CHAPTER TWENTY-SEVEN

FRIDAY, AUGUST 13, 1915

Olive had never been superstitious. But when the telephone rang at five o'clock in the morning on Friday the thirteenth, a shiver cycled down her spine.

Untangling from her sheets, Olive hurried from her bedroom to answer it before the sound woke her mother.

"Miss Pierce?" The female voice on the other end was unfamiliar.

"Speaking. Can I help you?" Dawn glowed around the edges of the curtains, turning the living room's grey walls an oyster-shell pink.

"Actually, I'm hoping I can help you." Her words carried a slight German accent. "My name is Mrs. Emma Mueller, and I work at Hawthorne Works. Word got around that you were looking for Clive Robbins. Is this right?"

Instantly, Olive felt like she'd just had three cups of coffee. "If Clive is C.W. from the cable plant who took pictures at the employee picnic last summer—then yes. It's a matter of some urgency."

"I was on the committee with Clive and took photographs, too. I understand you're trying to identify an *Eastland* victim who likely attended the 1914 event. A young woman, correct?"

"Yes, that's right."

"Clive covered the men's events. I have dozens of images from last year's suffragettes parade and beauty pageant. If it would help you to see them, you're welcome to."

"I'd love to," Olive breathed. She pressed the earpiece closer. "I can't tell you how grateful I am. When is the soonest we could meet?"

"My shift begins at seven. Could you meet me for breakfast at a cafeteria here at Hawthorne?"

Olive spun to look at the clock. She could already hear the El thundering by a block away and streetcars jangling below. "I'll be there by 6:15."

She was there at 6:08, breathless from hurry but trying not to show it. Smoothing her sand-colored suit jacket over the matching skirt, she inhaled the smell of eggs, bacon, and coffee. Silverware clinked on plates, punctuating conversations held in Swedish, Norwegian, German, Polish, Czech, Hungarian, and English.

In the corner, past the long line of folks sliding trays along metal rungs, a woman of middling years had claimed a table big enough for four. Grey threaded her coiled brown braid. Her tray held a crust of toast, a coffee mug half full, and a scrapbook, which Olive could only pray held the answer she needed.

Taking another deep breath, Olive approached. "Mrs. Mueller? I'm Olive Pierce."

With a soft smile, the woman stood and shook Olive's hand. The pleated white blouse topping her navy skirt strained a little at the buttons. "Please," she said. "Call me Emma. Would you care to get breakfast first?"

Olive hadn't come for the food. She slid into a chair and smiled. "Thank you. I had a little something before I left home. I so appreciate your taking time for this today."

Emma pushed spectacles up the bridge of her nose. "It is nothing. It is very little."

"Just the same. I brought some things to show you." Olive

withdrew from her satchel the sweater and scarf, explaining that she thought the woman might have worn the sweater to last year's event, as well. "Perhaps you remember seeing her," she added. "Or maybe you happen to know her already. Her left leg was shorter than her right by two inches. She may have worn special shoes or walked with a limp or a cane."

Emma's countenance seemed to open with every word Olive spoke. "Why, yes! Of course! That must be Nellie Timmerman. She works in the winding department with my niece."

Olive's heart lurched at hearing a name. "You're sure this sweater belongs to Nellie? And that Nellie's left leg is—"

"Yes, yes." Emma opened her scrapbook and flipped the pages. "She wears a special shoe, so usually no one even notices. But for long days of exertion, the cane helps. Look." She pointed to a photograph showing young women on parade, wearing sashes that read *Votes for Women*. At the rear of the columns was a dark-haired woman whose build and height were remarkably similar to Claire's. She clutched a cane. "Nellie is such a peach. She marched in that parade even though I'm sure it put a strain on her leg. You know what she said to me about it? She said, '*It would hurt me far worse to sit on the sidelines.*' That's exactly what she said to me. She and I aren't close, but I got a good sense of her that day."

The ache inside Olive expanded as she was reminded that her mission was to identify not just a body, but a flesh-and-blood person who had harbored hopes and dreams and personality. A girl who had loved and been loved.

"Do you have other photographs of her?" she asked. "Something closer up." Olive could tell that Nellie wore a white dress, but the image had been overexposed, and details didn't come through.

"I'm sure I do."

While Emma turned more pages, Olive felt torn between wanting Jane Doe to be Nellie Timmerman and hoping Nellie was still alive. She'd noticed that Emma referred to her in the present tense.

"There she is." Emma tapped the page triumphantly. "She won third place in the beauty pageant last year, so she sat for a photo with the winner and runner-up. Look, the sweater! Just like you said."

Olive's fingertips hovered over the photograph as she studied it. The sweater was exactly the same. She wore no scarf because she hadn't earned it until this year.

But that smile. Nellie had beamed for the camera.

"She looks so happy," Olive whispered. Without showing Emma, she pulled from her satchel the folder containing photographs of Jane Doe at the morgue. She located the image of the teeth. The right front tooth overlapped the left. It was a match for Nellie's smile.

"To tell you the truth," Emma was saying, "she seemed happier than the girl who won second. She couldn't believe it. Her whole family treated her as if she'd won first place. You'd never find prouder parents or a younger sister more in awe than Nellie's." She fell silent, her chin dimpling. "They're all gone now. For a second, I'd forgotten. But they all perished on the *Eastland*. I was supposed to be on it, you know, but I was late to the docks and watched the boat turn over."

Olive slipped the photographs back into her satchel, trading them for a folder holding passenger lists and the *Western Electric News*, which listed the dead. Four Timmermans, including Nellie, were aboard the *Eastland*, and three of them had perished.

"It's a miracle Nellie survived the disaster." Emma sipped her coffee. "But her recovery isn't a sure thing."

"What can you tell me about it?"

"Just that she's been at Cook County Hospital all this time with some broken bones and now pneumonia. We have a small hospital here at Hawthorne, but her case was too severe to be moved here. I went to visit her at Cook after she'd been there for about a week. I didn't get to see her, since the nurses were changing her bedclothes at the time, but it was just as well, since she was heavily sedated for the pain of losing her family. I did have a chat with her aunt Irene, who is watching over her."

"Her aunt," Olive repeated, weighing Emma's every word. "So her entire family *didn't* die July 24."

Emma set down her mug and dabbed a napkin to her mouth. "Her immediate family did. Her aunt isn't from here. Someone must have told the nurses who Nellie was, and then the hospital staff contacted Irene and she came in from out of town. Irene and Nellie's mother were sisters and had been estranged for years before this."

"How do you know?" It seemed a rather personal detail for Nellie to have shared with Emma, especially if they weren't particularly close.

"Irene said so. It's amazing what people will tell a sympathetic ear in a hospital. Tragic, isn't it? She came too late to reconcile. Before the disaster, Irene hadn't seen Nellie since she was a child."

Memories collided as Olive scribbled notes on the inside of her folder.

"Did we do it, then?" Emma checked her watch and adjusted her spectacles. "Nellie's the young woman you were looking for, isn't she?"

Eyelids burning, Olive nodded. "I need to visit that hospital room. And I need you to come with me, the sooner the better. Bring the photographs, if you please. I wouldn't ask if it weren't important. Could you get permission from your supervisor or have someone cover your shift?"

Emma's eyes rounded. "I'll try."

◆

Lowered voices and rubber-soled footsteps filtered up and down the corridor at Cook County Hospital. Olive stood at the door to Nellie's room, Emma at her side. She had been in this very spot twice before and had spied Irene bending over the patient, whispering her name. At the time, Olive had dismissed the scene, seeing all she needed to know. The young woman had been identified.

Olive had been quiet on the streetcar. The less she said to Emma, the better. She didn't want to risk influencing Emma's reaction to what came next.

A tall, angular nurse in a white uniform pushed open the door, gesturing that they could enter. "She's not had any visitors since her aunt left, the poor dear."

"When did her aunt leave town, Nurse Watkins?" Olive asked, recognizing her from her previous visits. Her chestnut hair came to a widow's peak, and she wore a gold suffrage pin on her collar. She couldn't be older than forty.

"Oh, after the first week, I'd say. Mrs. Collins has her own family to care for in Indiana. She did say we were to call her back when Nellie was ready to come out of sedation. But there was no point in her being here with her niece unaware of her presence."

Olive gaped. "Do you mean she's been sedated to the point of being insensible for three weeks?"

Bristling, Nurse Watkins pursed her lips. "You must understand the situation. Nellie suffered a concussion, a broken arm, and three broken ribs. She wasn't conscious when we admitted her, and then, when she did wake, she couldn't remember the disaster that had brought her here. Concussions will do that. She was completely confused and in great pain. We sedated her while the doctor set the bones in her right forearm and wrapped her ribs. We do let her come out of it enough to eat and drink a few times a day, but even then, her speech is slurred, and whatever she says is nonsense. As soon as her aunt arrived and broke the news to her that her entire family had perished, she went hysterical. Her wailing caused her broken ribs such pain, and we couldn't let her continue like that."

"So you've been keeping her sedated ever since?" Olive clarified.

"We've been keeping her quiet so her bones can heal, yes. It isn't fair for her to try to mend both a broken heart and a broken body at once. It's a shame about the pneumonia. But she's a fighter. As soon as she can be awake and calm, we'll let her, and we'll call her aunt back. But until then, this is really the best way for her. Go on in, ladies. She can likely hear you speaking, even if she can't respond."

Olive slipped in first, watching Emma as she entered.

"Her coloring is so much better," the nurse said, "and the laceration on the side of her face has all but healed. We've just washed her hair this morning. I think Mrs. Collins would be astounded by the improvement, especially with the bandage off her head and the swelling down."

Olive heard her. But she was so focused on Emma's reaction that she didn't respond.

Emma frowned, her complexion an uneven red. "Excuse me. But are you sure this is Nellie Timmerman's room?"

Nurse Watkins confirmed it was.

Mouth pulling down, Emma stepped to a small metal cart on wheels and opened her scrapbook to the photo of Nellie after the beauty pageant. She pointed to her likeness. "This is Nellie Timmerman." She looked at the patient in the bed. "That is not."

Olive's heart pounded with anticipation. "Nurse, would you please check the patient's—"

The patient yawned wide enough to glimpse inside her mouth. There was a slight gap between the two front teeth.

"Did you see her teeth?" Emma asked. "Those aren't Nellie's. Come see for yourself."

"Is she waking up?" Olive asked.

"Not for hours," Nurse Watkins replied, "but what do you mean, this isn't Nellie? Dr. Larson and I have been caring for this lamb since she was brought in July 24. Her own aunt was here."

"But not until she'd been told to come," Olive pointed out. "Who first identified her as Nellie Timmerman?"

The nurse consulted a clipboard. "Sigrid Halvorsen."

The name meant nothing to Olive except that she'd seen it on the passenger list of Western Electric employees, but not on the list of the dead.

"Sigrid Halvorsen?" Emma crossed her arms. "She doesn't work in the same department as Nellie. They live on the same block, but Sigrid's family just moved to town and started working at Hawthorne in June. The Halvorsens barely speak English. God bless them, they're trying, taking night classes and all that. But I'm afraid—" She placed a hand over her heart and licked her lips. "I'm afraid Sigrid made a mistake. Are the patient's legs the same length?"

Nurse Watkins paled. "Well, she hasn't been standing or walking, so I wouldn't be able to tell a small discrepancy."

"Two inches," Olive supplied. "Could you tell, even now, if her left leg is two inches shorter than the other?"

"Oh my. I would have noticed such a difference as I've exercised her legs and rubbed her feet to keep her muscles from atrophying. No, thank goodness she doesn't suffer that. I suppose Nellie Timmerman does?"

Emma nodded. Her face clouded, and she removed her glasses to catch her tears with a handkerchief. "I thought I'd helped you find Nellie, but I didn't after all, did I?" Her broken voice belied the breaking of something else inside her.

"Yes, you did. I just didn't know her name." Olive wrapped her arm around Emma's soft, round shoulders, willing the simple gesture to convey how deeply sorry she was. Even though Emma said they hadn't been close, she'd known Nellie when she was bright-eyed and hopeful, her life completely before her.

Emma's shoulders heaved as she pulled in deep breaths. Her lips drew a thin, brave line before she spoke. "They told us eight hundred and forty-three people died in that disaster. Eight hundred and forty-three." She repeated the number slowly, emphasizing each syllable as if it were a foreign language she struggled to understand. "Mostly young women and children. More than six hundred were from my Hawthorne family. That was a number we all had to get used to, and I have spent the last few weeks doing my level best."

Neither Olive nor Nurse Watkins interrupted her as she paused and then continued. "I was a checker that horrible Monday morning, July 26. It was my job to go to every department and check to see who was missing. On one bench—one *single* bench—there should have been twenty-two young ladies. There were two." Her brow knotted, and her composure cracked. "Now this. This isn't Nellie. And now I have to add one more number to the tally of lives cut short. *Eight hundred and forty-four*. Forgive me, please, but I find this new number unbearable."

It was. No one was ever meant to bear such grief, especially not all at once.

Squeezing Emma's shoulders once more, Olive bowed her head in respect for all the *Eastland*'s victims and for those left in its deadly wake. Her eyes stung.

Sniffing, Nurse Watkins studied the papers on her clipboard, then looked at the woman lying in the bed. "If this isn't Nellie, who is it?"

Olive knew. She suspected the patient had tried to tell the hospital staff herself but had been dismissed as confused and hysterical. Energy coursed through her veins, an onslaught of blended hope and sorrow. "Could you tell me, please, if the patient has a crescent-shaped birthmark on the inside of her upper right arm? About half an inch long, according to her husband."

Adjusting her starched cap, Nurse Watkins went to the patient's bedside and checked. "It's there." She carefully lowered the arm and patted the patient's hand. "But Nellie doesn't have a husband."

Olive gripped the bed's iron footboard. "Stella Petroski does."

The hours that followed were a flurry of phone calls and meetings involving Olive, Emma, the medical examiner, the coroner, the hospital administrator, Dr. Larson, and the dentist from Cicero who had treated both Nellie and Stella. The verdict was unanimous. Nellie Timmerman, aged twenty-six, had died on the *Eastland*, along with both parents and her seventeen-year-old sister. The blow to the head she'd suffered, which had made her features less recognizable, had most likely taken her life instantly. It was a small comfort to know she hadn't spent slow, dark hours in terror.

Dr. Larson would call Nellie's aunt, Irene Collins, to relay the regretful news and to ask if she wanted to claim the body. Later, Olive would call Howard at MetLife, who could follow up with the coroner and medical examiner to officially close the case. She'd send a telegram to Claire as well. Fleetingly, she considered sending word to Erik, too.

But right now, there was someone else she needed to see first.

"That's the one." Olive leaned forward from the Cadillac's back seat, pointing at the pale green bungalow. Her pulse buzzed along with the engine. Michael and Addie were playing in the front yard with their grandmother watching—or rather, napping—from the rocker on the front porch.

Mr. Sheridan, the hospital administrator, parked the car alongside the curb. After cutting the engine, he glanced at Dr. Larson beside him. "Ready, doctor?"

Dr. Larson tugged his homburg more securely in place. "I'm always ready to deliver good news, albeit delayed. A wife, mother, daughter once was lost and now is found."

Brave words. But the tic in his jaw betrayed his nerves. He didn't mention the fact that he'd kept Stella too sedated to clear up the matter herself. Worse, perhaps at some point she'd been lucid enough to tell him who she was, and he didn't believe her, attributing it to the concussion or hysteria or even to the sedation's tricks on the mind.

He and Mr. Sheridan might well fear being sued for malpractice. Olive doubted the Petroskis would take such action, but neither did she feel compelled to set these men at ease after the way they'd mishandled Stella's care.

Pneumonia, however, was a disaster of its own. "Can you tell if she'll fully recover?" Olive asked.

Dr. Larson twisted on the leather seat to look her in the eye. "I know better than to make promises, Miss Pierce. But once we bring her out of sedation, if she sees her family again and learns they are all safe and sound, she'll have more reasons to live than she's realized for the past three weeks. That can only be a positive thing."

Olive looked through the window at two of those reasons. The children, as untidy as their yard, had stopped playing to stare at the shiny vehicle. They'd been waiting long enough.

The second Olive emerged from the car, heels sinking into the soft ground, Addie squealed and toddled toward her. "Red!"

Olive jogged a little to gain more distance from the street before kneeling in the grass and letting the little girl climb onto her lap. Michael came to greet her, as well, suspicion in his too-wise eyes. After all, she had come before and had never brought back their mother.

Mr. Sheridan and Dr. Larson strolled up the front walk, their gaits full of purpose.

"Michael." Olive stretched out a hand, ready to embrace him, but he gave it a limp shake instead before stuffing his fist back in his trouser pocket. Scabbed-over mosquito bites dotted his arms, and green streaked his dirty knees.

"You didn't even bring Mr. Erik? I was going to play catch with him." His tone held accusation and a disappointment well on its way to resentment. It wasn't just about Erik's absence, she knew, but about his mother's. She didn't blame him. "Who are those men?" He hitched a thumb toward the strangers now standing on the porch, knocking on the door.

"They're here to talk to your father and grandparents," Olive told him. She removed the pins dangling from Addie's wispy blond locks and reinserted them to clear her little face. "And I'm here to talk to you in the meantime."

She wanted Jakob and the Adamskis to receive the news without the children present. For such a shock, thrilling as it was, they should have at least a moment to themselves to absorb it.

"You got fired from your job," Michael said. "You weren't finding people you said you'd find. My dad said you're not even trying to anymore, on account of not having a job. So I don't even know why you're here."

True, every word, or very nearly.

Her gaze shifted to the porch when Jakob answered the door. He did not invite Dr. Larson and Mr. Sheridan inside, but instead came out, Mr. Adamski following. Stella's father looked so worn and spent, standing beside Jakob. His shoulders rounded, his steps unsure. While Jakob remained standing, Mr. Adamski eased himself into the rocker beside his wife and held her gnarled hand.

"You don't care," Michael spat out like a curse. He moved a few feet away, his bottom lip trembling. "You lied to us."

"Oh, Michael." Olive stayed where she was on the ground, though she longed to reach him. She wrapped her arms around his sister instead. "I always cared. I still do."

Addie pointed one chubby finger. "Papa?"

Michael turned to see, and Olive bade him stay.

Both Mr. Sheridan and Dr. Larson removed their hats. One of them spoke.

Jakob collapsed to his knees and wept.

"Papa's sad!" Addie's voice approached a wail.

Michael spun back to Olive, paling. "Is he—is he sad?" he whispered.

Olive's heart dilated with joy and relief. It wasn't her place to tell Michael the news when Jakob was just yards away. But neither could she leave his pleading question unanswered. Not for one heartbeat did she want him to worry his mother had been found dead.

She shook her head.

His brave mask fell, his composure crumbled. Michael ran to Olive and threw his arms around her neck. With one arm she encircled him, while the other held Addie. Tears trailed her cheeks. She closed her eyes, and the three of them were back on the *Eastland*'s hull, then on the wharf, huddled together in the pouring rain. She was holding the children tight, unwilling to let go until she could release them to their parents.

Cicadas whirred. Sunshine soaked through her hat and warmed her scalp. Olive opened her eyes. She kissed both of their cheeks, then watched them race into Jakob's wide-open arms.

CHAPTER TWENTY-EIGHT

SATURDAY, AUGUST 14, 1915

The telephone rang once. A few beats of silence. Then two more rings. Silence. It rang again.

Erik.

Meg looked up from poking noodles into a pot of boiling water. "Are you ignoring that telephone because you aren't expecting a call or because you are?"

Olive stirred the ground beef, Italian sausage, garlic, and onion she was cooking on the stove. It was the second time today he'd tried using their special code. If he really wanted to talk to her, she supposed, he could skip the code and let the phone ring like any other caller. But he hadn't. He hadn't tricked her into answering the phone before she knew it was him, and she had to give him credit for that.

"I know who it is, and I don't need to speak to him." If she did, she couldn't guarantee that her wall of resistance would hold steady.

"I see." Her mother wiped her hands on her apron. "Do you think he knows you solved two cases yesterday?"

The phone stopped ringing, blunting the edge of her guilt. "He doesn't need to know." Neither did he need to know that the Petroskis had crowded into Mr. Sheridan's Cadillac last night and gone straight to the hospital to confirm Stella's identity. "Besides, he might simply point out that, eventually, they would have let Stella out of her sedation long enough for her to say exactly who she was and clear up the entire matter herself. I might have saved a few days or weeks of suspense for her family, but that's all."

"Oh no, you don't." Meg stretched her fingers away from her palms.

"Don't what?"

"Don't minimize what you've done. If you hadn't solved these cases, Stella might have been able to reveal her own identity, but when? And would they have believed her or declared her insane? And what about Nellie and her aunt? Mrs. Collins would suddenly find herself in the dreadful position of suspecting Nellie was dead but not knowing where her body was. You prevented Nellie's remains from being lost forever. Because of your diligence, Mrs. Collins will be able to lay Nellie to rest where she belongs, alongside the rest of her family. I'm sure she was gut-wrenched to learn her niece hadn't survived after all. But at least now she'll have closure. Her wounds can begin to heal. That's a gift, sweetheart." Meg gentled her voice. "One can live with scars, however constricting they may feel. But one cannot live long with open wounds."

Olive smiled her thanks and stitched the words firmly into her memory. Perhaps they would hold against the tugging self-doubt. It had occurred to her last night that for more than two weeks, she'd had Erik, an actual private detective. If she'd had more humility from the start, if she'd accepted his first offer to give her feedback, could she have solved the cases of Stella and Nellie any sooner? If she had known Erik's main profession, what could she have learned from him? She'd been so busy sleuthing in her own way that she'd missed untold opportunities. Part of her wanted to learn from him still.

The larger part, the one ruled by logic, reasoned that there could be no point in that. She could practically feel the weight of the bookstore's reins in her hands. Now she would be the one who must content herself with fictional mysteries.

Meg set a mixing bowl on the table, along with ricotta cheese and an egg. "By the way, how did Howard respond when you told him you'd found both Stella's and Jane Doe's identities?"

"More than anything, he sounded surprised and somewhat dubious. But he'll get everything he needs from the officials come Monday in order to close the case."

Monday would be a big day for Howard. He'd agreed to meet Raymond Murphy after the GAR meeting at the library and had insisted that Olive stay out of it, since it was his case and she'd been fired. It was just as well, since she had a different appointment to keep now. Irene Collins would be returning to Chicago on Monday morning, she'd learned, and Olive was determined to see her.

Shoving thoughts of Howard aside, she drained the grease from the meat, then added crushed tomatoes, tomato sauce, and tomato paste, and seasoned it with sugar, basil, oregano, and fennel. When her mother struggled to open the container of cheese, Olive did it for her with barely a thought, then cracked the egg into the mixing bowl and measured out the parsley.

"Thank you, dear. But I could have done that myself." Meg dumped the ricotta into the bowl and began to combine it all with a wooden spoon.

"It's no trouble," Olive replied. "I love helping you. I love *you.*"

A smile pushed creases into Meg's face. "I know you do. But you'd be surprised how useful I can be if only given the chance."

That stopped her. "What does that mean?"

"It means that you've done such a fine job tending to my every want and need that I'd forgotten how good it feels to do the tending myself." Meg's expression suggested she had far more to say. "Maria isn't doing very well, I'm afraid."

Olive set the meat sauce to simmer. "What's wrong?"

"She hasn't regained her strength since little Nathan was born in January. With three other children all under the age of five, it's a lot for her to handle on her own."

"But she isn't on her own," Olive pointed out. "She has Walter. Doesn't he have the summers off?"

"Oh, pish. He has plenty to do getting ready for fall classes and attending conferences, and he's trying to write and publish, too. The fall semester is nearly upon us already."

Olive considered this, absently stirring the pot. Caring for four small children, at least two of them in diapers, would be taxing on a woman even in the best of health. "Can they hire some help? A housekeeper, a nanny?"

"On Walter's salary?" Meg huffed. "No. And even if they could afford it, I don't believe they would."

"I'm sure they loved having you visit, then. I'll bet you read those little ones as many stories as they wanted. Did you give them art lessons, too?"

"We were very messy." Meg laughed. "That's part of the fun. And Maria didn't mind, since I cleaned everything up afterward. I really think it relieved her, knowing the children were well occupied."

"What a blessing you were to them."

"They blessed me too. We all wished you could have been there with us."

Olive smiled. "Is that so?" she teased. She imagined her mother relished having her grandchildren all to herself.

Finished mixing the cheese, Meg pulled the lasagna pan from the cupboard and moved to ladle meat sauce into it.

"I can do that, Mom."

"I know, dear." Meg patted her cheek. "So can I. In fact, we need to—"

The telephone jangled. After the third ring, Olive answered it to find Sylvie on the line from the bookstore downstairs.

"I've got a customer here who's determined to speak with you," her aunt said.

Olive frowned. "It isn't Erik, is it? Or Warren?"

Meg looked up from layering noodles in the pan.

"No and no. It's Leopold Rousseau the First."

"Leo?" The last time Olive had seen him, he was assuring her and Erik that he'd find his own ride home from the Lincoln Park Boat Club.

"So you are acquainted, good. He said you were. It's almost closing time, and this young man won't leave the building until he sees you. May I send him up? He won't bite. I already asked. I'd really like to close up shop."

After the slightest hesitation, Olive agreed and ended the call. "Well, Mom, we're about to have company."

After Meg slid the pan into the oven, Olive answered the knock at the door and made the introductions.

"*Enchanté.*" Hat to his heart, Leo bowed in Meg's direction with all sincerity, the crown of his head shining. Grasping the strap of a bag slung over his shoulder, he turned to Olive. "Erik doesn't know I'm here."

"Why don't you two have a seat, and I'll make the salad." Meg waved them out of the kitchen.

Olive stood her ground. "But I usually—"

"Yes, dear." Meg smiled. "You usually make it. Allow me to prove I'm equal to the challenge. Allow me to surprise you."

In the living room, Olive took a club chair and Leo took the sofa, unbuttoning his khaki suit jacket before he sat. Even here, the aromas of Italian sausage, onion, and garlic seasoned the air.

"I have never smelled anything so divine in all my life." He pushed his glasses up his hawkish nose.

"Tell me the truth, Leo," Olive said. "Are you really Erik's room-mate? Did you really grow up with him?"

"Yes!" His response carried the indignation of the falsely ac-cused.

"Was there any part of what you told me on our way to Venetian Night that was manufactured just for me?"

Leo straightened his spine. "Manufactured? I may talk a lot, mademoiselle, but I tell no lies. Scout's honor."

"Were you ever a scout?"

"I didn't say I was."

Olive trapped a sigh. "I understand you have something to tell me. Go ahead."

"Only this. Erik is miserable. When he came home Thursday night, he was wretched by all measures. I have never seen him like this."

She shifted, but with no hope of getting comfortable. "He should have known that his betrayal would not secure my affections."

"See, now, that's the thing." Leo crooked a finger at her. "He's told me everything, including the perspective that he betrayed you. But the person he actually betrayed was Warren. Although *betray* is a strong word. He terminated his work-for-hire agreement with Warren—which isn't so good for business, I might add. But he did that on principle, and he did it for you. He cares for you a great deal. That started almost right away. And I think you care for him, too. Am I wrong?"

Meg whisked in to deliver two glasses of lemonade before returning to the kitchen.

Olive swiped a thumb over the condensation beading the glass. She did care for Erik but was barely willing to admit that to herself, let alone to this man sitting on her sofa. "I miss him," she confessed. "But more importantly, I miss being able to trust him. Our entire relationship has been one humiliating sham. He was using me to get information."

"At first, that was the idea, yes. The friendship did begin under false pretenses, and you have every right to be upset about that. I would be." He paused, as if weighing his next words. "But I do wonder if, after the initial surprise wears off, you might consider forgiving my friend."

Olive leaned back in the chair, not yet ready to concede. "I thought he was *my* friend, even more than that, right up until he told me who he really is."

Leo's brow puckered. "Who he really is? Erik has always been Erik. The job title on his business card doesn't define who he is. Do you see the difference? What we do is not the sum of who we are. Is *your* identity as a human being tied completely to your job?"

The words landed inside her and burrowed deep. She couldn't remember a time when she hadn't measured her worth by what she did, first with her role in her family and then in her career. Which might account for how lost she felt when she lost her job. Erik had made it clear he didn't think less of her for it, but *she* felt less.

Leo took a drink of lemonade, then rubbed the back of his neck. "I'm not doing a very good job of convincing you to give him another chance. Look, we can agree on the facts. He wasn't completely honest with you from the start. If you'd let him talk to you, he'd apologize and beg your forgiveness. So I'm here on his behalf. Gladly would I give up the time I get to spend in his company if it meant he could be happy."

Olive shifted in the chair, fingers resting in the divots where buttons pulled leather tight. "And what makes you think he'd be happy with me?"

Leo smiled. "A perfect segue. I thank you." He opened the bag he'd brought and withdrew a notebook. "Do you know what this is?"

She did not.

"Ever since Erik started looking for clues about his parents and family, he's written everything down in here. The first entry is March 26, 1894. He was twelve years old." He opened the notebook and pointed to youthful handwriting.

Olive leaned forward to see. It held his parents' names and the dates of their deaths.

"Once he learned which church had baptized him, he went there and interviewed people in Humboldt Park, looking for neighbors who'd known them." Leo flipped the pages. "When he learned some had moved up to the Logan Square area, he went knocking on doors there, too. He recorded everything they said about his family."

Again, the juvenile script.

My father was left-handed. He read *Moby Dick*.
My mother loved to garden. Her favorite flower was the iris. She loved Easter more than Christmas. Mrs. Lovoll saw her through the window dancing in the kitchen with my father more than once.

His struggle for connection sprawled across the paper. Olive waited for her voice to regain strength. "Leo, this notebook seems private," she told him. "It's probably sacred to Erik. I'm not sure he'd want you showing this to me."

Leo waved a hand at her concern. "You need to see this. Have patience, and you'll understand why I'm convinced I'm not betraying his confidence. All right?" Adjusting his glasses, he pressed on. "He didn't stop with neighbors. Erik found an old Norwegian sailor willing to talk to him. This sailor didn't know Erik's parents from Adam, but he had stories to share, and Erik was eager to hear them. This page lists Norwegian proverbs translated into English. Erik memorized them and tried to work them into his daily speech."

He tilted the page to show her.

Every man's home is his castle.
That day, that sorrow.
What is honest never sinks.

There, her gaze snagged. Did that mean the truth would always come out? Or did it mean truth would always be rewarded? When Erik told her his initial motivations in getting close to her, Olive had punished him for it instead. She'd been hurt and embarrassed, she reasoned, but she couldn't deny that when he'd been the most honest he'd ever been, that was the point at which she shunned him. Not that she didn't have good reason.

Leo turned a few more pages. "Sometimes he wrote questions. Simple things. What did they like to cook at home? He also wanted to know what soap his mother used. What shaving soap did his father prefer? Did he smoke, and if so, what brand?"

"Those are all smells," Olive pointed out.

"Exactly. Have you ever noticed how strongly smells are attached to memory?"

She had. Without thinking, Olive inhaled. The smell of baking lasagna coming from the kitchen was not only the smell of a promised dinner. It was a tradition that stretched back to family dinners at their old house before Nate had died, but after Hazel and Walter had moved out. Olive was fifteen the first time she'd decided to cook spaghetti for her parents and aunt and uncle. She saw how much her mother loved her visits with Sylvie, and she felt this was a way to take care of both of them. Ever since, the aromas of an Italian dinner brought the reassurance of a steady routine, the comfort of family, and a reminder that whatever else was going on in the world, she could gather with her loved ones and belong.

That was what Erik had been looking for. Something, anything, to trigger a memory, to remind him of the family he came from. Sympathy pummeled through Olive.

"He was desperate, you see, for a place to belong," Leo said, flipping through the rest of the fuzzy-edged pages. The handwriting evolved from boyish scrawls to masculine, blocky letters. "Even after his mother's cousin took us both in, he was trying to piece together a puzzle that would tell him who his family had been. There's a flurry of notes from what Oscar shared, but then Erik's discoveries slowed down over the years and became more general in nature. For example, he'd write down any Norwegian customs he learned about—folk tales, songs, and basic vocabulary of the language, although his attempts to learn to speak it were never successful."

She looked at him and softened. "Like your attempts to speak French, Monsieur Rousseau?"

He slapped a hand over his heart. "The truth hurts, mademoiselle. But *oui*. All I know about my people is that, based on my surname, at one point we were French. *C'est la vie*. But I digress. We're talking about my best friend and his own quest. One day, he stopped." With a dramatic flourish, Leo turned to a blank page. "Not only did he stop adding to it, he stopped reviewing it, which he had done on a regular basis, even though I'm sure he had it memorized. It was like he didn't need it anymore."

Olive waited for him to explain the significance. Meg looked just as expectant, tomatoes untouched near her idle hands.

"He stopped looking for his family," Leo said at last, "soon after he found you. That's not a coincidence. And it has never happened before. Not even when he found Oscar."

Olive studied his expression and found something like resignation. The words would have meant more had they come from Erik himself, but she never would have listened had he tried. She'd been too stubborn, too hurt to give him the chance. She would have missed this completely.

"Are you sure?" she asked Leo.

He nodded, his thin lips a straight line on his face. "May I remind you that I have nothing to gain personally by inventing such a tale? Nothing, that is, save the satisfaction of telling the truth. I'm not asking you to send a message back with me. You're a grown-up. When you're ready to talk, talk to him yourself." He handed her a piece of paper bearing their telephone number.

The timer dinged in the kitchen, and Olive dashed to the oven to take out the lasagna.

"Stay for dinner, Mr. Rousseau?" Meg asked.

Tucking the notebook back in his bag, Leo stood and reseated his boater. "Oh, no. It ought to be Erik in that chair, not me. I could never do that to him."

Meg finally tossed the tomatoes in with the lettuce. "And what will you be eating tonight?"

Leo chuckled. "Madame, you don't want to know."

"Nonsense." Olive cut two generous servings of lasagna and heaped them into an empty tin, affixed the lid, and wrapped it in a dish towel to blunt the heat conducting through the metal. Into a mason jar she piled salad, drizzling homemade dressing over the top before screwing on the lid. She handed both to Leo, who tucked the jar into his bag and held tight to the tin with both hands.

"This is far too much for one person," he said.

Olive's shoulders lifted and fell. "Then you'll just have to find someone with whom to share."

Grinning like an imp, Leo bowed to her, then to Meg, and whistled his way out the door.

Olive was still mulling over Leo's visit during dinner. Beyond what he'd shared about Erik, what had struck her most was his unwitting exposure of her own flawed thinking. "I've been so consumed with the mistaken identities of other women, I didn't realize I'd misplaced my own," she admitted to her family.

Meg lowered a laden fork to her plate. "Your value comes from a much deeper place than who your employer is. You were made in the image of God, and who you are is bigger than what you do."

"Absolutely. You are cherished by God and your family no matter what." Grasping the water pitcher, Sylvie refilled Kristof's glass and then her own. "And you know you're welcome to more hours at the store anytime you're ready," she said gently, steering the conversation toward the practical. "I really do think a club for L. M. Montgomery fans would be a big hit with our customers, and I'd love for you to get that project off the ground. I have my hands full."

Finished with dinner, Olive tasted the cannoli her uncle had brought while considering her response. "I'd be happy to do that, Aunt Sylvie." She had no reason not to.

Claire would have been so much better at it. The rebellious thought brought a stab of longing for her friend. But, of course, Olive could manage this project if it meant lightening Sylvie's burden. She could certainly claim no other demands on her time. Her calendar had been wiped clean and loomed long and blank before her. It didn't make her worthless, she knew. But it did make her available.

"Then it's settled," Sylvie said with a satisfied sigh.

Meg's lips curled into a tremulous smile. But when she pushed back her plate of cannoli unfinished, Olive felt a clutch of dread. Her mother loved sweets almost as much as she loved painting.

"Are you feeling all right?" Olive took another bite. "I don't doubt that you pushed yourself too hard while with Walter's and Hazel's families." Especially Walter's.

"That's actually what I want to talk to you all about. I meant to talk to you, Olive, first, but then Leo came, and—well. Delaying won't make this any easier."

Sylvie blanched. "You're not sick, are you? Oh, Meg, what did the doctor say? What do we do?"

Laughter crinkled the corners of Meg's eyes. "That's enough of that, you goose. I mean only to say that I had a wonderful time helping Walter and Maria with their children."

"I'm sure you did, Mom. But they exhausted you. You'll need to rest and recover for a bit."

"My darling girl. Since when did exertion guarantee danger? Have you considered that growing tired in service to the ones I love is far preferable to—to growing weary with idleness? My hands can't paint as much as they used to. But that doesn't mean they're useless."

That word again. It stung. "I never meant to make you feel that way," Olive said quietly. "I only ever wanted to help you."

"I know." Meg grasped her hand. "I appreciate all you've done for me. But I cannot help but wonder if your efforts to protect me from any discomfort have also been a way for you to protect yourself."

Olive blinked back her astonishment.

Kristof leaned back in his chair, thoughtful. Sylvie leaned forward, and Lizzie leapt off a chair to join Jane in a patch of sun.

"You've always been my special gift," Meg continued. "You

284

cared more for me than you seemed to care about pursuing your own friendships, outside of Claire. And I let you. I love the bond we share. But I fear I've let you take care of me for far too long, and that this, too, has become too much a part of who you think you are, and so you're unwilling to let go of it. After your father died, it was the right decision to move into this apartment together. But you have poured yourself so much into my well-being that I fear you've neglected your own. I fear you've been protecting your heart by pouring all your devotion into me."

Kristof's eyebrows rose.

Sylvie clicked her tongue, shaking her head, then nodding. "I can see that."

This conversation had jumped the rails. "I disagree," Olive protested. "I risked my heart again just this summer, and we all know how that turned out."

"Don't misunderstand me. I agree that was awful. Of course you're upset. But please, don't let this experience convince you to close yourself off from future relationships. Don't pretend I'm all you need. I am not."

She didn't have to add that Olive was not all her mother needed, either.

"I see." Olive buried the hurt she felt and schooled herself to rise above it. "Walter and Maria need you now. Is that what you're trying to say?"

Meg squeezed and released her hand. "Let's leave the word *need* entirely out of it, shall we? But to your point: I have decided the time is right for me to move in with Walter and his family. I will miss all three of you dearly. But the truth is, I'm doing very little here, and I can do so much for Walter's family."

Olive set down her fork, no longer hungry. "Then you've already decided?"

"I have. It is the right thing to do. This city has grown too big for me."

Chicago's growth had been exponential, more than doubling

since Olive was a child. She tried to imagine the city as it had been when her mother and aunt were in their twenties—with only three hundred thousand people—and couldn't. It now held two and a half million souls.

Sylvie pressed a handkerchief to her eyes. "I can't say it hasn't crossed my mind that you'd want to be close to your grandbabies."

A slow smile warmed Kristof's face. "Those children, and their parents, will be so fortunate to have you."

"But, Upland, Indiana?" Olive parried. "They have little more than a thousand people there, correct?"

"Plus the students on campus." Meg smiled. "Believe it or not, I like the change of pace. It suits me. More importantly, being with Walter, Maria, and my grandchildren suits me. And I plan on visiting Chicago plenty."

Olive was stunned that they all spoke as if the matter had been settled and etched in stone.

Then she envisioned her mother there. She could go for walks with the children without worrying about crime on the streets. She would be surrounded by family and activity rather than waiting for Olive to come home from work. It was true that here she could see her sister whenever she pleased and that this building held precious memories. But Sylvie had her own work and husband, and perhaps Meg was ready to make new memories of her own. And oh, how Walter's children adored their grandmother.

At length, Olive gathered her composure enough to admit, "I always wished I'd known my grandparents. I know Maria's parents have already passed on. If you can be a part of their children's lives, I'm sure it's a blessing to all of you."

That didn't mean that her mother's leaving wouldn't hurt.

"When will you go?" Olive forced the question through a fast-closing throat.

"As soon as I get my affairs in order." The words left Meg on a sigh. "In other words, soon."

Too soon.

CHAPTER TWENTY-NINE

MONDAY, AUGUST 16, 1915

Early morning sunlight slipped between scalloped curtains and into Olive's bedroom. After fastening the belt at the waist of her smoke-grey dress, she tamed her hair into a loose twist at the back of her head. *Czerwony*, she could hear little Addie say. *Red*.

A block beyond her window, the El whooshed on its steel tracks, carrying thousands of Chicagoans on their daily commutes to work. Olive was unemployed but not without work to do. Now that Stella and Nellie were both accounted for, her thoughts returned to Raymond Murphy. His GAR meeting was in a few hours at the Chicago Public Library. Perhaps by today's end, that mystery would finally be solved.

There had to be a connection between Raymond and Blanche, possibly familial. If Olive had reached Erik yesterday, she'd have talked through the possibilities.

After a considerable amount of time working up the nerve, she had called him after church, ready to tell him about Stella and Nellie. Ready to hear whatever he wanted to say, too.

She also would have told him that Jakob had called her yesterday from the hospital to say that Stella was asking for her. Olive had gone right away and found Jakob, Mr. and Mrs. Adamski, and the children in a semicircle around Stella.

"Thank you," Stella had said to Olive, then fallen into a fit of coughing. *"Jakob told me everything. Michael and Addie, too."*

"If only the hospital staff had listened to you—"

More rattling coughs swallowed Olive's regrets, but it was no matter. Everyone in that room had cycled through their own batteries of "if only." Olive added nothing by voicing her own.

Stella's frail shoulders sank back against her pillows, her eyelids fluttering closed. The visit had exhausted her, likely even before Olive had arrived. The children, her parents, and Jakob all wanted their fill of her.

"I once was lost," Stella whispered through dry, cracked lips, *"and now I'm found. This is all that matters."* When she turned up her palms, Michael and Addie each put their little hands in hers. Her parents murmured to her in Polish.

"But when are you coming home, Mama?" By the look on Jakob's haggard face, it was not the first time Michael had asked.

"Soon." Jakob planted a kiss on his wife's forehead, answering so she wouldn't have to.

Olive had taken her leave shortly afterward, but not before inviting Jakob to bring his children to the bookstore Tuesday morning to enjoy a special event just for them. *"You could visit Stella alone while I watch them."*

He accepted, since his boss had given him sick leave to use this week.

All of this, she would have shared with Erik yesterday. But after the tenth unanswered ring, she hung up. A few hours later, she'd tried again with the same result.

Another train chugged by outside, snapping the cords of her reverie. She still had work to do.

After pushing silver combs into place in her hair, Olive greeted her mother at the kitchen table with a kiss on the cheek, resolved to be grateful for every day she had with her rather than bitter for the ones she didn't. She inhaled Meg's rosewater scent, combined with the aroma coming from her jasmine tea, and catalogued them in her memory as the essence of her mother. Not for the first time since Leo's visit did she realize how fortunate she was that she didn't have to wonder what her parents were like. She'd grown up in a secure, loving family while Erik had been hunting for clues about his.

Another injustice. Another wrong she could not right.

"What's on your agenda today, dear?" Meg asked, likely probing to see if she was officially on the bookstore's payroll yet.

Before Olive could reply, a knock sounded, fast but quiet. As soon as she opened the door, a woman slipped inside and slammed the door shut behind her, then locked it.

"Claire!" Olive captured her in a stunned embrace before standing back to look at her again.

"I had to come." Claire unpinned and removed a hat the same black as her dress. "I made sure I wasn't followed from the station. Warren wouldn't be up this early anyway, not on a Monday morning. You can have no idea how he drinks on Sunday nights."

Rising, Meg embraced Claire as a mother would a prodigal child. Her eyes shimmered. "It's so good to see you again. I thought—"

Claire grasped her hands. "I know. I'm sorry. I'm sorry for everything. When I got the telegram Friday, I decided to apologize in person to Nellie's aunt. I finally recovered Nellie's earrings from the pawn shop yesterday, and I want to give them to Irene myself since there was no time to mail them. I'd be too afraid they'd get lost in the postal system, anyway. I hate to surprise you like this, but I didn't send you a wire that I was coming in case your mail was being watched."

"I'm glad you were prudent," Olive assured her. "Please, sit down. Coffee?"

"Yes, please."

Olive set the coffee to brew and joined Claire and Meg at the table. "Mrs. Collins will be arriving by train this morning to sign off on Nellie's remains. I'm meeting her at the morgue to give her the sweater and scarf. I can bring the earrings with me."

Pink splotched Claire's neck and face. "I want to be there, too."

"You're sure you want to take the risk of being seen?" Olive asked.

"Doesn't Warren still work at Sears? If so, he'll be miles away."

"As far as I know, but let me find out."

With the coffee percolating in the background, Olive dialed his department. When someone answered, Olive asked for Warren Sterling.

"His shift doesn't start for another hour. Call back then."

"All right," Olive said to Claire as soon as she hung up. "By the time we need to leave for the morgue, he'll be at work. We have about two hours and fifteen minutes before then."

Claire's shoulders relaxed. "Thank goodness. I have so much I want to tell you, Olive. I just don't know if I ought to."

Meg, sensitive to the delicate situation, finished her tea and announced she was meeting her sister for breakfast. "Will I see you later today, dear?" she asked Claire.

"I'd like that, Mrs. Pierce. I'm heading back tonight."

With a nod, Meg uttered a brief prayer of protection over her and left Olive and Claire alone.

When the coffee was ready, Olive poured two cups, added cream, and placed them on the table before sitting beside her friend. "Are you safe where you are now?"

"Yes. I'm safer there than I've been in years. I no longer have to wonder if I'll be beaten on a given day. I keep to myself, and so far, that has served me well. But I am so lonely. I miss you, Olive, more than you could ever know."

"I miss you, too." The words were strangled by all the emotion she'd bottled up during the last few weeks and especially the last several days. "But it's worth it to know you're safe. Although I confess I'll feel better on that score once you're back wherever your new home is. Warren can never find you, Claire. If he does—"

"Please." Claire clutched her mug. "I have spent years thinking about Warren. I'd rather not give him one more second of the limited time you and I have together. Just because I can't share about my life doesn't mean you can't tell me about yours. Tell me everything that's happened since Claire Sterling died. Don't you dare leave anything out."

Olive obliged. For the next two hours, she mapped every mountain, valley, and lake in the landscape of her experiences since the day her best friend left. It was such a luxury to be able to share like this. She'd forgotten how well Claire listened, offering all the right questions to clarify or dig deeper, adding her own observations every once in a while, but never derailing the conversation.

When at last Olive declared her tale complete, Claire sat back, running her index finger round her mug's rim. "I caused so much confusion with my attempt to fool Warren. I don't know if Mrs. Collins will forgive me, or Stella's family either, for that matter. If I hadn't meddled with Nellie's clothing, maybe she would have been properly identified right away. And then Stella, who was injured and unconscious, might have been discovered, or if she had at least been labeled a Jane Doe, you would have found her in your search through the hospitals for unidentified victims. Those poor children." She covered a trembling mouth with her hand.

Olive knew she meant Michael and Addie. She didn't respond right away, because everything Claire had said was true. Rain tapped the windows, filling the silence. "All you can do is ask," she finally said. "Whether or not they grant forgiveness is up to them."

The clock from the mantel chimed the hour.

"That's our cue," Olive said. "I'd like to get to the morgue before Irene does so she doesn't have to wait."

She put both mugs in the sink, then went to her room for her gloves, hat, and her satchel, which contained Nellie's clothes. With thunder rattling the windows, she grabbed an umbrella, too.

"We'll take a cab," she said, unwilling to wait in the rain for the streetcar.

The phone rang once. Then stopped. It rang twice, then paused before ringing again.

Claire gasped. "It's the code! You have to answer it!"

Olive swallowed and lifted the earpiece. "Hello?"

"Olive, thank God." Erik's voice was sharp with alarm.

"I—I tried calling you yesterday, twice."

"Did you? Leo and I were surveilling Warren all day. I'm sorry I missed you. I'm sorry about a lot." The urgency in his tone banished any awkwardness she'd expected. She could almost believe they were teammates again.

"Yes, of course. Listen, Erik, I'd love to talk, but I'm on my way out the door right now. We've got an appointment at the morgue with Irene Collins. It's really important that we be on time."

"Who?"

So much had happened, and he didn't know. Quickly, she filled him in.

"Then I'll keep this short," he said, "but what did you mean when you said *'we've'* got an appointment? Who's going with you?"

"Claire's here," she breathed. "She came into town this morning. As I said, we're on our way out right now."

A beat of silence buzzed across the line. "Olive, listen to me. I'm calling from Sears. Warren didn't show up at work this morning."

Chills lifted goose bumps on her skin.

"I went to Warren's house, and his car is gone," he went on, "but he's not at work. I have no idea where he is. If I'd spent the night in the neighborhood, I would know. I could have followed him. But you and Claire cannot go out alone. Wait until I get there, and I'll accompany you. I urge Claire not to go at all, though. The risk that Warren might spot her, if he hasn't already, is too great."

Stones piled into Olive's gut. She told Claire what Erik had reported.

"No." Blanching, Claire stepped back, as if doing so could put distance between herself and Warren. "But I have to meet Mrs. Collins."

"It's raining. We'll use umbrellas, which will completely obscure our heads and shoulders. We'll step into a cab and get out at the morgue." But even as she said it, Olive knew it was no guarantee that Warren wasn't already watching the door in case she, or they, emerged. Perhaps he'd already seen Claire go in. "No," she admitted. "It's no good."

"What time is the appointment?" Erik asked.

Olive told him.

"I can't get to you and then to the morgue in time," he said. "But if you call the morgue and let them know to expect me, I'll meet Mrs. Collins there and, after her appointment, bring her to you. She can go in through the bookstore, like any other customer, and your aunt can send her up. You never have to leave the apartment. I'll wait for Mrs. Collins outside to make sure Warren hasn't somehow followed us. Ring for a cab to pick her up outside the store when she's through, and I'll stay and watch your building."

Olive had held the earpiece away from her head so Claire could hear, as well. As he spoke, Claire nodded. "Yes, yes," she said. "That's better."

"Let's do it," Olive told Erik. "I'll call the morgue right away, then tell Sylvie to expect Mrs. Collins."

"Do you have any other appointments today?"

She told him she didn't.

"Then promise me you'll stay right where you are all day. From across the street at the corner, I'll have a view of both entrances, the front and the rear. Do not leave under any circumstances, either of you. When Claire needs to go back to the train station, I'll take her there myself."

Once again, Olive had not asked for his help, but he was offering it all the same. "And then we'll talk," she added. "After you take Claire to the station, come back and meet my mother."

"I'd love nothing more."

"Good," she said. "Now, get a move on. We've got work to do."

Ninety minutes later, Irene Collins was sitting on Olive's sofa, her black dress spread against the pale yellow, with a cup of tea and lemon shortbread cookies. She looked to be in her forties, with a brown chignon and watery blue eyes. She'd already insisted they use her Christian name.

While Olive and Claire sat in the club chairs, Meg sat beside their guest, exuding compassion through her gentle smile and a brief but sympathetic touch to the woman's back.

"I find myself at quite a loss for words," Irene confessed. "I was going to bring her home with me, or at least offer to. She was a grown woman, after all, and that's something I kept forgetting. The last time I saw her, she was not more than twelve years old, her little sister only three. Still, I was determined that after this, I'd make up for lost time. I had no idea, those weeks we prayed for her recovery, that time was already up."

"It's a shock," Meg murmured. "You've done all you could."

Irene sipped her tea. "But it was too late, wasn't it? The coroner said she died instantly on the ship, which means that by the time I learned of the disaster at all, she was gone, along with her entire family. I was too late, not by minutes or hours, but by years. I ought to have reconciled while I had the chance. That's no one's fault but mine. And yet I was listed as a beneficiary of their life insurance policies. I was named in their will as the guardian for my sister's children, if it ever came to that." Thunder rolled outside, quietly rattling the dishes in the kitchen. "That's how I've been able to pay the hospital bills, you know. That won't stop now that I know the truth, though."

"Pardon me?" Olive asked.

Irene shifted on the cushion. Rain purled on the window behind her. "I intend to pay for Mrs. Petroski's medical bills out of the life insurance money that came to me from Nellie's family," she confirmed. "I can think of no better use for it than to care for the living. I do hope the gesture will be accepted by the Petroskis. I don't want to injure their pride, but neither do I suppose that extended hospital care would be easy for the family to pay for, especially since they've lost her brother's income, and hers, until she fully recovers."

Olive completely agreed. "How very generous," she said, nearly overcome by this unlooked-for grace. "It will ease a great burden, indeed."

"I'm glad of it." Irene's gaze traveled from Olive to Claire. "I understand you have some of my niece's personal belongings?"

Her nose already pink with emotion, Claire laid on the table between them the intricately crocheted cardigan sweater Nellie had worn that day. "She was wearing this. Nellie wore her very best clothes that day, because she was going to be in a beauty pageant at the picnic."

"Was she?" A smile curving one corner of her lips, Irene set down her cup and saucer.

"Last summer she won third place and marched in the suffragette parade, too," Olive offered, adding the heartwarming anecdotes Emma Mueller had passed on to her. She handed Irene the photograph Emma had let her have.

"Bless her." Composure buckling, Irene studied the image and hugged the sweater. "This was my sister's. I made it for her as a wedding present. Surely she must not have hated me if she let her firstborn daughter wear it. Do you know, I have this sweater's twin. It turned out so beautifully that I couldn't bear to part with it, so I crocheted one for myself as well. After the argument that estranged us, I convinced myself that in some small way, as long as we both had these sweaters, we maintained a connection, no matter how slender that thread."

Meg offered her a handkerchief. At length, Irene looked at Claire, an invitation to continue.

"This silk scarf was around her neck," Claire explained. "She earned it by completing her first year of employment with Western Electric. And the earrings—they look precious. A family heirloom, perhaps?"

Irene's eyes lit as Claire dropped the earrings into her palm.

"My mother's. My goodness, Nellie really did wear all her finery that day, didn't she? Thank you for preserving them."

Ridges grooved Claire's brow, and Olive could only imagine the guilt wreaking havoc beneath the surface. "I cannot tell you how sorry I am for what I did," Claire began, and her voice caught. The hospital administrator had explained the situation to Irene over the phone, so she'd had some time to process the information already. "I was thinking only of myself," Claire went on, "when I traded my things for hers. All I wanted was to escape my own life, to convince my husband I had died so I could live in peace."

Irene's expression gave nothing away. "He must have treated you poorly indeed for you to have taken such measures. I know a little something about what that feels like."

"But my actions were my own. I made the choice that caused so much confusion and hurt. I own it completely, and I apologize with everything I am for the sorrow I caused."

Irene softened as she regarded Claire. "There is enough guilt and blame to go around. The hospital staff could have tried harder to understand what Stella was trying to say. Instead, they drugged her. Well-intended or not, they kept her from being lucid enough to play any role in the matter herself. For my part, I could have—" Her posture sagged. "There are so many things I should have done differently over the years. I allowed a disagreement—between our husbands, no less—to separate me from my sister for so long that I didn't know my own niece."

"We all have our regrets," Meg said gently. "There was nothing you could have done to save Nellie or any of her family. The matter was decided before any telegram was sent."

"I don't deny that." Irene sniffed. "But I also cannot deny that my sister died without knowing I still love her and that I'm sorry I ever allowed such pettiness to steal the years away."

No one spoke for a few moments.

At last, Irene squared her shoulders. "You got away from him? Your husband?"

"I did."

Irene set her chin. "Good. I don't pretend to have known Nellie well, but if she's anything like her mother, she would not have been sorry to play a part in your escape. All I ask is that you remember that your freedom wasn't free."

"I do." Tears lined Claire's dark lashes. "I'll never forget."

None of them would.

CHAPTER THIRTY

The rest of the day passed at the unnatural speed that came only in the presence of a friend long missed. Irene left after announcing that Nellie's body would be interred at the cemetery with her family that afternoon. A reverend would meet her there to say a few words, and that was all the company she wished to have. Meg left the apartment to help Sylvie in the store shortly afterwards.

Olive wished the weather wasn't so bleak today, for Irene's sake. But then, she wished a lot of things. She wished she could have sent Irene off with some measure of hope, however meager. She wished Stella and her family hadn't gone through such an ordeal, and that Claire didn't have to leave tonight.

Neither mentioned it. It was as if Olive and Claire were in fierce denial that the clock ticked ever closer to their parting. When conversation veered toward Olive's future with Corner Books & More, she told Claire that her fictitious return address had inspired an actual L. M. Montgomery Fan Club and that Olive had been appointed to get it off the ground.

Instantly, Claire's entire countenance brightened. "Can I help?" she asked. "We've got some time. We can at least plan it out together."

And so they did. Curled up on the sofa, with the portrait of their childhood selves watching from above the fireplace, Claire transformed into a fount of ideas, and Olive played the part of her scribe.

"You're so much better at this job than I am," Olive told her.

"This isn't work, though, it's fun." Claire tucked her legs beneath her on the sofa. "I could do this in my sleep. When is the first meeting?"

Olive nearly laughed aloud at her childlike eagerness. "Want to come?"

"More than you can imagine." Her smile turned wistful. "Speaking of which, isn't there a big party downstairs right now? Your mother mentioned something about the store's sixty-fifth anniversary celebration."

"It's a week-long event, but yes, it does kick off tonight with a special buffet, and Uncle Kristof is playing the violin along with some musicians from the orchestra." Olive glanced at the time. "Aunt Sylvie and my mother are giving speeches in fifteen minutes, and then a guest writer is going to read for us."

"Who?"

Olive smiled. "Carl Sandburg was scheduled for seven o'clock. He's going to read his poem 'Chicago' and some from a collection that won't be published until next year. But he had to push back to eight. Aunt Sylvie is worried people will go home when they don't see Sandburg at seven, as advertised, even if she explains. If there's one thing she hates, it's the embarrassment of a small crowd for a speaker she brings to the store."

Claire murmured her understanding. "I don't suppose we can both go, can we? Add two more bodies to the room?"

A sigh feathered Olive's lips. "I don't think so. We can't risk Warren seeing you. For all we know, he could be there now, hiding among the stacks. Erik has been surveilling all day, but he could have attached himself to a group of customers and slipped in unnoticed."

"You're right. You should go without me. Before you say no, hear me out. This bookstore has been your family's for sixty-five years. That's no small thing. You ought to support your aunt and mother and hear their speeches. Even though the celebration continues throughout the week, this event launches it all."

Olive agreed. "There's another angle to consider. Let's say Warren *is* downstairs or perhaps watching through the windows. If I'm not present, he'll wonder why. He may even assume it's because I'm with you, given how suspicious he is. Honestly, Claire, you're the only reason I wouldn't be there. The last thing I want to do is give him a clue that something else is holding my attention."

"Go. Go now." Claire stood, pulling Olive up by the hand. "Get there before the speeches begin so you don't draw attention to your arrival by being late. Do not leave early. There would be no reason to. I'll be fine here."

Olive dashed to the mirror in the hall and repinned her hair. "But I have no idea how long this will go."

"Listen. If Warren sees you leave early, he'll wonder why. He may follow you and— Just stay to the end."

The logic was sound. "When do you need to leave for the train station?"

"Not until nine o'clock."

Olive stepped into her heels and buckled the straps at her ankles. "I should be back before then. Don't leave this apartment for any reason. Erik is watching from outside. If you need help, flash the lights. He'll come for you. Lock the door behind me."

Her mother and her aunt were glowing. Olive sat between them in a place of honor, Kristof on Sylvie's opposite side. The applause filling the bookstore began after Carl Sandburg's readings, but when Meg and Sylvie rose to give him a standing ovation, their patrons rose as well. When Olive turned, she saw by where their gazes were fixed that they weren't clapping only for the poet. These loyal readers were on their feet for the sisters who had resurrected the bookstore from ashes after the Great Fire of 1871.

Radiant, Meg turned to her younger sister and applauded her for the unwavering dedication that had weathered decades. Olive had never been prouder of them both than she was right now. Beside her, Kristof bowed to his wife.

The evening was a raging success, and Claire had been absolutely right that Olive should not miss it, especially since her siblings and Rozalia weren't here. Silent auction bids for Meg's paintings nearly overflowed the boxes that contained them. Kristof's sparkling music had carried sophistication to every corner of the store as patrons mingled over punch and pastries.

At last, the applause dimmed, and Sylvie joined Mr. Sandburg on the platform, shook his hand again, and began making her closing announcements, including a preview of the rest of the week's events.

Olive scanned the crowd and saw no sign of Warren. Good.

She leaned toward her mother. "I'm going home. Tell Aunt Sylvie I'll come congratulate her later."

All Olive wanted to do was bolt up the stairs and get back to Claire before she had to leave. But when a patron stopped her to chat, she forced herself to engage in small talk in case Warren was watching for undue hurry.

He probably wasn't. He probably hadn't dared to come inside, or if he had, Erik had already stopped him. But she'd rather err on the side of prudence.

Once she was back in her apartment, she closed and locked the door, then faced an empty kitchen and living room. "Claire?" she called quietly, whisking off to the bedroom to see if her friend was resting there. She'd need to get ready to leave for the train station soon.

But the bedroom, like the rest of the apartment, was empty.

Dread vibrating through her, Olive rushed back to the kitchen and spied a letter on the table, written in Claire's hand.

Dear Olive,

I heard noises from upstairs—the apartment I thought was empty—and didn't want to stay here anymore. I gave Erik the signal, and he came to get me. He's standing guard as I write this. Come see me as soon as you get this so we can have our good-bye before we need to go to the station. I'm asking Erik to take me to our special place. Hurry. I need to tell you something that must only be shared in person before I leave. Will be watching for you.

> *Yours,*
> *The Lady of Shalott*

Olive stared at the pseudonym and immediately recalled the scene from *Anne of Green Gables* when Anne found herself in a sinking canoe.

The *Eastland*?

Frowning, she picked up the letter and examined the handwriting more carefully. It wasn't forged, which she ought to have known from the Lady of Shalott reference. Only Claire would have written that.

She hurried to change her heels for rubber-soled pumps. The ship had finally been raised but was still in the river at the dock. It was the last place Warren would guess and smart to name it using a code in case he broke into the apartment and found the letter.

Olive never would have thought of the meeting place herself. She had no desire to revisit the ship that had tossed so many souls to their deaths.

Surely Warren knew that. And that was what made it the safest.

Besides, Olive couldn't think of another location nearby so easily identified by a phrase clear to her and hidden from Warren.

Grabbing a pen, Olive scrawled *Be back soon* on Claire's letter and left it for her mother to find.

Night draped the city, and fog ruffled its hem. Olive couldn't help but glance over her shoulder as she set off on the two-block jaunt to the river's edge. In a burst of inspiration, she'd worn one of her mother's old hats rather than her usual one in an effort to change her silhouette into one Warren wouldn't so easily recognize. The large brim hid her face, in case shadows and fog weren't enough.

Two blocks. It wasn't long, but Chicago after dark was not for cowards. The districts packed with vice were several blocks south, and she was headed north, but her senses were still on high alert. Being on guard for Warren made every stranger a threat.

Streetlamps buzzed, insects darting in and out of their hazy glow. The El roared overhead as she crossed Lake Street. In one more block, she'd meet Claire and laugh over her frazzled nerves.

She passed a policeman on his beat and felt somewhat mollified. From the shadows not far away, a fight broke out, and the officer gave chase, blowing his whistle, palm on some weapon at his hip.

The Clark Street Bridge loomed before her. At the foot of it, she turned left onto the wharf.

The *Eastland* rose up from the river, filthy and grey. It was still tied to the dock, and the ropes creaked as it shifted on the inky river. The floodlights that had been affixed to the Reid Murdoch Building had been removed now that the ship had been raised. Gone, too, were the tungsten-nitrogen lamps that had aided in the round-the-clock recovery of bodies. All that was left was the battered ship.

Olive did not believe in ghosts. She didn't have to. Memories alone were enough to haunt her. As she walked nearer to the *Eastland* with slowing steps, these came rushing back to her with the smells of rust and coal-dusted water. In her mind's eye, she was no longer alone but jostled and pressed by a merry crowd. She saw the boy on his father's shoulders, a toy ship in his hand. She heard the Norwegian woman on the ship repeating, *"I don't like the feel of this boat."* She felt Michael's and Addie's little hands in hers.

With her flashlight, she scanned the wharf's warehouses, shops, and market stalls. Surely Erik or Claire would show themselves, and they could all get in Erik's car for their rendezvous before Claire had to be at the station. Because being here felt more and more like a bad idea with every breath she took.

But that was nonsense. She was not afraid of the dark.

Nor was she afraid of the past that she had already overcome. Inhaling deeply, she faced the *Eastland* again. Gone were the smokestacks that had towered above it. And gone were all the lifeboats that had topped the hurricane deck. They had never been used. There hadn't been time. There hadn't even been time to unlock the cabinets that held the life jackets, let alone distribute them.

The sooner Olive could find Erik and Claire and get out of here, the better.

Strange. There was a gangway connecting the ship to the dock. Did Claire really mean Olive was to meet her *inside* it?

Footsteps sounded behind her, at least three pairs. As muffling as the fog was, they had to be close. As they grew even louder, so did male laughter, but she couldn't see anyone.

Unnerved, she stepped onto the gangway.

"Olive?" Claire called from inside the ship. "It's me, Claire Sterling. Come inside but watch your step. It's slippery in here. Dark, too, and I accidentally dropped my flashlight overboard."

Olive froze. Claire didn't use Warren's surname anymore. And there was no need to identify herself at all, since Olive was answering Claire's direction to meet her here.

This was a warning. A trap.

Her throat dried. "I'm here," she called. "Come down, and we'll talk out here. Is Erik with you?" She knew he couldn't be but wanted to see how Claire would respond.

Silence stung her.

"Olive," Claire said again, her voice now serrated and higher pitched. Movement caught Olive's eye, and she spied Claire waving from the promenade deck. "Of course he's here. Come in so we can have a private conversation."

Claire was lying. If Erik was there, he would have spoken and come out by now, and she wouldn't have called herself Claire *Sterling*. And she would only lie if she was forced to.

Erik hadn't come for her. Warren had.

Olive swung her flashlight's beam up to Claire, who angled slightly, exposing a fresh cut on a swelling cheekbone.

Then she was gone, jerked from behind with a yelp.

Chills shook Olive. Leaving Claire alone with him was out of the question. If Olive tried running for help, Warren would be free to do whatever he wanted to Claire while she was gone.

Warren was fishing, Claire was the bait, and Olive was hooked. She couldn't turn away from her friend.

CHAPTER THIRTY-ONE

Olive needed to think. She needed to act. And she needed to be flawless.

Warren held Claire hostage on the promenade deck. Olive had to get him away from her. Pulse whooshing in her ears, she walked the plank that led her inside the ship, feeling for all the world like Sir Henry Baskerville sent alone across the foggy moor to lure the murderous hound.

At the main deck, she turned on her flashlight. The floor wasn't where it ought to be. It had collapsed several feet, likely from the weight of the water as the crew lifted the ship. As a result, the warped decking was sunk well into the boiler and engine rooms. Wreckage sprawled along the port side.

She'd been prepared to see broken chairs and benches. She'd expected mud and decay. What plucked her nerves were the small signs of humanity still trapped here. A shattered picnic basket, an unmatched glove. A woman's high-buttoned shoe.

Olive swung the beam of light the length of the deck and back again to gain her bearings. This deck had boasted wallpapered parlors with private bathrooms attached. The rooms were distorted now, the paper streaked where it had managed to cling, rippling, to the walls. Large sections of it had simply peeled away. At one end, a bar remained, but the wood was splintered and warped.

Bottles still full of water, soda, and beer shifted on the floor among shards of glass filmed with silt.

She moved the light up the wall until she found the bottom of the staircase. Claire was two levels above, assuming she was still on the promenade deck. Olive sat on the doorway's ledge, legs dangling above the collapsed floor, and jumped. It would be a trick to get out the same way, now that the door was ten feet above her, even if she and Claire could manage to get this far uninjured.

She couldn't think about that now.

The air was thick with humidity and reeked of rotting fish. The floor complained as she made her way toward the stairs. A bottle of Coca-Cola slowly rolled into her path, then out of it with the gentle rocking of the ship. But Olive couldn't blame the turmoil in her middle on motion sickness. Fighting every urge to flee this haunted place, she made her next move. The way the floor had buckled, it remained high enough near the stairs that she could reach the bottom step and haul herself onto it. The balustrade had been knocked away by the crush of people trying to escape. Turning off the flashlight, she stayed well away from the edge as she climbed.

Once she gained the cabin deck, she studied the ceiling and imagined Warren and Claire above it. Judging by the absence of footsteps, Warren was waiting for Olive to come to him. If what Claire had said was true, he didn't have a light anymore, which gave her a distinct advantage. If Claire had been forced to say that, to pretend that was why she couldn't come down . . . Well. Olive prayed it was the former.

She had no idea when Warren's patience might run out, regardless of his ability to see, but she needed to refamiliarize herself with this deck. Praying she wouldn't lose her footing on some unseen piece of wreckage, she headed toward the staircase, then went beyond it. If she recalled correctly, the dining room was about half a block ahead.

There.

Once she was inside, she tried to close the door behind her so she could shine her light in the room, but the frame had twisted. And the door wasn't there at all. Heart racing, she covered the flashlight lens with her hand before turning it on. Separating her fingers slightly allowed the thinnest rays to seep between. It was enough for her to see but not enough to capture Warren's notice from the deck above.

The dining room was a shambles. As expected, battered chairs crowded the port side, along with shattered china and glassware. Tables that had been bolted down had sheared off and smashed against the bulkhead. Silt covered everything.

With the aid of the fractured light, Olive moved quicker now, following what would prove to be either a brilliant idea or reckless hope. The dining room was attached to the kitchen. At the kitchen doorway, she flicked off her light and tested the door on its hinges. It closed. Better yet, it latched. She opened it again and retraced her steps through the dining room.

Claire's muffled voice drew Olive back toward the staircase. Before she replied, however, she veered to the port side and bent, groping for anything to use as a weapon.

"Claire?" she shouted. Her fingers closed around the neck of a broken bottle. Her heart slammed against her chest as she stood again. "I don't want to come up there. Come on down to the main deck, and we'll talk."

She backed away, toward the dining room. If she could convince Warren she wasn't coming to him, he would have to come to her. And if she could lure him away from Claire, Claire stood a chance of somehow getting away, didn't she?

Those were two big *ifs*. But right now, they were all she had.

"Olive, run, he has a gun! He—" Claire's scream from the deck above sent a jolt through her, but the thud and silence that followed clutched her core.

She dropped the bottle into her pocket. It was no match for a bullet. Palms sweating, she listened for clues. Warren must have taken Erik out of play before he abducted Claire. If Erik had been able to help, he'd be here by now. She hated to think what that meant—both for him, and for Claire and herself. But where was the policeman who was supposed to be patrolling this neighborhood? He ought to have heard Claire's scream.

No one came running to their rescue.

Above her, the promenade deck groaned. "The jig is up, Olive." Warren's taunt floated down the stairs. "You and Claire humiliated me in front of the entire city. You made a fool of me." He was on the steps now, coming down. "No one makes a fool of Warren Sterling. Not without consequences." Five more steps, and he'd be on the cabin deck with her.

Her breathing grew quick and shallow. He wasn't close enough to harm Claire now.

She licked her lips. "Warren?" He needed to hear her so he'd know she was close.

Close enough to follow. To chase.

At the bottom of the stairs, he turned a slow circle, his silhouette barely visible. He had no flashlight. Thank God.

She shifted her feet, deliberately scattering whatever rubbish she'd been standing on. He couldn't know that she wanted to be found. He had to believe he was in control.

Warren turned toward her.

"Stay away from me." It was no ruse to give voice to her panic.

"I've stayed away from you for weeks. No longer."

She backed away.

He stepped forward. "You must have thought you were so smart, turning Magnussen against me like that. You were a worthy opponent. But every game must end. And in every game, there can only be one winner. Not two. One."

"Where's Erik?" she blurted. "What have you done?"

His footsteps slurred closer to her. He wasn't picking up his feet, which could only mean he preferred to bump into wreckage with the toe of his shoe rather than risk tripping on it.

Good.

"There was a moment this evening when I was sure he would best me. If it were merely hand to hand, he would have."

"What are you saying? Did you—you didn't shoot him."

"Someone had to."

Dizziness washed over her. She planted her feet wide to regain her balance. "You didn't. Not right there next to the courthouse. There would have been witnesses, including the police. You're lying." He had to be. But the longer she could keep him talking, the more time Claire would have to make her escape.

Another shuffling step. "You're right. I didn't shoot him there. I know enough to choose my location carefully."

"For murder?" Olive gasped.

"For justice."

The man was mad, and he had a gun, probably pointed at her.

"You have to understand," he went on. "I cannot abide injustice. Magnussen wronged me. You influenced him, granted, but he agreed to work for me, and then he broke the contract. He must be held accountable."

"By killing him?" It couldn't be true. He was playing her. Yet a sickening dread took hold.

"Enough about him. You hid my wife. You turned my private investigator against me." Something shifted in his tone, turning hard and dark. "You and Claire both must be brought to justice. And you must admit, there is no better justice than this. To end your lives here on the very ship you told me had taken Claire's. I'm about to be convinced that the *Eastland* really did kill my wife. And her best friend, too. At least they died together."

"You'll be locked away for the rest of your life." Olive spoke toward the starboard bulkhead, hoping the ricochet might confuse him rather than allow him to pinpoint her position. Every second she stayed near him was a gamble.

"Enough conversation. Claire's waiting."

Olive turned and ran, holding her skirt above her knees in the dark, gripping her unlit flashlight.

Warren gave chase.

She thrummed with alarm and exertion, but as long as he viewed himself as the predator and she the prey, she had a chance. She ran bent at the waist in case he should fire a bullet in the dark.

She could hear him slow at the threshold to the dining room, and she guessed he hadn't yet explored this space. In his hesitation, she reached the door to the kitchen, went inside to make a racket, then slipped out again, closing and latching the door behind her.

Another gamble.

Had he fallen for it? Would he be able to find the door in the dark?

Doubt seized her as she crouched several feet beyond, the broken glass in her pocket pressing into her thigh. Her gaze probed the darkness for his form, praying for his approach. She didn't want to hurt him, unless forced to in self-defense. All she wanted was to get Claire and get away. She held her breath.

His feet shuffled along the floor, but there was something else too—a constant brushing she could only hope was the slide of his fingers along the bulkhead, looking for an alcove or a closet or a room. Looking for her.

A beat of silence, then a *thunk*. Had his hand slipped from the wall to the recessed door?

Her heartbeat so loud she feared it would give her away, Olive stood and dared to inch closer as she listened to the handle turn. The hinges squeaked. The door was open.

"What have we here?" But his voice was turned from her and, if she could believe her senses, coming from inside the kitchen.

He was in.

It was a torture of suspense to wait until she thought he'd crept at least a few yards into the kitchen. Then she lunged for the door to close it. If she'd thought to do it stealthily, she failed, her nerves making her movements clumsy and forceful.

The door slammed, and she grabbed one of the only chairs she'd found in the wreckage that hadn't broken. With all her might, she wedged it up under the door's handle, preventing an easy opening.

It wouldn't hold long.

The flashlight beam bounced crazily over the cabin deck as Olive raced to the stairs and up to the promenade. Swinging around, she spotted Claire gagged and bound to a bench still bolted to the deck. But she was alive, thank God, and conscious.

Olive rushed to her and snatched the rag from her mouth.

"Is he coming?" Claire rasped.

"I'm sure he is." Olive shined her light on the knots binding Claire's wrists behind the bench and just as quickly gave up untying them. Instead, she turned off the flashlight and traded it for the broken bottle in her pocket. Veins buzzing with urgency, she gripped its neck and sawed the rope with the jagged glass. They were silent as she worked, listening for Warren. By small degrees, the rope frayed.

"That's good," Claire said. "I can get loose from here. My ankles."

Dropping to her knees, Olive attacked the last bond. One cord cut through. Then two. Olive abandoned the glass and tore the rest loose.

Claire shook them off and stood, rubbing her raw wrists. "Which way?"

"There's only one way off this ship." Warren's voice arrowed out of the darkness. His arrogance turned Olive cold.

She squeezed Claire's hand. "He's wrong," she whispered.

They could jump.

But they could barely see. The moon gave an ambient light, but the hurricane deck blocked the sky, enshrouding them in shadows.

At least that meant Warren could hardly see, either. "Time's up, ladies. Step to the rail."

Claire rushed to the starboard side, closest to the dock. "Help!" she cried over the empty wharf, the fog absorbing her words. "Up here, on the *East*—!"

Warren grasped her right arm and wrenched her back from the edge. "Port side," he snarled. "And don't waste your breath. The police aren't on this beat tonight." With a shove, he sent her stumbling across the deck.

When Olive caught her, Claire cried out in pain. "He dislocated my shoulder," she said through gritted teeth. The awkward angle of her arm proved something was wrong. "He's done it before. Olive, he'll kill us both."

"He'll only try." Mastering another surge of adrenaline, Olive slowed her steps as they walked across the deck, buying time to think and time to fear her plan might not work after all. Claire couldn't swim with a dislocated shoulder, and Olive had no idea how to set it.

The port side rail wasn't what it used to be. The once waist-high barrier had warped with the weight of the ship pushing it into the riverbed. In one place, the rod bent as low as the knees. That was where Olive steered Claire. At the rail, she looked down into a darkness thick and glistening. If they were going to live, they'd need to take the fall.

"Turn around," Warren said.

Olive whispered, "We'll have to jump. Stay under as long as you can." She didn't want to. She couldn't imagine how much pain it would cause Claire with her injured shoulder. But the way they'd come in was closed to them.

"I said turn around," Warren repeated. "I have something I need to say to you, Mrs. Sterling. The last thing you'll ever hear."

As they turned, Claire's expression bunched in pain and dread and fear.

"I loved you," Warren started. "It's because I loved you so much that I have to do this. If I can't have you, no one else can."

"That's not love," Claire told him. "That's a disease. You're sick, Warren."

Olive kept her eye on the outline of his gun. It was raised but not aimed. Not yet.

"If I didn't love you, I wouldn't care that you left me," Warren countered. "It's because I love you that I can't let you continue walking this earth unless you're mine."

His logic was as twisted as the metal chilling the backs of Olive's knees, but he kept talking, enamored with his faulty reasoning. Either he didn't notice the muffled sound of a car turning onto South Water Street, or he was so sure it would pass without incident that he didn't care.

Olive did. No one looking at the *Eastland* from the wharf would have any idea they were being held hostage in the dark on the opposite side of the steamship. She could change that. She whipped the flashlight from her pocket. She stood next to one of the supports connecting this deck to the one above it, and she slowly moved the flashlight until it was behind the pole, facing up. Breath held, she turned it on, sending a beam straight up into the sky.

Noise carried from the other side of the vessel as though from a great distance, but that could be the fog playing tricks. Doors slammed, at least two of them.

Warren halted his speech mid-sentence, listening at last. The hammer clicked back on his gun.

The ship shuddered. If others were on board now, they were only getting closer.

The instant Warren looked at the stairs, Olive and Claire leapt over the railing.

CHAPTER THIRTY-TWO

Some said time slowed in a moment of crisis. But for Olive, what happened next seemed to converge into one ragged heartbeat. Warren's shout. The crack of gunfire through fog. The distant *ping* of bullets hitting metal. Falling, falling, then hitting water so hard that it was like breaking through black ice.

She sank ever deeper, holding her breath while cold consumed her. All was darkness, without daylight to beckon from above.

But Olive had done this before.

It is only the lake, she told herself. *A canoe awaits, and so does Erik, and there are fireworks spangling the night. There is no madman with a gun, waiting for us to surface.*

Lies, and she knew it. Even so, they helped quell the rising urge to inhale. The river was only twenty feet deep, but in the surrounding dark, it might as well have been a mile. There was a current tonight that she hadn't felt before. Could she count on her instincts to guide her up, or in her panic would she swim the wrong direction?

Help, Olive prayed, lungs growing tight and hard. Just one word, over and again, for her slowing brain could form no other. The adrenaline that had gotten her this far faded into nothing more than violent shivering.

Something whizzed past her in the water. Then something bit

315

and tracked fire down her arm. Bullets. Warren was firing into the river, but she'd only been grazed, not hit.

Now she knew which way was up. She hoped he'd emptied his revolver.

Unable to bear the pressure any longer, she kicked furiously toward the surface and broke through it, gulping a giant breath. The *Eastland* towered next to her, close enough to touch. But where was Claire? They had entered the water within feet of each other. She couldn't be far.

Heart hammering a warning, Olive spun in a circle. Bubbles rose to the surface and popped. She dove under, eyes open and burning, blind. Her chest a corkscrew, she plunged deeper.

There. A cold hand grasped hers. Summoning her strength, Olive hooked her arms around Claire's waist, then swam with all her might until they reached air.

"Are you shot?" Olive guided Claire's left hand to find purchase on the hull. A seam in the metal held their fingertips, but barely.

Claire shook her head, still coughing and sputtering. She groaned. "It's my shoulder. I can't—I can't—"

From three decks above, Warren's laughter dropped like cold water. "Fish in a barrel," he declared. "Good thing I brought more bullets."

"Duck!" Olive yanked Claire beneath the water and swam deep while counting the shots she could barely hear from above.

After six, she knew he was out. She feared he would reload. But in that precious span of time, she brought Claire up to the surface for air.

Claire's stark white hand clung to the hull, her black hair cloaking the rest of her. "I can't do that again," she whispered. "I can't go on."

"You can't faint, that's what you can't do," Olive whispered back, though she worried the pain might be enough to cause it. "You can't give up, not now."

Another bullet hit the water, spraying her face. When another hit a few feet away, she held her breath and waited. He fired to her right, then again to the left of her.

Warren couldn't see them through the fog. He was guessing.

Olive clung to the side of the ship beside Claire, her fingertips cramping on the slimy hull seam. They couldn't stay here forever. They had half a city block to get to the end of the ship, and then they could make it to the wharf. With a nudge, she urged Claire to edge along slowly so as not to cause audible ripples.

But Claire only had one hand to hold her up, and she was fighting a losing battle with indescribable pain. Even so, this plan was a better bet than swimming for the opposite shore.

Shouts sounded above them. "Freeze!" a man called. "Drop your weapon and put your hands where I can see them!"

Claire was sinking, her head lolling to one side.

"Claire," Olive called, "float on your back, and I'll pull you to shore. But don't you dare faint, or we're both going down."

Moaning, Claire leaned back with her head on Olive's shoulder, her body floating among the ripples. While men struggled on the promenade deck, Olive blocked the noise from her mind and poured all her concentration into getting back to land.

Her muscles burned and trembled by the time they cleared the stern. "The docks are not twenty feet from here," she told Claire. Just because she couldn't see them through the fog didn't mean they were not there.

Memory knocked, but she would not admit it. She could not think of that drizzly July morning when hundreds had died with exactly the same view, or closer still.

"Almost there, sister," Olive panted.

But swimming in a dress, in the dark, with one arm around her injured friend, was getting the better of her. Her right calf cramped, and she flexed her foot to fight it off, but the muscle seized even tighter. She slipped down into the water and came back up spitting the river out of her mouth while Claire did the same.

Lord, she prayed, *I can't do this on my own. I can't save her.*

I can't even save myself. I need your help now and every day.
Whatever she did, it was through God's strength alone. If she had
ever denied it before, she'd been wrong. "Help!" she cried aloud.

Light swept over her, and she turned, only for the beam to slam
into her eyes.

"There you are, ladies!" a woman called from the dock. God's
help, in the form of Detective Alice Clement. "Lovely evening for
a swim! Look alive now, here comes a ring."

A life preserver splashed into the river beside Olive. Relief
flooded her as she looped an arm through it and with the other
held Claire fast. Together, they were towed away from the *Eastland*,
away from Warren, and to the safety of dry land.

"Careful," Olive called up as she helped Claire climb the ladder
to the dock. "Her right shoulder is dislocated."

"Claire, I presume? Charmed." Detective Clement helped her
up, and Olive climbed out after her.

Legs shaking, Olive sat on the dock and took a blanket from
the stack waiting beside her. Wrapping it around her, she massaged her calf and watched Clement guide Claire to lie down.
With bright and cheerful murmuring, Clement knelt and tucked
her strands of pearls into her jacket before leaning over Claire.
She bent Claire's right arm to ninety degrees and, with her other
hand firmly on the shoulder socket, shoved the arm back into
place with a loud *pop*.

"Atta girl!" Clement cheered while Claire gave a sharp cry of
pain. "Well done. That'll be sore for a while."

"But she's all right?" Olive asked.

"Right as rain, or will be," Clement announced.

Cautiously, Claire pushed herself up and accepted the blanket
Clement wrapped around her. "Where's Warren?" She cradled
her right arm. Water dripped from her sleeves and between the
wooden slats, back into the river below.

"In custody and en route to the station. Don't worry, either
of you. That man is going to answer for what he's done, or my

name isn't Alice Clement." The ostrich feather on her hat bobbed with every nod.

Claire covered her mouth but could not disguise the quaking of silent sobs.

Clement gave another nod. "I should say so. Now, if you're strong enough, what say we get off this creaky dock and back to terra firma?"

Olive's legs threatened to buckle when she stood but soon proved reliable enough to carry her. Claire leaned on Clement as they put the river behind them, but once on the wharf, she turned to Olive.

"I hate that Warren used me to get you on that ship."

Clement's police car remained parked on South Water Street, engine still running, headlamps muted in the fog.

"I knew before I stepped foot on it, thanks to you. Detective Clement, your timing was impeccable."

Clement smiled and shrugged. "I had help. How do you think we knew to come?"

"The cop on this beat?" Maybe he'd gone for backup. But if he'd left without even trying to stop Warren himself, he wouldn't be winning any medals for bravery.

"Not a chance. McAdams was patrolling this beat, but a fight broke out a few blocks from here, involving some theft from one of the warehouses. Distracted him well and good. Convenient, eh? He caught up with a few of the hoodlums, and they're cooling their heels in lockup now. I have a feeling we'll find out pretty soon that Sterling paid them to cause a ruckus, luring McAdams away. Snake."

Of course. Baiting was one of Warren's most practiced skills.

"Once we got here," Clement continued, "we had no idea where to look in that giant steamship. But then we saw a light shine straight into the sky like a beacon. Your signal, I take it? Good one."

Olive nodded. "But I still don't understand who tipped you off."

"Actually, your mother called us."

The tiny spark of hope that Erik had been involved guttered and died. "Thank God she did," Olive murmured. "But—"

Clement held up a hand, flicking a glance at a policeman approaching from the direction of the *Eastland*. "Listen. I know you want the full story, and we need yours, too. But she's worried sick, and I'd be a terrible woman if I didn't tell you to go straight home and put her at ease. Get cleaned up and into dry clothes, the both of you, and if you didn't get a typhus shot after your last dip in the drink, you'd better get it tomorrow. Now, get in my car, I'll drive you home before my partner over there insists on interrogating you while you catch your death of cold. We'll come by for your statements in an hour."

Olive felt like she'd done this before. Only this time, when she arrived home in a blanket soaked with the Chicago River, Claire was with her, and her mother was home to receive them both. The hugs that woman could give were nothing short of ferocious.

"Thank you for calling the police," Olive said when Meg finally released her and embraced Claire next. "I'm sorry you ended your beautiful night like this. Detective Clement said you're worried sick."

"What an understatement! There are no words for what I felt." Meg wiped her face with the back of her hand. "But look at the state of you two. Hurry and get out of those wet things and into a hot bath. We'll talk later. Claire, I'll take you down to Sylvie's place so you don't have to wait for Olive to finish."

The next twenty minutes were purely mechanical. Olive slammed the door on her questions about Erik and focused solely on washing the river from hair and skin. Knowing the police would be back, she changed into a white lawn shirtwaist and grey skirt, towel-dried her hair, and pinned it up again. When she emerged, she returned to the living room.

There, on the sofa beside her mother, sat Erik. He looked as ragged and worn as his clothing.

Olive launched herself at him as he stood, and he wrapped his arms around her, lifting her off the ground. She wept. Soon, she would demand answers about where he'd been and how he was here if he'd been shot. And if he hadn't been shot, how he could excuse his absence when he'd made her believe he'd keep them safe.

But right now, it was enough that he was here and strong enough to hold her. And that he hadn't yet let her go.

"It's all right," he said. But the shake in his voice suggested that he, too, had feared that it might not be. "Thank God you're all right," he whispered. "Thank you, God."

She didn't know how long they stayed that way, but it was long enough for her pulse to come down from its painful spike. It was time enough for her to realize that her mother had seen it all, and for Olive to recognize that she didn't mind.

At last, her feet touched solid ground again as Erik set her down. Olive heard Meg busying herself in the kitchen with the teakettle, most likely to give them as much privacy as the small apartment could afford.

Olive's initial relief faded, and her questions returned. Every fear and frustration poured into her fist, and she pounded his chest. "Where *were* you tonight? I needed you. Claire and I both needed you. I thought—" Her voice buckled under the fear she couldn't name.

Swallowing, Erik blinked his red-rimmed eyes. "You thought I would keep you safe. You thought you could trust me. And I failed on both counts, betraying your trust all over again."

"I thought you were dead!" She sluiced the tears from her face. "I was terrified. For Claire and for myself, but also for you. I couldn't imagine what happened to you, other than that Warren had killed you to get to us. He implied as much. I thought your death was our fault, and that's not something I could live with."

"I would have given my life for yours. That was Warren's plan."

321

Olive stared at him. He looked terrible but, as far as she could tell, uninjured. He certainly hadn't been shot. Then her gaze snagged on the scorched, torn fabric of his shirt. She pressed her fingers to the spot but couldn't feel his heartbeat. Something was in the way.

She drew back. "Tell me everything. Please."

A quiet knock at the door preceded Claire's return. Sylvie and Kristof came with her. After Olive embraced them both, Erik extended his hand to Claire.

"We meet at last." His smile was grave and apologetic. "I'm so sorry for all you've been through, especially on my watch."

Olive pointed to the kitchen table. "Now we can talk," she said.

Everyone sat, filling all six chairs, and the story of the evening's events unspooled. As Olive had suspected, Warren had deliberately shown himself to Erik after Olive had gone down to the bookstore.

"So I followed him on foot." Erik sighed as if disappointed in his decision.

"He lured you into a dark alley or something, didn't he?" Claire asked.

"That he did. I was ready for the confrontation, man to man. Turned out, it was man to thugs."

"What?" Olive gasped.

"He wasn't going to get his hands dirty," Erik went on. "But he isn't above hiring others to do the dirty work for him. There were at least two young men waiting for me when I turned into the alley behind that German saloon on Dearborn. One acted like he wanted to fight me, but I told him I had no quarrel with him. All I wanted was to chase Warren, who I could still see at that point. Then someone hit me over the head from behind and knocked me out."

He glanced from Olive's mother to her aunt and uncle, as though wondering if his story was too much for them.

"Well? What happened next?" Sylvie urged, her hand firmly ensconced in her husband's.

A small smile hooked Erik's lips. "The next thing I knew, I woke up in an alley in the Levee district, where muggings gone wrong are commonplace. They must have hoisted me into a car and driven me away. After they dumped me, one of them shot me. When I awoke, they were nowhere to be found, and neither was my hat, jacket, or wallet. All I had was an ache in my chest."

"You're kidding," Olive said. "You were shot, and you were *sore* afterwards? I thought you were mortal."

"One-hundred-percent, I assure you. And one-hundred-percent suspicious of Warren Sterling." Erik unfastened the top buttons of his shirt and spread it open. "I wear this for special occasions."

Kristof squinted at the dull, grey-yellow fabric. "What are we looking at, Erik?"

"A vest made of tightly woven silk, linen, and wool. It's a half inch thick." He buttoned his shirt again.

"And this stops bullets?" Claire asked.

"I'm living proof. Whoever shot me ran off right afterwards and had no idea I'd survive." He pulled a handkerchief from his pocket and opened it. A bullet nested inside.

Murmurs circled the table. Incredulous, Olive slid the handkerchief closer so she could inspect the misshapen metal. "But how did you know it would work?"

"The magic of the written word, of course." He smiled at Sylvie. "I read a couple of articles about silk's impenetrability, even to bullets. It was a priest in Chicago who engineered a vest like this, proving its effectiveness by voluntarily being shot. He was unharmed. If it worked for the priest, I figured it would work for me, too."

"So you woke up, alive but in the most vice-ridden section of the city, without money to pay for a cab out of there," Olive said. "I imagine that's about the time things started heating up for Claire."

Claire nodded. "Warren had a key to the building. He found the spare key you gave me years ago, Livvie."

"Did he come other times? Before tonight?" Olive asked.

"He mentioned once. All he found was ashes in the hearth, but it was enough to convince him that you knew where I was and that you were worth his surveillance. All he had to do was make sure Erik was no longer watching, and then, when he saw you in the bookstore, he let himself in as if he owned the place."

Olive felt her color drain. "But how did he know you were here at all? Once you arrived, we kept the drapes drawn and we didn't leave once."

"He noticed," Claire said. "He's become an expert on all your routines, including what time you open and close your drapes. So when he swung by before work this morning and saw them still closed though it was well past seven, he figured there was a reason. He called in sick from the hotel down the street, then came back to watch the drapes that never opened."

"And once he caught a glimpse of my car," Erik added, "he assumed you were hiding Claire. That's the thing about paranoid, suspicious folks. Every once in a while, they're actually right."

Claire rubbed at her cuticles. "He made me write that letter to you, Olive. I hated doing it, but he was literally holding a gun to my head."

"What about the code you used, pointing to the *Eastland* by calling yourself the Lady of Shalott?"

"He told me to write it as though I was afraid he might see it. He told me to write something only you would understand so you'd believe it wasn't forged."

"It worked," Olive admitted. "It shouldn't have!" The note still lay on the kitchen table. She spun it around and pointed. "There are blot marks at key places. One in the beginning, one in the word *Erik*, and one when you signed your name. At the time, I figured the pen was faulty, but you were hesitating at those places, weren't you? You were pausing to think or argue."

When Claire confirmed it, Olive groaned. Anyone who had read *The Hound of the Baskervilles* ought to have noticed such an anomaly. If she had, she could have notified the police right away.

Erik picked up the thread of the story. "While Warren was abducting Claire, I was scrambling for change to make a phone call, let alone hail a taxi. It took me several precious minutes to find my way to the Pacific Garden Mission to use their telephone. I'm afraid my first conversation with Mrs. Pierce was a terrifying one for her."

"I'll not deny it," Meg said. "But it was the situation that scared me. Not you, dear."

Olive raised an eyebrow at her mother.

"In any case, she told me about the letter and explained the Lady of Shalott, so I knew the three of you had gone to the *Eastland*. I knew I couldn't get there in time, so I asked Mrs. Pierce to call the police and send them right away. I told her to connect with Detective Clement if she could, since Clement knew the background and would take the situation seriously. By the time I got to the *Eastland* myself, Warren had been arrested, and you ladies were already recovered. I was too late."

Olive opened her mouth to speak but was so overcome that she found no words.

"But without your call to Meg," Kristof said, "and hers to the police, this story would not have this happy ending. By all accounts, son, you were right on time."

Olive grasped Erik's hand with both of hers, trusting that her touch would say what her voice could not.

The police had long since come and gone. Erik, Sylvie, and Kristof left shortly after, and Meg had retired for the night. But Olive was not ready for sleep.

Neither was Claire, who curled beside her on the sofa, head resting on a cushion. They were together, safe, whole. Alive. None of these had seemed likely mere hours ago. Olive still couldn't fully grasp what had happened tonight. What *could* have happened and what had *almost* happened felt more impossible still. Her statement to the police sounded so outlandish that it could have been a story from a novel.

But in a novel, the story would end soon. The villain had been caught, and justice was imminent. The would-be victims had escaped. All that was left was to wrap it up in a shiny bow.

Life didn't work that way. Chapters upon chapters remained unwritten, stretching out far beyond the point of escape. Surviving trauma wasn't the end of the story. It was only the beginning.

"It's going to take me a while to believe that Warren can't reach me now," Claire said, dispelling the quiet.

"He won't be reaching anyone but his lawyer," Olive reassured her.

The possibility of acquittal seemed remote. When the police came to take their statements, Detective Clement had informed them that during the struggle on the *Eastland*, Warren had shot an officer. Doctors predicted a full recovery for the wounded policeman, but the consequences for Warren would be severe. It was another serious crime added to the charges of abduction and conspiracy to murder. Soon the police would find the men Warren had hired to kill Erik, and with Erik's testimony, combined with the evidence of his vest and the bullet that couldn't penetrate it, Warren was sure to go to prison.

"You don't have to stay away," Olive added. "Please don't rush off tomorrow morning."

"I won't." Claire rubbed the muscles in her neck. "I don't think I'll be able to carry trays and wait tables for a while anyway. I'm going to lose my job at the restaurant over this." She pointed to her shoulder.

"Would that be so very bad?" Olive tucked a leg beneath her. "You were only there to get away from Warren. He'll be sent to prison in Joliet soon enough. Come back to Chicago for good. You do realize I'll have an opening for a roommate soon, right?"

"Don't tease, Liv. I won't be able to resist."

"Well, that is the general idea."

Outside, the fog rolled away. A moonbeam fell through the window and lay like a silver benediction upon the painting of Olive and Claire.

"It's a sign," Olive whispered. "Kindred spirits aren't meant to be parted."

The clock in the hall struck midnight.

A new day had begun.

CHAPTER THIRTY-THREE

TUESDAY, AUGUST 17, 1915

Olive straightened her apple-green suit jacket. After checking the angle of her hat, she inhaled deeply and entered the MetLife office.

Blanche was not at her desk. Gwendolyn leapt up to greet her, tucking a wayward blond lock behind her ear. "Olive! I read in the paper about what happened last night at the docks. Did you really escape death by gunshot and drowning, you and your friend, on the *Eastland*, of all places?"

Olive assured her it was true but offered no further details. It wasn't why she'd come. "You called me in for a meeting with Mr. Roth, correct? I'd hate to keep him waiting." She was ten minutes early, in fact.

"Oh! Yes, of course. He's in the conference room. Knock 'em dead, honey. And don't give 'em an inch, you hear me?"

Olive had no idea what the young secretary was talking about but could only hope it meant vindication was at hand. By now, Roth would have seen that he'd been wrong about her. Why else had he called the meeting, if not to apologize?

This was right. Olive loved the bookstore, and she loved what it had meant for her family. She could work there, but it didn't set her heart racing. It didn't make her want to jump out of bed in the morning.

Investigating did.

Thanking Gwendolyn, Olive threaded between desks and entered the conference room adjacent to Roth's corner office. Roth and Howard stood to greet her. Blanche was there, too, but she didn't rise or speak, transfixed by the handkerchief in her hand.

Olive sat across from them, an expanse of mahogany before her.

"Miss Pierce," Roth began, "thank you for coming. I understand you've been through another ordeal, so I appreciate your being here all the more."

She sat up straighter in the hardback chair. "I'm eager to hear what you have to say. I assume this is about the cases I closed after I was terminated. Nellie Timmerman and Stella Petroski?" She glanced at Howard, just now remembering that he was to have met with Raymond Murphy yesterday. She hoped for an update on that score, too.

"In part, yes." Roth waved dismissively.

Olive tried not to bristle. Solving those mysteries had meant a great deal to two families. For Roth, was it mere paperwork?

"Penrose?" Roth prompted.

Straightening the tie at his collar, Howard leaned forward in his chair and then back again, obviously ill at ease. "I found Murphy yesterday at Memorial Hall."

She waited. "And?"

"Let me back up a little, lest you think you did *all* the work." Howard shifted. "I went to the courthouse and looked at the policies filed there, and those beneficiary amendments weren't attached. So I looked at the page you copied from the ledger and contacted Raymond Murphy's banks. It turns out he had accounts at more than one. And the amounts he received as death benefits he didn't fully deposit. He put in ten percent of the amount and took the rest out as cash." He produced the ledger Olive had found in Blanche's desk. "The amounts listed here aren't the same as the amounts Murphy received," Howard explained. "They're lower by ten percent. To the penny."

Olive looked at Blanche. "You partnered with him for the money? Who was he?"

"He's her brother. Isn't that right, Blanche Murphy Eaton Holden?" Howard strung her maiden and married names together, emphasizing each one. "After I told her I talked to him yesterday, she confessed everything."

"Olive, I can explain!" Blanche bleated. "Just let me explain from the beginning. Raymond's my brother. And yes, I did partner with him, but it wasn't for me. It was for my son. It was for Geoffrey." She placed on the table the photograph that had been in her locked desk drawer. "He's grown now but an innocent still. Simple, but loving and harmless. He's the joy of my life and was the joy of my first husband, Joe, as well. We didn't mind taking care of him into his adulthood. He was a child in his mind, a child in our hearts. He kept us young, you understand? That's how we felt, anyway. It wasn't until Joe became ill that we realized how old we really are."

"Then Joe passed away," Olive said gently, "and you married Darryl."

"I did. What else was I to do, a widow supporting a child who would be a child forever and never leave home or get a job himself? Yes, I remarried. Darryl is kind and decent and promised to provide for us both."

"But he didn't, did he?" Howard prodded.

"For me, he always has." Blanche sniffed into her handkerchief. "But he decided soon into our marriage that he didn't want to share me or his house with another grown man, even though that man was my son. My *child*."

"Oh, Blanche," Olive said quietly. "I'm so sorry."

"Darryl said Geoffrey ought to be in the asylum. It was free and for the public good, and he could live out his days there with others like him. But there is no one else like my Geoffrey. He's one of a kind, a human being, not a category! Darryl never understood that. He wanted him gone or he'd leave me, and God help me, I didn't want that either. I could think of only one solution."

"The Evercrest Sanitarium," Olive said.

"But it's expensive. And Darryl could never know. I was able to afford the first few payments myself, but after that I needed more funds to keep him at that beautiful, peaceful place."

"You found that our client, Ernest Murphy, conveniently shared a last name with your brother," Olive said. "And you saw that Ernest's named beneficiary had already passed on and he didn't have a secondary. So you made an amendment that would benefit Raymond, who agreed on the condition that he could keep a cut of the amount."

"It wasn't hurting anybody," Blanche said. "Ernest was old and sweet, but he didn't have anyone else to leave the benefit to. He wouldn't have minded if he knew where the money went."

"Did you ask him, Blanche?" Roth skewered her with his gaze. She only lowered her lashes in response.

"But there was a problem," Olive continued, following the thread. "He wasn't dying fast enough, and you needed money urgently. So a few months later, you found another policy to amend. The widow Mathilda Schmidt, another elderly client, who had no children of her own. You named your brother instead. Did you realize she was sick by reading all those church newsletters? When you were writing get well cards, were you also amending their policies?"

"It didn't hurt anyone!" Blanche cried out with the force of someone in pain. "What do our clients care about money after they've gone on to glory? But those funds kept my bills paid up at Evercrest, and my sweet boy sheltered and well fed, with nurses and doctors that treat him well. He's happy there. He gets to paint and make crafts and learn music. Isn't that what every mother wants for her child, for him or her to be happy? I'd do anything for that, as long as it didn't harm anyone else."

"Including break the law," Roth added. "And you would have gone on doing just that, right under my nose, if Miss Pierce hadn't clued in."

Olive exhaled. "That's why you sabotaged my investigations. You retyped my notes and gave them to Roth, throwing the originals away, which is why you started taking out your own trash. Did you toss incriminating evidence every day?"

"No. Not every day. But I feared that I'd forget to dispose of my own trash someday when I needed to, so once I started, I made it a habit. I never dreamed it would be the receipts to Flo's Kitchen that would expose all of this."

A growl sounded from Roth's throat. "Did you deliberately not tell Miss Pierce about meetings that should have been on her calendar? Did you not arrange for that translator to slow her down, too?"

Blanche nodded.

The cords in Roth's neck pulled taut.

Olive turned back to Blanche, who was twisting her wedding ring around her finger. "Don't tell me you somehow siphoned the gas out of the company car that day I ran out of fuel in Cicero."

"Impossible," the secretary claimed. "I was right here in the office the entire day."

Howard tapped a pen on the table. "So you had Raymond do it for you."

Blanche's eyes filled. "I didn't want to, you must understand that. But you found the altered files and didn't return them, so I assumed that when things settled down after the *Eastland* disaster, you'd look into them again. I had to discredit you. You understand. It had nothing to do with those poor *Eastland* victims' families."

"And everything to do with protecting yourself," Howard said.

"Not me," she insisted. "It was never about me. It was always about protecting Geoffrey. The end justifies the means."

At last, Olive's name was cleared. But only because Blanche Holden's was forever stained. There was no joy or comfort in that. Blanche's actions were not violent. She'd deceived and stolen, but her motivation was rooted in love for her son. It was another sobering example of good intentions gone wrong, and that was something Olive understood.

Glowering, Roth signaled to someone behind Olive, and a security guard stepped into the room. "Mrs. Holden, please come with me."

Blanche flinched. "What will happen to Geoffrey?" she asked as she stood. "Please, Mr. Roth. What will happen to my boy?"

The door closed on her queries as she was marched from the room.

Grunting, Roth expelled a frustrated sigh. "I owe you an apology, Miss Pierce, and I'm not too proud to say it. I called you careless and unprofessional, and you were not. You were wronged. What Blanche did to you was wrong, and I was wrong to allow my assessment of your work to be so easily swayed when I've had eight months of your track record proving your consistent quality. You did fine work finding Miss Timmerman and Mrs. Petroski, too, in case I didn't mention it before."

"Thank you." Olive resisted looking over her shoulder for Blanche. The former secretary had been escorted to the elevator by now, but her story stayed in the room like a physical presence. "What will happen to Blanche?"

"I haven't decided yet," Roth said. "Termination is just the beginning of a long and prickly road for her. You deserved to be here to hear her confession. That should give you some sense of satisfaction and closure."

It was not satisfying to bear witness to the unraveling of a woman she'd respected and been fond of. It was not satisfying to have done some of the unraveling herself. But Olive knew what he meant and thanked him.

When he stood, however, she was thrown off guard. "Are we finished, then? Was there nothing more?" She stood to look him in the eye.

His lips flattened into a slash across his face.

Howard squeezed past Roth. "Good-bye, Olive," he said as he left the room.

She managed to return the sentiment before turning back to her former boss. "I heard you were hiring." She tried a smile. "Would it be worth my time to apply?" She was practically begging for her old job, and here she thought he'd called her back to offer it on a silver platter.

"Don't."

"Sir?" She stood her ground.

"Don't ask me to burst your bubble when you know I can't give you what you want. I've already had one crying woman in here this morning. Let's not make it two."

"Mr. Roth, Blanche confessed to sabotaging my work. Is this not grounds for a second chance?"

He rubbed the back of his neck. "Under normal circumstances, sure. But you're ignoring what I cannot. These new revelations don't erase the fact that you knew Claire Sterling was alive and allowed her claim to be processed. That was your choice alone, Miss Pierce. If you believe the end justifies the means, as Blanche does, you two have more and more in common. You're both fired. You both think you were justified. But neither of you will find employment here—or at any other life insurance agency, for that matter—again."

The short walk from the Conway Building to Olive's apartment would not be enough to distance herself from the disappointment that trailed her. So when she reached Corner Books & More, she kept right on walking.

What had she been thinking, to imagine herself back on staff at MetLife? Roth's parting words had struck a blow too near the mark. It was true that Blanche had obstructed Olive's investigations, but Olive had interfered in MetLife cases too, in an uncomfortably similar way. She had almost let a death benefit be paid when it shouldn't have been. This was Blanche's crime precisely.

Were they the same?

Guilt needled her. A gust of wind pulled at the brim of Olive's hat, and she tugged it firmly back into place. She waited at the corner for a streetcar to pass, then a Model T in its wake. Around and around the block she went, with the courthouse and City Hall at its center, though her legs were still sore from last night's exertion. Once, twice, three times she passed the same shouting newsie, the same man leaning against a lamppost, and the same bunch of children feeding pigeons.

At last, she decided the answer was no.

It was a thin glimmer of difference, but what separated her from Blanche was that Olive was full of remorse. Blanche was still justifying her choices as she'd been escorted away. That God forgave Olive for all she'd done, and for every unintended consequence, was a grace both humbling and liberating. She wasn't tied to her guilt. From now on, she would remember that her value came from Him, no matter what she did for a job. She was free to begin anew. It was time to leave the past where it was and pay attention to the path before her.

Looking up, she smiled. She'd come full circle again, and the path before her led back to Corner Books & More. A banner hanging above the entrance announced, *Celebrating 65 Years of Serving Chicago*. Would her family's bookstore remain for sixty-five more? Perhaps her place truly was as one more link in that chain of generations.

Upon entering, she felt her hunch confirmed. Though it was only half past ten o'clock, the store was packed. And no wonder. She'd forgotten that today's theme was Our Fair City, a pun on Chicago's hosting of the World's Fair in 1893. This evening, the guest speaker was local author Clara Louise Burnham, whose novel *Sweet Clover: A Romance of the White City* was called the best depiction of the Fair in any fiction.

The daytime event, however, was a treat for children of all ages. In his book *The Wonderful Wizard of Oz*, L. Frank Baum was said to have modeled his Emerald City after the White City of the Chicago World's Fair. And since his illustrator, William Wallace

Denslow, was a Chicagoan, it only seemed fitting to celebrate by having actors from a local theater dress up as the main characters to delight store patrons.

One of her mother's paintings was on prominent display near the front. The subject was Corner Books & More in different decades, with Chicago growing up and around it. The title of the piece was *There's No Place Like Home.*

Well. If Olive had asked for a sign, that would have been it.

"Livvie!" Holding her right arm close, Claire threaded through a tangle of customers as the actor dressed as the Cowardly Lion let out a comical roar. "Look at this crowd!" One would never guess by looking at her what a harrowing experience she'd come through last night, let alone the last few weeks. Claire glowed with as much pride as if she were still employed by the store herself.

Olive laughed with her friend, indulging in the nostalgia of when they both worked here together.

"Come on, you've got to see these characters. Your mother and aunt are standing over there and having the time of their lives, by the looks of it."

In the bistro area in the back of the store, on the stage where Sandburg had been last night, a very convincing Scarecrow spoke to an utterly captivated audience. "It is such an uncomfortable feeling to know one is a fool," he told them.

Olive smiled at the children's reactions. "I know the feeling," she muttered.

Claire spun toward her. "Your meeting. What happened?"

In a lull in the Scarecrow's monologue, the front door opened, and the tinkling bell turned both Meg's and Sylvie's heads. When they spotted Olive, they wove between customers to reach her.

"Come." Sylvie gestured, and they followed her to a quieter place in the store. "Dorothy and Toto—a real dog, I might add, which I hope I don't regret—are due to make their grand entrance in a few minutes. But we want to know what happened at MetLife."

336

As briefly as she could, Olive told them about Blanche.

"Okay," said Claire. "That's one more mystery solved. But what are you not telling us?"

Olive sighed. "Let's just say I was prepared to apply for a job at MetLife again if Mr. Roth had been open to it. He wasn't."

Too late, she realized that her confession had likely surprised her mother and aunt and possibly hurt their feelings. After all, they assumed the plan was for Olive to work at Corner Books & More full-time and to the end of her days. For the good of the family business.

"It's for the best, I'm sure," she rushed to say. "I already have a job lined up here, don't I?" She produced a smile. "I'll work with you, Aunt Sylvie. You've always been my favorite aunt."

An eyebrow quirked up as Sylvie crossed her arms. "I won't argue with that. But, dear, I want you to love what you do rather than just work here because you love me."

"This is my home too, and you know what they say. There's no place like it." This store, this building, would be Olive's home forever.

It ought to have been a comfort, but what she felt was a squeeze, a constricting of her entire world. Which was ridiculous, since the books within these walls could carry her anywhere.

In the quiet that followed her cheeky quip, the Tin Woodman's voice carried between the stacks. "You people with hearts have something to guide you, and need never do wrong," he said. "But I have no heart, and so I must be very careful."

Sylvie looked at Meg and then to Olive. "This *is* your home for as long as you want it. But I don't believe the idea of taking over the bookstore has fully captured your heart. Follow your own yellow brick road, dear. Where will it lead you?"

But that was the thing about yellow brick roads. One could follow a set path, hoping for fulfillment at the end, and yet one never knew what lay around the corner.

"Isn't there a Bible verse about the heart being deceitful and impossible to understand?" Olive asked. "I know mine has not always been a reliable guide."

"Indeed," Sylvie agreed. "I could say the same. So we must balance the heart with the brain. Your experience, gifts, interests, and skills probably point in a certain direction. It's wise to pay attention to that."

"Oh!" Claire snapped her fingers. "I meant to tell you. Erik's here."

Olive scanned the crowd until she found a trio that looked familiar. "With Michael and Addie?"

"Jakob brought them," Claire explained, "saying that you offered to keep an eye on them while he visits Stella this morning. When you weren't here, Erik volunteered to play guardian in your stead."

A smile lifted Olive's lips. Addie sat on Erik's lap, holding one of his large hands with both of her small, dimpled ones. Michael sat beside him, while Erik hemmed him in with his arm. You couldn't fit a baseball between them. Filling both children's faces was not the fear, sorrow, or anger Olive had come to know, but wonder.

"Olive." Meg touched her arm. "The bookstore might be the family business, but it is not the only family tradition. There are two we hold very dear. The first is starting over in spite of all odds. When met with obstacles and challenges, we have found different ways to do what we love while understanding that we're loved no matter what."

Olive nodded. "And the second?"

Meg handed her a folded newspaper with one small box of text circled.

HELP WANTED
RIVER NORTH DETECTIVE AGENCY
REFERENCES REQUIRED
MEN NEED NOT APPLY

Wide-eyed, Olive looked at her mother, surprise snatching her speech.

"Your father and I, your aunt and uncle, and even your grand-father—we have all solved our own mysteries in our day. If investigating is your yellow brick road, dear, please follow it. You honor your family best when you honor what you feel God is calling you to do."

Sylvie firmly agreed. "Never believe that your family ties are bonds to keep you from what you love."

In the next moment, the actress playing Dorothy arrived toting a trembling, barking basket on her arm, and the store went wild. Olive laughed when Toto pushed up the lid on the basket and showed his little black face and a flash of pink tongue. As Sylvie and Meg stayed close, keeping a sharp eye out for any little fingers that might reach too near the dog's teeth, Erik caught Olive's eye.

Claire didn't miss it. "I want a turn with those babies." Winking at Olive, she made her way to Erik and took his place, gathering Addie and Michael into her arms and kissing them each on their cheeks.

Erik made his way to Olive, hat in hand, uncertainty his shadow.

"Nice day for a walk," she said.

Shoulders relaxing, he gave her his arm.

All about Olive were the sounds of Chicago on a weekday morning. The El, the trolleys, honking horns, hoofbeats. Tugboats on the river. A policeman whistling, newsies and shoeshine boys calling. But all she wanted to hear was Erik's voice.

Neither of them spoke, however, until they'd traveled the two and a half blocks to the Clark Street Bridge. Somehow she knew this was where they would land. It was as if they were both drawn by the river and by the current that had brought them together. In silence, they regarded the *Eastland*, which was tethered to tugboats and being slowly towed off at last.

What a horrible wake it left behind.

Twice, she had survived that ship. She wouldn't mind if she never saw it again, and yet right now she couldn't look away. Here she was, whole and healthy, while eight hundred and forty-four people had died right here less than a month ago. She wanted the ship out of sight. She didn't want to relive her experiences. But neither could she dismiss the pain suffered by hundreds of others. Would it all be forgotten once the *Eastland* was no longer here to remind them?

"How are you?" Erik asked. It was more entreaty than question. Never had she known so much feeling could be poured into such a commonplace phrase.

She was many things and most of them contradictory. "I'm grieved for the families of those who died here," she told him, "and relieved for those who didn't. Sorrowful for Mrs. Collins and others who lost their loved ones. Overjoyed for the Petroskis. Horrified by Warren, optimistic for Claire. Grateful for God's providence. For grace and second chances."

His head bowed. "You gave me a second chance to prove myself, and I failed you miserably."

"You didn't."

The muscle bunching at Erik's jaw told her he wasn't convinced. "I made you a promise," he said hoarsely. "A promise to keep you safe."

Fords and Buicks rolled by, shaking the bridge. Olive glanced at the water beneath, sifting through all the memories she'd catalogued of their conversations together. "I don't recall you ever making that promise."

"Perhaps not in words, but in every other way, I thought I made that clear. Almost from the very start, you were my priority. Not the information I could get out of you, but you. Whatever I may have said or left unsaid, I vowed to myself that I would protect you at all costs. The only other time I've broken my word was when I canceled my contract with Warren. You could have

340

died last night, Olive. If you had, I would have been as much to blame as him."

Sunshine poured in from the east. Olive stood in Erik's shadow as she looked up at him. "Listen to me. You did the best you could, and your best kept us from a tragic end. Thank you for that. But I need to tell you something else. A promise to keep me safe wasn't yours to make. Ultimately, my life is in God's hands, not yours. That's something I've had to remind myself since we parted last night, too." The realization had kept her awake long after she'd said good night to Claire.

"What do you mean?" The earnestness in his blue eyes suggested that a great deal hinged on her answer.

"I mean that relying too much on any one person is a mistake. No one, no matter how strong and good and clever, can stand in for God or be everything another person needs. For years I tried to be all things for my mother, and I'm finally realizing that not only is that impossible, it isn't healthy. So when I prayed for you to rescue us last night—"

At this, he looked agonized.

"—I was wrong. I should have been praying for God's help all along, not just when it was clear you weren't coming. I ought not to rely on you for impossible things. God can help in all manner of ways. Last night it came from your phone call to my mother, and from her phone call to the police, and from the person of Alice Clement and her life preserver."

"If this is supposed to make me feel better about not being there for you . . . it isn't."

On a bold impulse, she grasped his hands, willing the physical connection to translate. She needed to help him understand. "Have you read *The Wonderful Wizard of Oz*?"

"Of course."

"Good. Then you'll remember the part at the end of the book, after Oz, the great and powerful wizard, fails to grant Dorothy her wish to return home. As the story goes, '*Oz had not kept the promise he made her, but he had done his best. So she forgave him. As he said, he was a good man, even if he was a bad Wizard.'"* Olive watched Erik, waiting for understanding to dawn. "You're not a very good wizard, either, Erik," she said gently to bring the point home. "Or a Norse god or a hero who can make all things right."

Cringing, he lowered his head. "This I know." But he didn't release her hands.

"If you promised to keep me safe and feel that you've failed, I forgive you. Please forgive me for punishing you when you pulled back the curtain and let me see that you are a private investigator who, for a short time, was investigating what I knew. I don't blame you for taking the case to find Claire. I don't want a wizard or a Norse god or a hero. I do want the mere mortal in front of me, the one who did his best."

He stood intensely still. "What are you saying, exactly?"

Warmth bloomed over her skin as she cast about for how to frame her feelings.

Then she had it. The answer was in another story, but this time it was her own.

"For my eighth birthday, my family and I went to the Midway at the World's Fair here in Chicago. I wanted to see Hagenback's Animal Show, which was like a petting zoo. My parents let me go with my older brother, my sister, and my cousin Rozalia. I went from one animal to another without waiting for Walter, Hazel, or Rose to come with me. I did what I wanted, and I didn't look back. I was having a grand time until all of a sudden, Rose and Hazel ran at me, crying, and nearly scared the living daylights out of me."

"Why? What was wrong?" He shifted, and sun spilled over his shoulder.

She squinted, and he adjusted his position to shield her again. "I was lost, Erik. I just didn't realize it. I didn't know I'd been lost until I was found. That's what it's like being with you. I'm not saying I was lost, but rather I never realized I was alone—or if I

342

did, I didn't *mind* being alone—until I met you. I never understood this kind of companionship, this kind of joy, until you brought it to me yourself. With you, I feel known and cared for. Sheltered. I can't think of any other way to describe it."

"I can't think of a better compliment." His expression softened. "And I know exactly what you mean. Leo told me he showed you my old notebook. He's not one for keeping secrets, as you might imagine."

"Were you upset that he shared it with me? I told him I thought it was too private."

A chuckle rumbled in his chest. "No, I was indifferent. I'd already told you about my search for my family. When I asked Leo why the notebook mattered to you, he told me if I didn't know the answer without him telling me, I didn't deserve to know."

"And he left it at that?"

A horse-drawn wagon rattled over the bridge, and Erik waited until it passed. "He did. In fact, he added a few choice words along the lines of, 'You'd better investigate your heart before signing on any new clients.'"

"And did you?"

He answered with a smile. "He was right. I stopped looking for my family when I found you. For years and years, I had been wondering where I belonged. And now—well, let's just say I don't wonder that anymore. I think I know." He searched her face, his own full of feeling. "But what do you think?"

A wedge pressed at the base of her throat. "I think we're still getting to know each other. It's been an intense month, full of excitement and emotion. But I think I know where you belong, too."

"By any chance, is it somewhere close to you?"

Her smile broke into a laugh. "Very close."

The relief in his expression kindled into something far less fleeting. His hands moved to the small of her back, drawing her near.

A door unlocked inside of her, and she felt her world expand. "I see you now."

He chuckled, suggesting he knew what she meant. Twice, Olive had told him she hadn't seen him. And she hadn't. She hadn't known him then as fully as she did now.

"And you still want me near?"

"More than ever before."

Eyes drifting closed, she lifted her chin, and his mouth met hers. Automobiles rumbled past them, and river traffic glided beneath their feet. If anyone stared or clucked their tongues, Olive didn't care. The wind cast his hat cartwheeling into the river, and he didn't seem to mind that, either.

Then she pushed him away. "Wait, stop," she said. "This probably isn't a good idea."

Erik leaned back. "Too public?"

"I'm going to apply for a position at the River North Detective Agency, and they require references. Mr. Roth isn't likely to give me a glowing report. I thought I'd ask you for one, as an established P.I. But it would seem disingenuous if you and I were romantically involved. A conflict of interests, you see?"

He rubbed his jaw. "So, it's not the involvement that you're opposed to but the timing of it. You'd like my objective assessment of your skills without a hint of personal bias. And then, once you've secured your position, I'm free to court you properly. Do I have that right?"

"Yes. Would you mind that very much?"

Amusement lit his eyes. "You want to be my competition? And I had so hoped we could be allies."

"It's a job, not my entire life," Olive countered. "We could still be partners in all the ways that really matter. Couldn't we?"

Wind ruffled his blond hair, gilded by the sun. "We do make a great team, Sherlock."

"Yes, my dear Watson." She laced her fingers with his. "We do."

EPILOGUE

CHICAGO
SUNDAY, JULY 23, 1916

Sunlight caught the diamond on Olive's finger as she gripped the port-side rail. Three levels below the promenade deck where she stood, water ruffled against steel. The steamship *Theodore Roosevelt* cleaved through the Chicago River, headed for the lake and ultimately to Michigan City, Indiana. She did, after all, owe her best friend the trip she'd promised her one year—and a lifetime—ago.

She linked her arm through Claire's. "Happy birthday, sister."

Claire smiled, eyes glimmering. "It is. Thank you."

Tomorrow was the anniversary of the *Eastland* disaster. In the morning, there would be special services at two Catholic churches in Cicero, and a memorial event at Pilsen Park in the evening. Olive planned to take the day off from work and attend them all. But this excursion, falling on Claire's birthday, seemed another fitting way to honor the memory of those who had died and to celebrate those who still lived.

Olive breathed in deeply. The breeze rushing between Chicago's downtown buildings twirled the hem of her dress. Traffic below filled the air with hoofbeats and honking. From the wharf, produce sellers called out prices for cherries and blueberries.

"Ready?"

Claire opened the lid of a basket packed with loose rose petals.

Olive began. "Marie Adamkiewicz, age 19. Henryk Adamski, 24. Augusta Adler, 29. Caroline Schroth Affeld, 36. Marie Albertz, 20. Lena Albrecht, 17." As she spoke each name from a list of those who'd perished, Claire released a petal into the river below.

Pages later, heat rushed to Olive's eyes. "John Braitsch, 42. Anna Braitsch, 17. Frederick Braitsch, 9. Gertrude Braitsch, 11. Hattie Braitsch, 7. Marie Braitsch, 5 months and 16 days only." Tears spilled for them and for the childless widow left behind.

Passengers within hearing distance quieted. Some of them moved closer, doffing hats and bowing heads, while others watched the falling petals in respectful silence. Not trusting her voice to hold steady, Olive passed the list to Claire and accepted the basket in trade. Noticing the onlookers, Olive beckoned the nearest to come, and in seconds they formed a line, each taking a petal from the basket and setting it free over the rail.

On and on and on, Olive and Claire took turns speaking the names of the dead.

"Frank Leff, 37. Edward Leff, 9. Frank Leff, Jr., 12. Elizabeth Lemke, 23. Emily Lemke, 18. Wilhelmine Lemke, 21." Claire pressed a fist to her mouth, struggling for composure.

After nearly thirty minutes of steady reading, half the list still remained. The river behind them now, the *Theodore Roosevelt* steamed across the tip of Lake Michigan, puffing thick black clouds into the marbled sky. Most of the crowd ebbed away to some less somber section of the ship.

Not everyone, however, had gone. Olive held the basket out to the next person in line. With a ripple of welcome surprise, she saw that it was Erik. His throat constricted on a swallow as he wiped the tears from her cheek with his thumb, then silently accepted a petal and gave way to the next in line.

It was Sylvie, who had poured so much of herself into Olive, especially this last year. She approached with a wavering smile and a wrinkled handkerchief in her grip.

Behind her came Kristof, the steadfast and tenderhearted uncle who would stand in her father's place and give Olive away to Erik at their wedding in two weeks.

He was followed by Rozalia. Her wet cheeks and bright pink nose betrayed how deeply she felt the loss of the *Eastland* victims. They'd been her neighbors, after all. Her coworkers, her friends.

Just when Olive believed she could not be more surprised, there was her mother, too. With no one waiting behind her, Meg captured Olive in an embrace that felt like both sorrow and gratitude.

Claire faltered on the list, overcome and clearly as emotionally wrung-out as Olive.

"May I?" Rozalia offered to read, and Claire let her.

For fifteen minutes, Rose read, until she came to the Sindelar family of seven and could not go on.

Kristof took over then, his sonorous voice clear and strong, until the last name had been pronounced. Olive checked the bracelet watch on her wrist, a gift from Erik last year. *"A time for everything,"* he'd said, quoting Ecclesiastes 3. *"A time to weep, and a time to laugh; a time to mourn, and a time to dance.'"* She rubbed her thumb over its face. It had taken fifty-seven minutes to read all eight hundred and forty-four names. Time to mourn, indeed.

Water churned against the ship, and Olive watched the petals in its wake. Erik's hand, warm and calloused, came to rest on the nape of her neck as she bowed her head and prayed for the families of the departed, asking for grace and strength on their behalf.

Then she lifted her face to the sun.

Surrounded by the people she loved most in the world, Olive turned to her friend for an explanation.

After a shuddering sigh, Claire smiled. "I invited them to come."

"Walter and Hazel and their families are coming next week as planned," Meg said. "But when Claire suggested a day at Michigan City for all of us to spend together, and an extra week with you, how could I say no to that?"

"Claire also told us how you planned to honor the *Eastland* victims," Sylvie added. "We wanted to be part of that, too."

Erik slid his arm around Olive's shoulders. "She said she didn't want to celebrate just her life today, but yours, as well."

"A celebration of life, in general," Claire confirmed, her luminous face wiped clean of tears.

Olive recalled Claire's desperate words when they'd been trapped in the *Eastland* last year and she'd thought death was her only way out: *"But you, you will live."*

By the grace of God, they both had. By grace they survived, and by grace Olive had learned to accept that. Grace was their safe harbor.

"We wouldn't miss this, dear." Rose embraced Olive and kissed her cheek, then tapped the violin case she carried. Smiling at Kristof, she said, "Shall we?"

Moments later, the maestro and his former student were playing a duet, "The Blue Danube" lifting on the wind.

Olive guided Claire to sit with her on a wooden bench. "Do you really not mind sharing your birthday with my entire family?"

"They're practically my family, too."

That was true. Soon after Warren's imprisonment last summer, Claire had moved in with Olive, filed for divorce, and started working again at Corner Books & More. As assistant manager, Claire was being trained to take over as owner upon Sylvie's retirement, which would likely be within the next few years. Soon Olive would move out of the building and into a house with Erik, and Claire would stay. Claire would be the one to keep an eye on Olive's aunt and uncle. They, in turn, loved Claire like a daughter.

"Besides, doesn't a day at the beach with family sound like a good idea to you?" Claire pressed. "A pre-wedding party, of sorts."

"Marvelous."

"I thought so."

While Claire joined Sylvie to enjoy the concert being given by Kristof and Rose, Olive found Erik and Meg chatting at the bow of the ship.

Her mother looked wonderful. Nine months of living with Walter's family had reawakened a vivacity that Olive hadn't even realized had waned until she saw her now. "I see that life with children agrees with you."

The laughter that spilled from her mother was musical, a resounding, chiming thing. It was confirmation that Meg reveled in her newfound calling to serve and love Walter's family. She'd also been working with art students at the university on an informal but clearly gratifying basis. Her skirts billowing, she held her hat to her head while they swapped news and stories.

When Meg went to find Sylvie, Erik kissed Olive's gloved hand and then held it. "Did you tell Stella and the kids I was sorry to miss them yesterday?"

"Of course. They missed you too, but not overmuch. The children were so excited to try on their 'fancy clothes,' as they call them, and Stella was equally enthralled, even as she pinned hems and cuffs for alterations." Michael was to be their ring bearer and Addie their flower girl in the upcoming nuptials.

Erik grinned. "I can't wait to see them. Wouldn't mind having a pair just like them someday."

"I'll see what I can do." Olive blushed, despite all her efforts not to.

Laughing, Erik caught his Panama before it vaulted overboard. He didn't bother to reseat it. "Speaking of life after the wedding, I expect you'll be giving your notice at River North soon."

She angled toward him. "You want me to quit working at the detective agency? I love that job. It hasn't gotten in the way of our relationship so far, so I don't suppose it will start."

"So far," he said, "you haven't been in the family way. That'll change, Lord willing. You'll want to take care of yourself and, more importantly, let *me* take care of you."

Surprise threatened to steal her composure. "Once I *am* in the family way, of course I'll take it easier. When we have a baby, I'll want to stay home with him or her—at least for a while. But I see no reason to stop working before that. My job doesn't define me, but it is important to me. I thought you knew that."

"But you'll have *me*. What more could you possibly want?"

Stunned, Olive gaped at him. They'd long ago agreed that no one person could meet all the emotional needs of another. One needed other relationships too, and a fulfilling occupation of one's time, even if one also had a spouse. "You're joking."

Erik's seriousness cracked into the pleasant lines she knew so well, and his laughter rolled over the water. He pulled a small card from his pocket. "Before you call off the wedding, read this."

It was a business card. It was hers.

Olive Magnussen, Private Investigator. Magnussen & Magnussen Detective Agency. Their new address followed.

A thrill shot through her. She peered into Erik's dancing eyes.

"I don't want you to stop working, Olive. I was only hoping you might agree it's time to work together. What do you say? A husband-and-wife team? After all, the commute would be much better for you."

"Erik!" She punched him in the arm, laughing. "Of course I'll work with you. But only because you've already printed the business cards," she teased. Strains of Mozart eddied around them.

"All part of my master plan." Grinning, he winked at her.

"So, next time I want something, I'll just print it on a business card, shall I, and consider it a *fait accompli*?"

He cupped her cheek. "And what is it you want, beloved?"

Gratitude flared hot in her throat. "I want this." She swung her arm in a gesture meant to encompass the abundance she already had: her best friend, her family, time together, the beauty of lake and sky, freedom from fear. Life itself, and the grace to enjoy it.

The gift of coming days, and the man she loved with whom to share them. "I want you."

An answering warmth filled his eyes. Drawing her close, he bent his head and pressed a kiss to her lips that said he was already hers. Holding to the lapels of his jacket, Olive stood on her toes, breathing in his sandalwood scent, and replied without words that she was his, as well. Some days he was her anchor, and others, the wind at her back. Always, her friend. Always, her partner. Soon and forever, her husband.

Sea gulls winged overhead, and the deck shifted beneath Olive's feet. Erik held her steady as she turned toward the lake, enclosing her in the shelter of his arms. Her family behind her, the unknown before her, they faced the horizon together.

Author's Note

I wish I could tell you that the *Eastland* disaster is fictional. But though the main characters in this story come from my imagination, the SS *Eastland* really did turn over in the Chicago River on July 24, 1915, and the best estimate we have is that eight hundred and forty-four people lost their lives because of it. At the time, the number of reported victims varied between eight hundred twelve to eight hundred thirty-six, but for the sake of simplicity, I chose to use the most authoritative number we now have, thanks to the research published by George W. Hilton in 1985.

My goal was to represent the event and its aftermath as accurately as possible within the scope of the plot. For those who want more details, especially about the causes and the years of criminal investigation that followed, I recommend *The Sinking of the Eastland: America's Forgotten Tragedy* by Jay Bonansinga, *Eastland: Legacy of the Titanic* by George W. Hilton, and *The Eastland Disaster* by Ted Wachholz.

The misidentification of several bodies was an unfortunate reality in the wake of the disaster. Not only did I find articles in the *Chicago Tribune* confirming this (see the editions from July 27, 1915, and July 28, 1915), but in Ted Wachholz's book, he describes a case involving three bodies and two misidentifications that was only resolved a month after the sinking when one of the bodies was exhumed. This three-way complication served as the inspiration for my plot. (As a side note, I'd already been exploring this idea based on a tragic accident that occurred in April 2006, which led to the mistaken identities of two college students from my alma mater, Taylor University. For that incredible story, check out the book *Mistaken Identity: Two Families, One Survivor, Unwavering Hope* by Don and Susie Van Ryn and Newell, Colleen, and Whitney Cerak.)

Some of the minor characters Olive and Claire interact with on the *Eastland* were real people. The Norwegian woman who says "I don't like the feel of this boat" was Marianne Aanstad, and her thirteen-year-old daughter was Borghild, also called Bobbie. Olaf, who saves Olive from being drowned by a desperate passenger, was Olaf Ness, Bobbie's uncle. He helped as many victims as he could. Olaf and the Aanstad family were trapped for hours in the hull but survived.

The young man in the novel who dives to try to recover Michael and Claire represents the real person of Charles "Reggie" Bowles. Over the course of eight hours, this fearless eighteen-year-old removed thirty-six dead bodies from the wreck. Western Electric Nurse Helen Repa was also based on the real woman.

In the epilogue, every name and age from the list of the perished was real, with the exception of Henryk Adamski, who I invented for the story. The entire list is in an appendix in Hilton's book, *Eastland: Legacy of the Titanic*. The Petroski family and Nellie Timmerman are fictional.

Other historical figures who appear or are referenced in the novel include Cook County Coroner Peter Hoffman; Chicago writers Carl Sandburg, Edgar Rice Burroughs, Upton Sinclair, and Clara Louise Burnham; illustrator William Wallace Denslow; Alice Clement, the first female detective for the Chicago Police Department; and Jun Fujita of the *Chicago Evening Post*, the first Japanese American photojournalist. He really did make a scrapbook of all the photos from the *Eastland* disaster, something he never did for any other event. The photographs I described from the scrapbook are images he captured.

The Conway Building in which Olive worked is now an office building called the Burnham Center. The Chicago Public Library Olive visits is now the Chicago Cultural Center. It's well worth seeing, either in person or via the virtual tours on YouTube. Of the original forty-acre Sears, Roebuck, and Company complex, three buildings survive. The Western Electric Hawthorne Works closed in 1983. A Hawthorne Works Museum is operated by Morton College. Lamb's Café, beneath the Olympic Theater, was also a real place.

Drawn by the Current is one of the most emotionally taxing books I've ever written, but also one of the most fulfilling. More passengers died on the *Eastland* than on the *Titanic*, although when counting crew, the *Titanic* did have a greater loss of life. Yet this shocking Chicago disaster seems to have largely faded from public memory. My intention is that this novel will bring attention to the tragedy and honor those who lost their lives that day.

My hope is that this story will touch your life in some way, too. The theme of identity—mistaken, misplaced, or otherwise—is one we can all relate to. Perhaps, like Olive, you've misplaced your identity in work or works. Please remember where your value comes from. You were made in the image of God. Who you are is bigger than what you do, and it's bigger than what you don't do. You are cherished and loved by God, not because of anything you've done, but because of who God is and what Christ has already done for you.

DISCUSSION QUESTIONS

1. In chapter eleven, Olive realizes that "ignoring wounds didn't mean they were not there." Have you ever tried ignoring your own wounds or someone else's? What was the result?

2. In chapter thirteen, we learn that Olive feels her job is to take care of everyone and that she feels valuable when she's helping others. Can you relate to this? If not, what makes you feel valuable?

3. In chapter sixteen, Erik says, "You're never as alone as you think." In what ways have you found this to be true or not true?

4. In chapter nineteen, we learn that when Olive isn't helping someone, she often feels invisible and overlooked. She wonders if her motives are selfish or selfless. Do you think it's right or wrong to do a good thing because of how it makes you feel about yourself?

5. In chapter twenty-eight, Meg says, "One can live with scars, however constricting they may feel. But one cannot live long with open wounds." What scars have you had

to learn to live with? Do you have open wounds that still need tending?

6. In the same chapter, Leo says to Olive, "What we do is not the sum of who we are. Is your identity as a human being tied completely to your job?" Later, Meg says, "Who you are is bigger than what you do." How much of your identity is tied to your work? What else do you base your identity on?

7. During the climax in chapter thirty-one, Olive and Claire need to leave the ship, but the way they came in is closed to them. They need to take a fall in order to escape. Think back over some hard situations you've had in your own life. What risks did you take in order to improve your circumstances?

8. In chapter thirty-two, it reads, "Just because she couldn't see them through the fog didn't mean they were not there." This refers to the docks that would give Olive and Claire safety. Has there been a time in your life when help was near and you just couldn't see it? What happened?

9. The end of the same chapter contains these lines: "Surviving trauma wasn't the end of the story. It was only the beginning." What new beginnings have you experienced after surviving some kind of trauma or challenge?

10. The epilogue states, "By grace they survived, and by grace Olive had learned to accept that. Grace was their safe harbor." When and how has grace been a safe harbor for you?

ACKNOWLEDGMENTS

I'm humbled by all the help I've received to bring this novel to life. My sincere gratitude goes to:

My editors, Dave Long and Jessica Sharpe, for letting me tell this story, and for your insights that made it better.

My copy editor, Elisa Tally, and to Noelle Chew, Amy Lokkesmoe, Brooke Vikla, Serena Hanson, and all the marketing, publicity, design, and author support staff at Bethany House who have a hand in the process.

My agent, Tim Beals of Credo Communications, for his continued and enthusiastic support.

To Kevin Doerksen, whose personalized tours of Chicago through his company Wild Onion Walks were invaluable. Your passion for your city's history fueled mine.

To Ted Wachholz, president of the Eastland Disaster Historical Society, not only for answering my questions but for reading this manuscript to make sure I presented the *Eastland* disaster as accurately as possible. (Any mistakes are my own.)

To Lesley Martin of the Chicago Historical Society, and to Laura Adler and Will Sumner of the Chicago Public Library, for helping me find the perfect resources on the historic Conway Building.

To Dylan Hoffman of the Chicago Maritime Museum; Leo Belleville of the National Archives at Chicago; and Harvey Moshman, executive producer of the documentary *Eastland: Chicago's Deadliest Day*. All of you helped me find what I was looking for and pointed me in the right direction to learn more.

To Dr. Michele Catellier, associate medical examiner for the state of Iowa, for explaining the decomposition of bodies according to several variables, ways to identify them, and the exhumation process.

To Special Agent Scott Reger, Iowa Division of Criminal Investigation, for generously sharing about police procedure, missing persons cases, and methods of investigation.

To Ann Meyer, one of my favorite readers and retired police officer with the Waterloo Police Department here in Iowa, where she was the first female sergeant and first female lieutenant for the WPD. I'm in your debt for the perspective you shared as a woman working in a male-dominated field, and the insights gained from your work in the area of domestic abuse.

To Brad Jacobsen, my own insurance agent, for answering all my questions about insurance protocols and procedures.

To nurse and author Jordyn Redwood, for helping me create a credible medical situation for Stella.

To long-time reader and friend Sheri Lesh, for sharing information about her relative, William Fisher, who died on the *Eastland* at the age of twenty-one. I pray this novel honors his memory.

To Susie Finkbeiner, a true kindred spirit of my own. The writing life, and life in general, is so much better with you as my friend.

To my husband, Rob, and my kids, Elsa and Ethan. Such adventures we've had together in Chicago while I've been working on this series! Thank you for literally coming with me on the journey—actually, three of them. You're my favorite research assistants, even though you kids are still building up your museum stamina. What a team!

To God, again and always. For the gift of life, for whatever time we get on this earth, and for daily grace and strength. For dying in our place so we can break free from bondage, and live.

Jocelyn Green inspires faith and courage as the award-winning and bestselling author of numerous fiction and nonfiction books, including *The Mark of the King, Wedded to War,* and *The 5 Love Languages Military Edition*, which she coauthored with bestselling author Dr. Gary Chapman. Her books have garnered starred reviews from *Booklist* and *Publishers Weekly* and have been honored with the Christy Award, the gold medal from the Military Writers Society of America, and the Golden Scroll Award from the Advanced Writers & Speakers Association. She graduated from Taylor University in Upland, Indiana, and lives with her husband, Rob, and their two children in Cedar Falls, Iowa. She loves tea, pie, hydrangeas, Yo-Yo Ma, the color red, *The Great British Baking Show*, and reading on her patio. To learn more, visit her online at www.jocelyngreen.com.

Sign Up for Jocelyn's Newsletter

Keep up to date with Jocelyn's news on book releases and events by signing up for her email list at jocelyngreen.com.

More from Jocelyn Green

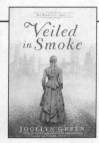

As Chicago's Great Fire destroys their bookshop, Meg and Sylvie Townsend make a harrowing escape from the flames with the help of reporter Nate Pierce. But the trouble doesn't end there—their father is committed to an asylum after being accused of murder, and they must prove his innocence before the asylum truly drives him mad.

Veiled in Smoke • THE WINDY CITY SAGA #1

You May Also Like . . .

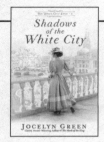

When Sylvie Townsend's Polish ward, Rose, goes missing at the World's Fair, her life unravels. Brushed off by the authorities, Sylvie turns to her boarder and Rose's violin instructor, Kristof Bartok, for help searching the immigrant communities. When the unexpected happens, will Sylvie be able to accept the change that comes her way?

Shadows of the White City by Jocelyn Green
THE WINDY CITY SAGA #2
jocelyngreen.com

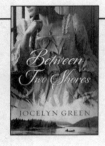

With a Mohawk mother and a French father in 1759 Montreal, Catherine Duval finds it easiest to remain neutral among warring sides. But when her British ex-fiancé, Samuel, is taken prisoner by her father, he claims to have information that could end the war. At last, she must choose whom to fight for. Is she willing to commit treason for the greater good?

Between Two Shores by Jocelyn Green
jocelyngreen.com

Vivienne Rivard fled revolutionary France and seeks a new life for herself and a boy in her care, who some say is the Dauphin. But America is far from safe, as militiaman Liam Delaney knows. He proudly served in the American Revolution but is less sure of his role in the Whiskey Rebellion. Drawn together, will Liam and Vivienne find the peace they long for?

A Refuge Assured by Jocelyn Green
jocelyngreen.com

More from Bethany House

A very public jilting has Theodore Day fleeing the ballrooms of New York to focus on building his family's luxury steamboat business in New Orleans and beating out his brother to be next in charge. But he can't escape the Southern belles' notice, nor Flora Wingfield, who is determined to win his attention.

Her Darling Mr. Day by Grace Hitchcock
AMERICAN ROYALTY #2
gracehitchcock.com

When Beth Tremayne stumbles across an old map, she pursues the excitement she's always craved. But her only way to piece together the clues is through Lord Sheridan—a man she insists stole a prized possession. As they follow the clues, they uncover a story of piratical adventure, but the true treasure is the one they discover in each other.

To Treasure an Heiress by Roseanna M. White
THE SECRETS OF THE ISLES #2
roseannamwhite.com

More than a century apart, two women search for the lost. Despite her father's Confederate leanings, Clara is determined to help an enslaved woman reunite with her daughter; Alice can't stop wondering what happened to her mother in the aftermath of Hurricane Katrina. Faced with the unknown, both women will have to dig deep to let their courage bloom.

Where the Last Rose Blooms by Ashley Clark
HEIRLOOM SECRETS
ashleyclarkbooks.com

BETHANYHOUSE